SLAUGHTER
OF THE
MOUNTAIN MAN

SLAUGHTER
OF THE
MOUNTAIN MAN

WILLIAM W.
JOHNSTONE
AND J.A. JOHNSTONE

PINNACLE BOOKS
Kensington Publishing Corp.
www.kensingtonbooks.com

PINNACLE BOOKS are published by

Kensington Publishing Corp.
119 West 40th Street
New York, NY 10018

PUBLISHER'S NOTE
Following the death of William W. Johnstone, the Johnstone family is working with a carefully selected writer to organize and complete Mr. Johnstone's outlines and many unfinished manuscripts to create additional novels in all of his series like The Last Gunfighter, Mountain Man, and Eagles, among others. This novel was inspired by Mr. Johnstone's superb storytelling.

All Kensington titles, imprints, and distributed lines are available at special quantity discounts for bulk purchases for sales promotion, premiums, fund-raising, educational, or institutional use.

Special book excerpts or customized printings can also be created to fit specific needs. For details, write or phone the office of the Kensington Sales Manager: Attn.: Sales Department. Kensington Publishing Corp., 119 West 40th Street, New York, NY 10018. Phone: 1-800-221-2647.

PINNACLE BOOKS, the Pinnacle logo, and the WWJ steer head logo are Reg. U.S. Pat. & TM Off.

First Printing: December 2021
ISBN-13: 978-0-7860-4059-9
ISBN-13: 978-0-7860-4060-5 (eBook)

10 9 8 7 6 5 4 3 2 1

Printed in the United States of America

THE JENSEN FAMILY

FIRST FAMILY
OF THE AMERICAN FRONTIER

Smoke Jensen—*The Mountain Man.*

The youngest of three children and orphaned as a young boy, Smoke Jensen is considered one of the fastest draws in the West. His quest to tame the lawless West has become the stuff of legend. Smoke owns the Sugarloaf Ranch in Colorado. Married to Sally Jensen, father to Denise "*Denny,*" and Louis.

Preacher—*The First Mountain Man.*

Though not a blood relative, grizzled frontiersman Preacher became a father figure to the young Smoke Jensen, teaching him how to survive in the brutal, often deadly Rocky Mountains. Preacher fought the battles that forged his destiny. Armed with a long gun, he is as fierce as the land itself.

Matt Jensen—*The Last Mountain Man.*

Orphaned but taken in by Smoke Jensen, Matt Jensen has become like a younger brother to Smoke, and even took the Jensen name. And like Smoke, Matt has carved out his destiny on the American frontier. He lives by the gun and surrenders to no man.

Luke Jensen—*Bounty Hunter.*

Mountain Man Smoke Jensen's long-lost brother, Luke Jensen, is scarred by war and a dead shot—the right skills to be a bounty hunter. And he's cunning, and fierce enough to bring down the deadliest outlaws of his day.

Ace Jensen and Chance Jensen—*Those Jensen Boys.*

The untold story of Smoke Jensen's long-lost nephews, Ace and Chance, a pair of young-gun twins as reckless and wild as the frontier itself . . . Their father is Luke Jensen, thought killed in the Civil War. Their uncle Smoke Jensen is one of the fiercest gunfighters the West has ever known. It's no surprise that the inseparable Ace and Chance Jensen have a knack for taking risks— even if they have to blast their way out of them.

Denise "Denny" Jensen, and Louis Jensen— *The Jensen Brand.*

Denny and Louis are the adult children of Smoke and Sally Jensen. Denny is the wildcard tomboy, kept in line by the more levelheaded Louis. The twins grew up mostly abroad, but never lost their love of the Sugarloaf Ranch, or lost sight of what it means to be a Jensen.

In 1880 Rutherford B. Hayes, nineteenth President of the United States, embarked on a seventy-one-day tour of the American West, becoming the first sitting President to travel west of the Rocky Mountains. Hayes's traveling party included his wife, two of their children, General William Tecumseh Sherman, who helped organize the trip, and the general's daughter, Rachel, Secretary of War Ramsey and his wife, General McCook, and Colonel and Mrs. Barr. Hayes began his trip in September 1880, departing from Chicago on the transcontinental railroad. He journeyed across the continent, ultimately arriving in California, stopping first in Wyoming and then Utah and Nevada, reaching Sacramento and San Francisco. By railroad and stagecoach, the party traveled north to Oregon, arriving in Portland, and from there to Vancouver, Washington. Going by steamship, they visited Seattle and then returned to San Francisco. Hayes then toured several southwestern states before returning to Ohio in November, in time to cast a vote in the 1880 Presidential Election for which he was not a candidate.

Though this book draws upon that authentic historical event for inspiration, the author has taken "poetic license" to add even more drama to the adventure, in order to develop this story.

CHAPTER ONE

On board the Pacific Flyer

In the pre-dawn darkness, Smoke Jensen stared through the window at the moonlit Kansas prairie passing outside. Smoke and Sally, occupying a private roomette, were two days into their return trip from Chicago where Smoke had been investigating the commodities market, not just the price of cattle, but, specifically, the going price for registered bulls and dams. Over the last few years Smoke had gotten into raising registered cattle to be used for breeding, rather than to provide beef.

As Smoke sat there, watching the sun rise, Sally stirred in the bed.

"You awake?" Smoke asked.

"No."

"What do you mean, you aren't awake? You just answered me."

"I'm talking in my sleep."

Smoke laughed. "How about breakfast?"

Sally yawned, stretched, and rolled over. "You go without me," she mumbled.

Smoke went into the dining car where he was met by

the waiter, a relatively small man, swarthy complexioned with what had once been very dark hair, though a considerable amount of gray had gathered at the temples.

"What's for breakfast?" Smoke asked.

"Why, Mr. Jensen, I'm sure you are aware that we have a most extensive menu," Peabody replied.

"What do you suggest? No, tell me what the engineer and fireman chose for breakfast."

"They have not eaten, sir. They'll do without until the next stop," the waiter replied.

"Really? That doesn't sound very good. All right, put together some biscuit-and-bacon sandwiches and drop them in a bag, would you?"

"Yes, sir," Peabody replied. "You wish to take breakfast back to Mrs. Jensen, do you?"

"No, I think I'll have breakfast with the engine crew."

"Mr. Jensen, how do you plan to do that? Why, there is no way to reach the engine crew from here."

"Leave that up to me," Smoke replied. "Please, just put the biscuits and bacon in a bag."

"Yes, sir." Peabody smiled. "I expect that Mr. Barnes and Mr. Prouty are going to be quite surprised. Pleased, but surprised."

A few minutes later Smoke, carrying the sack, climbed over the top of the express car then crawled across the tender and dropped down onto the platform of the locomotive.

"Here!" the fireman asked, startled by Smoke's sudden appearance. "Who are you, and what are you doing here?"

Smoke smiled, and held out the sack. "I'm Smoke Jensen, and I've come to have breakfast with you," he said.

The fireman opened the bag and looked down inside.

"Hey, Clyde, what do you think? You just said you was hungry. This feller has brought us some biscuits 'n bacon."

"They aren't all for you, one of them is mine. I plan to eat with you," Smoke said. "I just heard the engineer's name. What's yours?"

"Austin Prouty. The engineer is Clyde Barnes."

"It's good to meet the two of you," Smoke said, taking a bite of his biscuit. As Smoke looked at the two men, he could see scars, like little pits on their faces and necks. He was puzzled at first, then he realized that they were actually scars made by the red-hot sparks that over the many years and miles of railroading, had found their skin.

It was hot in the engine, and Smoke saw how Clyde was dealing with it. The engineer's arm was laid along the base of the window, the sleeve open to catch the breeze created by the twenty-five-mile-per-hour forward speed of the engine. That had the effect of causing the air to pass through the sleeve to the inside of his shirt, then circle all around his body.

"Pretty good idea," Smoke said, pointing to the shirt-sleeve.

Clyde smiled. "The feller I apprenticed under taught me this little trick," he said. "I don't know who taught it to him."

As Smoke watched the two men the difference in their jobs could not be more obvious. Clyde was standing at the throttle cooled by the breeze, casually eating his breakfast, the small raft of chin whiskers that stuck forward waving up and down as he chewed.

By contrast the fireman was sweating profusely, not only from the heat of the locomotive cab, but also from the effort of his labors. He tossed a few shovels full of coal into the boiler furnace, closed the door, then checked the steam pressure gauge.

"What's it reading, Austin?" Clyde asked.

"A hunnert forty 'n holdin'," Austin replied.

"Good, good," Clyde said with an approving nod of his head.

Austin sat on his bench and wiped the sweat from his face. The fire was roaring, the steam was hissing, and the rolling wheels were pounding out a thunder of steel on steel.

"What brought you up here, Mr. Jensen?" Austin asked. "I know you said it was to have breakfast with us, but what really brought you up here?"

"Curiosity, I suppose," Smoke answered. "Also, I have an appreciation for work, and for men who know what they are doing. I'm always honored to spend some time with such men."

"You're the feller that owns Sugarloaf Ranch, ain't you?" Clyde asked.

"How did you know that?"

"We're always told when we got someone important travelin' with us," Clyde replied. "We was told about you." Clyde chuckled. "Sure didn't expect you to come crawlin' down over the tender, though."

Smoke laughed. "I had no idea I was considered important enough to be reported to the cab crew. But the concept is interesting. Who is the most important person you ever had on your train?"

"I've had two Presidents ride on my train, only there warn't neither one of 'em President then. I drove a train durin' the war 'n President Grant rode on it, only he was a general then. 'N President Hayes rode on my train when he was the Governor of Ohio. But I reckon the most important one would be General Custer. Fact is, the last train he ever rode on was one I was drivin'."

"You've had an interesting career," Smoke said.

"Yes, sir, I reckon I have."

Back in the roomette, Sally was awake now and dressed, waiting for Smoke to return. When he didn't return, she thought perhaps he was in the parlor car, but he wasn't there either, so she went to the diner, thinking perhaps he had lingered in conversation. When he wasn't there, she decided she would have her breakfast without him.

"Mr. Peabody, have you seen my husband this morning?" Sally asked the waiter when he approached her table.

"Yes, ma'am, Mr. Jensen was here, earlier this morning," Peabody replied.

"Really? That's odd, I haven't been able to find him."

"He's in the engine," Peabody said.

"I beg your pardon?"

"Mr. Jensen ordered a sack of biscuits and bacon to take up to the engine. If you can believe it, he stated that it was his intention to have breakfast with the engine crew."

Sally laughed. "Yes, I can quite easily believe that. Such a thing would be just like him."

At that moment, Bob Dempster came into the dining car. Dempster, who was an officer at the Bank of Big Rock, had made the trip to Chicago with them, as Smoke's personal banker.

"Mr. Dempster, won't you join me for breakfast?" Sally invited.

"Where is Smoke?"

"He's driving the train," Sally said with a little laugh.

"I beg your pardon?"

"Mr. Peabody said he took some biscuits and bacon up to the engineer and fireman."

"My word, why would he do something like that?"

"You can ask him yourself," Sally said. "Here he comes now." Smoke had just stepped in through the door of the car.

"I thought you weren't going to eat," Smoke said as he joined them.

"And I thought you had already eaten," Sally replied. "Mr. Peabody said you had decided to take your breakfast up in the engine cab."

"Yes, I did. I just came back for some coffee. Hello, Bob. Did you sleep well?"

"Not particularly well," Dempster replied. "I did nothing but run numbers through my head last night. Smoke, are you sure you want to reduce your herd? You would be giving up quite a large source of revenue."

"We've been all through this, Bob. If I take five hundred head to market, I'll do well to clear four dollars a head. That's two thousand dollars. You may recall that I made two thousand five hundred dollars for Prince Dandy. He was sired by HRH Charles, and three of HRH Charles's issue have given me six more bulls, all who can trace their lineage back to HRH Charles."

"But you are forgetting one thing," Dempster said.

"Five hundred head spreads out your risk. If you lose one cow, you will lose, at most, thirty-five dollars. If you lose one registered bull, you can lose twenty-five hundred dollars, or more."

"There are always trade-offs," Smoke replied. "You should know that, Bob. You're in a business that deals with money."

"I know, I know," Dempster replied. "I just feel that it is my job to point out every contingency to you."

"And I appreciate that," Smoke replied. "That's why I asked you to go to Chicago with Sally and me."

"Tell me, Smoke, did you show the nice men how to drive the train?" Sally asked with a smile.

"I did indeed," Smoke replied. "I pointed to those two long strips of iron, rails I think they are called, and I said, 'Boys, keep this train on those rails, and it'll take us exactly where we want to go.'"

Both Sally and Dempster laughed.

CHAPTER TWO

Smoke and Sally were met at the Big Rock depot by Pearlie Fontaine and Cal Wood. More than employees, the two men who had shared many dangers with both Smoke and Sally were practically members of the family.

"How was your trip?" Cal asked as he put their luggage into the back of the buckboard.

"It was a good trip," Smoke replied. "The market for registered bulls is quite good right now. Did you get the flyers printed?"

Pearlie laughed. "What'd I tell you, Cal? I told you that the first thing Smoke would say soon as he got back would be 'Did you get the flyers printed yet?'"

"Yeah? Well that wasn't the first thing he said. First thing he said was, 'It was a good trip.'"

"He wasn't saying, he was answering."

"Which is what I would like now," Smoke said, laughing at the argument between the two. "An answer, I mean. Did you get the flyers printed or not?"

"Here it is," Pearlie said, unfolding the paper that he had kept in his pocket.

REGISTERED BULLS FOR SALE

Mr. Kirby Jensen, owner of
SUGARLOAF RANCH
Big Rock, Colorado
Has five registered bulls for sale;
HRH Charles III, Prince Oscar, Sir McGinnis,
Count Edward, and Sir Victorious
Papers available price negotiable
Inquire of Kirby Jensen Big Rock Colorado

"Good job," Smoke said, examining the flyer. "I'll get these sent out to every major rancher in Colorado, Wyoming, Nevada, and Texas."

"I hope nobody wants Sir McGinnis," Cal said.

"You mean you don't want Smoke to make money?" Pearlie asked.

"He has to keep some back, doesn't he? I think he should keep Sir McGinnis back."

Washington University, St. Louis, Missouri

As Smoke, Sally, Pearlie, and Cal headed toward Sugarloaf Ranch from Big Rock, nine hundred and fifty miles east in St. Louis, Missouri, Clemente Pecorino, Doctor of Philosophy, and a professor at Washington University, was responding to the invitation of William Elliot, the chancellor. It was an invitation he had been expecting, because he was certain that he was about to be offered a "chair" at the university.

"You sent for me, sir?" Pecorino asked, sporting a confident smile.

Elliot opened the drawer of his desk, and took out the copy of a book that the university press had printed.

"Empiricism and Human Experience," Elliot said, reading the title. "I believe this is your book, Dr. Pecorino?"

"Yes, sir, it is," Pecorino replied, the smile of confidence changing to one of pride.

"And in this book you address the practical problems of implementing Empiricism into society? You say, and I am reading here, 'Under the motto of love, order, and progress, organized religion will eventually be replaced by Humanism.'"

Pecorino raised his hand. "Chancellor Elliot, I realize that you, being an ordained minister, probably don't appreciate that position, but I think my thesis is well-documented in the body of the text."

"No, I don't appreciate it," Chancellor Elliot said. Reaching into his desk, he pulled out another book. "I also didn't appreciate it when I read it in Auguste Comte's book *A General View of Positivism.* But what I most don't appreciate, Dr. Pecorino, is having our university publish a volume replete with plagiarism."

The smile froze on Pecorino's face.

"I . . . uh, admit that I was influenced by Comte's work, but I wouldn't go so far as to say I plagiarized his work."

"Oh? It was one of your students who pointed it out to me, Dr. Pecorino. I then read the work in comparison with Comte's own book, and I had two others read both books and give me a report. Yes, you change some of the language here and there, but more than eighty-five percent of your book, *Empiricism and Human Experience*, is a direct English translation of the French in Comte's work

A General View of Positivism. What do you have to say for yourself, Doctor?"

"I don't agree with that. I will admit only to being influenced by Comte, to publish my own thoughts on the philosophy."

"Yes, well, whether you agree or not, we are pulling back all the books we have published under your name, and we are apologizing to all the other universities and colleges who are using your book as text. We are also terminating your position with us. Please vacate your office as quickly as possible."

"I have a class at ten," Pecorino said.

"No, you don't. Professor Walker has assumed all of your classes."

Pecorino reached for the copy of his book. "If you don't mind, I would like to keep this book as a souvenir," he said.

"By all means," Chancellor Elliot said. "I want no copies left here, at the school, and I've no doubt but that this will soon be the last such book in existence."

Pecorino returned to his office where he saw a maintenance man already scraping his name off the frosted glass of the door. Without exchanging greetings, he went inside and began removing his belongings. When he had everything packed that he intended to take, he sat down to contemplate what had just happened to him. After the publication of his book, which had become a text in colleges all over the country, he had received several invitations to lecture, which would have provided a lucrative second income for him. There was talk of establishing a chair in his name. Now his academic career was ruined.

Comte's book had been published almost forty years ago, in France.

It had a very limited circulation in the United States and had never been translated into English. What were the chances, he wondered, of anyone making the connection between Comte's book and his?

Pecorino picked up the book he had received from the chancellor and opened it. That was when he saw something written on the title page.

This book has been plagiarized from Auguste Comte's book A General View of Positivism. I think Dr. Pecorino should be held to account for it. Jason Kennedy

Jason Kennedy, Pecorino thought. Yes, it would be him. Kennedy was one of his students, intelligent, but a real problem who showed him none of the respect due a man of his position. Kennedy constantly questioned his authority and challenged the information he imparted in his lectures. Those were insults and could only be regarded as insults by design.

But this was the ultimate insult, for this challenge as to the legitimate authorship of the book had cost Pecorino his career in academia.

Half an hour later, Pecorino was standing in front of the university building on Washington Avenue, holding a satchel that contained the personal belongings he had removed from what had been his office. He was waiting for one of the horse-cars to take him to his apartment on Olive.

"Going somewhere, Professor?" a young man asked, his voice clearly meant to be taunting.

"Shouldn't you be in class, Mr. Kennedy?" Pecorino replied.

"Oh, you mean the philosophy course? I've still got fifteen minutes, plenty of time to make it. What about you? Aren't you in danger of being late, as well? After all, you have to teach the class and . . . oh, wait, you can't teach it, can you? You have been . . . what is the word they used? Terminated, yes, that's it. You have no class, because you have been terminated."

"Tell me, Mr. Kennedy, do you consider destroying a man's career to be an accomplishment?"

"If that career is built upon deception, I believe destroying that career to be not only an accomplishment, but a necessity, to prevent students from being influenced by someone who operates under false colors. The book you are so proud of, the one you were using as the text for the class, was not your work. It was the work of the French philosopher, Comte."

"Did you read Comte, Mr. Kennedy?"

"Yes, I read it."

"Then, I have opened your eyes to the subject, haven't I? You'll have to excuse me now. I see the horse-car is arriving."

"You're a fraud, Professor Pecorino. No, wait, you aren't a professor anymore, are you?" Kennedy added with a little laugh. "You're a fraud, Dr. Pecorino. Wait, you probably lied and cheated to get your Ph.D., so you don't deserve to be called Dr. Pecorino either. No doubt you will be relieved of that title, as well."

The horse-car arrived, and with his satchel in hand,

Pecorino mounted the steps, paid his fare, then moved to the back, choosing a seat by the window.

"You're a fraud, Pecorino," Kennedy called through the open window. "You're a fraud, and never again will you be in a position to fill vulnerable students' minds with your lies and deceit."

The car started down the tracks, the team of horses pulling it at a brisk pace.

"You're a fraud, Pecorino!" Kennedy shouted again, though mercifully, his shout was dimmed by distance as the car moved quickly down the track.

Leroy, Wyoming

The small town of Leroy was in the extreme western part of the territory. It had not even existed until the spur line was built that connected Granger, Wyoming, with Echo, Utah. Like any boomtown, it was suffering from the effects of growing too fast. Saloons, brothels, and gambling halls were being built faster than stores, schools, and churches, so that many of the town's newly arrived residents were less-than-desirable citizens.

A recent article in the *Leroy Times* bemoaned that fact when the editor, Dean McClain, wrote:

> From all outside appearances, the town of Leroy is making a rapid growth. But I ask the good citizens of this town, is this really the kind of growth we want? Instead of boardinghouses, we have bordellos, saloons rather than family businesses, dance halls where there should be churches.
>
> We are a town that attracts, not families

upon which there can be real growth, but the very dregs of humanity. Our streets are filled with drunken and debased men and women who have no regard for decency, nor respect for the rights of others.

When five men, Franklin, Logan, Moss, Mason, and Jenner, came riding into the town of Leroy, no one paid any particular attention to them. If they had, some of the more informed might have noticed that they were all wanted men.

Although saloons and brothels would normally be an attraction for such men, these men were here for a different reason. They were here to rob the bank.

"There it is," Franklin said. "Logan, Mason, you stay out front with the horses. Moss, Jenner, you come in with me."

As soon as the three men stepped into the bank, they drew their pistols.

"This is a holdup!" Franklin shouted.

There were two customers in the bank, and they looked around, shocked at the sudden intrusion.

"You two, get up against the wall!" Franklin shouted.

There was only one teller in the bank, and taking advantage of the temporary distraction, he grabbed a gun.

"The teller has a gun!" Moss shouted, shooting, even as he gave the warning. The bank employee went down.

"Now what are we going to do?" Jenner asked. "How are we goin' to get the safe door open?"

They heard shots from outside.

"Franklin! Get out here, fast!" Logan shouted.

"Let's go," Franklin said.

"We ain't got no money, yet," Jenner complained.

"You want to wait around?"

The shooting outside grew more intense, and as the three failed robbers started toward the door, one of the two men who had been in the bank as a customer drew his own pistol. Franklin, sensing the movement, shot the would-be hero.

"Hurry, hurry!" Logan was shouting as the three rushed outside. Leaping into the saddle, the five men galloped out of town, shooting anyone who got in their way. By the time they rode out of town they had killed four, but had come away from the bank with not one dollar.

CHAPTER THREE

Sugarloaf Ranch, Colorado

Smoke Jensen's Sugarloaf Ranch consisted of fifty thousand acres of titled land, with an additional one hundred thousand acres of adjacent, free-range land. With ample water and grass, a rather significant herd of cattle could be accommodated. There was little chance that the herd could wander off because it was fenced in by nature, with mountains to the east and south, and a mesa to the north and west.

When Smoke Jensen began his ranch, he raised only horses, and was, for a while, one of the principal suppliers of remounts for the U.S. Cavalry. But with a growing demand for beef in the East, and premium prices being paid for Herefords, Smoke switched to raising cattle, and his ranch, Sugarloaf, was now the biggest in Colorado, on par with some of the largest ranches in Texas.

He was still a major supplier of beef for the nation's meat market, but he had expanded into the raising and selling of quality registered stock. And these registered animals were kept in their own personal corrals.

Smoke and Pearlie were working on the gate to one of the corrals when Cal rode up.

"I mailed out all the flyers," Cal reported.

"To the newspapers as well as to the ranches?" Smoke asked.

"Yes, sir, just like you said."

"Good, thank you, Cal."

"I'd better go check on Sir McGinnis."

"He's fine," Pearlie said. "I just checked on all of them."

"Yeah, but you don't understand, Pearlie. All the others are satisfied just to have food and water, but Sir McGinnis is different. He expects me to come talk to him ever' day, and if I'm late, he starts looking for me, wondering where I am. So, like I say, I need to go check on him."

Cal started toward the corral where Sir McGinnis was kept.

"Cal sure sets a lot of store by that bull," Pearlie said.

"Yes, well, if you recall when Sir McGinnis was born, his dam had a difficult delivery, and if Cal hadn't been there, the calf might have died. Cal's taken a real personal interest in him, ever since," Smoke said.

Smoke, you know Cal is goin' to be some upset when you sell that pet of his."

Smoke smiled. "He will be, I'm sure. But since I wouldn't even have Sir McGinnis to sell if it weren't for Cal, I've decided to give him a personal bonus when I do sell him. That might make it a little easier for him."

Pearlie laughed. "Yeah, I think it will."

Medicine Bow Mountain Range, Wyoming

The letter didn't have a return address, though it was postmarked in Rawlins. Sheriff Sharples selected it first, from all the mail he had received today.

"This is strange," he said.

"What's that, Sheriff?" Dinkins asked. The deputy was sitting at his desk working on a disassembled kerosene lantern that was spread out before him.

"This letter has no return address. Who would send a letter without a return address?"

"Only way you're goin' to find out is if you open it."

"You don't say," the sheriff replied. He held the letter up to his forehead. "You mean you don't believe I could figure it out just by thinkin' about it?"

"I don't know, maybe you can. You're a pretty smart man," Dinkins replied with a little chuckle.

Sheriff opened the envelope and removed the letter. "I'll be damn," he said. "Listen to this, Dinkins."

Sharples read aloud:

> They was four what got kilt during the bank robbery in Leroy but I didn't kill nobody and I dont want to hang for somethin I didnt do. So what I'm goin to do is tell you how to capture ever one but me. We done got word that the stagecoach on the 10th will be carryin a lot of money, and were a plannin on robbin it. We'll be at the top of Bridgers Pass. I'll be a wearin a yeller shirt sos that when you commence a shootin you will know which one is me and you wont shoot me.

Sharples looked up from the letter. "What do you think about that?"

"Who wrote it?"

Sharples reexamined the missive. "I don't know, he didn't sign it."

"Then how are we supposed to know who it is that helped us?"

"I guess we'll figure that out just by lookin' for the man in the yellow shirt," Sheriff Sharples replied.

Bridger Pass

Franklin, Logan, Moss, Mason, 'n Jenner were waiting at the top of the pass, which, because it was a long, uphill road from the valley below, gave them a position of advantage. Logan was sitting on a rock, eating from a can of peaches; Moss and Jenner were playing a game of mumblety-peg, and Mason was pacing about, nervously. Tony Franklin was looking down the road that climbed up from the valley below.

"Mason, I don't know what the hell for you decided to wear that yeller shirt," Logan said. "Damn if it don't stick out. Iffen we have to hide for somethin', don't you be comin' 'round me."

"Maybe he thinks the women would liken 'im more iffen he'd look like a daisy," Jenner said.

The others laughed.

Franklin paid no attention to the talk going on behind him, as he was too busy keeping a lookout. Then he saw a plume of dust, shining in the mid-afternoon sun. It was too much dust to be coming from a single rider and as he watched for a moment longer, he saw the stagecoach.

"Here it is, boys," he said. "Here comes the stagecoach."

"How much longer you think it'll be 'fore it gets here?" Logan asked.

"Fifteen minutes, maybe. If any of you got to take a

piss, best you do it now. I don't want none of you runnin' off to do it in the middle of the job."

"Hey, Franklin, tell us again how much money the coach is a' carryin'?" Jenner asked.

"Ten thousand dollars," Franklin replied. "It's bein' took from Medicine Bow to the bank in Blodgett."

"Ten thousand dollars," Jenner said. "Ha. I'll have enough money for the prettiest whore in all of Miner Switch."

"There ain't no pretty whores in Miner Switch," Logan said, and the others laughed.

"Get ready, boys, it'll be here any minute, now," Franklin said. "Mason, you stay the farthest back, that damn shirt of your'n is shinin' so bright you can be seen real easy. I ought to make you take the damn thing off."

"I got my long handles underneath, 'n they is red," Mason said. "They'd be seen just as good."

"It's gettin' closer," Logan said.

The five men waited patiently for the coach, knowing that when it reached the top of the pass it would have to stop to give the horses a blow. They knew, too, that there would be no passengers inside the coach, as it was the routine for the passengers to walk behind the coach on these long climbs in order to make it easier on the horses.

The coach reached the top and stopped, but it stopped about twenty yards short of the normal stop . . . the normal stop being a little cleared area with some benches and a couple of privies for the gents and ladies. It was a place that would allow the passengers to rest, as the team recuperated.

"What are they stoppin' back there, for? How come

they ain't up here where they are a' s'posed to be?" Logan asked. By now, he and the others were hidden in a stand of junipers.

"I don't know," Franklin replied.

The five men waited a little longer, but when the coach showed no indication of coming the rest of the way, Franklin lost patience.

"All right, if the coach won't come to us, we'll go to it," Franklin said. "It ain't likely that any of the passengers are carryin' a gun, 'n even if they are, they won't none of 'em know how to use it."

As the five robbers approached, they were so focused on the coach that they didn't notice Mason dropping off behind them.

The driver of the coach was busy with the traces and was standing on the opposite side of the team from the approaching men.

"You, driver!" Franklin called. "Climb up on that box, 'n throw down the money pouch. You passengers, step around here where we can see you!"

The four "passengers" stepped out from behind the coach, all four of them carrying double-barreled shotguns that were leveled at the approaching men.

"Drop them pistols!" one of the men said. "We're loaded with double-aught shot, and we can purt' near cut you in two."

"Do what they say, Franklin," Mason called out. "Or I'll kill you from back here."

"What?" Franklin replied.

"Damn!" Logan said. "The traitor has sold us out!"

Washington, D.C.

General Sherman held a match to President Hayes's cigar, then to his own. Shaking his hand to extinguish the flame, he took several puffs until his head was enveloped by an aromatic cloud of smoke.

At the moment, President Hayes was sitting behind his desk, a recent gift to him from Queen Victoria.

There was a story behind the desk, pertaining to the British vessel, the HMS *Resolute.* That ship had formed a part of an expedition sent in search of Sir John Franklin in 1852, and was abandoned in the far northern ice in 1854. Eventually discovered and extracted by Captain Buddington of the United States whaler *George Henry,* the ship was purchased, fitted out, and sent to England, as a token of goodwill and friendship between the two countries. Later, when the *Resolute* was broken up, a desk was made from her timbers, and presented to President Hayes who accepted it, not for himself, but for the office of President of the United States.

General Sherman and the President were meeting in what had become known as the Lincoln Office.

"You asked to see me, Mr. President?" General Sherman said.

"Yes, General. I have been giving a lot of thought to my last few months in office, and I have decided to take a trip."

"Sir?" Sherman was still unclear as to what he might have to do with any trip the President might have in mind.

President Hayes chuckled. "So, you want to know what that has to do with you, right?"

"It might be good for me to know," Sherman replied with a smile.

"I want to go out West. I want to visit parts of this country no other President has ever visited. Unless you think that would be a bad idea."

"No, sir, I think that would be a great idea. The West is a vibrant and growing part of our nation. I think it would be very good for a President to see the West, and more importantly, for the people of the West to see a President. Sometimes I almost get the impression that the people who live out there feel a little detached, as if the rest of the country has forgotten all about them. Yes, sir, I think it is a wonderful idea."

"Good, good, I'm glad you feel that way," President Hayes said. "Because I want you to plan the trip, make all the arrangements down to the last detail. And I also want you to go with us."

"Us?"

"Yes, that's another thing. I intend to take Lucy, Birchard, and Rutherford with me, and anyone else that you think should go. I'll leave those decisions up to you."

Sherman nodded. "All right, Mr. President, I'll get started right away."

CHAPTER FOUR

St. Louis

It had been two months since Pecorino was fired by Chancellor Allen. Pecorino had applied for teaching positions at St. Louis University, and even at two small colleges over in Illinois, McKendree and Blackburn. But like Washington University, those three schools had been using *Empiricism and Human Experience* as textbooks in their philosophy course until they learned the book had been plagiarized, so when Pecorino approached them, he was turned down. He soon found that all other positions in academia were closed to him, as well, so he had to earn money by tutoring, but that was barely enough to sustain him. Then, he happened to think about something, and he went to Boatman's Bank to make an inquiry.

"How much money is in the building fund for Washington University?"

"Sir, I can only give that information out to the account holders," the officious bank teller replied.

"If you will check, you will see that I *am* an account holder, duly authorized to make withdrawals."

Because Pecorino had been a member of the building

committee before he was fired, he had been one of the signatories, authorized to draw against the account. He was taking the chance, now, that his name had not been withdrawn.

"Very good, Dr. Pecorino," the bank clerk said a moment later. "You are an authorized signatory, so I am at liberty to tell you the amount of money that is in the account. At present, the balance of the account is twenty-one thousand, six hundred and twenty-seven dollars."

"Ah, good, good," Pecorino said with a wide smile. "We need to expend some of the money now, but we didn't want the account to go below fifteen thousand dollars. I'll withdraw only five thousand dollars, and that will leave—the account will be in very good shape."

He had thought about taking all the money, but decided that doing so might arouse enough suspicion that the bank would check on him. Limiting it to five thousand dollars meant no questions were asked.

Pecorino withdrew the money just before the bank closed on Friday afternoon. It would be impossible for anyone to find out about the withdrawal until Monday morning, and Pecorino had every intention of being gone by then. He had only one more task to accomplish.

Monday morning, Pecorino boarded a train in Union Station, heading for Laramie, Wyoming. It was a destination he had chosen at random. He was traveling first class, and as he sat in the Wagner Parlor Car, sipping wine, he began reading the *St. Louis Post-Dispatch*. He found the article he was looking for, even before the train left the station.

WASHINGTON UNIVERSITY
STUDENT FOUND DEAD

Jason Kennedy, a student at Washington University, was found dead Sunday morning. Cause of death was a bullet wound to the head. The assailant is unknown.

Laramie, Wyoming Territory

"Hear ye, hear ye, hear ye! This court of Laramie is now in session, the Honorable J. Bernard Zoller presiding. Ever' body stand up 'n be quiet," the bailiff shouted.

There was a scrape of boots and rustle of skirts and petticoats as the gallery stood.

Judge J. Bernard Zoller was a portly man, bald headed, but with a full, gray beard. He came into the courtroom with his black judicial robe sweeping out behind him, then he took his seat behind the bench.

"Be seated," he said.

The scrape of boots and rustle of skirts was repeated.

The trial of Tony Franklin, Mack Logan, Simon Jenner, William Moss, and Tobias Mason had lasted but half a day. The prosecution had paraded witnesses who testified they had seen the five men leaving the bank, and one of the witnesses, who had actually been in the bank during the robbery attempt, told of seeing the teller and the other customer being shot down.

The jury had adjourned half an hour earlier, and, having announced they reached the verdict, the court was now reconvened.

Judge J. Bernard Zoller turned toward the jury. "Would the foreman of the jury please stand?"

A tall and very slender man responded.

"Has the jury reached a verdict?"

"We have, Your Honor."

"Would you publish that verdict, please?"

"Your Honor, we find ever' one of these killers guilty of murder," he said.

"Oh, oh, that don't look all that good for you fellers, does it?" Mason said quietly with a wide smile on his face.

During their time of incarceration, Mason had been kept in a separate cell from the others.

"Attorney for the defense, please bring your clients up so they may present themselves before the bench."

Morley Gilmore was their defense attorney, only because he had been appointed as such by the judge.

"Your Honor, by prior agreement with the prosecution, we ask that the sentence be adjudicated to Mr. Mason, separately from that of Franklin, Jenner, Logan, and Moss."

"Very well, bring Misters Franklin, Jenner, Logan, and Moss before me now."

Gilmore, with the help of the bailiff, urged the four men toward the bench. It was difficult for them to move, because they were shackled hand to foot.

"Franklin, Logan, Jenner, and Moss, you have been found guilty of murder, and are hereby sentenced to hang."

"Oh, now," Mason called from the defendants' table. "You boys is all goin' to hang. Ain't that just too bad?" He laughed out loud.

Judge Zoller rapped his gavel on the bench. "Order in the court," he said.

The four condemned men were returned to the table.

"Please bring Mr. Mason before me," the judge said.

"I'll be right there, Judge," Mason said with a big smile as he shuffled up to the bench. Although his movement was as restricted as that of the others, there was almost a jauntiness to his approach. When he reached the bench, he turned toward the four men who had retaken their seats at the defendants' table, and laughed out loud. "Watch this," he said.

"Mr. Mason, I have brought you before me on your own, to honor the agreement made between defense and prosecution that you wish to have your sentence pronounced separately from the others. Am I correct in assuming that you wanted your sentence to be pronounced separately from the others?"

"Yeah, that's what I want, all right," Mason said, his response bordering on cockiness.

"Very well, Mr. Mason. You, like the others, have been found guilty of murder. I will separate from the others your sentence pronouncement, as per your request, but I see little reason to do so, as your sentence is exactly the same. You are to be taken along with the others to Cheyenne, and there, to be led up the thirteen gallows' steps where a rope shall be placed around your neck, and you, along with the four men with you, will be hanged by the neck until dead, thus hurled into eternity."

"What?" Mason screamed out loud. "No, that ain't right! We had a deal! I'm the one set it up so's you could capture 'em!"

"Bailiff, please return the prisoners to their cells, to await transportation to Cheyenne," Judge Zoller said.

"No!" Mason screamed again as the bailiff, with the

help of the sheriff, removed the prisoners from the courtroom. "This ain't right! This ain't in no way right!"

The gallery had to wait until the courtroom had been cleared of its prisoners before they were allowed to leave, and as the prisoners were leaving, Franklin was laughing manically.

"Mason, your neck is goin' to be stretched same as ours," he said, and he laughed again.

Sugarloaf Ranch

"I picked up the mail," Cal said. "There's two from Wyoming."

"Let me have them. One of them might be just the letter I've been looking for," Smoke said, reaching for the envelopes. Removing the first letter, he read it and smiled.

"Well, I've got one bite. This is from a man named R. D. Cummings. He wants me to come to Wyoming to visit with him."

Smoke removed the second letter, and his smile grew larger.

"This one is from Albert Barrington. He's also interested in Sir McGinnis."

"You're really going to sell Sir McGinnis?" Cal asked.

"You think we should keep him, and maybe cook him over a pit?" Pearlie asked.

"No, of course not, nothin' like that," Cal answered.

"Cal, whoever winds up buying him, whether it is Mr. Barrington or Mr. Cummings, they are going to pay a lot of money for Sir McGinnis. You know that means that McGinnis is going to get very good treatment," Smoke said.

"I know," Cal said. "It's just that . . ."

"Damn, Smoke. I think Cal's goin' to cry," said Pearlie.

Smoke flashed a stern look toward Pearlie.

"Cal," Pearlie said, his tone considerably softer now. "Smoke's right. Whoever buys him is going to pay a lot of money for Sir McGinnis, and that means he will treat him well. And you know why he'll pay a lot of money? He'll pay a lot of money because you helped bring Sir McGinnis into the world, and you took good care of him. Why, McGinnis wouldn't even be here if it weren't for you."

"That's right, isn't it?" Cal said, brightening a bit.

"He's not going up right away," Smoke said. "First thing I have to do is visit with the two men, and make the sale."

"Why don't they come down here? Why do you have to make the trip?" Pearlie asked.

"I don't mind going up there to see them. I'm the one trying to make the sale."

On Board a train somewhere in Nebraska

At a stop in Kansas City, Clemente Pecorino bought the book *The Trial of Aaron Burr,* written by David Robertson. Pecorino had a particular interest in the book because after he wrote *Empiricism and Human Experience,* he had found a very limited edition of an 1807 book about Aaron Burr, and he had planned to republish it as his own work.

"Apparently, you beat me to it," Pecorino said aloud, though he mouthed the words so quietly that no one heard him.

Pecorino read Robertson's Author's Foreword:

*In 1805, Burr traveled down the Ohio
River where he met with Harman Blennerhassett,
who owned an island on the Ohio River. It was
Burr's plan to use this island as a storage space
for men and supplies. He then recruited
volunteers to raise a western army and "to form a
separate government," in the Louisiana Purchase
Territory.*

*In 1806 he recruited more volunteers for a
military expedition down the Mississippi River,
while using the island in the Ohio River to store
men and supplies. The Governor of Ohio grew
suspicious of the activity there, and ordered the
state militia to raid the island and seize all
supplies. Blennerhassett, Burr's second in
command, escaped with one boat and met up with
Burr at the operation's headquarters on the
Cumberland River. With a significantly smaller
force, the two headed down the Ohio to the
Mississippi River and New Orleans. James
Wilkinson, a general of the U.S. Army and
Governor of Northern Louisiana Territory, became
a co-conspirator, vowing to supply troops at New
Orleans, but he concluded that the conspiracy was
bound to fail. Rather than providing troops,
Wilkinson revealed Burr's plan to President
Jefferson. Aaron Burr, the slayer of Alexander
Hamilton, and the former vice-President of the
United States, was actively seeking to form a new
nation, with himself at its head. Burr failed, and
was subsequently tried for Treason, thus giving*

birth to this book, an accurate, and word by word account of the trial.

"I'll be damn!" Pecorino said, as a wide grin spread across his face.

"I beg your pardon, sir?" someone else in the parlor car asked. "Did you say something?"

"If I did, I'm terribly sorry," Pecorino replied. "I must have spoken aloud over having read something in this book." He held the book up.

The questioning passenger returned Pecorino's smile. "That's quite all right, sir. I too, have found that it is quite easy to lose myself in a book."

Pecorino turned his attention back to the book. I didn't lose myself, he thought. I found myself.

As he continued to read, he began to develop a plan. One learns best by observing past failures. It had been Burr's intention to create a new nation. He had failed because he had divided his authority, giving both Harman Blennerhassett and James Wilkinson power equal to his own.

Pecorino had no intention of making that same mistake.

CHAPTER FIVE

Railroad depot in Denver, Colorado

Smoke was making the trip alone, having left Big Rock just before noon and arriving in Denver around supper-time. After making certain that his luggage was checked on through, he stepped into the dining room and was waiting to be seated when someone called out to him.

"Hello, Smoke!"

Looking toward the sound of the voice, he saw Clyde Barnes, the engineer he had met a few months earlier when he and Sally were returning from Chicago. Clyde, and his fireman, Austin, were sitting at a table.

"Won't you come join us?" Clyde invited.

"Sure, I'd be happy to," Smoke said, then, as the maître d' approached him, he pointed to the table where the two men in striped overalls were sitting.

"I'll join them," he said.

"Very good, sir," the maître d' replied.

"So, what are you doing here? You taking a trip some-where, or are you meeting someone?" Clyde asked.

"I'm going to Medicine Bow, first, then I'll be stopping at Cheyenne on the way back."

"Is that a fact? Well, Austin and I are taking the run all the way to Rawlins, so we'll be on the same train. I'll try and give you a nice ride."

"I'm sure you will," Smoke replied.

When the waiter came to get Smoke's order, Clyde asked that his and Austin's orders be held until Smoke's was ready so they could all dine together. Over the next several minutes they visited, Smoke explaining that he was going to Medicine Bow to meet with R. D. Cummings, a rancher who might be interested in buying a prize bull from him.

As they were talking an officious looking man wearing a Union Pacific Railroad hat approached the table and handed Clyde an envelope.

"Thanks," Clyde replied.

"Do we have a change of orders?" Austin asked.

"I don't know, we may have. Won't know until I look at it," Clyde replied, removing the paper from the envelope. After a moment, he whistled softly.

"What is it?" Austin asked.

"We'll be carrying a money shipment of fifty thousand dollars," he said.

"Damn, that's a lot of money," Austin replied.

"Oh, it's not all that much," Clyde said. "If you saved all your money, and didn't spend one cent of it, you'd have that much by the time you were sixty years old."

Austin laughed.

Smoke enjoyed the company during supper, then when the two train crewmen left to get ready for the trip, Smoke went out into the waiting room until boarding time.

Six hours later, Wahite Creek

Five men were waiting below the track berm where the trestle crossed Wahite Creek, just south of Cheyenne. It was dark, though the brightly shining moon provided a surprising amount of illumination. One of the men was eating beans from a can.

"Damn, Connor, don't you never get filled up?" one of the others asked.

"I didn't eat all my beans at supper," Connor replied, putting another spoonful into his mouth.

"Hey, Dewey, how much longer do you think it'll be?"

Dewey, who had just chided Connor about his eating, was the head of the little group.

"It should be any time now," Dewey replied. "Baggett, climb up to the track and look back toward the west. If the train is within half a mile, you should be able to see the head lamp."

"All right," Baggett agreed.

"Hey, Dewey, I can see the light," Logan called down. "The train's a' comin'."

"All right, boys, get ready," Dewey ordered.

Connor took the last mouthful of beans, wiped the spoon clean on his shirt, then stuck it in his pocket. He tossed the can over his shoulder and it landed with a soft clanking sound. Standing up, he brushed his hands together.

Connor and Hastings walked over to join Dewey and Baggett who had come back down from the track.

"Now, do you understand what we are to do?" Dewey asked.

"Yeah," Connor replied. "We're goin' to build a fire to stop the train. Then when it stops, me 'n Hastings is goin' to make the engineer 'n fireman come down from the cab. You'll be watchin' out for the conductor or anyone else on the train, while Baggett puts a stick of dynamite on the door of the mail car. When it goes, me 'n Hastings will get the money from the mail clerk, then clear out."

"Very good, Mr. Connor. All right, get the fire lit, then get mounted."

The firewood already having been laid, Baggett dashed a little kerosene onto the pile, then lit it. Within a moment a large fire was burning in the middle of the track.

Baggett ran back down and joined the other three to wait, as the train approached.

"Austin, look up ahead. What is that?" Clyde asked.

Austin stuck his head out from the left side of the engine and peered ahead, into the night.

"Looks like a fire," he said. "You don't reckon it's the Rock Creek bridge, do you?"

"Damn, I don't know! It could be!" Clyde replied. Grabbing the brake handle, he pulled it, putting the train into an emergency stop.

Smoke was awakened from a sound sleep by the sudden stopping of the train. He opened his eyes and looked around in the dimly lit car to see what was going on. The other passengers on the train were just as startled by the sudden stop as Smoke, because he heard them talking in confusion. One of the passengers went forward to the vestibule.

There was a heavy, stomach-jarring noise from the front of the train.

"What was that?"

"Sounded like an explosion!"

The passenger who had gone forward, now returned to the car, his eyes wide with excitement.

"It's a holdup!" he said, excitedly. "They just blew the door off the mail car, and I seen some men on the ground pointin' guns at the engineer and fireman!"

"Oh, my!" one of the women said in a frightened voice. "Do you think they'll be in here?"

"I don't know, but iffen I was you folks, I'd be hidin' my valuables," the passenger who had seen the train robbers said.

Taking his advice, the other passengers quickly began to poke billfolds, coin purses, and jewelry into the various nooks and crannies on the train. They were so distracted by what they were doing that none of them noticed Smoke as he eased out the back door. Once outside, he climbed the ladder to the top of the car where he lay down on the roof, using the center ridge for concealment. He pulled his pistol, then surveyed the scene unfolding before him.

There were six men on the ground, and the passenger had been correct in pointing out that two of the men were the cab crew. Smoke saw Clyde and Austin with their hands up. He heard a shot fired from inside the baggage car. That was followed almost immediately by more shots from outside the car, the gun blasts lighting up the darkness with their muzzle-flashes.

"No, no, don't shoot no more!" a muffled voice called from inside the car. "You done kilt the guard!"

"Throw out the money pouch, or we'll kill these two men we're a' holdin'," one of the robbers shouted.

Smoke saw the money pouch being tossed from the train. He aimed at the robber who was waiting for it, then squeezed off a shot just as the money pouch hit the robber's hands.

The robber was knocked down and he landed on his back with both arms spread out to either side. The money pouch lay on the ground beside him.

"Dewey, someone shot Hastings!" one of the riders shouted.

"Where'd that shot come from?" Dewey shouted.

"I don't have no idea!"

"Connor!" Dewey shouted. "Grab the money pouch, 'n let's get outta here!"

Connor had been one of the men holding guns on the cab crew, and as he started toward the money pouch, that left only one man with a gun on Clyde and Austin.

Smoke shot that man, and he went down.

"Drop your guns!" Smoke called down to them. He was now standing on the roof of the car, so the robbers could see him.

"There he is!" Dewey shouted, and the two of them shot at Smoke. The bullets whizzed by his ear, and Smoke returned fire, dropping both of the shooters.

"Clyde, Austin, are you two all right?" Smoke called.

"Yeah," Clyde called back. "But it sounds like they killed Dusty."

"I ain't kilt," a voice called back from inside the car. "We just told 'em that to stop 'em from shootin'. There ain't neither one of us hurt."

Smoke climbed down from the car, and he and the train crew extinguished the fire, then got the track cleared.

"What'll we do with them?" Dusty asked, pointing to the bodies of the men Smoke had killed.

"We can throw them in the express car," Clyde said. "That is if you and Mr. Phillips don't mind."

Phillips, the express agent, wasn't actually a member of the train crew, but worked for an express agency that handled the rail shipment of money and other valuables.

"I don't mind at all," Phillips replied.

CHAPTER SIX

Cheyenne, Wyoming Territory

The arrival and departure of the trains were always big events at the towns and whistle-stops along the Western railroads. It didn't matter whether the citizen was waiting to board the train or meeting an arriving passenger or even seeing someone off. It was the arrivals and departures themselves that were the great attraction, for the trains were a direct, and physical connection with the rest of the world.

There was always a carnival atmosphere in the towns as the people waited to meet the train. The crowd would begin to gather at the depot about half-an-hour before the train was due to arrive, growing with each passing minute until, at the appointed hour, there would be two score or more on hand. Then would come the high point of the evening, the arrival of the engine. The whistle could be heard first, far off and mournful.

"Here she comes!" someone would shout, and the laughter and talking would stop as if everyone were consciously giving the approaching train center stage. The initial sighting would be closely followed by the hollow sounds of puffing steam, then the glowing sparks that were whipped away in the black clouds that billowed up from the flared stack to leave a long line of smoke, hovering over the speeding train.

Finally the engine would rush by with white wisps of steam escaping from the thrusting piston rods, sparks flying from the pounding drive wheels, and glowing hot embers dripping from the fire box.

Then would come the long line of windows of the cars, the passengers inside looking out at the town, which was just like the town they had left, and like the next one they would see. The expressions of the faces of the passengers rarely showed any interest.

The arriving train slowed, and finally ground to a halt with a shower of sparks and a hissing of air from the Westinghouse air-brakes.

"Look!" someone shouted. "Look at the door on the mail car! It looks like it's been blowed off!"

The arriving passengers began to detrain then, met by family and friends. Very quickly after that the stories they carried were repeated throughout the crowd, even among those who were meeting no one.

"Did you hear? Someone tried to hold up the train!"

"Tried? You mean they didn't get away with it?"

"Nope. They was four of 'em what tried, 'n they was all four kilt."

"Sounds like the guard the bank hired earned his money."

"The guard hell. He didn't have nothin' to do with it. It was one of the passengers that shot 'em."

Sheriff Sharples and Deputy Dinkins were pushing their way through the crowd toward the mail car.

"Get back," Deputy Dinkins was saying. "Get back, ever' body. Make way! Let me an' the sheriff through here!"

Phillips, the mail clerk, climbed down from the train. He had a bandage wrapped around his head, covering the wound he received when the door was blown.

"What happened here?" Sheriff Sharples asked. Sheriff Sharples was a large man, at least six feet four, and well over two hundred pounds.

"Someone tried to rob us, Sheriff," Phillips said.

"Did they get the money?" an overweight, middle-aged man asked, pushing through the crowd. This was Joel Adams, the banker.

"No sir, Mr. Adams," Dusty said, proudly. "The money pouch is safe."

"We got four bodies on board, Sheriff," the conductor said. "And I would like to get them off the train as quickly as I could."

Sheriff Sharples turned to Deputy Dinkins. "Get 'em out of the car, Bobby, and lay 'em on the platform," he said. "Let's take a look at 'em."

Soliciting help from a couple of men in the crowd, Dinkins soon had the bodies lying out on the brick surfaced loading platform. Sheriff Sharples walked over to take a good look at them.

"Hey, Sheriff, I know two o' them boys," Dinkins said. He pointed. "That there 'n is Connor, 'n that 'un is Hastings. I don't know them other two."

"Dewey and Baggett," Sheriff Sharples replied. "I've had 'em in jail a couple of times."

"Really? That's funny. How come I don't 'member them?" Dinkins asked.

"I wasn't sheriffin' here then. I was city marshal over in Rock Creek," he said.

Sheriff Sharples looked up at Dusty Fields, the guard who had been hired to keep watch over the money.

"If you didn't kill 'em, who did?"

"He did," Dusty said, pointing to a tall, lean man who was standing next to the baggage car, watching the luggage as it was being off-loaded.

Sheriff Sharples walked down to him. "It seems the town owes you a vote of thanks," the sheriff said. "I'm told you killed all four of the robbers."

"Yes," Smoke said. "I would rather not have killed them, but it just sort of worked out that way."

"What's your name?"

"Jensen. Kirby Jensen."

"You shoulda seen ole Smoke, Sheriff!" Clyde said, approaching the two men then, a wide smile spread across his face. "He was standin' up there on top of the baggage car, hurling death down on them four critters like lightnin' bolts from the angel Gabriel."

"Smoke? Wait, you said Kirby. You're Smoke Jensen?" Sheriff Sharples asked.

"Yes."

The sheriff smiled and extended his hand. "I've heard a lot about you, Mr. Jensen. It's an honor to finally meet you, at last."

The sheriff straightened up, then looked up and down the platform. Most of those who had come to meet the train, as well as the passengers who had arrived and those who planned to continue on with the train, were gathered around for a closer view of the grisly sight. The women were holding handkerchiefs over their noses, though that was more symbolic than anything else for the men had been too recently killed for their bodies to be ripe. The men were somewhat bolder, though Sheriff Sharples noticed that the expressions on the faces of more than a few of them showed that, like the women, their stomachs were just a little queasy.

The engineer, Clyde Barnes, was off the train, while Austin remained in the cab to keep up the steam pressure.

"Smoke, I intend to tell the UP Railroad folks about you. And I guarantee you that you'll have a free ride on any train I'm drivin', from now on. Me 'n Austin owe our lives to you, 'cause I'm sure them ole boys planned to kill us so as to stop the train 'n give 'em time to get away."

Smoke grinned. "I'm glad I was there, Clyde. I consider you and Austin friends, and I don't like losing friends."

"Clyde?" the conductor called.

"Yeah?"

"Better get back into the cab, now. We have a schedule to keep."

Clyde chuckled. "Lonnie let's that conductor position go to his head sometimes, but he's right. We need to get underway again." He started back toward the engine.

"All aboard!" the conductor called, and those who had left the train joined those who were just starting their journey, in re-boarding.

"Well, Mr. Jensen," the sheriff said, "I don't know why it is that you happened to come to Cheyenne, but whatever it was that brung you here, I'm glad you was on the train when you was. You not only kept a couple of good men from gettin' kilt, you saved the money shipment, 'n that'll be mighty important for a lot of the folks here. By the way, why did you come?"

"I'm here to meet with a couple of cattlemen, Mr. R. D. Cummings and Mr. Albert Barrington."

"Barrington lives here. Or, very close."

"Yes, I know, but I thought I would go on to Medicine Bow and meet with Mr. Cummings, first, then meet with Barrington on the way back through."

"Well then, I won't hold you here, any longer, looks like the train is about ready to pull out. Colonel Cummings is a big man in the territory, and he's good man, but I know for a fact that he drives a very hard bargain, so I wish you good luck in dealing with him.

"Barrington, not so much."

"What's wrong with Barrington? Is he not an honest man?"

"Oh, as far as I know he's honest. But he's an Englishman," the sheriff said, as if that explained everything.

The RDC Ranch

Once he reached Medicine Bow, Smoke rented a horse from the livery to ride the five miles that separated R. D. Cummings's ranch from the town of Medicine Bow. Along the Medicine Bow River, he saw a stretch of prairie with grasslands watered by summer rains and winter snows. It was a large open area, impressive in its very loneliness, but good cattle country.

Two of the RDC Cattle cowboys were at the east end of the twenty-thousand-acre spread, just south of where Muddy Creek branched off from the Medicine Bow River. They were keeping watch over the fifteen hundred cattle that had gathered here as a place that would provide them with shade and water, and as Smoke approached, one of the cowboys rode out to meet him.

"Would you be Mr. Jensen?" the cowboy asked.

"I am."

The cowboy smiled. "Yes, sir, I thought maybe it was you, seein' as the colonel is lookin' for you." He twisted around in his saddle and pointed. "This here is the Medicine Bow River, 'n if you'll just follow it for 'bout half a mile, or so, why you'll see a big house with a red roof 'n red shutters. That's where you'll find Colonel Cummings."

"Thanks," Smoke said.

After a ride of a little less than half a mile, Smoke saw a grove of cottonwood trees that stretched out along the east bank of the river. The main house was as the cowboy had described. It was a two-story, white clapboard house with a red roof and red shingled windows. The pillared porch stretched all the way across the front of the house, then wrapped around to the left side, and below it, where the trees stretched down into the valley, there were several buildings, including a barn, the machine shed, and bunkhouse. From here he could see horses in the pastures and cattle dotting the valley.

Even as Smoke was dismounting, he was met on the front porch by a heavyset man with a squared jaw, a full mustache, and intense, dark eyes. Though Smoke had never met him, he had been described. Smoke knew this would be Colonel Cummings.

"Mr. Jensen?" Cummings asked.

"I'm Smoke Jensen."

The colonel smiled. "Good, good. Come in, won't you? I'd like for you to meet Mrs. Cummings. I've had the cook make some pastries for us. We can talk as we have our coffee and sinkers."

"Sounds good to me," Smoke replied with a smile.

When Mrs. Cummings met them, Smoke could see that she must have been exceptionally beautiful as a young woman, because now, in her late forties, or early fifties, she was still quite attractive, the streaks of gray in her hair seeming to augment, rather than detract from, her looks.

"Mr. Jensen, I'm Grace Cummings. It's so nice to meet you," the woman greeted with a smile and an extended hand. "Won't you join us in the keeping room?"

When they stepped into the room, Smoke saw a large painting of R. D. Cummings in the uniform of an army colonel.

"I was with General Crook," Cummings said. "We arrived at Little Big Horn too late to help Custer."

"Given as everyone calls you colonel, I assumed you had some sort of military background," Smoke said.

A couple of servants arrived then, one carrying a silver coffeepot and cups, the other carrying a silver tray, piled high with doughnuts.

"Now, tell me about this bull I'm buying," Colonel Cummings said a few minutes later as the two men and Mrs. Cummings enjoyed coffee and doughnuts in the parlor.

"Well, the first thing I must tell you is that you aren't the only one who has expressed an interest in it. I'll also be calling on Albert Barrington before I go back home."

"Barrington? The Englishman?"

"I'm told he is an Englishman," Smoke said. "I've never met him."

"Yeah, well, if you want my opinion, he's more of a charlatan than he is a rancher."

"Why do you say that?"

"He doesn't really know anything about ranching. He represents a bunch of English investors, and he's losing all their money in that ranch of his, the . . . it's some number, I can't think of what he calls it, right now."

"Three," Smoke said. "The Three Mountain Ranch. That's what he called it in the letter I received."

"Yeah, the Three Mountain Ranch. You aren't really going to sell the bull to him, are you?"

"Well, I'm not going to get the two of you into a bidding war, but I am going to consider an offer from each of you."

Cummings nodded. "All right, that's fair enough. You are in business, after all. Now, tell me more about this bull."

"The bull's name is Sir McGinnis, and he is out of Silk Lady, by HRH Charles III," Smoke said. "HRH Charles has been adjudged 'best of show' in more than a dozen exhibits, from Wyoming to Texas. And Sir McGinnis is as fine a bull as his father is."

"He sounds just like the kind of bull I could use to improve my line," Colonel Cummings said. "Now, how much are you asking for him?"

What followed was a spirited discussion with prices being tossed back and forth until Cummings made an offer of three thousand, five hundred dollars.

"And I guarantee you that Barrington won't be able to match that figure," Cummings said with a satisfied smile.

"I'll promise you this," Smoke said. "He may offer

more, but if his offer is less than five hundred dollars more than the offer you just made, the bull is yours."

Cummings nodded. "That's fair enough, Smoke. And if he does go five hundred dollars higher, you can go ahead and sell to him."

"I doubt very much that he will go five hundred dollars above your offer, but I feel honor-bound to visit him and give him the opportunity, especially since he also expressed an interest," Smoke said.

"I understand, and I'm not worried, because there is no doubt in my little military mind, but that I will wind up with the bull."

"How soon do you want him delivered?" Smoke asked.

"Not until this fall. I'm going to be very busy getting cattle to the railhead and off to market." He smiled. "Besides, I'll need the income from the sale of my cattle in order to be able to pay for Sir McGinnis."

"September?" Smoke asked.

"Yes, that would be a good time. I don't expect you to keep him that long without some money," Colonel Cummings said. "I'll give you half now as earnest money, and the balance when he is delivered."

"There's no need for that," Smoke said. "Especially since I'll be making an offer to Barrington."

"All right, but I did want to make the offer."

"I think we've made a good bargain here," Smoke said with a smile as he extended his hand.

"I do as well," Colonel Cummings said, accepting the handshake. "But it really doesn't matter, because I have no intention of passing on the opportunity to get a bull like Sir McGinnis. I say that Barrington won't beat the offer by five hundred dollars, but to be honest, there's no telling what that crazy Englishman might do. After all, it isn't his own money he is dealing with."

"On the other hand, since it isn't his own money, he might be even a little more cautious," Smoke suggested.

"Yeah, I hope so."

"Oh, Mr. Jensen? When you do bring Sir McGinnis, assuming that my husband's bid stands, please do bring your wife," Grace Cummings said. "I would love to meet her."

"Thank you, I will bring her," Smoke replied. "She loves to travel and meet new people. I know she would enjoy it very much."

CHAPTER SEVEN

Medicine Bow, Wyoming

Satisfied that he had made a good deal, Smoke rode back to town from the RDC Ranch where he returned the rented horse at the livery stable.

"Horse give you any trouble?" the groom asked.

"No trouble at all. He was a good horse," Smoke replied, patting the horse on the neck.

"You coulda slept on your ride out, 'n Coffee here would have taken you to the ranch with no problem," the stable man said as he began removing the saddle. "Coffee knows the RDC well, seein' as Mr. Heckemeyer bought him from the Colonel."

Concluding his business with the livery, Smoke walked back to the train depot to make arrangements to take the steam cars to Big Rock, but first arranging a stop in Cheyenne.

Albert Barrington's ranch, the Three Mountain Ranch, was on the Powder River, near Cheyenne.

* * *

Barrington had offered to meet him at the Cheyenne Cattlemen's Club, but Smoke declined, saying he would rather do business at the ranch. Though he didn't tell Barrington why he chose to meet him at the ranch, the reason was he wanted to see what kind of operation Barrington was running. Cummings had not spoken too highly of him, and he had no wish to leave Sir McGinnis in a tenuous situation.

As he had in Medicine Bow, Smoke rented a horse to ride out to the ranch. When he arrived, it was the house that caught his attention. It was a big two-story pitched-roof house made of squared pine logs. The house was larger than his own house at Sugarloaf and larger than Cummings's house at the RDC Ranch. Smoke had been told that the house was called "Barrington's Castle," and he could see why.

A tall man, wearing buckskins, came out to welcome Smoke.

"I am Albert Barrington, Esquire. You would be Mr. Kirby Jensen?" the man said in a very, cultured, British accent.

Smoke chuckled.

"You laugh, my good man? May I inquire as to what you find so amusing?"

"Hearing that accent coming from someone who is wearing buckskins," Smoke replied.

Barrington laughed as well.

"Yes, I suppose it could be. But I wear such attire because I very much want to fit in. Do come in, won't you? We'll have a spot of tea."

Barrington fit in, all right, Smoke thought. He was like

any other cowman who identified himself as "esquire" and invited someone for a "spot of tea." Smoke didn't give voice to his thoughts, but followed Barrington into the house. Besides, it wouldn't be that unusual for Smoke to drink tea. Sally actually preferred tea to coffee.

Once they were inside, a small, bald-headed man entered the room carrying a tray with a silver salver with a gilt encrusted, porcelain teapot, two cups, and a small platter of scones. He set the tray on a small table that was between two tufted brown leather chairs. They sat in front of one of the stone fireplaces that flanked each end of the great baronial hall.

"Will that be all, sir?" the man asked.

"Yes, thank you, Jules," Barrington said. "Mr. Jensen, this is Jules Plumbly. Mr. Plumbly was the best damn manservant in all of Great Britain, and now he is the best in America."

Smoke stood to meet him. "Congratulations on being the best manservant in America."

"My pleasure, sir, but I prefer the title, valet," Jules replied, pronouncing the "t."

"I thought the 't' was silent," Smoke said.

"Sir, apparently the French lack the dexterity of the tongue that will allow them to say the letter 't' in a great number of words. However, 't' is a perfectly good letter, and as I am a va-Let, I choose the right to pronounce the word as it was intended."

"I've never heard a more vigorous, or effective defense of the letter 't,'" Smoke said with a laugh.

Barrington laughed, as well. "Tell me truthfully, Mr. Jensen, have you ever heard the letter 't' defended at all?"

"I can't say that I have."

"I hired Mr. Plumbly to groom horses, but I soon found out he was better at grooming me, so I keep him around. He's a good man."

"Shall I pour, sir?"

"Please do. Will you join me?" Barrington asked, indicating the empty cups.

"Thanks," Smoke replied as he accepted the cup.

"Now, about the bull you have for sale," Barrington said.

"Mr. Barrington, as I indicated in the letter, you were not the only person who expressed an interest in buying Sir McGinnis. And I feel that I must also tell you, that I received an offer of three thousand five hundred dollars from Colonel R. D. Cummings."

"Oh, my, that's quite a sum of money," Barrington said. "I've read all the information you included about the bull, and I'm sure he is worth that, and more. And I do think he is just what I need now . . . I am sorry to say that my ranch is not doing as well as I and my backers hoped."

Smoke cleared his throat. "I also told Colonel Cummings that I wouldn't sell unless his offer was topped by five hundred dollars, and if an offer of four thousand dollars is made, I will sell the animal. I've no intention of getting you two gentlemen into a bidding war."

"Yes, well, that is most decent of you," Barrington said. "However, I don't think I can afford to be out four thousand dollars. As I said, my ranch is in great difficulty right now . . . you might even say it is bordering on extreme."

"I'm sorry to hear that. What is your biggest problem?"

"My brother," Barrington answered, cryptically.

"Your brother?"

"Richard has assumed the duty of . . . I believe you Americans call it ramrod, though using the term of a device meant to load weapons as foreman seems rather strange to me. At any rate Richard is in charge of the cowboys and the actual operation of the ranch, and he is failing, miserably."

"Why don't you fire him?"

"Oh, that would cause great familial stress, and I would rather not do that." Barrington smiled. "At any rate, this isn't your problem, and, as it is quite impossible for me to meet the required sum for the purchase of Sir McGinnis, I will have to let that pass. In the meantime, perhaps you'll be my guest for dinner at the Cheyenne Cattlemen's Club while you wait for the train to take you back to Colorado."

"I would be glad to join you for dinner, but please allow me to buy it. I think I should, seeing as I am unable to provide the bull for you."

Barrington shook his head. "Only members may make purchases at the club." He smiled. "So I win this one."

When they returned to Cheyenne, they stopped by the depot for Smoke to check on his train. He would have to change trains in Denver, where there would be a two-hour layover. Smoke calculated what time he would be back home, then stepped up to the Western Union office to send a telegram back to Sally.

WILL BE HOME IN TIME FOR SUPPER
TOMORROW STOP CHICKEN AND
DUMPLINGS WOULD MAKE A GREAT
WELCOME HOME MEAL STOP LOVE
SMOKE

The train would not leave until ten thirty that night, which gave Smoke time to have dinner with Barrington.

"How did your roundup go, this spring?" Smoke asked over dinner.

"There was no roundup to speak of. We had a very difficult winter, the cattle were scattered everywhere, we lost cattle to predators and no few rustlers. As a matter of fact, and you've no idea how it pains me to say this, but I would estimate that over the last two years, we have lost fully one half of our herd, and Richard is totally incapable of handling the situation." Barrington pinched the bridge of his nose. "I'll tell you the truth, Mr. Jensen, I am quite at my wit's end."

"You need a good foreman."

"Oh, I quite agree. But the problem is I'm English. Well, it isn't so much that I'm English, it is that my brother is also English. It has been my observation that the American cowboy seems to have a difficult time taking orders from someone who says, you 'cohn't' do that, rather than you 'cain't' do that."

Smoke chuckled. "Cohn't or cain't, it's been my observation that cowboys don't like to be told that they can't do anything."

The two men continued with their friendly conversation until Barrington said that he needed to get back to the ranch. "I'm sorry I wasn't able to come up with the extra money to buy the bull," Barrington said. "But to tell you the truth, I don't think I could have even met Colonel Cummings's offer, let alone top it by five hundred dollars. But I do appreciate you extending me the opportunity."

"And I appreciate the dinner," Smoke said.

After Barrington started back to the Three Mountain Ranch, Smoke, seeing that he still had a lot of time to kill, decided to have a beer. It was mid-August, and as he walked away from the club, the heat bore down on him like some great weight. The false-front buildings of the town were somewhat blurred by the shimmering heat waves.

He hurried from the shade of one building to the next, taking every opportunity to get out of the sun. After a walk of less than two blocks he was drenched with sweat, and the cool interior of the Watering Hole Saloon beckoned him. A sign outside the saloon promised cold beer, and he thought nothing could be better than that. He pushed his way through the batwing doors and went inside, moving as he always did to place his back against the wall as he perused the saloon.

It was so dark that he had to stand there for a moment or two until his eyes adjusted. The bar was made of burnished mahogany with a highly polished brass foot rail. A bartender with pomaded black hair and a waxed handlebar mustache stood behind the bar industriously polishing glasses.

Smoke stepped up to the bar. "Is the beer really cold?"

The bartender looked up at him, but he didn't stop polishing the glasses.

"It's cooler than horse piss," he said, in a matter-of-fact voice.

Smoke laughed. "That's good enough for me." He put a nickel on the bar as the bartender drew the beer and set the mug before him.

"Hey, wait a minute," the bartender said, pausing with his finger on the nickel. "You're the feller that broke up that train robbery, ain't you?"

"I was on the train," Smoke replied, deliberately being as circumspect as he could be, not wanting any unnecessary recognition.

"You was more than just on the train. Mister, you might not know it, but if that money hadn't got through to the bank, there's a lot of folks in this town that woulda been hurt by it, includin' me."

The bartender pushed the nickel back. "This beer's on the house," he said.

"And the next one is on me," another man said. "I own the boot and leather shop, I woulda lost a lot of money, too."

"And the next one's on me," another said.

"Don't leave me out!" a third put in.

Smoke laughed. "What are you men trying to do, get me drunk?"

"No, sir, not at all. We're just tryin' to be neighborly, is all," one of the well-wishers said.

There was one man standing at the far end of the bar who had not taken part in the accolades. He was a thin man, with very black hair, a pock-marked face, and full mustache that curved down over his mouth. Although he had said nothing, he hadn't escaped Smoke's notice, and there was something about him that put Smoke on alert. Perhaps it was the fact that, unlike the others in the saloon, he had not vocalized his appreciation of the bank shipment being saved.

"You can do that, can you, mister?" the man said, and the expression and timbre of his voice was in direct contrast to the laudatory tones of the others.

"I'm sorry, I don't understand," Smoke replied. "What is it that you are questioning that I can or can't do?"

"You can commit murder, then come in here and have a drink and talk with others as if the murder you done didn't mean nothin' to you?"

"That's enough, Dewey," the bartender said. "It wasn't murder and you know it."

"Your name is Dewey?" Smoke asked.

"Yeah. Ethan Dewey."

"One of the train robbers was a man named Dewey."

"That would be Emmet, my brother," Dewey said. "You kilt 'im."

"I'm sorry about that, Mr. Dewey. But your brother left me no choice." At that moment, Smoke saw in the mirror that Dewey had already drawn his pistol, and was holding it down by his side.

"Mr. Dewey, I suggest that you put your pistol away. Holding it down by your side isn't going to give you any advantage."

"You murderer!" Dewey shouted, swinging his gun up toward Smoke and thumbing the hammer back as he was doing so. Even though he had the advantage of the pistol already being in his hand, Smoke drew and fired. His bullet struck Dewey in the chest, and his would-be assailant's eyes opened wide in surprise, even as he pulled the trigger on his pistol. Because he had been hit, his shot was erratic, and it crashed into the mirror behind the bar and Dewey fell to the floor.

Someone said in awe, "Did you see that? Dewey already had his gun out, 'n this feller still beat 'im."

"Yeah, Burt, we seen it. We all seen it," one of the others replied.

Smoke looked at Dewey, and knew, without having to check any further, that the man was dead.

"Somebody ought to go get the sheriff," one of the card players suggested.

"We don't need the sheriff. We need an undertaker," another said.

"I don't know 'bout you boys, but one day I'll be tellin' my grandkids 'bout this day, 'n me seein' Smoke Jensen bestin' another feller in a gunfight."

"Who you kiddin', Smitty? How you goin' to have grandkids to tell your story to, seein' as you ain't never goin' to find no woman that'll give you any kids in the first place?"

The others laughed.

CHAPTER EIGHT

"What's going on in here?" a loud, gruff voice asked, pushing in through the batwing doors.

"Hello, Deputy Dinkins," the bartender said. "We was just about to send for you. Ethan Dewey got hisself kilt."

"Who done it?"

"I did," Smoke said.

"Deputy, if there was ever anyone who needed hisself kilt, it was Ethan Dewey," one of the customers said.

"Did you see it, Hillis?" Dinkins asked.

"Yeah, I seen it," Hillis replied. He proceeded to tell the deputy all the events leading up to the shooting, including the fact that Dewey had already drawn his gun and was holding it down by his side before the confrontation had advanced to the showdown stage. Hillis's story was validated by everyone else in the saloon.

"Mr. Jensen, would you come down to the sheriff's office with me?" Dinkins asked. Before Smoke could respond, Dinkins held out his hand. "Don't worry, there ain't goin' to be no charges, or nothin', but the sheriff will be needin' to get a statement from you."

"Do I have time to finish my beer?" Smoke asked, holding up his mug.

"Sure, go ahead. I'll talk to some of the witnesses."

"Ain't no need to talk to nobody," one of the patrons said. "You done got the story of what happened, 'n there ain't nobody goin' to tell you nothin' no differn't."

"You know how this works, Sandy. I need to talk to as many people as I can. Besides which, you heard Mr. Jensen. He needs time to finish his beer anyhow."

A few minutes later, Arthur Welsh came in to the saloon. Welsh was the local undertaker. He walked over to look down at the body. "Someone said that the man who killed the four train robbers, is the same one that killed this man," Welsh said. "Is that true?"

"It surely is," the bartender said. "Smoke Jensen did it. He's standin' there at the bar, drinking a beer."

Welsh looked over toward the tall, broad-shouldered man the salon patron had pointed out. Smoke was drinking his beer, looking across the bar at the now-cracked mirror.

"He's sort of a cool fellow, isn't he?" Welsh asked.

"I'd say so. He's about as cool as they come. He warn't the bit flustered, even though Dewey already had his gun out 'n was bringin' it up on Jensen before Jensen even draw'd his."

"That's five bodies for me today. Sometimes I don't get that many subjects in an entire month." Welsh glanced over at Smoke. "I may have to put that gentleman on a retainer."

* * *

"Do you have anything to add to the story?" Sheriff Sharples asked after Deputy Dinkins gave his report.

Smoke shook his head. "I can't say that I do. Deputy Dinkins got all the details right."

"Did you know Ethan Dewey?"

"I met him for the first time today," Smoke said.

"Well, I don't intend to suggest that any charges be filed, but I'd like to have the judge sign off on it, nevertheless. And it just so happens that he's in town today. So if you don't mind, we'll just go see him now."

"All right," Smoke said. "I've got plenty of time before my train leaves."

It took but one inquiry to find the judge having his dinner at the Palace Café.

"Sheriff, I hope you aren't bringing me any business for me to deal with in the middle of my dinner," the judge said, lifting the bottom of the napkin that was tied around his neck, and using it to dab at his lips.

"No, sir, I ain't bringin' you nothin' to work on," Sheriff Sharples replied. "I'm bringin' you just the opposite. I'm comin' to tell you that I won't be filin' no charges against Smoke Jensen."

"Isn't he the one who interrupted the attempted train holdup?" the judge asked. "I thought I had already signed off on that."

"Yes, sir, you did, only this killin' ain't that killin'."

"You mean he killed someone else?"

"Yes, Your Honor, 'bout an hour ago, over in the saloon."

"My word, you have been a busy man, haven't you, Mr. Jensen?" the judge asked.

"I have, Your Honor, but not by design."

Quickly, Sheriff Sharples told the story of Smoke's encounter with Ethan Dewey. "Dinkins talked to ever' one in the saloon, 'n ever' one of 'em has told the same story. So, I'm recommendin' that there don't be no charges made, only thing is, you're the one that'll have to say that."

"Done, done, no charges," the judge said.

"Thank you, Your Honor."

Sheriff Sharples walked with Smoke down to the depot.

"I'll wait for the train with you," the sheriff offered.

Smoke chuckled.

"What is it?" Sheriff Sharples asked.

"If I didn't know better, Sheriff, I'd say you are staying with me just to keep me from getting into any more trouble."

"What makes you think you do know better?" the sheriff asked. "That's exactly what I'm doing."

"What?" Smoke replied in surprise.

Sheriff Sharples laughed out loud. "I got you on that one," he said. "Truth is, Smoke Jensen, I'm glad you come to town. You've done us a huge favor, not only by savin' the money, but takin' care of some folks that's been a big problem for us."

"Yes, well, as I said, my running into these people was certainly not by design," Smoke replied.

"I reckon not. Damn, all this come up, 'n I haven't even had a chance to ask you how things went with Colonel Cummings 'n Mr. Barrington. Were you able to do business with either one of 'em?"

"Yes, I was, thank you."

"I'm bettin' it was with Colonel Cummings, 'n not the Englishman."

"What makes you think that?" Smoke asked.

"Well, sir, from what I've heard, them two Englishmen, Albert, 'n his brother, Richard, have damn near gone bust. 'N all them fellers back in England that's put up the money 'n all is gettin' pretty dissatisfied. Problem is Richard is the ranch foreman, 'n he don't know no more 'bout runnin' a cattle ranch than I do 'bout runnin' a ladies' tea room. If he don't get someone else in here, he's goin' to go belly up, sure as gun is made of iron."

"You are right . . . about Colonel Cummings, I mean. He's the one that bought the bull."

"Colonel Cummings is a big man in these parts, and he's a good man, but I know for a fact that he drives a very hard bargain, so I know that, if you made a deal with him, he's satisfied. The question is, are you satisfied?"

"I'm very satisfied."

"You don't say. Well, you can't ask for nothin' better than for both of you to be satisfied. I guess that means you'll be comin' back to town before long."

"Yes, to deliver the bull."

"Well, I hope that all goes through without any trouble." They heard a distant whistle.

"Sounds like the train's a' comin'," Sheriff Sharples said.

Within a few minutes the floor of the building began to shake, slightly, and the windows rattled as the heavy train approached.

Smoke and Sharples walked outside to watch the train approach. The fireman was leaning out the window of the cab as the locomotive rolled into the station. Smoke was a little disappointed that it wasn't Austin, but then, he knew that the chances were very much against that.

CHAPTER NINE

Laramie, Wyoming Territory

Clemente Pecorino sat at a desk in his room at the Mixon Hotel in Laramie. On the desk before him was a bottle of ink, a fountain pen, and a sheet of newsprint he had purchased from the local newspaper.

He heard a knock at the door, and because the knock was not unexpected, he opened it without concern. A man with a mutton chop beard and wearing a vertically striped, blue and white shirt with garters on his sleeves stood there, holding a large camera in one hand, and a tripod in the other.

"Mr. Pecorino?" the man asked.

"I am a Ph.D.," Pecorino replied.

"I beg your pardon?" the visitor replied, confused by the answer.

"I am a Ph.D. The proper form of address would be Dr. Pecorino, not Mr. Pecorino."

"Oh. Well, anyway, you asked for a photographer?"

"I did indeed. Come in."

"Yes, sir. May I ask, where is the photograph to be taken?"

"It is to be taken here, of me," Pecorino replied.

"Oh, sir, if it is to be a portrait, this isn't the best place for me to take the picture. If I could talk you into coming down to the studio, I assure you, the conditions would be much better for photography."

"Perhaps that is so. But such a photograph would not be historically accurate."

"Historically accurate? I don't understand."

"There is no need for you to understand," Pecorino said. "The only thing I want from you is the photograph."

"Yes, sir."

"I will be sitting at that desk, and I will be writing on that sheet of paper. Will you be able to get everything in the picture? By that, I mean me, the paper, the inkwell, and the pen?"

The photographer set up a tripod and camera, then stared diligently through his viewfinder.

"Yes, sir," the photographer said. "I have established the perfect angle. If you would just look at me, I can take the photograph now."

"No, I don't want to be looking at you," Pecorino said.

"Sir? I don't understand. What is the purpose of a photograph, if the face of the subject cannot be seen?"

"The purpose of the photograph is to see me writing," Pecorino said.

"You want me to take a picture of you writing, even though I will only get the side of your face?"

"Yes, that is exactly what I want," Pecorino replied.

"I don't understand."

"Of course, you don't understand, but I'm not hiring you for your intellectual acuity. I'm hiring you to take a photograph."

"Very good, sir. Begin writing. I will take some photographs."

"I only want one photograph taken."

"Oh, but sir, we always take two or three, in order to make certain that we get at least one good one that will satisfy the customer," the photographer replied.

"Very well, you can take more than one, but after I make my choice, I want the other pictures destroyed. I also want the photo plates destroyed. It is very important that there be but one official photograph."

"Official?"

"Perhaps I have used the wrong word," Pecorino replied. "What I mean is, I shall want only one *authentic* photograph. That will greatly enhance its value."

"Yes, sir," the photographer replied.

Pecorino grasped the pen and, bending over the newsprint paper, held the pen as if writing. He maintained that same position for four takes, each take requiring a reloading of the plate, and the magnesium flash.

"How soon can I have the prints?" Pecorino asked.

"You can have them this very afternoon," the photographer replied.

"Very good. Get on with it," Pecorino said.

After the photographer left, Pecorino picked up the pen again, loaded the tip with ink, and began working diligently to set his thoughts to paper. He was filled with a sense of importance as he penned the words, and he wrote them in a beautiful, flowing cursive, because he was certain that in school classrooms one hundred years from now, children would be reading about him, honoring him as the founder of their nation. And what he was writing, right now, would, no doubt, be reprinted and posted in classrooms as the founding document of the new nation. And unlike the signers of the Declaration of Independence, reproduced only in the imagination of artists, the birth of this nation had just been captured by the modern science of photography.

Pecorino wrote the title, looked at it with pride, then continued with the document.

FOUNDING PROCLAMATION OF NOVA AMERIGO REGNUM

A DECLARATION TO WITHDRAW THE TERRITORIES AND STATES OF WYOMING, COLORADO, UTAH, NEVADA, AND CALIFORNIA, FROM THE ENTITY KNOWN AS THE UNITED STATES OF AMERICA, IN ORDER TO ESTABLISH ITS INDEPENDENCE, AND ASSUME ALL THE RIGHTS AND POWERS THEREOF

Whereas, the above-mentioned territories and states are too distant from the federal government in Washington, DC, and whereas the laws of the United States are applied unequally upon this area because of said distance, therefore be it proclaimed that there be a separation, and subsequent establishment of a new nation to be known as Nova Amerigo Regnum.

The new nation, formed by the joining of Wyoming, Colorado, Utah, Nevada, and California, shall be established as one contiguous kingdom, uninterrupted by state or territorial lines, to be ruled by the absolute authority and power invested in His Royal Highness, King Clemente Benito Pecorino, first sovereign of the new kingdom. Succeeding sovereigns of Nova Amerigo Regnum shall be from the first male issue of King Pecorino and the first male issue of all Kings subsequent. By the affixation of the signature of His Royal Highness, hereto attached, this proclamation is hereby in force.

HRH Clemente B. Pecorino
Monarch of Nova Amerigo Regnum

Over dinner that evening Pecorino thought about the proclamation he had written earlier in the day. He considered having it framed, but decided it would be easier to keep it rolled up and in his valise.

Pecorino was well aware that one could not conduct a revolution without an army, and one couldn't raise an army without money. But even as he considered the situation, he realized that the two requirements were not incompatible. He would gather an army, and use that small army to raise money to fund the revolution. It would be a small army at first, one that would be easy to control. He would use his army to strike at targets of opportunity, balancing target vulnerability with overall effect.

Pecorino realized that, initially, his army would not consist of men of vision and purpose for the new nation. They would have to be men that were driven by the promise of economic reward. And, of course, they would have to be men of absolute and unquestioned loyalty, not to the Nova Amerigo Regnum, but to him, personally.

All right, he had established the requirements, all he had to do now was respond to those needs, and an article in the *Laramie Sentinel* gave him an idea as to how to take his first step. This is where he would raise his first recruits.

SENTENCES TO BE CARRIED OUT

On the twelfth Instant, five murderers, whose horrendous crimes defy description, were tried in a court of law. Had the murderers, Tony Franklin, Mack Logan, Simon Jenner, William Moss, and Tobias Mason been taken from their cells and hanged by an enraged mob of citizens, there would be few who would lament the violation of prisoners' rights.

But the faint hearted need have no fear over the destiny awaiting these five murderers, for though they will hang, their demise will be the result of legal trial and sentencing. One week hence, the five will be transported to Cheyenne in a barred wagon, driven and guarded by two armed deputies.

Sugarloaf Ranch

When Smoke returned home late the next afternoon, Cal was waiting under the arched gate of the drive that ran from Big Rock Road up to the house.

"Hello, Cal."

"We hear you had some excitement on the train on the way up," Cal said.

"I suppose you could call it excitement," Smoke said. "How did you hear about it?"

"Ha! All I had to do was read the newspaper, seeing as there was a story about it in the *Big Rock Journal*."

"If that is the case, I guess there is no need for me to tell the story."

"You can still tell it, Smoke. I mean, yeah, it was in the newspaper, but it'll be a lot more interestin' comin' from you." Cal smiled. "Oh, and Miz Sally has made you a surprise for supper."

"I hope it's chicken and dumplings."

"Yeah, it is, 'n that's the surprise . . ." Cal paused and flashed a sheepish grin. "Only, if you already know about it, I don't reckon it's that much of a surprise."

Pearlie was sitting in the front porch swing when he saw Smoke and Cal approaching.

"Miz Sally!" he shouted. "Come look who's here."

Sally came to the front door.

"Oh, it's Smoke!" Sally said happily. She stepped out onto the front porch and stood at the steps, holding on to one of the supporting posts of the porch as she watched

Smoke and Cal coming up from the arched gate at the end of the long drive.

The two riders rode on up to the house, then Smoke dismounted and handed the reins of Seven to Cal. Sally hurried down the steps, and they kissed and embraced as Cal rode toward the barn to take care of the two mounts.

"I read about your little adventure," Sally said, after the kiss. "It seems like I can't send you anywhere without you getting in trouble."

"You know me, Sally. Trouble just seems to follow me."

"I can't argue with that," Sally replied. "And I knew that when I married you, so I don't have anyone to blame but myself. Come on in, dinner is about ready."

"Cal told me that you got my order about having chicken and dumplins."

"Order? Smoke Jensen, you had better amend that statement to request."

Smoke laughed. "I requested chicken and dumplins, and Cal said that you had, most graciously, granted me that request."

Sally smiled and kissed him on the cheek. "Now you are learning," she said.

"So, what is the verdict?" Sally asked over supper that evening.

"Verdict?"

"Correct me if I'm wrong, but you did go to Wyoming to sell a bull, didn't you? Who did you sell it to, Cummings or Barrington?"

Smoke laughed. "Yes, I did, and here we have been

talking about everything but the bull. I sold it to Colonel Cummings, and I got quite a good deal, I think. Three thousand, five hundred dollars."

"Oh, Smoke, that's a great deal!" Sally said enthusiastically.

"Three hundred and fifty dollars of it goes to you, Cal," Smoke said.

"What? You're givin' me three hundred fifty dollars? Why?"

"So you won't cry when we take Sir McGinnis away from you," Pearlie teased.

"Pearlie! That's not nice. You take that back," Sally said, sternly.

"Sorry, Cal, I didn't mean anything by it," Pearlie said. "And the reason you're getting the money is because Smoke wouldn't even have a bull to sell, if it hadn't been for you."

"Pearlie is right, Cal," Sally said. "Everyone knows how you saved his life when he was first born, and how well you've taken care of him ever since. You have, truly, earned the bonus."

"When will you deliver him?" Cal asked.

"Sometime in September," Smoke replied. "And Sally, when I take Sir McGinnis up, I would like you to come with me. Mrs. Cummings wants to meet you, and I think the two of you would get along just real well."

CHAPTER TEN

Laramie County, Wyoming Territory

Luke Jacobs and Clay Waters were transporting seven prisoners in a locked, and barred wagon.

"You think a fella really could dig a hole all the way through the middle of the world, and come out in China?" Waters asked.

"I suppose you could, seein' as it's on the other side of the world," Jacobs replied. "But what I'd be wonderin' about is, you would start out by diggin' down, right?"

"Well, yeah," Waters said. "How else would you dig?"

"Well now, see, that's the problem. You'd start out diggin' down here, in America, but when you dug all the way through the middle of the world 'n reached China, why you'd have to be diggin' up to come out of the hole. Now how do you think that would happen?"

"That's easy," Waters said. "When you'd get to the middle of the world, why, you'd stop diggin' down, 'n start diggin' up."

"That sure is somethin' to ponder on, ain't it?" Jacobs said.

"Yeah, but not too much 'cause if you thought about

somethin' like that too much, why, you'd plumb go crazy,"
Waters insisted.

"Hey, what's that up there?" Jacobs said.

"Looks like a buckboard."

"Yeah, only what's it doin' just sittin' there?"

"Why, there's the problem," Waters said. "Lookie
there, it's got a broke wheel."

As the prison transport wagon approached, a very
well-dressed man stepped out into the road and held up
his hand. He was neatly groomed, with dark hair and a
well-maintained dark mustache. He was wearing a three-
piece suit and a bowler hat that he removed and held in
his hands.

"Am I glad to see you gentlemen," he said.

"Who are you?" Jacobs asked.

"Yes, I suppose that was rude of me, wasn't it? My
name is Clemente Pecorino. Dr. Pecorino to be exact. And
as you can see, the vehicle I rented has a broken wheel."

"Yes, I see that."

"I was wondering if I could get a ride with you gentlemen? Just into Cheyenne, you understand. Once there, I
shall make arrangements for the vehicle to be recovered."

"Doc, I'm sorry but we can't give you a ride," Jacobs
replied. "For one thing, it would be against the rules for
any citizen to ride on a prison wagon, 'n for another thing,
you more 'n likely wouldn't want to ride with this bunch,
anyhow. Why, they're all murderers, 'n are bein' took to
Cheyenne to hang."

"Well, that ain't entirely true," Waters added. "Only
Franklin, Logan, Moss, Mason, 'n Jenner is goin' to be
hung. Them other two is more 'n likely just goin' to spend
a few months in jail."

"Oh, dear me," Pecorino said. "Does that mean I'm to walk all the way to Cheyenne? How far is it, anyway? I'm a stranger in these parts. I'm a college professor from Washington University in St. Louis, and I've come out West to conduct a lecture tour."

"You got a couple of horses there," Waters said, pointing to the two animals that were standing patiently in their harness. "You could ride one of them."

"But I have no saddle," Pecorino complained.

"You don't need no saddle, Doc. I rode bareback 'til I was sixteen. There ain't nothin' to it."

"But you don't understand. I'm from the city. I know nothing about horses. I don't even know how to get this animal disconnected from its harness."

"Well, hell, we can take care of that, for you. Come on, Luke, let's get the doc fixed up here."

"All right," Jacobs said.

"Hey! Jacobs! Waters!" someone shouted from the wagon. "Seein' as we're stopped anyway, how 'bout you let us out so's we can take a piss?"

"Go let 'em out," Jacobs said. "I'll take care of the doc's horse, while you watch over 'em."

After the two men climbed down from the high seat of the wagon, Jacobs started toward the buckboard and team, while Waters went to the back of the wagon and let the six prisoners out.

"Who is that fancy lookin' feller?" one of the prisoners asked, as they all shuffled over to the side of the road to relieve themselves.

"He's a doctor," Waters replied, "a gentleman, which is more 'n likely somethin' there ain't nigh a one of you ever even seen before."

As Jacobs began working on the horse, Pecorino stepped up behind him, reached around to put his hand over Jacobs's mouth while, with his other hand, he drew a knife across the front of Jacobs's throat. The blade cut through the jugular and the wind pipe, which not only started massive bleeding and cut off his supply of air, it also silenced him. Jacobs dropped to the road and died without a sound.

Because the whole thing had happened in silence, and behind the backs of Waters and the prisoners, they were unaware of the murder that had just taken place.

Pecorino, who had been holding the knife secreted in his hat, now put the knife away and, from an inside jacket pocket, pulled a pistol and stepped up behind Waters.

"Sir, can you be of some assistance?" he said.

"Better ask Luke. I've got these men to see to."

"He can't help me," Pecorino replied.

"What do you mean he can't help? All he has to do is cut the horse loose," Waters replied, the tone of his voice showing his irritation.

"I'm afraid he is deceased," Pecorino said.

"He's what?"

"He is dead."

"How the hell . . ."

When Waters turned and saw the pistol in Pecorino's hand, he gave a start.

"Here! What is this?" he called.

Pecorino pulled the trigger. A black hole appeared in the middle of Waters's chest, and he went down.

"What the hell?" one of the prisoners shouted. Because they were all shackled together, it took them an awkward moment to turn around and see what had just happened.

"Gentlemen," Pecorino said, still holding the smoking gun in his hand. "I am in the process of raising a group of men who would be willing to be one hundred percent loyal to the cause. In response to your loyalty, I will grant you your freedom now, provide you with a generous income, and guarantee a place for you in the future I plan to build. Who of you, now, are willing to make that pledge to me?"

"Hell, I will, for sure!" one of the men said. "I mean we was bein' took to hang anyway. What have I got to lose?"

"You can count me in, too," another said, and two more prisoners joined in the affirmation of loyalty.

"Yeah, well, you can count me out," another prisoner said. "Them five was bein' took to prison to hang, but me 'n Floyd here, ain' fixin' to hang."

"And what is your name, sir?" Pecorino asked.

"Toone. The name is Tucker Toone."

"And you would be Floyd?" Pecorino asked the other man.

"Yeah, Floyd Simpson."

"Mister Simpson, do you agree with Mr. Toone? Do you not wish to join the group I'm assembling?"

"No, why should I ask for more trouble? Six months from now, I'll be out of jail."

"Too bad," Pecorino said as he shot both Simpson and Toone.

Getting keys to the ankle shackles from Jacobs's

pocket, Pecorino freed Franklin, Logan, Moss, Mason, and Jenner."

"What do we do now?" Logan asked. "If we take the prison wagon, we'll for sure be seen."

"I have a spare wheel," Pecorino said. "We can put it on the buckboard and proceed onward. There is plenty of room for six of us."

"We only need room for five," Franklin said.

"What do you mean?"

Franklin pointed to Mason. "This man is a traitor. If you take him, he will betray you, just as he betrayed us."

"Is it the consensus of all, that he is a traitor?" Pecorino asked.

"Damn right he's a traitor. He turned us in to the law," Jenner said. "Hell, we wouldn't all be goin' to hang, iffen it warn't for him."

"No, wait, I won't never do that no more," Mason said. "You can count on me."

Pecorino turned his pistol toward Mason and shot him.

"Now, gentlemen, shall we go?"

"Damn, you've thought of ever' thing, haven't you?" Franklin asked.

"That will be my position in the group I am organizing," Pecorino said. "I will do all the thinking. Do any of you have any difficulty with that?"

"I've been sort of the chief, but you doin' it is fine with me," Franklin said.

To the surprise of everyone, Pecorino shot Franklin.

"Wha . . ." Franklin gasped, as he put his hand over the hole in his chest. Blood began oozing through his fingers. "Why'd you do that?"

"I couldn't take a chance on you deciding to resume your position of leadership," Pecorino said. He looked at Logan, Jenner, and Moss, the only three men remaining from the nine who had started the journey. All three were wearing an expression of shock.

"Before you lament the passing of your former chief, I hasten to remind you that under his leadership you were caught, tried, convicted, and sentenced to hang," Pecorino said.

"Yeah, that's right, ain't it?" Jenner said.

"You will not be caught under my leadership. And, if you follow my instructions, you will be amply compensated."

"We'll be what?" Moss asked.

"You'll make a lot of money," Pecorino said.

The three men who, but moments earlier had been prisoners, smiled broadly.

"Makin' a lot of money, you say? Well now," Logan said. "That sounds awful good to me."

"You men get the wheel changed so we can get out of here. If my research is correct, there will be a stagecoach coming through here in about another hour. I've no wish to be here when the coach arrives."

"Are you really a doctor?" Moss asked.

"Yes."

"That's good. If one of us was to get shot, doin' whatever it is you're goin' to have us do, why, you could tend to us."

"I'm not that kind of a doctor. I'm a Ph.D."

"Well, that's all right. If one of us gets a toothache, you can take care of that, too."

* * *

Pecorino supervised the replacing of the wheel. While Jenner and Logan held the back of the buckboard up, Moss fitted the replacement wheel, then tightened down the lug nut.

"All right, gentlemen, get aboard," Pecorino ordered, and after the three recruits climbed into the back, Pecorino urged the team on. As they drove off, vultures began to gather over the unexpected feast of the six bodies left lying in the dirt behind them.

One hour later the Walbach to Silver Crown stage-coach was approaching the scene. Because it was, at the moment, climbing Bufford Butte, neither the abandoned prison wagon, nor the bodies, could be seen.

"You goin' to stop by the Peacock 'n have a beer before you go home, Pete?" the shotgun guard asked.

Pete shook his head. "I told Lily I'd come on home, soon as I got in."

"I swear, Pete, ever since you got married, you ain't been no fun at all."

"Hell, Junior, me 'n you spend most of the day sittin' next to each other on this box, why would I want to spend more time with you when we ain't workin'?"

Junior chuckled. "I reckon you've got a point there."

Just as they crested the hill, they saw a wagon about one hundred yards in front of them.

"Damn," Pete said. "Look up there, Junior. Ain't that the Black Maria?"

"Yeah, I believe it is. Why is it stopped? Broke down, do you reckon?"

"Whoa," Pete said, pulling back on the reins to bring the team to a halt. He didn't have to answer Junior's question. The circling of vultures, and the black lumps lying on the road, answered the question for both of them.

"What the hell?" Junior asked quietly.

"Driver, why have we stopped?" one of the passengers called.

"Come out here 'n see for yourself!" Junior replied.

"No!" Pete said. "You ladyfolk, it would prob'ly be a good idea for you to stay in the coach. Menfolk, if you want to take a look, climb down 'n see for yourself."

The men climbed down and one of the women, but upon seeing the carnage displayed before her, the female passenger quickly climbed back into the coach.

"What are you going to do, driver?" one of the men passengers asked.

"What do you mean, what am I going to do? What do you expect me to do?"

"We can't just leave them here," the passenger said.

"We don't have room to put six bodies in the coach," Pete replied. "And even if we did have room, why, I couldn't do nothin' like that to the ladies."

"I tell you what. If the other men will help me load them into the prison wagon, I'll drive it on into Cheyenne."

"All right," Pete said. "And if you'll do that, I'll drive along behind you."

* * *

From the **Cheyenne Sun**

TERRIBLE MURDER
ON LARAMIE ROAD

Pete Malone and Junior Allman, driver and shotgun guard of the Walbach to Silver Crown stagecoach, while making the transit on Wednesday previous, encountered a terrible sight on Laramie Road. Coming across the prisoner transport vehicle, known to many as the "Black Maria" they discovered the wagon stopped, the horses standing dumb in their harness, and the bodies of the two drivers, as well as four of the prisoners lying dead on the road.

Three of the prisoners known to have been among those being transported: Mack Logan, Simon Jenner, and William Moss were missing. It is being assumed one of the three may have, by some means yet to be determined, secreted a firearm on their person prior to being transmitted. In such a way, they may have arranged their escape, but the mystery remains, why did they kill, in addition to the two transport officers, four of their own?

CHAPTER ELEVEN

Pecorino had been reading the newspaper as his order was being loaded into the buckboard. He looked up as the proprietor of the gun shop approached.

"There you are, Mr. Smith," the proprietor said. "Ten Winchester repeating rifles, ten Colt .45 caliber pistols, one thousand rounds of .45 caliber ammunition, and one thousand rounds of .44-40 ammunition, loaded into your buckboard."

The proprietor chuckled. "You plannin' on startin' a war, Mr. Smith?"

"Didn't I pay you enough money for me not to be bothered by a lot of silly questions?"

"Yes, sir, I suppose you did."

"Then I'll be taking my leave of you," Pecorino said as he climbed into the driver's seat of the buckboard, then snapped the reins against the back of the team.

He had enough weapons to get started now. The next thing he would need would be mounts and tack.

And uniforms. Even before he had recruited his first three men, he had designed . . . and had made . . . ten uniforms. The uniforms were green with red trim. When questioned by the tailor, he explained that they were for a band.

Pecorino's own uniform was the most distinctive. While the other uniforms were trimmed in red, his uniform was trimmed in gold. And on the epaulets of his uniform, he had embroidered two silver stars, separated by a small gold crown.

His next stop, before leaving town, was the tailor shop where he picked up the uniforms, which were neatly packed in cardboard boxes.

He smiled as the buckboard rolled out of town. He had taken the first tentative steps toward building the Royal Army of the nation of Nova Amerigo Regnum. Now he had only to start the revolution, and he would start it by raising the money needed to fund it.

His first operation would be robbing the bank of Livermore. It was across the line, into the state of Colorado, and Pecorino had chosen it as his first, specifically for that reason. For one thing, by conducting a raid in Colorado, then withdrawing back into Wyoming, it would make it difficult for the law to pursue them. He knew that officers of the law were very jealous of their jurisdictional territories, and by crossing those jurisdictional lines, not only county lines, but by state and territory, he would be able to sow confusion among the authorities.

And the second reason he was crossing the line was one of principle. Once he had the nation of Nova Amerigo Regnum established, states and territories would cease to exist. There would be only one kingdom.

Washington, D.C.

The cigar had been chewed down to half its size so that now only a stub protruded from General Sherman's mouth. He was holding a couple of sheets of paper as he approached President Hayes's desk.

"I've got the details for the trip all worked out, Mr. President," he said. "They're all here."

President Hayes picked up the papers, glanced at them for a moment, then dropped them back on the desk.

"I can read them, but I would rather you tell me about them."

"We will proceed from here to Chicago, much as you would go anywhere, with your private car being attached to a regularly scheduled train. It is when we reach Chicago that we will actually assemble the Presidential train.

"There will be six cars in the Presidential train, one carrying the baggage, the second a dining car, you and Mrs. Hayes will occupy the entire third car by yourselves. The fourth car will be occupied by Secretary of War Ramsey and his wife, Anna, myself and my daughter, Rachel. The fifth car will be a Pullman Sleeper occupied by General McCook, Colonel and Mrs. Barr, Captain Gutterman, and your sons, Birchard and Rutherford. The last car will be a caboose, which will be occupied by the four porters, and the off-duty engine crew, as we will have two crews. Union Pacific has assured me that they will select only the most skilled and experienced engineers and firemen. We will also have a chef, but he will have a bed in the kitchen area of the dining car."

"That sounds good."

"In addition, I have made arrangements for you to visit

every military installation along our path, as well as Indian reservations, and points that I believe would be of particular interest to you."

"You haven't mentioned Alaska," President Hayes said.

"I know. I tried, Mr. President, but the logistics are just too difficult to handle. You said you wanted to be back in Washington in time for the election, and I think you should be. But that won't be possible, if you go to Alaska."

"All right, General, I shall continue to leave all aspects of this trip in your capable hands."

Sugarloaf Ranch

"Pearlie, when I go back to Wyoming to deliver Sir McGinnis to Colonel Cummings, I would like for you to come, as well."

"Sure, I'd be glad to," Pearlie said. "But don't you think Cal would be better? I mean the way it is between him and that bull."

Smoke chuckled. "Cal will be with us. I think I owe it to him to let him say goodbye, but it isn't the bull I'm thinking about. I have something else in mind for you . . . that is if you are willing to do it."

"Smoke, if you told me to go to the moon 'n open a line shack, 'n I could figure out how to get there, I'd do it for you. Hell, you know that by now, so whatever it is you're wantin' me to do, I'll do it."

"There's an Englishman up there who is hard up against it right now. Apparently he has backing from people back in England, and his ranch is on the edge of failing. His brother is acting as foreman, and from what I can understand, he's making things worse.

"What I would like for you to do is help out the

brother, without it being too obvious that you are helping him out."

"Damn, and just when I said that I'd do anything you ask me to do," Pearlie replied.

"You don't want to do it?"

Pearlie laughed. "I have to tell you, it doesn't sound like it'll be much fun. But I'll do it . . . and I'll do everything I can to save the ranch. What's the man's name?"

"Barrington. Albert Barrington. Esquire," Smoke added with a laugh.

"Esquire? What does that mean?"

"I asked Sally what it means, and she says it's someone of high social rank, but he has no title."

"Wait, I'm goin' to be takin' orders from someone who is an 'esquire'?"

"No, you'll still be working for me, and that means you won't have to take any orders from Albert Barrington or his brother Richard. I want you to do what you can to help them, Pearlie, but I'm not throwing you to the wolves. You'll be free to pack up and come back home anytime you want."

Pearlie nodded. "All right," he said. "As long as I'm still workin' for you, I'll take anything any of them want to put out."

Four days after that conversation, Smoke and Sally had driven a buckboard into town, and Smoke tied it off in front of Murchison's Leather Goods store on Front Street, then, as Sally went into the store, Smoke stepped next door into Longmont's Saloon. The piano player was filling the room with music, though the music was more of an underlying presence than an intrusion. Louis Longmont, owner of the saloon, was sitting at "his" table, with Sheriff Monte Carson, and when he saw Smoke, he lowered the newspaper he had been reading, smiled, and waved Smoke over.

Smoke nodded, then stopped at the bar to pick up a mug of beer that the bartender had already drawn as soon as he saw Smoke come in. Smoke put a nickel on the bar, then carried his drink over to the table to join his two friends.

"Smoke, what brings you to town today?" Louis asked.

"Sally wanted to buy a new pair of boots," Smoke said. "So I volunteered to bring her into town."

"That was nice of you," Longmont said.

"Especially since it gave you a chance to stop in for a beer," Sheriff Carson added with a smile.

"Monte, you know all my secrets," Smoke replied.

"Heavens, Smoke, I don't want to know all of them. If I did, I'd probably have to put you in jail."

Smoke laughed. "You might at that."

"If he knew all mine as well, I'd be in there with you," Longmont said.

"All right, fellas, let's drop it right here," Sheriff Carson suggested. "If we keep this up, you'll be wantin' to know my secrets, too, and the truth is, I've got my own past I'd just as soon keep to myself."

Smoke and Louis Longmont laughed.

"Is it true you're going to sell Sir McGinnis?" Louis asked.

"Yes, I found a man in Wyoming, Colonel R. D. Cummings who has agreed to give me my price, for him. I'll be delivering him in a few more weeks."

"Sir McGinnis is quite a bull. I'm sure Colonel Cummings will be quite pleased with him," Sheriff Carson said.

"So, you're going to Wyoming, huh? Who knows, you might meet the President," Longmont said.

"Meet the President? President of what?" Smoke asked, confused by the comment.

Longmont laughed. "Why, I'm talking about the President of the United States, of course, Rutherford Hayes."

"Ruthe-*fraud* Hayes, don't you mean?" Smoke asked. "Seeing as Sam Tilden won the election."

"Oh, for heaven's sake, Smoke, you aren't still upset over that, are you? That was four years ago," Carson said.

"Yeah, four years ago, but that hasn't changed anything. If you ask me, Hayes is dishonest."

"Tilden won the popular vote, but he didn't win enough electoral votes," Carson said.

"He was only one vote short, and there were twenty votes in dispute. But congress gave Hayes every one of those twenty disputed votes. Why if Tilden had gotten only one of those votes, he would be President today."

"He's not running for reelection this year," Louis said.

"What do you mean, 'reelection'? As far as I'm concerned, he was never elected in the first place."

"Ha!" Louis said. "Maybe you can tell him that, when you see him."

"That's the second time one of you has suggested that I might meet the President. What are you talking about?"

"Here, read this," Sheriff Carson suggested, sliding a copy of the *Journal* across the table toward Smoke.

PRESIDENT HAYES'S
WESTERN TRIP

A special train is being assembled in Chicago for the President's visit to the West. The President is being accompanied by Mrs. Hayes and their sons, Birchard and Rutherford.

The cars will be set up with all the conveniences of a home on rails, complete with a private lavatory, cooking facilities, and comfortable chairs and beds. Their meals will be served upon fine china, silverware, and elegant crystal. Fresh bouquets of flowers will be provided at every stop.

President Hayes will be the first sitting President ever to go west of the Rocky Mountains, and his schedule calls for visits in Wyoming, Utah, Nevada, California, Oregon, and Washington.

"What makes you think I might see the President?"

"Well, you're going to Wyoming and the President is going to Wyoming," Louis said.

"Wyoming is a big area," he said.

Sally laughed. "And what did Louis say when you told him that Wyoming was a big area?" Smoke had joined Sally in Delmonico's Restaurant.

"He said, 'I know that, but it has only one railroad.' You know, Sally, I think he really believes that I might meet the President."

"What would you do if you did meet him?"

"What do you mean?"

"Come on, Smoke, you know what I mean. You didn't vote for him, and like many Americans, you have never considered him to be a legitimate President."

"He didn't win the election. Sam Tilden, the man I voted for, won the election."

"No, Governor Tilden won the popular vote, but you know how the election process works. In order to be President, one must win the majority of the electoral votes, and though Tilden got more popular votes, he got fewer electoral votes than the President."

"In the words of Ebenezer Scrooge, bah humbug."

Sally laughed again. "Well, if you want to be technical about it, those are actually the words of the author, Charles Dickens."

"All right, Charles Dickens."

"You will be nice to him, won't you?"

"Nice to who? Charles Dickens?"

"You're a little late for that. He died ten years ago. No, I mean nice to the President. I know you don't like him, but Smoke, he *is* the President of the United States, and you should respect the office, even if you can't respect the man."

"I'm about as likely to run into him, as man is likely to walk on the moon someday. But, if I do run into him, you may rest assured that I will be as nice as I can possibly be."

"Yes, it is the 'possibly' that worries me," Sally replied.

CHAPTER TWELVE

Bitter Creek, Wyoming

Pecorino, Jenner, Logan, and Moss waited at the outskirts of the town of Bitter Creek, listening to the music of the night creatures. A cloud passed over the moon, then moved away, bathing in silver the twin rails that passed through the town. At this edge of town, stood a big white house, its cupolas, dormers, balconies, porches, and gingerbread trim all shining brightly in the moonlight. The property was surrounded by a white picket fence, which enclosed, not only the house, but a carriage house and stable as well.

As the four men rode into town, they avoided the main street, choosing instead to approach by a way that would be least likely to be noticed. When they reached the stable behind the big white house, they dismounted, then stepped out into the relative brightness of the moon. The back door to the house was locked.

"We'll have to go in through a window," Pecorino suggested.

"No, we don't," Jenner replied. Pulling a knife from the sheath on his belt, he stuck it in between the door edge and the lock plate and, within seconds, had the door unlocked.

A spill of moonlight illuminated the parlor and showed, clearly, the bottom of the stairs. They started up the stairs and were on the third step when there was a sudden whirring sound, followed by two "bongs." It was the clock, striking two A.M.

"That scared the bejesus out of me," Logan hissed.

"Keep quiet," Pecorino replied, hissing the order.

When they reached the second floor, Pecorino began peeking through the doors until he saw what he was looking for. The same splash of moonlight that had illuminated the parlor, also illuminated this room and they could see a young girl, sleeping alone.

Pecorino looked at Moss, and nodded. Moss stepped into the room and scooped the little girl up, clasping his hand over her mouth at the same time.

The little girl awoke instantly, and when she saw the four men, her eyes opened wide, and she tried to cry out, but was able to manage only a squeaking sound.

"Do you want to see your mother and dad, little girl?" Pecorino asked.

Her eyes still open wide, the little girl nodded in the affirmative.

"Point out their room for us," Pecorino said.

Moss carried her out into the hallway, and she pointed at one of the doors.

Quietly, the four men moved on into the room, then stood over the bed, looking down at the little girl's parents, both of whom were sound asleep. Pecorino pulled his pistol, as did Jenner and Logan.

"Call out for your parents," Pecorino said, while at the

same time signaling to Moss to drop his hand from over the little girl's mouth.

"Mommy, Daddy?" the little girl said, her voice amazingly calm under the circumstances.

The woman groaned. "Oh, Suzie, go back to bed," she mumbled.

"There are some men here," Suzie said.

"What? What are you talking about?" The woman had still not opened her eyes. "Go back to bed, sweetie."

"I can't. There are some men here."

The woman opened her eyes then, and seeing four men in the bedroom, one of them holding Suzie, she screamed.

"What? What is it?" the man asked, awakened by the scream.

"Hello, Mr. Boyle," Pecorino said, easily.

"What the hell? Who are you? What are you doing here? And what are you doing with my daughter?"

"You are the president of the bank, are you not?" Pecorino inquired.

"Yes."

"Well, we are here to do some banking business with you."

"Banking business? What kind of banking business?"

"I am General Clemente Pecorino, Regent of the nation of Nova Amerigo Regnum. Our army is in need of funds, and I intend for your bank to supply those funds."

"Are you serious? You have come to my home in the middle of the night to take out a loan?"

"Perhaps you misunderstood, Mr. Boyle. I am not asking for a loan. Some of the more crass might say that I am robbing the bank, but as this is a military operation, I would prefer to refer to it as a logistical acquisition."

"Are you crazy? I don't keep any money in my house."

"I know you don't. But you are the banker, as well as the father of this precious child." Pecorino flashed a pernicious smile toward the frightened little girl. "And this is your wife," he added. At Pecorino's signal, Jenner stepped up to the side of the bed, and put the barrel of the gun against Mrs. Boyle's temple.

"Now what I want you to do, Mr. Boyle . . . no, what I demand *you* do, is, go down there to your bank, remove all the money you have in the safe, and bring it back to me. And there had better be more than fifty thousand dollars there."

"Why on earth would I want to do such a thing?"

"Because if you don't do it, I'm going to kill your wife and your child, then I will kill you," Pecorino said.

"My chief teller is in charge of the vault."

"Do you have the combination to the safe?" Pecorino asked.

"Yes, but as I say, my chief teller deals with that. I'm not certain I can open it."

"Make a concerted effort to do so, and pray that you succeed. The lives of your wife and child depend upon your success."

"Herman, for heaven's sake, do what they ask," the woman said.

"Just be calm, Martha," Boyle said. "I don't believe they really mean you any harm."

"Disabuse yourself of any thought that we don't mean what we say," Pecorino replied.

"If I do what you say, will you let us go?" Boyle asked.

"Yes, of course, I will. We are revolutionaries, we aren't savages."

"Moss, put the little girl down and let her crawl into bed with her mother."

Moss put Suzie down, and, quickly, she got into bed with her mother.

Martha wrapped her arm around Suzie, and Suzie still stared at the men through wide open eyes.

"All right, all right," Boyle said, holding his hands out toward them. "I'll get dressed. I'll get the money."

Quickly, Boyle pulled on his trousers and a shirt, then he slipped on his shoes. Finally he was ready to go.

"You go with him, Jenner," Pecorino ordered, and the outlaw followed the banker out of the room.

For several minutes Pecorino, Moss, and Logan, as well as Martha and Suzie Boyle, just sat quietly.

"What are you going to do with us?" Martha asked in a frightened voice.

"Why, nothing, my dear, if your husband does what I have asked of him," Pecorino replied.

Moss walked over and looked out the window. "Here they are, comin' back," he said.

"Are they carrying anything?" Logan asked.

"Jenner's carryin' a big sack."

Logan smiled, broadly. "That's our money!" he said. "We done it! We took this bank!"

A moment later the two men came up the stairs.

"I got the money," Jenner said, a big smile spreading across his face as he held up the bag.

"How much is there?"

"A whole lot, but I don't know, exactly," Jenner said.

"Mr. Boyle?" Pecorino asked.

"Sixty-two thousand, five hundred and twenty-seven dollars," Boyle replied.

"Thank you, sir. I like a man who is precise with his figures."

"Damn! How much is that for each of us?" Moss asked.

"Nothing," Pecorino replied.

"What? What do you mean, nothing?"

"We must not think of ourselves as individuals, but as a collective," Pecorino said. "This money will be used for the new nation we are establishing."

"Oh, yeah, I forgot," Moss said.

"See to it that you do not forget in the future," Pecorino scolded. "From this moment on, until Nova Amerigo Regnum is recognized by the rest of the world as an independent nation, we must think only of our ultimate goal."

"New nation?" Boyle asked, confused by the statement.

"Perhaps this will explain everything," Pecorino said, handing Boyle an envelope. "If you would be so kind as to take this to the newspaper, I would be very appreciative."

Denver, Colorado, one week later

"Yes, sir, Mr. Jensen," the train master said. "We have it all set up so that the cattle car will be attached to the rear of the three fifteen for Cheyenne. There it will be attached through to Medicine Bow."

"Thank you, Mr. Eddington," Smoke replied.

"I took a look at your bull. I must say, he is a fine-looking animal."

"He is, indeed," Smoke said. "Only, technically, I suppose, he isn't my bull any longer. He belongs to Colonel R. D. Cummings now. Or at least, he will as soon as I make the delivery." Smoke smiled. "And that's what this trip is all about."

"Smoke, maybe I'd better go look at 'im, just to make sure he's all right," Cal said. "He's got to be nervous and wonderin' what this is all about. I'll tell him not to worry."

"All right, Cal, you do that," Smoke replied with a condescending smile.

"You sure you don't want to ride all the way up to Wyoming in the same car?" Pearlie teased. "Why, I'll bet they would put a little extra straw down, just so you'd have a place to sleep."

"Well, if I'm goin' to have to listen to you yappin' at me all the way up there, I'd just as soon sleep in the cattle car," Cal replied.

"Boys," Sally said. "Don't be . . . *boys.*"

"Sorry, Miz Sally," Pearlie said. "I won't be teasin' him no more."

"Any more," Cal corrected. You won't be teasin' me ANY more."

"That's what I said."

"No, you used a double negative, and Cal was quite right in correcting you."

"Yes, ma'am, I'm sorry," a contrite Pearlie replied.

Smoke, Sally, Pearlie, and Cal had come to Denver by way of the shuttle train from Big Rock today. Here, Smoke made all the arrangements for transporting Sir McGinnis to the right train, while Sally managed their transfer from the train they had arrived on to the train that would take them to Cheyenne where, once again, they would have to change trains.

After taking care of the cattle car transfer, Smoke returned to the waiting room where he found Pearlie and Sally.

"Did you get the tickets?" Smoke asked.

"Yes," Sally replied.

"Where's Cal?"

"Where do you think he is?" Pearlie asked.

"Well, if I had to guess, I would say that he is checking on Sir McGinnis."

"Give the man a silver dollar," Pearlie replied, sarcastically.

"Smoke, I'm worried about Cal. Is he going to be all right after Sir McGinnis is transferred to Colonel Cummings?" Sally asked.

"He's a big boy, Sally, he'll adjust."

"I don't know, it's just that he . . ." she started to say.

"Here he comes now," Smoke said.

"Is the train on time?" Cal asked as he came over to them.

"Yes."

"Good. I told Sir McGinnis it would be. You know what? I think I've actually got him looking forward to moving to Colonel Cummings's ranch. I told him it would be a new adventure for him."

"Smoke!" someone called.

"That man over there is calling you," Sally said. "Do you know him?"

Smoke smiled. "That would be Clyde Barnes, the engineer that I told you about."

Smoke waved for Clyde to come over.

"Clyde, I would like for you to meet my wife, Sally. Sally, this is Clyde Barnes."

Sally extended her hand. "It's very nice to meet you, Mr. Barnes. Smoke has spoken highly of you, and your friend . . . uh," Sally hesitated.

"Austin," Clyde said. "It's all right, you can call him that. That's what everyone calls him."

"And these two august gentlemen are Pearlie and Cal," Smoke added, turning toward the two men who were standing with them.

Clyde took Cal's hand. "You two work for Smoke, do you?" Clyde asked.

"Yes, sir," Cal answered.

"When I can actually get him to work," Smoke said.

"Smoke, Cal is a wonderful hand," Sally said.

"Smoke's just teasin', Miz Sally," Cal said. Then he glanced toward Smoke. "Aren't you?"

"I'll just let you think about that," Smoke replied.

Clyde turned back to Smoke. "What are you doing here? Off on another trip?"

"I'm going back to Medicine Bow, only this time I'm taking four others with me."

"Four?" Clyde saw only three.

"Sally, Pearlie, Cal, and . . ."

Before Smoke could finish, Sally broke in. "And Sir McGinnis."

"Who is Sir McGinnis?"

"That would be his bull. And Pearlie, Cal, and I should be very flattered that the bull didn't get top billing over us."

"You might remember, Clyde, that when I made this

trip before, I said I was coming north to sell a bull. Well, I sold him, and Sir McGinnis is the bull I was talking about."

"Yes, I do recollect hearin' you mention a champion bull. So he's goin' with you, huh?"

"He is, yes, in his own cattle car. Will you and Austin be taking us to Cheyenne?"

"Well, we were scheduled to," Clyde said. "Until we got this." With a huge smile, he pulled a piece of paper from his pocket and held it up.

"What's that?"

"This is from the home office of the Union Pacific Railroad. Me 'n Austin has been ordered to go to Chicago right away."

"Oh? Why are you going to Chicago?"

"Maybe you ain't heard nothin' about it yet, but President Hayes is makin' him a trip out West."

"Yes, I read about it in the newspaper," Smoke replied.

"Yeah, well, this here is somethin' you ain't read in the newspaper, 'n you ain't read it, on account of it's just been decided." Clyde's smile grew even larger. "Me 'n Austin is the ones that's goin' to be a' drivin' the President's train while he's travelin' around out here."

"Oh, Mr. Barnes!" Sally said. "What a wonderful honor has been bestowed upon you and your friend."

"Yeah, that's what I'm a' thinkin'. Only thing is, I just now got the message, 'n Austin, he's gettin' the steam up for the trip up to Cheyenne. He don't know nothin' a-tall about it, yet. I'm fixin' to go tell 'im right now."

"Congratulations, Clyde," Smoke said. "The President may not realize it, but he has, at least in my opinion, the finest engineer and fireman on the entire UP line."

CHAPTER THIRTEEN

Medicine Bow Mountains

Pecorino had recruited seven more men: Bilbo, Cooper, Easton, Garrison, Graves, Keller, and Reynolds. The first thing he had them do was build an encampment, complete with a palisade to surround the grounds. He called the encampment Fort Regency, and when it was completed, he issued the uniforms. Three of the uniforms had a gold stripe around the cuff of the tunic, and these, he gave to Logan, Jenner, and Moss.

"These men are your officers," he told the others. "They will take their orders from me, and you will take your orders from them.

"Anytime you encounter one of your officers, or me, you will dip your head slightly."

"What?" one of the men said. "You mean bow?"

"In a manner of speaking, yes, I suppose you could call it a bow."

"No, hell no, there ain't no way I'm a' goin' to do that. I done deserted from one army with all the salutin' and sirrin' and such," one of the men said. "I don't intend to join another'n, most especially if I have to go 'round bowin'. That's worse than salutin'. 'N if you think I'm a' goin' to wear this here funny-lookin' suit, why, you're just full of it."

The speaker was Adam Keller, and he pushed the uniform away.

"So, you are telling us that you are not ready to swear allegiance to me, and to the army of Nova Amerigo Regnum?" Pecorino asked.

Keller shook his head. "No, sir, I ain't swearin' no allegiance to no damn army, I can tell you that, right now."

Pecorino looked over toward Jenner.

"Lieutenant Jenner, would you take care of this"—he paused for a moment before he said the next word, setting it apart from the rest of the sentence—"problem . . . for us, please?"

Jenner pulled his pistol and pointed at Keller's head.

"Wait, no!" Keller shouted, holding his hands out in front of him. "I'll join your army, I'll be . . ."

"It is too late," Pecornio said, and he nodded at Jenner.

Jenner pulled the trigger, and Keller went down with a black hole in the middle of his forehead.

"What the hell?" one of the others shouted.

"I told you men when I recruited you, that this would be a life-long commitment," Pecorino said, the calmness of his voice displaying no emotion over what had just happened. "Just how long that life is, depends upon your loyalty and service. You are the foundation of my new empire. Loyalty to me, now, will pay handsomely when our new nation is established. You are the first of what will grow to be a mighty army, and because you are the first, you will be richly rewarded. All of you will be put in positions of great authority and power over the subjects of our new land. And with that authority and power, will come riches beyond your wildest imagination.

"Are there any more complaints about the way I am organizing us?"

Pecorino expected no further complaints, and he got none.

The mood of the men picked up once they were in uniform. They felt as if they belonged to something bigger than themselves, and they were inspired by the promise of power and wealth to come.

The Three Mountain Ranch

During the meal, Albert Barrington regaled Smoke, Sally, Pearlie, and Cal with amazing tales of adventure, from riding a steeplechase in England, to big game hunting in Africa, and mountain climbing in Switzerland. All these stories were told with humor and self-deprecation, and Smoke and the others found themselves truly enjoying the evening.

"I'm pleased and honored that you decided to visit me on your way to delivering the bull to Colonel Cummings," Barrington said after dinner when he and his brother Richard entertained in the library. "But I can't help but have the feeling that the visit is more than social."

Unlike Albert, who was almost as tall as Smoke, and had a pleasing countenance, Richard was considerably shorter, and wore a well-manicured goatee. And whereas Albert's hair was light brown, Richard's hair was so dark as to nearly be black.

Smoke chuckled. "You have good instincts," he said. "I do have something in mind."

"I hope you aren't about to make an offer for the

ranch," he said. "Because I know you can't offer enough to cover all the losses, and indeed, I wouldn't expect you to."

"I do have an offer," Smoke said. "But it isn't to buy your ranch, it is an offer that may help you cut the losses on your ranch."

"Oh? And what would that be, may I ask?"

"I propose a cultural exchange," Smoke said.

"A cultural exchange? I'm afraid I don't understand what you mean by that."

"I would like to leave Pearlie here with you. Pearlie is the best foreman I have ever seen. I think he could help you in . . ."

"My brother already has a foreman," Richard interrupted quickly. "I am the foreman."

"You misunderstand, Richard. I'm not proposing that Pearlie be the foreman. But I think he might be useful to you. Didn't you say that you believe some of your losses are from cattle rustlers?"

"I do believe that to be so," Albert said. "I must confess that we have never caught anyone in the act, so we don't know who it is, or even if for sure we are being rustled."

"Pearlie has had a good deal of experience in dealing with rustlers and would-be rustlers," Smoke said. "If you are being plagued by rustlers, he can not only find that out for you, I have every confidence that he can stop it."

"My word, I must say that you are expressing a great deal of reliance upon the ability of a mere hireling."

"A what?" Pearlie asked, not understanding the word.

"Pearlie is much more than a hired hand," Smoke said, speaking quickly enough to keep Pearlie from expanding his question. "Pearlie is to me what Richard is to you. I admit that he isn't a blood brother, but Pearlie, and Cal, are as close as any brother can be."

"Very well, your confidence in Pearlie has sold me on his worth to me, but the question remains, why? Why are you willing to spare such a valued, uh, associate, to allow him to work for me? Surely you realize that under the current state of affairs I can ill-afford to pay another hand."

"There's no need for you to pay him. Consider this a neighborly act."

"And it isn't as if we aren't getting anything in return," Sally said, joining the conversation for the first time.

"Oh? And what would that be?"

"I can't help but think that being around the proper culture as exemplified by you and your brother, Richard, can only have an ameliorating effect upon Pearlie's own demeanor. Don't get me wrong, Pearlie is one of the most decent men I have ever encountered in my entire life." She smiled at Pearlie. "But a little more refinement would be good."

"Well then, Mister . . ." Albert paused in mid-sentence. "What is your name?"

"Pearlie. Just Pearlie. No need for the mister."

"All right, Pearlie. Welcome to the Three Mountain Ranch."

Fort Regency

Pecorino began planning some military operations that would include attacks on money shipments, whether by train or coach, banks, and any other target of opportunity. But first, he needed to conduct a test run, to see how his men would perform, and an article in the newspaper gave him an idea for just such a trial operation.

REGISTERED BULL PURCHASED

Colonel R. D. Cummings, noted rancher, states that he has recently purchased, for a great deal of money, Sir McGinnis, a registered bull, from Smoke Jensen of Colorado. Sir McGinnis can trace his lineage back to HRH Charles, a prize bull. Such a fine animal, Colonel Cummings believes, will help improve his stock.

"We're goin' to steal a cow?" Jenner asked when Pecorino told him of his plans.

"It isn't just a cow, it is a registered bull."

"What are we goin' to do with a bull?"

"We will hold it for ransom," Pecorino said. "If this man, Cummings, paid a great deal of money for it, as is noted in this article, then he will be willing to pay a ransom for its return."

"How much do you think he will pay?" Jenner asked.

"It doesn't matter how much he pays, it only matters that he will pay."

Jenner shook his head. "Boy, now, I don't get that at all. How come it don't matter how much he'll pay for the bull?"

"Because the important thing isn't the amount of money we will raise for the operation, the important thing is that it will give us an opportunity to see how our men work together. Whether this operation is successful or not, it will give us a valuable lesson for any future endeavor.

It will also give us visibility. People will know of our existence."

"Really? You want people to know about us? Back when I was ridin' with Franklin, we most wanted to stay out of sight. I thought the reason we built this here fort was so we would have a place to hide out."

Pecorino shook his head, slowly. "Lieutenant Jenner, when will you learn that we are not a gang of outlaws? We have no need to hide. Quite the contrary. Our ultimate success depends upon establishing a presence, declaring that we are the rightful rulers of the new nation we are building, and winning the citizens to our side. That's why I say that it doesn't matter how much Cummings is willing to pay for his bull. It matters only that we establish the fact that we exist. And it is for that reason that the men I send to do this job will be in uniform."

"Who will you be sending out?" Jenner asked.

"I'll leave that up to you, Lieutenant. I'll let you choose the personnel as you will be in command of the operation."

Cheyenne, Wyoming

After Pearlie told Smoke and the others goodbye, he decided to stop by the Mud Hole Saloon for a beer before going back out to the Three Mountain Ranch. He was standing at the bar, nursing his beer, when he overheard a conversation from a nearby table.

"They're Englishmen, him 'n that brother of his'n both. 'N both of 'em is hoity toity bastards."

"And dumb," the other one said. "Hell, they're getting stoled blind, 'n they don't even know who it is that's a' doin' it."

"One of 'em knows."

"What do you mean, one of 'em knows?"

"I don't mean nothin'. I was just mouthin' off, is all," the other speaker said. Pearlie thought he detected a bit of nervousness in the man's response.

Leaving the saloon, Pearlie rode back out to the ranch, wondering just what the two men were talking about. Could it be that some of Barrington's own men were rustling the cattle?

"It's about time you got back," Richard Barrington said when he saw Pearlie dismounting. "That horse you are riding is property of the Three Mountain Ranch, and, as I am not yet that familiar with you, I must confess that I was made somewhat uncomfortable with your prolonged absence."

"I was just seeing Smoke and the others off," Pearlie said. "By the way, how are you called?"

"What do you mean?"

"Your name is Richard. Are you addressed as Dick, Rich, Rick, or Richard."

Richard got a stern look on his face. "I am addressed as *Mister* Barrington. I heard you address your employer in a familiar fashion, but you will *not* address me so."

"You got it . . . Mister . . . Barrington," Pearlie replied. He had intended to tell Barrington about the conversation he overheard in the saloon, but decided, for the moment at least, to keep it to himself.

"Smoke, just what the hell have you gotten me into?" he mumbled, quietly, as he removed the saddle from the Three Mountain Ranch horse.

CHAPTER FOURTEEN

Medicine Bow

They had been underway for four hours when the conductor, as he had at every stop since leaving Cheyenne, passed through the car calling out the name of the town they were approaching.

"Medicine Bow, folks, Medicine Bow," he called. "We won't be here long enough for anyone to leave the train, unless of course this is your destination. Medicine Bow."

Smoke was sitting near the window, and he watched the approach into the town. The first indication that any town existed was a few sod houses, which looked exactly like the ground from which they arose.

The sod houses slid by to be replaced by a few wood-frame structures, then as the train ground to a halt, Smoke looked out onto Beech Street, and the row of false-front business buildings: saloons, an apothecary, a leather goods shop, a mercantile, and a hardware store among others.

Smoke, Sally, and Cal were the only ones to leave the train here.

"Smoke, if you don't mind, I'm goin' to check on Sir

McGinnis," Cal said as soon as the three of them stepped down onto the depot platform. "I mean, what if they don't disconnect his car 'n was to take him on to . . . who knows where? Why, Sir McGinnis would be scared to death."

"Sure, go ahead," Smoke said.

Hurrying off, Cal disappeared in the crowd that had gathered to meet the train.

"Smoke! Smoke Jensen, over here!" someone called.

Looking toward the sound of the call, Smoke smiled. "There's R.D. over near the depot," he said.

Smoke wasn't surprised to see Colonel Cummings, as he had wired ahead to give him the date and time of his arrival. He was a little surprised to see that Grace was with him. There were also two of his cowboys standing nearby.

The two men with Colonel Cummings were Paul Burke and Dusty Shields. Cummings asked, "Any trouble getting Sir McGinnis here?"

"Not a bit of trouble. He had his own car, food, water. He traveled like a king," Smoke replied with a wide smile.

"That's only fitting, wouldn't you say?" Cummings replied. "I mean, seeing as Sir McGinnis is royalty."

"Don't say that around him, he's arrogant enough as it is," Smoke replied with a laugh. "I brought one of my top hands, Cal Wood, with us. Cal is with Sir McGinnis now."

Cummings said, "My boys. Paul and Dusty will take Sir McGinnis on out to the ranch. We brought a reinforced wagon to transport him, and while they're doing that, Mrs. Cummings and I would like for you and Mrs. Jensen to be our guest for lunch at The War Drum Restaurant. Oh, and of course Mr. Wood, as well."

"We would love to," Smoke replied.

"Oh, R.D., for heaven's sake don't be so formal," Cummings's wife said. She smiled at Sally. "My name is Grace, dear."

"Sally," Sally replied, returning the smile.

Cal came walking up to them then.

"It's a good thing I checked on him," Cal said. "Why, they didn't even know they were supposed to disconnect his car here. Next thing you know, Sir McGinnis might have wound up somewhere in Oregon."

"Well, you saved us a lot of trouble, then," Smoke replied. "Colonel Cummings, this is the man I told you about, Cal Wood."

Cummings extended his hand. "It's very nice to meet you, young man. Oh, and these men work for me, Paul and Dusty."

Cal, Paul, and Dusty exchanged handshakes.

"Cal, I've just issued an invitation to Smoke and Mrs. Jensen to dine with my wife and me while Paul and Dusty take Sir McGinnis out to the ranch. We would love to have you join us as well."

"Thanks for the invitation," Cal replied. "But, Smoke, if you 'n Colonel Cummings, 'n Paul 'n Dusty don't mind, I'd like to rent a horse 'n ride on out to the ranch with 'em. Don't you think Sir McGinnis would take it easier if he was with someone that he knows?"

"We sure don't mind, none," Paul said. "That is, if you don't mind, Colonel."

"No, of course I don't mind," Cummings said.

"You want to say one last goodbye to him, do you?" Smoke asked.

Cal grinned, sheepishly. "Yeah, I reckon I do."

"Goodbye?" Cummings asked.

"It's a personal thing between Cal and Sir McGinnis. Go ahead, Cal. We'll be spending the night here. I'll get you a room in the hotel."

"Thanks!" Cal replied with a grateful smile.

Later, as Smoke, Sally, Cummings, and Grace enjoyed their meal in The War Drum, Cummings showed Smoke a newspaper in which there was an article announcing that he had bought a prize bull.

"As you can see, Sir McGinnis made the news," Cummings said with a broad smile.

"Yes, I can see that," Smoke replied. He started to hand the newspaper back when he saw something else that arrested his attention.

"Wait a minute, what is this?" Smoke asked. "Do we have some fool threatening a revolution?"

"You got it right, when you called him a fool. He robbed the bank over in Bitter Creek, and now he's trying to justify it by saying that he isn't your run of the mill outlaw bank robber, he is a revolutionary."

Smoke read the article in the Medicine Bow newspaper.

REVOLUTION IN PROGRESS?

The following is a letter to the editor of the Bitter Creek Union Report. It is not the normal policy of this newspaper to reprint letters to the editors of other newspapers; however, this particular letter is of note because it suggests the possibility that a revolution is brewing. Readers should pay close attention to the words herein printed, as they could, if acted upon, have a deleterious effect upon the lives of the citizens of the states and territories mentioned.

The Aforementioned Letter

To the loyal subjects of Nova Amerigo Regnum, I bring greetings from your sovereign. I am taking this opportunity to communicate with you, to tell you that your liberation is soon at hand. You, the people of this magnificent and inalienable New Amerigo Kingdom, have shown by your indomitable spirit, and by your willingness to seek new horizons, that you are the strength, and the future, of the regencies of Wyoming, Colorado, Utah, Nevada, and California.

Even now plans are in motion to provide you with a future free of interference from far off governments, and free from the scourge of Indian depredations. As your sovereign I can tell you now that we, the Exercitus Salus, that is, your Army of Deliverance, are your Milites Honorem, your knights of honor, and we will bring liberation to you.

Any plan so ennobled will of necessity require funds. It was to provide seed money for this noble cause that we called upon Mr. Boyle to provide us with a non-redeemable loan from the Bank of Bitter Creek. I ask that you not blame Mr. Boyle for his role in this, as he was coerced to do so by

*the fact that we held hostage his wife and
daughter in quasi captivas, as it were.*

*In order to have sufficient funds for the
revolution to proceed, we will, from time to time,
be required to resort to other extra-legal
activities, such as relieving trains, stagecoaches,
and even banks of such specie as may be in their
keeping. Think not of these activities as robberies,
think, rather, that they are but a tax applied to the
moneyed in order to provide independence to the
commoner, without burdening you, the commoner,
with the financial responsibility to build your new
nation.*

*To some, this forceful acquisition of funds may
seem contrary to our espoused intention of
bringing liberation to all, but under actum de
bello such transactions are justified, and these
operations are, indeed, acts of war. I ask you to
consider this as a matter of violating a lesser law,
in order to obey the greater law of success.*

*I will, as conditions warrant, issue other
communiques to keep you, the loyal subjects of
Nova Amerigo Regnum, apprised, both of our
goals, and our progress.*

> *Clemente Rex the First,*
> *Nova Amerigo Regnum*

"What do you think of this, Sally?" Smoke asked,
handing her the letter.

Sally read through the letter quickly, then handed it
back. "Colonel Cummings, Grace, if you will excuse my

language, I will say that whoever wrote this letter is arrogant and trying to show off his education."

"Whoever he is, he has just come out of the woodwork," Cummings said. "I don't know anyone named Clemente Rex, and I've never even heard of him."

"Rex means 'king,'" Sally said. And 'Regnum' means kingdom. This man, Clemente, has just declared himself king of Wyoming, Colorado, Nevada, California, and Utah."

"The hell he has? Ahh, like we said, he's just a fool," Cummings said with a dismissive wave of his hand.

"I don't know," Smoke said. "I'm not sure I would be that quick to dismiss him. He is obviously an educated and intelligent man, and as Sally said, he is arrogant, and that makes him even more dangerous."

When they left The War Drum, they were met by a young man who was passing out flyers. Sally took one, then, with a broad smile, showed it to Smoke.

"Look at this."

BALLOON ASCENSIONS
East of Town
YOU MAY
FLY THROUGH THE CLOUDS
For only Ten Dollars per person
See World Famous Aeronaut
PROFESSOR JORDAHL

"Oh, heavens!" Grace said after she read the flyer. "He expects people to pay him to go up in that thing? I wouldn't do it if you paid me one hundred dollars."

"Smoke, I want to do it," Sally said.

"Are you serious?" Smoke replied with a grin.

"I'm very serious," she said.

"Sally, no! What if you were to fall out of that thing and break your neck?" Grace asked, concerned that Sally would really do such a thing.

"I'll hold on tight," Sally promised.

CHAPTER FIFTEEN

Half an hour later, Smoke and Sally showed up at a field where a large silver balloon was being filled with gas. A rather smallish man, wearing a one-piece suit of clothing, was standing by, watching the operation.

"Are you Professor Jordahl?" Smoke asked.

"I am, sir."

"My wife and I would like to go up in your balloon. Will it be able to hold all three of us?"

The professor smiled. "Oh, indeed it will, sir, and another, as well."

"It's too bad Cal went on with Paul and Dusty," Smoke said. "I think he would have enjoyed this. Are there others in front of us?"

"No, sir, you are the first to inquire," Professor Jordahl replied. He looked back at the growing crowd who had gathered to watch the ascension. "To be honest with you, I think they are all just a little nervous about it. I tell you what I will do, sir. I will take you and your wife aloft for free . . . though we shouldn't let anyone else know that I'm doing such a thing. Perhaps if they see you go up and come back down, safely, they will be emboldened to try such an adventure for themselves."

Smoke shook his head. "I wouldn't want to do that."

The smile left the professor's face. "Sir, I assure you, it is quite safe. I have made more than a thousand ascensions, including those I made for Professor Lowe during the war."

"Oh, you didn't understand me," Smoke said. "I have every intention of going up with you. What I meant was, I wouldn't want you to forgo the fee. I am more than willing to pay the full amount for my wife and myself."

The smile returned to the professor's face now, wider than before. "Yes, sir!" he said. He looked over toward the balloon, which had now lifted from the ground as the inflation continued. "We shall achieve buoyancy very soon, now."

A short while later, Professor Jordahl informed them that enough gas had been put into the balloon to provide the lift they would need.

Professor Jordahl climbed into the rather large wicker basket, then invited Smoke and Sally in.

"Let the lady in first," the professor instructed. "You can help her from out there, I'll help her from in here."

Smoke knew that Sally was athletic enough to need no help, but he acquiesced to the professor's instruction, then he followed Sally into the basket.

"We shall go up one thousand feet," the professor said.

"Is that as high as the balloon can go?" Sally asked.

"No, my dear, we could go over ten thousand feet high, but we are limited to one thousand feet, because that is the length of our tether."

When both Smoke and Sally were in the basket, Professor Jordahl jettisoned his ballast, and the balloon started up.

"Look at those fools," someone on the ground said. "You sure as hell ain't goin' to get me into one o' them things."

The voice was as audible as if the speaker had been standing right beside them. Sally looked at the professor in surprise, and he smiled.

"That is one of the stranger aspects about ballooning," he said. "It is so quiet, and sound travels up, so that conversations from the ground are quite easy to hear." He chuckled. "During the war, it wasn't just what we observed while aloft, that proved valuable to our generals. It is also what we heard, and there were times when were able to report specific details of an operation being planned by the enemy, just because we could overhear them."

"Oh, Smoke, isn't this the most wonderful sensation?" Sally asked. "I wonder if some clever person will ever design a balloon that can be guided from point to point so that they may be used as a source of transportation, like stagecoaches, or trains."

"They are already working on such a thing," Professor Jordahl said.

"It makes one feel a bit strange, doesn't it?" Sally asked. "I mean being able to observe someone, without them knowing they are being observed."

Fifteen minutes later, Professor Jordahl began venting off enough gas to allow them to come back down.

"Thank you for having the courage to go first," the professor said.

"Oh, it was great fun!" Sally said, enthusiastically.

"Have you ever seen a parachute leap?" Professor Jordahl asked.

"A parachute leap? I don't know what that is," Smoke said.

"Stay for a while longer. I am about to give a demonstration."

Jordahl attached a large cloth to the side of the basket, from which ran several small ropes. The bottoms of the ropes were attached to two larger ropes, and those ropes were attached to a wide strip of leather, that resembled a swing seat.

"How does that work?" Smoke asked.

"You'll see," Professor Jordahl replied with a smile.

Once the balloon was sufficiently re-inflated, it lifted from the ground and rose to a great height. Several had gathered to watch the ascension.

"If you ask me, a feller would be crazy to go up in such a thing," someone said.

"Call me crazy then, 'cause I'm plannin' on doin' just that," another said.

"Oh, my God! He fell out!" someone shouted.

There were additional shouts and screams as a body plummeted down from the balloon, with a piece of cloth fluttering above. Then, there was a gasp as the trailing cloth suddenly popped open into a canopy, and the rapid descent was halted. The crowd watched in fascination as Professor Jordahl floated down as gently as dandelion puffs.

Jordahl touched down, and ran a few steps as the canopy collapsed behind him.

"That, my friends, is known as a parachute leap," the

professor said, and as he was cheered and applauded, he took a deep bow.

"Hey, Professor, if we go up in the balloon with you, you ain't goin' to make us jump out of it, are you?"

"Only if you wish to," the professor replied.

"I'll do it," Smoke said, the balloon now back on land.

"Smoke, you aren't serious!" Sally said.

"Yeah," Smoke said. "I am."

"If you really are serious, Mr. Jensen, I will not charge you for the experience."

For the second time in as many hours, Smoke found himself ascending in a balloon. He experienced the same sensation of seeing the buildings of the town grow smaller as the balloon climbed higher, and again, he had a panoramic view of the rivers, creeks, and mountains that surrounded Medicine Bow. He also saw, in the distance, an approaching train and felt a sense of power that he knew the train was coming before anyone in the city knew.

It was, as it had been on his first time aloft, very quiet.

"If you are going to do this, you should do it now, while there is very little wind to disturb you," Professor Jordahl said. He spoke in a conversational tone only, but they could have been sitting in a parlor, so clearly could he be heard.

"What do I have to do?" Smoke asked.

"Before I tell you, I want to make certain that you really want to do this. You don't have to, you know. You can still back out, and no one will think any the less of you."

Smoke chuckled. "I will think less of me."

"Very well," the aeronaut said. "First, grab hold of these two iron rings. Then, when you have a secure grip, climb over the side of the gondola, and position yourself in that strap seat. When you are so positioned, I will release the parachute. You'll be sitting in that seat, but you must continue to hold tightly to the rings, lest you fall out of the seat."

"All right," Smoke said. He hooked one leg over the edge of the basket, then looked at the ground, far below. For just a moment, he had a second thought, and almost drew his leg back in. But he recalled his comment to the professor a moment earlier. *"I will think less of me."*

What the professor hadn't told him was, during the transition from climbing over the edge of the gondola, until he was positioned in the seat, he would be hanging a thousand feet above the ground by his hand-hold on the rings only.

It was much more difficult to get into the seat than he had thought it would be, because each time he tried, his bottom would merely push the leather strap away from him.

"I can't get into the seat," he said.

"Lift yourself up higher, so that you are over the seat . . . then you can push yourself through it," the professor replied.

Smoke was getting a little tired of hanging on to the rings, but he pulled himself up higher, as directed, then, feeling the seat strap against the back of his legs, he was able to push himself on through and, with a sigh of relief, found himself in a good position on the seat.

"Are you ready?" the professor asked.

"I'm ready."

The professor cut the parachute loose from the gondola, and Smoke felt himself plunging down. He felt his stomach coming up to his throat, and for a second, he wondered if he hadn't made the biggest mistake of his life. No, not the biggest mistake of his life, the *last* mistake of his life.

He heard a popping sound above him, and his rapid descent was arrested so sharply that, for a moment, he had the sensation that he had come to a complete stop. He was just hanging here, in mid-air.

Then, as he looked down, he saw that the buildings of the town were gradually expanding in size as he drifted down. The people, gathered at the ground just outside of town were but small, indistinguishable figures, though he found Sally, and saw her looking up at him. As he grew closer, he could see the expression on her face change from apprehension, to relief, and then to pride.

He hit the ground a little harder than he expected, but no harder than jumping down from a barn loft. He made a few quick steps, then turned as the parachute collapsed behind him.

Cummings and Grace had been among the many who had come to watch Smoke and Sally make the balloon ascension, then stayed to see Smoke make his parachute leap.

"That was, without a doubt, the most amazing thing I have ever seen!" Colonel Cummings said.

"Weren't you just terrified?" Grace asked.

Smoke recalled what he had felt just as he was crawling over the edge of the gondola. "I had a moment," he replied with a sheepish grin.

"Well, thank God for that," Sally said.

"Wait a minute, you are thankful that I was a little frightened?" Smoke asked.

"Indeed, I am," Sally replied. She smiled back at him,

then reached up to put her hand on his cheek. "I wouldn't want to think that I am married to a complete fool."

The others laughed.

"What do you say we go to the Wyoming Lounge to celebrate?" Cummings invited. "I would say this calls for Champagne."

"I think that would be a wonderful idea," Sally agreed.

By the time they reached the Wyoming Lounge, several had heard of Smoke's parachute leap, and many came to congratulate him.

"I appreciate the accolades," Smoke said, "but don't forget, Professor Jordahl did it before I did."

"Yes, but he does it all the time," Colonel Cummings said. "For you, a person with absolutely no experience to do it . . . well, that required a great deal of courage."

"And a total suspension of good sense," Sally added with a proud smile.

"Ha, look who is talking," Grace said. "And didn't Miss 'good sense' herself defy gravity and float up to the clouds?"

"We didn't quite go high enough to get into the clouds," Sally said. "But I should like to do so, some day. I would love to see the clouds from above."

Chapter Sixteen

Pecorino had sent Bilbo, Cooper, and Easton out, with Jenner in charge, to intercept and steal the registered bull that would be coming along the road from Medicine Bend to the RDC Ranch. They were waiting, two men on either side of the road, for the bull to come.

"There's somebody comin'," Bilbo said. "It's a wagon, 'n two riders alongside."

"You don't see no bull?" Jenner asked.

"Like I said, it's just two riders, 'n someone drivin' a wagon."

"What's in the wagon?" Jenner asked.

"I don't know, could be the bull, I reckon. We'll find that out when it gets here."

"Stay out of sight 'til I give you the signal," Jenner said.

The wagon and two riders that Bilbo had spotted were moving at the pace of a quick walk down the road, their passage marked by the crunching sound of the wheels, rolling through the dirt, and the creak and groan of the heavy wagon. It was getting on into late September, and there was a bit of a chill in the gentle breeze that came from the north.

Cal was riding on one side of the wagon, Dusty on the other side, and Paul was driving the wagon which was in between them.

"You two boys just don't know how good a bull it is you're getting," Cal said.

"You know this bull pretty well, do you?" Paul asked.

"Do I know him well? I'll have you know that I'm the one that pulled him out of his mama when he first came into the world," Cal said. "I know this bull better than any other creature I've ever been around."

"You sound like you don't want your boss man to sell 'im."

"If I had my say, he wouldn't sell Sir McGinnis," Cal said. "But the bull doesn't belong to me, so I don't have any say so in it. But, like Smoke said, if someone is willing to pay as much money as your boss paid for Sir McGinnis, I can be awfully sure that he will be treated well."

"I can see what a store you set in 'im," Dusty said. "So I can promise you, personal, that this bull will be treated just real good."

"Thank you. That's sort of an easing of my mind to know that."

"Why is he called Smoke?" Paul asked.

"His real name is Kirby, but nobody ever calls him that. We just all call him Smoke."

"All of his hands call him Smoke?"

"No, mostly it's just Pearlie 'n me . . . that is, Pearlie and I. Miz Sally, once bein' a school teacher, sets a great store about usin' proper grammar and all. But what I was going to say is that, of all his hands, it is really only Pearlie and I who call him that. But now, among all of his friends, I mean the folks in town and the other ranchers 'n all, they call him Smoke. Are you telling me you've never heard of Smoke Jensen?"

"I ain't never a' heered of 'im," Paul replied. "Should I have?"

"Well, I won't go so far as to say that you should have heard of him, but he is pretty much what most folks would call famous."

"Hey, I read a book oncet about a feller named Smoke Jensen," Dusty said. "He was s'posed to be real good with a gun."

"That's Smoke, all right."

"But this can't be the same one you're a' talkin' about, on account of this here book warn't even true," Dusty insisted.

"There have been a lot of books written about him, and none of them are true," Cal said. "They are what you call novels and that means that the stories are all made up. But the main character of the novels is Smoke Jensen, and he is true."

"I'll be damn. Then he is famous, ain't he?" Dusty asked.

"I'd say he is," Cal responded. He smiled as he thought about it, but didn't add that both he and Pearlie had appeared as themselves in several of the dime novels about Smoke.

"Hey, what's that up there?" Paul asked, pulling back on the reins to halt the wagon.

"I don't know," Cal said. "But I don't have a good feeling about it."

"What's that they're a' wearin'?" Dusty asked. "Looks like they're in a fireman's band or somethin'."

"They're wearing uniforms all right," Cal said, puzzled by the approach of the four, uniformed men. "But I sure don't think they're members of any fireman's band. I've never seen anything like this, and I have to tell you that I don't like it."

Three of the four men were carrying rifles, but at the moment, the rifle barrels were pointing toward the road.

"What do you think they are about?" Paul asked, nervously.

"I don't know," Cal replied. "I guess we'll just have to find out." Cal moved his hand to the butt of his pistol and waited as the four men approached, one riding in front, and three riding abreast behind him. Cal noticed that the one riding in front had a gold stripe around the cuff of his blouse, whereas the three behind him did not. He assumed from that, and from the way they approached, that this man was the leader of the group.

"I see that you have the bull in the wagon," the leader of the group said. "That's good. That'll make it easier for us to take him."

"Take him? What do you mean, take him?" Paul asked. "This here bull belongs to Colonel R. D. Cummings, 'n unless you are ridin' for the brand, which I know that you ain't, 'cause I ain't never seen you before, you ain't comin' nowhere close to this bull."

"This bull is bein' taken for the new country. Taxes, you might say," the leader said.

"What new country?"

"Why, Nova Amera . . . uh . . . Reg somethin' or the other." The leader stopped in frustration at not being able to come up with the words he was looking for. "It don't make no difference what the name of it is, all that matters is that you folks are in the new country right now. 'N that means that we can take this here bull for taxes 'n there's nothin' you can do about it, 'cause it'll be legal."

"I know of no federal, state, or territorial law that would allow you to take this bull," Cal said. "And unless you show me a warrant to that effect, you'll not be taking this animal."

"I told you, this here is a new country, 'n none of them laws matter anymore," the leader of the group said. "Now we are going to take the bull from you, 'n it can either be peaceable, or not peaceable at all, but one way the other, we will be takin' that bull."

"The hell you are," Paul replied.

"Are you saying you ain't goin' to give up that bull?"

"That's exactly what I'm sayin'," Paul replied.

"Shoot them," the leader said, and, as one, the three men lifted their rifles.

When Cal saw the rifle barrels come up, he drew and fired, knocking one of the shooters out of his saddle. The other two fired their rifles. Paul was hit by one of the bullets, and Cal heard the other bullet as it fried the air just by him.

The two uniformed road agents who had fired realized now that before they could fire a second time, they would have to cock their weapons to chamber a new round. But seeing one of their own down, and seeing the pistol in the hand of the man who had done the shooting, the three remaining men turned and galloped away.

Dusty started after them.

"No, Dusty, we need to get Paul back in town to the doctor!" Cal called out to him.

"They're getting away!" Dusty replied.

"Let them. Paul is more important."

"Yeah," Dusty agreed. "Yeah, you're right."

Half an hour later, just as Smoke, Sally, Cummings, and Grace were coming out of the Wyoming Lounge, they were surprised to see that the wagon that had been designed to carry Sir McGinnis was back in town. They were even more surprised to see Dusty driving it and Paul slumped against him. Cal was riding alongside, leading Dusty's horse.

"Cal!" Smoke shouted, at the same time Cummings called out to Dusty. "What happened?"

"Paul's been shot, Colonel!" Dusty called back.

The doctor's office was only three buildings down from the Wyoming Lounge, so Smoke and the others hurried down to it, then stood by as Cal and Dusty eased Paul down from the seat. All seven of them went into the doctor's office.

"What is it? What do we have here?" the doctor asked, coming over to them.

"My friend's been shot, Doc," Dusty said.

"Get him into the back so I can have a closer look at him. Who stuffed this cloth into the bullet hole?"

"I did, Doc," Cal said.

"Well, you did well to stop the bleeding. Probably

wasn't good for infection, but I'll clean the wound, and maybe that will stop it."

Everyone started in the back with the doctor, but he held up his hand to stop them.

"Not enough room back there for everyone. Mrs. Cummings, I know that you used to be a nurse, why don't you come back with me? I could probably use your help."

"I'll be glad to," Grace said.

"Cal, what happened?" Smoke asked, after Grace disappeared inside with the doctor and patient.

"It's the damndest thing, Smoke. It was four men, and they were all wearing uniforms, like the army, or something."

"Soldiers?" Cummings asked.

"No, sir. Well, I don't know. I mean they were all wearing uniforms and they were sort of acting like they were soldiers, because there was one man who seemed to be giving orders. But it wasn't army uniforms, because they were green, instead of blue."

"Yeah, and don't forget, he said something about taxes and a new country," Dusty said.

"It has to be the fool who wrote the letter to the editor," Smoke said.

"My word, Smoke. You don't think someone is insane enough to actually try and start a revolution, do you?"

"Revolution? What revolution?" Cal asked.

Smoke told Cal about the letter to the editor of the newspaper.

"Do you think that's who I ran into?"

"Cal, you've been studying grammar," Sally said.

Cal smiled. "Yes, ma'am, from you. And I don't figure

I would get a better background in grammar, no matter where I went to school."

"Thank you for the compliment. But the reason I asked is, by now you are a pretty good judge of grammar and speech patterns. The man who spoke to you . . . do you think he was an educated man?"

Cal laughed out loud. "No, ma'am, if you want to know the truth of it, he was as dumb as dirt."

Sally looked over at Smoke. "This obviously isn't the man who's calling himself King Clemente."

"So this isn't the beginning of the revolution," Cummings said.

Smoke shook his head. "Not necessarily," Smoke replied. "The fella whose calling himself a king, wasn't with them. That just means that he has enough people to send others out to do his bidding."

"That may be, but one of 'em that he sent out to do his bidding won't be coming back," Cal said.

"You shot one of them?"

"I sure did. He's lying out there on the trail now, deader than a doornail."

"I'll get Sheriff Sharples to send a deputy out there," Cummings said. "Maybe someone will know him."

The doctor came into the room then, and even before he spoke, Smoke could tell by the expression on his face, that it wouldn't be good news.

"I'm sorry, Colonel," the doctor said. "I did all I could for him, but the bullet hit some vital organs inside. It's a miracle he lived as long as he did."

"Damn," Cummings said, quietly. "Paul was a good man, a damn good man."

Fort Regency

"There was a man with them who warn't like no ordinary man," Jenner reported. "He got his gun out and commenced a' shootin' even while Bilbo, Cooper, 'n Easton was shootin' at him. Cooper, he got kilt, so the rest of us high-tailed it out of there."

"Why did you not stay and engage him?" Pecorino said.

"We was shootin' rifles, 'n we would 'a had to cock 'em a' fore we could shoot again," Jenner said. "He had a pistol in his hand, 'n all he had to do was pull the trigger."

"Then you were right to order a strategic withdrawal," Pecorino said. "At this point, we can't afford to lose any more men. Was there any effect from your shooting?"

"What?"

"Were any of them hit?"

"Oh, yeah, the man that was drivin' the wagon was shot, 'n I'm purt' nigh sure he was kilt. He was sure slumped over like he was."

Two days later Pecorino, dressed in ordinary clothes, rode into Medicine Bow. He was unknown in this town, and thus was able to move through the people without generating any attention, all the while listening to the conversations. He had learned long ago that the best place to pick up information was in a saloon.

"Paul Burke was a good man," one of the patrons of the Double Down Saloon said.

Pecorino was standing at the bar, nursing his beer.

"Do you believe it, what they are a' sayin', that he was kilt by some army soldiers?"

"There ain't nobody a' sayin' that there was army soldiers that kilt 'im."

"Yeah? Well, the feller they brought in was damn sure wearin' some sort of uniform."

"Well it warn't no army uniform, that's for sure. You goin' to Burke's funeral?"

"I reckon so. Me 'n Paul wasn't what you'd call just real good friends, but I did know 'im, 'n me 'n him always had a kind word for one another."

"Yeah, I'll be a' goin', as well."

"What time is the funeral?" one of the other patrons asked.

Pecorino was glad someone else asked the question so that he wouldn't have to call attention to himself by asking.

"Well, the fella they brung in, one o' the ones that actual kilt Paul, he's goin' to be buried 'round one o'clock I heard, only there ain't goin' to be no funeral for him. Actually, there couldn't really be no funeral for him, 'cause there don't nobody even know his name. But the one for Paul, now, it'll be at two thirty."

CHAPTER SEVENTEEN

At one o'clock Pecorino walked through the cemetery to the Potter's Field area where he saw two men digging a grave. There was a plain, pine box lying alongside the grave and Pecorino stepped up to it. One of the grave diggers looked up.

"Somethin' we can do for you, mister?"

"No," Pecorino replied. "I'm just here for the interment of this poor soul."

"You know who he is?" the other grave digger asked. "'Cause there don't seem to be nobody else who does know 'im."

"I'm afraid I have no idea who it is."

The two grave diggers exchanged curious looks. "Well, I don't understand, mister. If you don't even know who this feller is, what are you here to see him buried for?"

"He was a fellow human being, passing through this fragile globe with hopes, ambitions, fears, and failures like all the rest of us. Don't you think that, in that case, he deserves at least one other soul to be present as he shuffles off this mortal coil."

The two grave diggers chuckled and shook their heads, then continued with their shoveling.

"Mister, you're welcome to stay here and say as many o' them words about 'im as you want. There don't me nor Dooley understand nothin' you said, but they sure did sound purty."

Pecorino waited only until Cooper's coffin was lowered into the ground, then left, even as he heard the dirt falling upon the pine box.

After leaving the cemetery, Pecorino went back to town. He had two articles that he wanted the newspaper to run . . . one to be run immediately, and the other to run a day or two later. At first he wondered how he could do that without making himself seen to prevent specific instructions to the editor, then he hit upon a plan. He would leave the first article directly with the newspaper, and he would mail the second article. That would give him the separation he was looking for.

He thought about hiring some boy to deliver the first article for him, but when he saw the publisher close the door to the newspaper office and walk away, leaving a sign on the door behind him, he decided to take advantage of the opportunity.

After the publisher was gone, Pecorino crossed the street to read the sign.

CLOSED
GONE TO THE FUNERAL
BACK IN TWO HOURS

Pecorino smiled. That made it easy for him. He slipped the first article in through the mail slot on the door, then he, too, left for the funeral.

There was no church funeral for Paul Burke, the decision having been made to have a grave-side service only.

"Hell, Paul never went to no church a-tall, anyway, much as I can remember," Dusty said. "Iffen you was to put him into a church buildin' now, I mean even what with him bein' dead 'n all, why, the Good Lord would most likely send a lightnin' bolt to strike us down."

There were a few laughing agreements from some of the other cowboys, then shortly before two o'clock, two wagons carrying cowboys, handymen, the cook, and his helpers made the trip into town.

Smoke, Sally, and Cal joined Colonel Cummings, Grace, Dusty, and the rest of the cowboys from the RDC Ranch for the burial of Paul Burke. Under ordinary circumstances, there would have been only a few of Paul's friends from among the cowboys to attend the funeral. But today the cemetery was crowded with townspeople, most of whom didn't even know him.

"Lord, Colonel, look at all these people," Dusty said in awe. "I ain't never seen so many people at one time, 'n they've all turned out for Paul's funeral."

"Yes," Cummings replied. "I'm sure it is because of the circumstances under which he was killed."

Word had gotten around that Paul, Dusty, and Cal had been attacked by men in uniform, and there was a great deal of nervous discussion among those who had come to the interment. Smoke realized that, while Paul Burke did, obviously, have friends, most of the people who had come for the funeral did so out of curiosity, more than a sense of sorrow for the deceased.

"Do you think there's actually going to be another civil war?" someone asked.

"I don't see how there could be," another answered. "Hell, they said they was only four of 'em that tried to steal the bull, 'n one o' them was kilt."

"Yes, but they was wearin' uniforms," another said. "You ever heard of outlaws . . . any outlaws, wearin' army uniforms?"

"I keep tellin' ever' one, these weren't actual army uniforms. They was green, they wasn't blue," Dusty said.

"Yeah? Well, the Confederates wore gray, instead of blue. And there sure as hell can't nobody say they wasn't an army."

Someone said that he thought Paul Burke had a brother somewhere, another said he thought it might have been a sister, but nobody was sure enough to know whether he had any relatives or not. It was for certain that he had no relatives in Medicine Bow, so instead of an awning that was normally reserved for family, a couple of long benches were laid out beside the open grave for the cowboys who had worked with Burke. Colonel Cummings, Grace, and Dusty set on the front bench, closest to the grave. Dusty was accorded that honor because everyone knew that he had been Paul Burke's closest friend.

The service was conducted by the Episcopal priest because Colonel Cummings was Episcopalian. Father Tuttle, fully vested, conducted the service, concluding it with the burial prayer.

"Oh God, whose mercies cannot be numbered; accept our prayers on behalf of the soul of Paul Burke, thy servant departed, and grant him an entrance into the land of light and joy, in the fellowship of thy saints; through Jesus Christ our Lord. Amen."

Father Tuttle concluded by making the sign of the cross, then with a nod toward Dusty, signaled that it was time for him to drop the first handful of dirt onto the casket.

The very next day, an alarming article appeared in the Medicine Bow newspaper.

Editor's note:

As your publisher, I must confess to some hesitation about printing these letters today. On the one hand, printing them does naught but gather more attention to the man who calls himself King Clemente. And it is obvious that such a megalomaniac craves attention. And yet, despite my abhorrence in providing publicity to such a person, I feel that under the circumstances it is very necessary that I do so. I consider this story to be no less than a declaration of war against the good citizens, not only of Wyoming, but Colorado, Utah, Nevada, and California as well. We can, and should, take this as a warning because as the old saying goes: "Forewarned is forearmed."

First, I shall print his "Proclamation":

FOUNDING PROCLAMATION OF NOVA AMERIGO REGNUM

A DECLARATION TO WITHDRAW THE TERRITORIES AND STATES OF WYOMING, COLORADO, UTAH, NEVADA, AND CALIFORNIA, FROM THE ENTITY KNOWN AS THE UNITED STATES OF AMERICA, IN ORDER TO ESTABLISH ITS INDEPENDENCE, AND ASSUME ALL THE RIGHTS AND POWERS THEREOF

Whereas, the above mentioned territories and states are too distant from the federal government in Washington, DC, and whereas the laws of the United States are applied unequally upon this area because of said distance, therefore be it proclaimed that there be a separation, and subsequent establishment of a new nation to be known as Nova Amerigo Regnum.

The new nation, formed by the joining of Wyoming, Colorado, Utah, Nevada, and California, shall be established as one contiguous kingdom, uninterrupted by state or territorial lines, to be ruled by the absolute authority and power invested in His Royal Highness, King Clemente Benito Pecorino, first sovereign of the new kingdom. Succeeding sovereigns of Nova Amerigo Regnum shall be from the first male issue of King Pecorino and the first male issue of all Kings subsequent.

By the affixation of the signature of His Royal Highness, hereto attached, this proclamation is hereby in force.

HRH Clemente Rex
Monarch of Nova Amerigo Regnum

And, no doubt using this proclamation as his justification, the man would be king, has "declared" war upon we, the citizens of the United States:

War Has Been Declared

By means of this letter I announce that a state of war exists between Nova Amerigo Regnum and the United States of America. The first blood has already been spilled when an attempt was made to confiscate a prize bull for taxes. Representatives of the Nova Amerigo Regnum were met, not with cooperation, but with hostility. In the gunfire that ensued, a disloyal subject to the new nation, one Paul Burke, was killed. Also killed was Ely Cooper, a soldier in Exercitus Salus. Ely Cooper will be immortalized in the history of Nova Amerigo Regnum, as the first person to be killed in the service of our new nation.

By this exchange of gunfire, I hereby put all my subjects on notice. You must submit to the demands of my soldiers, as they are carrying out my will. Failure to do so will be prima facie evidence that you are a traitor to the kingdom, and as such, shall be subject to any penalty my soldiers deem appropriate, up to and including death.

These terms may seem harsh to you, but in any revolution, be it the one by which the United States established its position in the world population of independent nations, or the failed revolution of the Confederacy, blood will be spilled. The amount of blood spilled in this revolution shall be entirely dependent upon the willingness of my subjects to submit to my absolute authority over them.

Clemente Rex the First

Two days later, the Medicine Bow newspaper carried another letter to the editor from the mysterious Clemente Rex.

To the Subjects of Nova Amerigo Regnum

I bring you greetings from your sovereign. As I reported but two days previous in my missive to this newspaper, Ely Cooper, a soldier of my army, a hero whose loyalty to our realm, manifested in his fealty to me by giving his life in service, and by extension to you, the subjects of this new nation we are building, was killed in service to his king.

By royal edict, I now declare that this brave young man is henceforth to be recognized as "Hero of the Realm," and the second day of September shall be celebrated in perpetuity, as "First Blood

Day." School children in Nova Amerigo Regnum will, for the next one hundred years, honor Ely Cooper as one of our kingdom's earliest heroes. We are now actively seeking men to join the revolution and fight for the independence of our new nation from the oppressive government of the United States.

In order to prevent any unauthorized and ill-meaning intrusion into the birth process of our new nation, at this point we are not accepting unsolicited applications for membership. However, we will be examining the merits, qualifications, and loyalty of those people we find worthy of membership, and if you are deemed to be such a person, we will approach you. Should you be propositioned for membership, it will be because you have been adjudged worthy of the honor of being one of our new nation's founding fathers.

The rewards for such membership with be great, for the founding fathers will share in the faustum et virtutis (power and prosperity) as shall be accrued by the Nova Amerigo Regnum. But the true patriot will realize that this power and this prosperity, rich though it may be, will be less important than the knowledge of having participated in the birth of a new nation.

> Faustum et virtutis
> Clemente Rex the First,
> Nova Amerigo Regnum

"Who is this person, anyway?" Smoke asked.

Cummings shook his head. "Nobody knows. He just seemed to show up one day. Well, he has never actually shown up. By that, I mean that far as I know, nobody has ever even seen him. But he has made himself known by these letters to the editor . . . and . . . I guess it's news because every newspaper in the country, it seems, is printing his drivel."

R. D. Cummings and Grace were at the depot now with Smoke, Sally, and Cal, waiting with them for the train that would take them back to Colorado.

"I've known people like him," Sally said. "Educated men who, for some reason, feel aggrieved. If I were guessing, I would say he is a politician who may have lost an election, and feels that the people were just too dumb to reelect him. Such men have tremendous egos, and that ego often crowds out any other sense of humanity.

"I must admit, though, that anyone who declares himself king, and speaks of others as subjects in his realm, has more than just a little ego."

"Yes, but for someone to actually talk about turning a republic into a kingdom, that's beyond all reason. He has a sense of self-importance bigger than can be carried in a Studebaker Wagon. You don't really think he might actually wind up causing trouble for us, do you?" Cummings asked. "I mean, a lot of trouble . . . more so than just another ordinary outlaw," he added.

"Well, France was a Republic, and it fell to an egomaniac named Napoleon," Sally replied with a little laugh.

"Oh, Lord, I hadn't even considered that. I wonder if someone should go to Fort Laramie and talk to the army?" Grace said.

"It might not be a bad idea," Smoke said.

"No, not yet anyway," Cummings said. "I mean folks didn't mind the army so much when we were still having Indian trouble. But for the army to come in here, just to deal with a band of outlaws, well, I think maybe our lawmen should be able to handle that."

Cummings's response was punctuated with the distant sound of a whistle, denoting the approach of the train.

"Here comes your train," Cummings said. "We'll walk out onto the platform with you, to watch you board."

Thank you so much for your hospitality, Grace, and Colonel," Sally said. "You must come to Colorado to see us some day."

"I look forward to it."

Fifteen minutes later, Smoke, Sally, and Cal were on the train, headed toward Cheyenne, where they would change trains for the trip down to Denver.

"Smoke, you said it might not be a bad idea for them to go to the army," Sally said. "Do you really believe that?"

"I don't know," Smoke replied. "R.D. has a point in that the civilians may not welcome the interference of the army. And he's right, no bigger than it seems to be now, it may well be something that the law can handle on its own. But, like you said, this man does seem to be awfully full of himself. And who knows where it might lead?"

Fort Regency

Pecorino started every day in the fort exactly as such a day would be started in an actual army post. There were no bugle calls, but the men, in uniform, did stand at morning formation.

The army had grown, slightly, and this morning after telling the men they could stand at ease, Pecorino addressed his troops.

"I know that some of you have been wondering when there would be some compensation for your service." Pecorino paused and smiled. "Well, gentlemen, that is about to occur. Today we are going to conduct our first, full-scale military operation. I intend to lead you in an attack on a bank. With our numbers, and under my leadership, there will be nothing anyone can do that will prevent us from relieving the bank of every cent it has in reserve. One half of the money we get will go into the treasury of Nova Amerigo Regnum. The other half of the money will be divided into twenty-five equal parts, to be distributed among you."

One of the men raised his hand.

"Yes, Harris?"

"How come it is that you're a' dividin' the money into twenty-five equal parts, when there is only ten of us?"

"That is a good question," Pecorino replied. "The answer is in the method of distribution. Each of you shall get share equal to one twenty-fifth of the half of the money that is available for disbursement. Jenner, Logan, and Moss, as your officers, shall each get two twenty-fifths of the bounty, and the remaining seven shares will be mine."

"How much will one share be?"

"I know, for a fact, that the bank I have chosen, has a reserve of at least fifty thousand dollars," Pecorino replied. "Twenty-five thousand dollars will go into our treasury. The remaining twenty-five thousand will comprise the payroll, at one thousand dollars per share. That means each of you will get a minimum of one thousand dollars. Your officers will get two thousand dollars apiece. The remainder will go into my own personal reserve."

Jenner, Logan, and Moss exchanged smiles of pride and gratification over their good luck.

"Where is this here bank?" one of the other soldiers asked.

"It is the Bank of Alford. This bank is just across the line into Colorado, which makes it even more attractive. By conducting a raid in Colorado, it will extend our presence, thus validating our position of a true, regional revolution."

CHAPTER EIGHTEEN

Alford, Colorado

Alford, Colorado, was just across the line from Wyoming. Its proximity to Wyoming made it an easy target for Pecorino to conduct his operation and, as he had explained to his men, it also gave him an opportunity to expand his presence.

The citizens of the town looked up in surprise, then confusion, as they saw several men riding in columns of twos as they came into town. One man was riding in front, and though they were all wearing uniforms, the uniform of the man in front looked a bit more ornate than the others. But his uniform, like the others, was different from any army uniform any of the residents had ever seen. The uniforms were green, rather than army blue, though it certainly appeared to be a precise military formation.

There were at least forty or fifty of Alford's citizens going about their daily business, and curious as to this strange parade, they paused to watch as the men rode right down through the middle of the street.

"Hey! Who are you fellas?" one of the citizens called. "What is it you're a' supposed to be?"

Not one of the men responded, nor even glanced around. Instead, they kept their eyes glued to the front.

"Damn, them fellers is just like an army. Look at 'em."

"If it is an army, it ain't no American army."

"I bet it's Mexicans."

"Mexicans? We ain't at war with Mexico."

The formation continued on down the street until they reached the Bank of Alford.

The man who was riding in front of the formation held his hand up.

"Company, halt!" he called.

The riders stopped.

"Dismount!"

The riders dismounted.

"Horse holders, to horse."

Three men moved into position so that they were holding four horses each. A fourth man held his own horse, and the horse of the leader, and the curiosity among the citizens of the town grew.

A quick appraisal of the townspeople satisfied Pecorino that only a few of the men were even wearing weapons. He allowed himself a smile. This was goin' to be even easier than he thought it would be.

"Lookouts post!" he ordered, and two men moved into position in the middle of the street, holding their rifles at the ready, and peering up and down the street.

"Those so designated, follow me."

Four men followed Pecorino into the bank.

"Here, what is this?" the teller asked. He looked at the five uniformed and armed men.

There were four other customers in the bank, an old man with white hair and a long, white beard, a young woman holding a baby, and a young man who was obviously a cowboy.

"In the name of the nation of Nova Amerigo Regnum, I am placing a one hundred percent tax upon all the funds herein held by this bank," Pecorino said.

"What? What does that mean?"

"It means that I am taking every cent this bank has."

"The hell you are."

Pecorino shot the old man. Grabbing the wound on his chest, the old man's eyes registered shock as he went down.

"What the hell did you do that for? Mr. Travers don't have nothin' to do with the bank!" the startled teller shouted.

"Did I get your attention?" Pecorino replied in a voice as calm as if he was asking the time of day.

"Yeah, yeah, you got my attention," the bank teller said, barely able to control the anger and the fear in his voice.

"Good. Then you know that the next person I kill will be the baby," Pecorino said. "Then the woman, then you."

"You won't kill me. You'll need me to open the vault for you."

Pecorino smiled and pulled out a couple of sticks of dynamite. "No, I won't. It might be a bit messy, but believe me, I will get the safe open."

"You're too late, anyway. Most all our money's done been shipped out. We don't have more than a hundred dollars on hand."

"That ain't true, Gilbert. You was just sayin' as how you got more 'n a hunnert thousand dollars right now," the young cowboy said.

"Parker, you fool!" the bank teller shouted. "Why would you tell these men such a thing?"

"Maybe it's 'cause no more 'n fifteen minutes ago you turned me down for a fifty-dollar loan," Parker replied. He smiled at Pecorino and the other armed men. "And, maybe it's 'cause I want to ride off with 'em."

Pecorino handed the cowboy a cloth bag. "Mr. Parker, if you would be so good, sir, as soon as the teller opens the vault, I would like for you to fill this bag with what currency you can find, eschewing of course, all the coins. Your help in this matter would greatly expedite our withdrawal."

Parker's smile grew broader. "I'm not sure what all that means, but I think you're 'a sayin' for me to scoop up all the money, 'n then I can ride out with you."

"Open the vault," Pecorino ordered, pointing the pistol at the baby's head.

"No!" the young woman screamed. "Kill me, spare my baby!"

"I'll open it, I'll open it! There's no need for you to kill anyone else," the teller said.

Parker, holding the cloth bag, followed Gibson back to the vault, then stood by as the vault door was unlocked, then swung open. Quickly, the bag was stuffed with money, then Parker came back around to the front side of the teller cage.

"You have your choice, Mr. Parker," Pecorino said. "You may take one hundred dollars from the bag, to keep for yourself. Or, if you pass the test, you may ride with us."

"What is this test you're a' talkin' about?" Parker asked.

Pecorino drew his pistol and handed it to Parker.

"Kill Mr. Gibson," Pecorino said.

"What? No!" Gibson shouted.

"You shoulda give me the loan," Parker said as he pulled the trigger.

Gibson went down with a bullet in his forehead.

"What is it? What's the shootin' that's goin' on in there?" one of the townspeople called out.

"It ain't nothin' you need to be a' worryin' about," Jenner, who had remained outside, replied.

A moment later, Pecorino and the men who entered the bank with him came back outside. Pecorino was holding the cloth bag and, even from here, Jenner could see that it was filled with money.

"Company, to horse!" Pecorino called, and though his voice was raised loud enough that everyone in town could hear him, there seemed to be no sense of urgency, either in his voice or his action.

The men recovered their horses, then stood by them until Pecorino gave the order.

"Mount up!"

As one, and with precision, the men swung into their saddles.

"Right by twos, forward!"

The men left town in the same orderly fashion by which they had arrived.

* * *

"What do you think that was?" one of the townspeople asked, as the formation rode out of town at a brisk trot.

"You know what I think? I think it was most likely a bank robbery," one of the other citizens replied.

"The hell it was. You ever know'd any bank robbers to just ride out of town like that, as if there warn't nothin' that just happened?"

"But they was them two gunshots and . . ."

"Help!"

The scream came from Mrs. Margrabe, who stepped out from the bank clutching her baby to her. "Those men just killed Mr. Travers and Mr. Gibson!"

Big Rock, Colorado

Sheriff Carson met Smoke, Sally, and Cal when they stepped off the train.

"Where's Pearlie?" the sheriff asked.

"I've loaned him out," Smoke said, explaining that Pearlie would be working at Albert Barrington's Three Mountain Ranch to try and get the ranch back into a financially stable condition.

"It's like nothing I've ever seen before," Smoke explained. "His ranch is every bit as large as Sugarloaf, and his herd is as large, but he is losing money."

"Rustlers?" Sheriff Carson asked.

"Yes, I'm sure that's what is causing the immediate loss. However, I have no doubt but that the long-time cause is the result of bad management."

"So you left Pearlie to help him out." It wasn't a question. Sheriff Carson had simply made a statement.

"Yes. I don't know how much success he'll have in changing the mindset of two of the most self-assured men you'll ever meet in your life, but with the least to be comfortable about."

"Sort of full of themselves, are they?"

"They are the height of arrogance," Sally put in.

"What about the man you sold the bull to?" Sheriff Carson asked.

"He is a gentleman by any way you measure," Smoke replied.

"Well, I'm glad it all worked out for you. I mean, after that aborted train robbery, I figured someone might come after you."

"Someone did," Cal said, explaining how the brother of one of the train robbers came after Smoke.

"Well, what do you three say to dinner at Lamberts, my treat? Feel like dodging a couple of throwed rolls?" Sheriff Carson invited.

"Hungry as I am, I'll have at least two of 'em et before we even reach the table," Cal said.

"Cal?"

"Sorry, Miz Sally. I'll only have one of them et . . ." Seeing the expression on her face, Cal smiled, and corrected himself, "Eaten."

Lamberts was a rather unique restaurant, not in the fare it served, but in the way it was served. As soon as someone stepped in through the front door, someone would throw a couple of rolls at them.

"Look out!" Cal shouted as one was heading directly for Sally's face.

Smoke, demonstrating the reaction and determination that made him a very good gunfighter, stuck out his hand

and grasped the roll from mid-air, a second before it would have hit Sally.

"Oh, my, I had better be more careful, hadn't I?"

"Uh-huh," Smoke said, though his reply was mumbled because he was already eating the roll.

During lunch, Cal told the story of how while he, and two others, were taking Sir McGinnis out to the ranch, they were set upon by four men who attempted to take the bull from them. "And what was strange about it," Cal said, concluding his story, "is that they was . . . were," he corrected himself and threw a quick glance toward Sally, "wearing uniforms. Not army uniforms mind you, these were . . ."

"Green?" Sheriff Carson asked.

"Yeah, green. How did you know that?"

"Earl?" Sheriff Carson called, holding up his hand toward one of the waiters.

"Yes, Sheriff. You want something else?"

"Bring me a copy of today's paper, would you?"

"Yes, sir," Earl replied.

A waiter came by their table with a large pan of fried okra. Known as "pass arounds," this was another feature of Lambert's Restaurant.

"Here's the paper, Sheriff," Earl said a short while later.

"Thanks." Sheriff Carson showed the paper to Smoke. "What do you think about this?"

UNIFORMED ARMY ROBS BANK

Alford, Colorado was the scene of a bank robbery on two days previous. The bank robbers, all of whom were wearing military-cut uniforms, entered the town in formation, as if they were an army troop. The uniforms, being green, aroused the curiosity of the citizens of the town and they watched as the "army" proceeded to the bank, and there, in precise military action, deployed lookouts and horse holders while four of their number entered the bank.

A short while later the "army" left town, having stolen $102,019 dollars and leaving in the bank two dead men, 85-year-old Edward Travers, a retired barber, and Roger Gilbert, the teller. The departing army took with them, Emmitt Parker, a local ne'r-do-well. There was some speculation that Parker had been taken as a hostage, but Mrs. Frank Osgood, who witnessed the hold up, has stated to the sheriff that Parker volunteered to join the band of robbers.

It is believed that these men might be related to the recent missives sent to area newspapers, proclaiming a revolution of sorts, with the intention of separating Colorado, California, Wyoming, Nevada, and Utah from the United States of America, for the purpose of establishing a new nation, to be called Nova Amerigo Regnum. The name of this so-called new nation is itself an anathema to all freedom-loving people, for it means New American Kingdom.

The self-proclaimed king of this "kingdom" is known only as Clemente.

CHAPTER NINETEEN

Chicago, Illinois

Clyde Barnes, Austin Prouty, Mule Blackwell, and Vernon Mathis were shown into a hotel suite and asked to wait.

"Any of you fellas ever seen a hotel room like this 'n?" Austin asked, looking around at the luxurious furnishings.

"It is very elegant, all right," Clyde agreed.

"It ain't that," Austin said. "What I mean is, where does a fella sleep? There ain't no bed here."

"Of course, there is no bed in here. This is the sitting room," Clyde said. He pointed to a door. I expect the bedroom is in there."

"The hell you say? I ain't never heard of no hotel room that had a sitting room and a bedroom."

"That's because this isn't a hotel room. It's what they call a suite," Mule said.

"A sweet? Yeah, I reckon it is sweet, all right, for someone as could afford it," Austin said.

A moment later the door opened, and a white-jacketed

bellhop pushed in a cart, upon which sat a silver tray, silver coffeepot, and five cups.

"You can leave it there, Mr. Collins," a man said, coming into the room behind the bellhop.

"Yes, sir, General," the bellhop said.

The man who had just entered was a tall, thin man. He was wearing a uniform with shoulder boards that bore two stars. He had a high forehead, and a beard that was more white now than its original rust color.

"Gentlemen, I'm General Sherman," he said, extending his hand.

"Lord a' mighty, I was never more 'n a private," Austin said. "And here I am, shakin' hands with a general."

"Did you wear the blue?" Sherman asked.

"Yes, sir, I'm just real proud to say that I did."

Sherman smiled. "Then we were brothers in arms."

Austin returned the smile. "Yes, sir, I reckon we was at that."

"What do you gentlemen say we have a cup of coffee and talk for a few minutes?" General Sherman said, indicating that they should take a seat. He poured coffee for each of them.

"You four gentlemen will be driving the President's train," Sherman said, as he sat, now holding his own cup of coffee.

"Yes, sir," Austin replied. "Well, actually it's Clyde 'n Mule that'll be a' drivin' the train, General. Me 'n Vernon is just the firemen."

Clyde chuckled. "The train won't run without the fire."

"I reckon you got that right," Vernon said.

"At what speed will you be driving?" Sherman asked Clyde.

"Well, I suppose I can drive at just about any speed you want," Clyde answered. "I understand that they'll be clearin' the high iron for us, so there won't be no other trains that'll get in the way."

"What is the fastest you can run, and guarantee the safety of President Hayes and his family?"

"Well now, General, what you done there is, you asked two different questions," Clyde replied. "First thing you asked is, how fast can this engine run. And it can actual run seventy miles to the hour."

"Seventy miles to the hour?" General Sherman gasped. "You can run that fast, and keep the President safe?"

Clyde chuckled. "No, sir, 'n that's what I meant by a' sayin' that you was askin' two different questions. We can make the train go seventy miles to the hour, just like I said. But I don't reckon nobody can actual guarantee that train travel will be for sure 'n certain safe, seein' as there could near 'bout be anythin' that could happen. And most especially iffen we was to be runnin' that fast. But I reckon that we could run purt' nigh thirty-five miles an hour 'n be safe. Wouldn't you say so, Mule?"

Blackwell nodded. "I'd say we could run thirty to thirty-five miles to the hour 'n not be worryin' none 'bout runnin' off the rails."

"Good. I want the President to be able to move as rapidly as possible, without being endangered." Sherman chuckled. "And, as my daughter, Rachel, and I will be riding on the same train, I don't want myself to be endangered either."

Clyde laughed. "Well, now General, since the four of us will all be ridin' up in front of the train, whenever it's our time to drive, that is, we'd be the first ones to be in danger if somethin' was to happen, so you can bet that we sure don't plan on doin' nothin' that'll get us kilt, or even hurt."

General Sherman smiled and nodded. "That's a good point. I was assured that you four were the best the railroad has to offer, and now that I have met you, I am inclined to agree with that assessment."

"Is there any particular schedule you want us to keep as to who is drivin' the train, 'n who is restin'? Or do you want us to work it out ourselves?" Mule Blackwell asked.

"Work it out among yourselves," General Sherman said. "We will want the train to be underway for twenty-four hours, with only the limited stops for the President's personal appearances. In order for us to be able to do that, you will have to spell each other."

"We can rotate ever' eight hours," Clyde said.

General Sherman eased the tone of his voice. "There will be times where you will have two to four hours of not having to do anything because of the time the President will spend visiting."

"All those times will be in the daytime, won't they?" Mule asked.

"Most of them will be, yes, but I expect some of his appearances may be as late as ten o'clock at night."

"We can work with that," Clyde said.

"Good," Sherman said. "I have to meet with the President now. Come, I'll escort you down to the lobby."

General Sherman accompanied the four train crewmen down to the lobby, then went back upstairs where he knocked on the door to the President's suite. The door was opened by Birchard, one of the President's sons. Rutherford, the President's other son, was standing at the window with General Sherman's daughter, Rachel, looking down at the busy streets of Chicago.

"Hello, General," Birchard greeted. "I'll tell Father you're here."

"Papa, you must see this lovely view," Rachel said. Rachel, who was twenty years old, was an exceptionally pretty young woman who had fired the fantasies of many a young army officer.

General Sherman stepped over to the window and was standing there when President Hayes came out of the master bedroom, this particular suite consisting of a sitting room, dining room, and two bedrooms.

"Hello, Bill," President Hayes said.

"Mr. President," General Sherman replied. The general waited until the President was seated before he sat.

"Did you talk to the train crew?"

"Yes, sir, I'm well satisfied with them."

"Good, good. I just had an interview with a reporter from a Chicago newspaper. He assures me that the story will appear, not only in the *Tribune,* but in dozens of newspapers all along our route of travel."

"Oh, I don't know, Mr. President. Do you think that was a good idea?"

"Why not? Isn't the reason for this trip to allow me to get out among all the people? And, since I will not be running for re-election, nobody can accuse me of doing this for political reasons."

"It isn't that, it's just that . . ." General Sherman hesitated a moment before he continued. "Ah, never mind.

I suppose I'm being overly cautious when there is no real need for me to be so."

President Hayes chuckled. "My term will be over very soon. I'm no threat to anyone."

Fort Regency, Wyoming Territory

Pecorino was reading a newspaper *The Cheyenne Leader,* when Jenner, Logan, and Moss came over to talk to him. There was a fourth man with them.

"Dr. Pecorino?" Jenner said.

"I believe I have instructed you to address me as General," Pecorino replied.

"Oh, yeah, I keep forgettin'."

"You three men are my officers, and once my kingdom is established, you will be elevated to a peer of the realm. If I can't depend upon you three to follow the rules, I can always dismiss you and appoint someone else to your place."

"No, sir, now, uh, General, there ain't no need for you to be a' doin' nothin' like that now. No need a-tall. We'll not be a' forgettin' that no more," Jenner said.

"No, sir, 'n me 'n Moss won't be forgettin' it none, neither," Logan said.

The three had already seen, first hand, examples of how Pecorino "dismissed" those with whom he was displeased.

"Now, what have we here?" Pecorino asked.

"This here is Luke Dobbins," Logan said. "Me 'n him used to work together some."

"Oh? And in what capacity, may I ask?"

"Dobbins used to be the telegrapher up in Wilcox. Sometimes when he'd get or send a message that me 'n

Franklin 'n the others could use, why, he'd tell us about it. They didn't hardly ever have no money shipments comin' in, or goin' out of Wilcox that we didn't know about."

"Oh? You are a telegrapher, are you, Mr. Dobbins?" Pecorino asked.

"Yeah, I . . ."

"Sir," Logan said.

"What?"

"When you talk to General Pecorino you'll call 'im general, 'n you'll always say sir to 'im."

"Oh."

"You were saying, Mr. Dobbins?" Pecorino asked.

"Oh, yeah. Uh, I mean sir. What I was about to say is that I *was* a telegrapher workin' at the railroad depot in Wilcox, only I got fired on account of I did not always keep all the telegrams secret like I was s'posed to."

"But you do have the skill of a telegrapher, do you not?"

"Oh, yeah, I can still handle the key all right. I mean, sir."

"I would like for you gentlemen to step outside with me for a moment, if you would, please," Pecorino invited.

Curious as to why Pecorino wanted them outside, Dobbins, Logan, Jenner, and Moss followed him outside.

"About one mile in that direction is a telegraph wire," Pecorino said.

"Yes, sir, it's the main wire."

"Who all uses that wire?"

"Oh, ever' station betwixt Cheyenne 'n Granger uses it."

"So, what you are saying is that any telegram, originating in any station between Cheyenne and Granger will pass over that line?"

"Yes, sir. 'N if it starts in Cheyenne, no matter where it goes, it'll also be on that line."

"Tell me, Mr. Dobbins. If we were to attach a line to that wire and run it here to Fort Regency, would you be able to read all the telegrams?"

A big smile spread across Dobbins's face. "Yes, sir, I sure as hell could."

"Problem is, General, that there wire is a mile away, 'n that means we'd have to have us at least a mile long wire," Jenner said. "Where would we get such a thing?"

"At Fort Laramie," Moss said.

"At Fort Laramie?" Pecorino asked, interested in Moss's comment.

"Yes, sir. When I was in the army at Fort Laramie I worked in supply. We always had two or three miles' worth of wire just in case."

"Do you know anyone who is still in the army there? And by, know someone, I mean someone who could be paid to make a mile of wire available to us."

"There's a fella there by the name of Largent. Frankie Largent. It wouldn't take much to make him desert the army, 'n I reckon iffen we was to let him join up with us, he'd brang the wire along with 'im."

"Very good, Lieutenant, see to it," Pecorino said.

"Oh, and speakin' of Fort Laramie," Moss added, "I don't got no doubt but that Largent will know whenever it is that they take the payroll from Cheyenne up to the Fort. 'N from what I remember they don't never have no more 'n four guards that rides with it. While we're a' stealin' the wire from 'em, seems to me like it'd be just real easy to take the money from one of those payrolls."

"Money is not our main concern, right now," Pecorino

said. "As a matter of fact, it would be a tactical error for us to acquire any more funding at this juncture."

"What? What does that mean . . . tactical error to get more money?" Jenner replied, confused by the comment.

"Look at it this way," Pecorino replied. "Every man in our army now has more money than he has ever had before, in his entire life. Isn't that correct?"

"Well, yes sir, but . . ."

"There is always the danger that someone with money will no longer feel a connection to the revolution, and leave us. And if we increase their wealth, they might feel even more constrained to do so. And it would be a very big mistake for anyone to leave right now, because that could compromise our operation, and that, I will not let happen. Once the revolution is completed, those who have been loyal to me from the beginning shall be rewarded beyond their wildest dreams."

"The revolution," Moss said. "Yeah, uh, I almost forgot about the revolution."

"Never forget the revolution!" Pecorino shouted, angrily. "That is the entire purpose of our existence!"

"Yes, sir, I guess that's right," Moss said.

Pecorino glared at Moss, and the other two men. "What's wrong?" he asked. "Do you three men have something against power and wealth?"

"No, sir, it ain't nothin' like that," Jenner replied. "It's just that . . ."

"It's just what?"

"Well sir, there ain't but ten of us, all told. 'N I can't help but think about the Confederates durin' the late war. They was thousands of them, more 'n likely they was

millions of 'em, 'n yet with all them soldiers, all put together, why, they still got whupped."

"So, you are concerned because there are so few of
us, is that it?"

"Well, yeah, somethin' like that," Jenner said.

"Have any of you men ever heard of a tragedian by the
name of Euripides?"

"You rip a what?"

"Euripides. He was a tragedian of classical Athens,
who lived some four hundred years, B.C. There are many
intelligent quotes ascribed to Euripides, one of which, I
have read, is being taught in West Point. It was his observation that, 'Ten soldiers, wisely led, can defeat a hundred,
without a head.' We more than satisfy that premise, for
we have ten soldiers, and I am providing leadership that
exceeds the definition of merely wise."

"Yes, sir, but, if we start fightin' a revolution, why
they's a lot more than a hunnert of 'em."

Pecorino smiled, shook his head, and thumped the
newspaper he was reading.

"No, at the moment there are only nineteen of them.
And four of them are women."

Jenner, Logan, and Moss looked at each other, clearly
confused by Pecorino's comments.

"Gentlemen, I have just been reading about our next
mission," Pecorino said. Again, he thumped this finger
on the newspaper. "You may not be aware of it, but the
President of the United States is making a trip through
the West and, in so doing, he will be traveling, by train,
through Wyoming. We will be waiting for him."

"Yeah," Jenner said with a broad smile. "I see what

you're talkin' about now. Iffen we was to kill the President, why, more 'n likely the government would have to give up, 'n we'd win."

"Right," Pecorino replied. "Just as when Abraham Lincoln was assassinated, allowing the South to win the war."

"What? Uh, no, sir, that ain't right, on account of the South didn't win the war. The North won the war," Jenner replied.

"Ahh, so, killing the President had nothing to do with the outcome of the war, did it?"

"No, sir."

"Then what makes you think that, by killing Rutherford Hayes, that the government in Washington would be willing to surrender to us?"

"I don't know. It's just that . . . well you said we was goin' to be waitin' for the President's train, so I just reckoned you was plannin' on killin' 'im."

"It won't be necessary to kill him. All that will be required is for us to capture the President and hold him hostage. That will give us some leverage with the U.S. government. Once we have the President in our custody, we will declare our intention to kill him, unless our demands are met."

"What if they don't pay no attention to us? What if they don't believe we would actual kill him?"

"As I told you, there would be nineteen people on board the train. Two of them are generals, one of them is a colonel, four of them are women, and two of them are the sons of the President. If they don't believe us, we'll just start killing our hostages, one at a time, starting with the two generals and the colonel. Then, we'll start killing the women who are not a part of the President's family, then we will kill Mrs. Hayes, then we will kill the President's sons. But long before we get to that point, the entire nation will be clamoring for the Washington government to negotiate a peace with us."

"Yeah," Jenner said, a huge smile spreading across his face. "Yeah, they will do that, won't they?"

"Indeed, they will."

"Damn, you know what? I'll just bet that if you had been the President of the South instead of Jefferson Davis, why, the South woulda won that war."

"I think you might be quite correct in that assumption," Pecorino replied, as if such accolades were his due.

"All right, what do we do now?"

"I think we need a rehearsal," Pecorino said.

"A rehearsal? What does that mean?"

"It means we need to find a train, stop it, and take as our hostage an important passenger."

"Oh, I see. We're goin' to hold 'im for ransom, are we?" Moss asked.

Pecorino shook his head. "There wouldn't be enough money in it, and it would only detract from our ultimate mission. No, this operation will be purely for practice. After we accomplish the mission, we'll let him go."

"When will we do this?"

"We aren't in any hurry. We have plenty of time remaining before the Presidential train rolls into Wyoming, and I'll need that time to plan, and to perfect, the mission. And to put in our own private telegraph line."

As Jenner, Logan, and Moss left the small log house that had been constructed as both headquarters and living quarters for Pecorino, they discussed among themselves some of the things Pecorino had told them.

"You think that's true, Jenner?" Moss asked. "You think if we was to grab a' holt of the President 'n tell the government that we'll kill 'im iffen they don't do what we tell 'em to do, that they would actual do it?"

"Yeah," Jenner said. "I believe it. You heard what Peco . . . uh, I mean the general said. Iffen the government don't do what we tell 'em to do, we'll commence a' killin' the others that we've got."

"Pecorino said that four of 'em was women," Logan said.

"We ain't s'posed to call him Pecorino," Jenner reminded him.

"Yeah, well, when I talk to him, I'll call him General, but I ain't talkin' to him right now, I'm talkin' about him."

"Yeah, 'n you think there won't nobody hear us talkin', and go tell 'im what it was you called 'im? I mean, if he gets rid of you, who do you think he'll put in your place? The feller that told 'im, that's who."

"Yeah, well, I hadn't quite thought about that," Logan said.

"Look at it this a' way," Jenner said. "This here is 'bout the smartest feller I've done ever seen, 'n I think somebody as smart as he is really can do all the things that he says. 'N iffen he does do all that, why then he's already told us that we would be . . . what's that he said we would be?"

"Peers of the Realm," Moss said.

"Yeah, I don't know what that is, but it sounds good."

"He said that oncet before," Moss said, "so I asked him what it means. It means that we'll all be lords and such . . . like that Barrington fella, you know, the English-man that owns that big ranch near Cheyenne. Folks will have to call us Lord Jenner 'n Lord Moss 'n Lord Logan," Moss said. "And lords 'n such have big castles 'n lots of women 'n lots of servants."

"You know what I think?" Logan asked.

"What's that?"

"I think we ought to stay with this here general we've hooked up to."

CHAPTER TWENTY

Cheyenne

When Pecorino stepped into the Catttlemen's Club he saw Richard Barrington setting alone, at a table, staring into his drink. This was just the man he was looking for, and he walked over to address him.

"Lord Barrington?"

Richard looked up. "We aren't allowed to use our titles here."

"Yes, that's a shame. But it is also a condition that can be remedied."

"What are you talking about?"

"I am Dr. Pecorino. May I join you?"

Richard nodded, and Pecorino took his seat across the table from him.

"So, you are a physician, are you?" Richard asked.

"No, not a physician. I am a doctor of letters. A college professor."

"A college professor. Well then, my good man, I welcome your company. When one must interact with the barely literate on a daily basis, it is refreshing to speak with someone who, at least, has command of the English language. What do you teach?"

"You might say that I am a professor emeritus. I have disassociated myself from academia, because I am engaged in a new pursuit . . . in fact, that is why I wish an audience with you."

"I see. What can I do for you, Professor?"

"Before I commit myself any further, I need to know the depth of your commitment to your country?"

"That's a rather odd question to ask of an English expatriate. I still have roots there, I suppose."

"I was asking about the United States," Pecorino said.

"I am not an American citizen, thus I have no commitment to the United States," Richard replied. "I can't use my title, the laws of this country limit what I can do with the cretins who are in my employ. My brother and I came to this country as an economic endeavor, sponsored by investors in England, and we are in the process of losing not only all of our money, but our social standing as well."

"Suppose I were to tell you that there was a way that you could assume your rightful position as a titled nobleman, right here, and that your social standing would be elevated to a position where you could command a vast amount of prestige, authority, and wealth."

Richard finished the rest of his drink before he responded.

"You have my attention," he said.

Pecorino smiled, then showed him the founding proclamation.

Richard read it, then looked up at Pecorino. "You are the Clemente Rex who has been corresponding with area newspapers?"

"I am."

"I see. And what do you want with me?"

"You are a titled nobleman. You have lived in the world of peerage, you were, as they say, 'to the manor born.' I need someone like you and your brother to help me establish this new kingdom. I would expect one of you to be the Lord Chancellor, and the other to be the Prime Minister."

"My brother would never go along with this," Richard said, sliding the document back across the table.

"That's too bad," Pecorino replied.

Unexpectedly, a broad smile spread across Richard's face. "But Albert need never know," he said.

"Hmm, it is interesting that you would have that reaction. Fortuitous, as well, for I have a proposal that would require your participation."

"What is the proposal?"

Two days later,
Four miles west of Granite Canyon

"Put the torpedoes on the track here," Pecorino directed. "When the engine runs over them the detonation will alert the engineer. Parker will be just ahead of the curve, waving a red flag. That will signal the engineer to stop and when he does, we will approach the train. Sergeant Easton, you will be in charge of the engineer and fireman. Lieutenant Moss, you will take charge of the conductor. Lieutenant Jenner, you will place a man in every car to make certain no one attempts to interfere with us. You and your men will take charge of the conductor and porters. Lieutenant Logan, you and three men will board the train with me, and it will be our task to locate, and remove, Mr. Albert Barrington."

Although it was only a six-hour trip from Cheyenne to Rawlings, Albert Barrington had taken passage in the Wagner Parlor car. It was an added expense, and given the failing economic conditions of the Three Mountain Ranch, some might say that it was an unnecessary expense. But the day cars were filled with passengers who couldn't afford anything better, some of whom had come for a thousand miles or more without bathing or changing clothes. Albert was of just too sensitive a nature to be able to ride in a car with such people, even for a distance as short as this trip.

Albert was going to Rawlings to meet with Joseph Carey. It had been Richard who set up the meeting, much to Albert's surprise. Richard had become more and more negative about their ranching operation of late, and Albert was pleased to see that he was finally showing an interest. Moreton Frewen, The Swan Brothers, R. D. Cummings, and Duff MacCallister were the most successful ranchers in all of Wyoming. It had been Albert Barrington's belief, when he started his operation, that the Three Mountain Ranch would be as productive as any of the others. In fact, he had used the success of those ranchers to convince his backers in England that the money would be well invested. As he sat here, watching the countryside roll swiftly by outside, he recalled the conversation he and his brother had, which led to this trip.

* * *

"I'm glad you're beginning to come around," Albert had said when Richard proposed the meeting.

"Yes, well, I got the idea while I was in town a few days ago, so I sent a telegram to Carey, and he agreed to meet with you."

"Why don't you come with me?" Albert suggested.

"One of us should stay here to look after the ranch."

"Pearlie has been here long enough that I'm sure he can handle anything that might come up."

"I am second in charge, not Pearlie," Richard said.

"Of course, you are," Albert said by way of assuaging his brother's feelings. "And, perhaps you are correct. Perhaps it would be better if you remained here." Albert smiled. "I will send you a telegram as soon as my meeting with Mr. Carey is completed."

Albert was hoping that Carey would be able to offer him a way out of his current situation, if not by the actual offer of cash for debentures, then at least some information that he could use.

Albert's thoughts returned to the present, and looking toward the front of the car he saw a very attractive young woman, traveling alone. He wondered if he might be so bold as to approach the woman, perhaps before lunch, and ask if she would dine with him. He was just beginning to work up the courage to do so, when, shortly after leaving Granite Canyon, the train came to a rapid and unscheduled stop. As it so happened, the conductor was passing his seat at that moment.

"Conductor, what is this?" Albert asked. "Why are we stopping like this?"

"Yes, why *are* we stopping?" another passenger asked.

"I don't know," the harried conductor answered. "But I shall find out as quickly as I can."

The conductor stepped down from the train, and a moment later five men came aboard. All five were wearing military-style uniforms.

"Everyone just stay in your seats, and no one will be hurt," one of the men said.

"Here, what is this? Is this a robbery?" someone asked.

"No, you may disabuse yourselves of any idea that we are here to rob the train or any of its passengers. This is a military operation being conducted by the army of Nova Amerigo Regnum. As soon as our mission is completed, we shall allow the train to continue its journey, with no harm coming to any of you."

The speaker, who was obviously the leader of the group, stepped over to Albert's seat.

"Lord Barrington, if you would please, I would like for you to come with us," he said.

"What? Why on earth would I do such a thing? I shall remain right here, thank you very much."

"I'm afraid you don't understand, sir. I issue that in the form of an invitation, but I assure you, that it is an invitation you will not be allowed to refuse. You will either come with us as our guest, or we will start killing passengers until you acquiesce." The leader smiled. "The choice is yours, and I would suggest that you choose wisely."

"I'll . . . come with you," Barrington replied.

"Thank you. You will be much more comfortable, being treated as our guest, than you would as our prisoner."

The leader turned to one of his men. "Sergeant Bilbo, would you ask Lieutenant Moss to bring the conductor back aboard?"

"Yes, sir."

A moment later a frightened conductor, with Moss holding a pistol to his head, stepped back onto the car.

"Conductor, if you would, please, give this letter to Lord Richard Barrington. It is most important that he receive it with all dispatch, for the life of his brother hangs in the balance," the leader said.

"That would be your brother, sir?" the conductor asked Albert.

"Yes."

"Where will I find him?"

"He is on our ranch, Three Mountain Ranch, which is slightly north of Cheyenne."

The conductor looked back toward the leader. "Sir, surely you understand that Cheyenne is east of us, whereas this train is headed west."

"I will leave it to your ingenuity to find a means of seeing that this letter reaches Sir Richard," Albert said.

"Sir Richard?" the conductor asked.

"The 'Sir' isn't necessary," Albert said. "Although my brother and I are both titled, such appellations are not authorized in the United States."

"That is so," the leader said. "But it is a condition I intend to correct. Therefore, as a courtesy, I will refer to both you and your brother by your rightful title. Come now, we must go. Conductor, I shall allow the engineer and fireman to return to their positions in the engine cab so that this train may resume its transit."

"Thank you," the conductor said. "And Mr. Barrington . . ."

"That would be Sir Albert," the leader corrected.

"Sir Albert, don't worry, sir." The conductor held up

the letter. "I'll get this letter to your brother as quickly as I can."

"Thank you," Albert said.

"Sir Albert, my name is General Pecorino. You are going to be my guest for a while."

"An unwilling guest, I might say," Albert replied.

Pecorino chuckled. "Indeed, that will be the case. But I shall endeavor to make your stay with us as pleasant as possible, under the circumstances. I am afraid, however, that there will be some minor discomfort for you at the beginning. We shall have to blindfold you, and tie your wrists to the saddle horn of your mount, so that you won't be able to escape."

Albert was led over to a saddled horse and told to get mounted. The first thing he noticed was that there were no reins for him. Instead, there was a line between his horse, and the one being ridden by the man Pecorino had addressed as Lieutenant Jenner.

"We shall wait until after the train has departed," Pecorino said. "That way, there will be no one who can report to the authorities, which way we go."

"Where are we going?" Albert asked.

"We are going to Fort Regency."

"Fort Regency? I've never heard of the place."

Pecorino smiled. "That's good," he said. "It is my intention to keep the location a secret."

Once the train departed, Albert's hands were tied to the saddle horn and a hood pulled down over his head. After that, they started moving, though he had no idea which direction they were going.

CHAPTER TWENTY-ONE

Fort Regency

"You can take his hood off, now," Albert heard Pecorino say, and a moment later Albert felt a pair of hands remove the hood that had kept him blind for at least four hours. Once the hood was lifted, he blinked his eyes a few times in reaction to the very bright sun. He would like to rub them, but he couldn't, because his hands were tied, very tightly, to the saddle horn.

When his eyes cleared, he looked around and saw what appeared to be an army fort. It wasn't Fort Laramie, because he had been there before, and would be able to recognize it. Pecorino had identified this place as Fort Regency, but he had never heard of it before, and even though he was here, now, he had no idea where "here" was, and of course, he knew that was by design.

As they rode through the front gate of the palisades that surrounded the fort, a man came to attention and brought his rifle up in salute, then dipped his head as in a bow.

Although Pecorino stared straight ahead without

responding to the gate guard, three of the members of Albert's escort returned the salute.

"Detail, halt!" Pecorino called. "Dismount. Dismissed."

"Very impressive," Albert said.

"Yes, I have instructed my army on the tactics of drill and ceremonies as written by General Hardee," Pecorino said.

"General Hardee? I am familiar with his manual of arms. It is a document I studied when I was a Leftenant Colonel in the Third Dragoon Guards of the Royal Army. But didn't Hardee leave the U.S. Army to join the Southern revolt?"

Pecorino smiled. "Indeed, he did, which makes our use of his manual even more significant."

"What do you mean by that?"

"Have you not figured out yet who I am?" Pecorino asked. "Have you read none of my missives to the newspapers?"

"I'm beginning to have my suspicions," Albert replied. "Would you be the gentleman who is calling himself Clemente Rex?"

"I would be."

"Are you actually declaring yourself a king?"

"Since you recognized my name, perhaps you are also aware that I am launching a revolution. I am taking the territory and states of Wyoming, Colorado, Utah, Nevada, and California, and creating a new nation, a new kingdom. That being the case, why would I not declare myself king? I believe the people of my new nation would be much better served by a beneficent king than by a distant and detached President."

"Do you seriously believe that you can raise an army

that can defeat the United States Army? Surely you know that was just tried. They called themselves the Confederate States of America, I believe, and they not only failed, their effort cost almost a million lives."

"That's because they fought a revolution."

"Did you not just tell me that you would be fighting a revolution?"

"No, I said I was *launching* a revolution. The Confederacy fought and lost. I shall *finesse* the revolution, and I will win."

Albert was quiet for a moment before he responded. "How am I to address you? I can't bring myself to call you King Clemente."

"You may address me as General." Pecorino smiled. "I have also appointed myself general, and as you can see, I have an army."

"The army that you won't be using to fight the revolution."

"Yes, the army that will finesse the revolution."

"What do you want with me, General? Why did you take me from the train?"

"Did you not see me pass the letter to the conductor, with direction that he give it to your brother?"

"A ransom note? You are actually asking my brother to pay a ransom for me?"

"He is your own brother. Do you think he won't pay a ransom to get you back, safely?"

"You don't understand. Three Mountain Ranch is nearly bankrupt. I was going to Rawlings to meet with Mr. Joseph Carey to arrange a loan. I don't know how much money you asked for, but the chances are that we not only don't have the money, we also are quite limited in our ability to raise any more."

"Yes, I'm quite aware of that, but the ransom isn't the real reason I took you from the train. At the moment, money is of no concern. In fact, we have recently conducted two very successful operations, each of which brought significant funds into our treasury."

"Then I don't understand. If you didn't do this for money, why did you do it?"

"One of the reasons I did it is because I would like to recruit you to our cause."

"Why in heaven's name would I want to do a thing like that?"

"For title, prestige, and money. As you said, Three Mountain Ranch is in debt. As an independent nation, I will declare any money owed by my subjects to anyone outside the boundaries of our new nation to be nullified. That will relieve you of the burden of debt. In addition, as a Lord of the Realm, I shall deed land to you from among public land."

Albert shook his head. "No," he said. "I appreciate the offer, but I've no wish to be a part of a revolution, whether it is fought or finessed."

"I'm sorry you feel that way."

"Now, since I've no wish to join you, and I'm quite sure my brother will be unable to come up with the ransom, what will happen to me?"

"Nothing will happen to you. In fact, the very exercise by which we took you from the train was a rehearsal for our finesse operation. Whether you wish to join our revolution or not, you have provided us with valuable help.

Within the week, we will take you into the town of Tie Siding, where you can catch a train back home."

"You aren't concerned that I will tell others what you plan to do?"

Pecorino laughed. "My dear sir, I have been going out of my way to tell others what I plan to do. That is the purpose of my many letters to the editors. Tell anyone you want . . . tell to as many as you wish. The more people who know of our activities, the greater the reality of our revolution."

"General?" someone said, approaching Albert and Pecorino.

"Yes."

"Largent is here with the wire," the man said with a broad smile.

"Is there enough wire to accomplish the task?"

"I'd say there is, sir. There's six thousand pounds of it in the wagon, 'n that's near two miles."

"Excellent, excellent."

Three Mountain Ranch

"Say, do you have any idea when Albert will be back?" Pearlie asked Richard.

"You mean, Mr. Barrington, don't you?"

"I'm sorry. Mr. Barrington, do you have any idea when Albert will be back?"

"No, you idiot! I mean when you speak of my brother Albert, you will speak of him as Mr. Barrington."

"Yeah, well, he told me to call him Albert."

"You'll not do so around me," Richard replied.

"All right, *Mister* Barrington, when will *Mister* Barrington be back?"

"I do not see how my brother's travel schedule has anything to do with you. If you have a question pertaining to your duties, or anything about the operation of this ranch, you will come to me."

"No, I don't have any questions," Pearlie said. "I was just curious, is all. I thought maybe that letter you got might have something to do with him."

"What made you think that?"

"I don't know, it's just that it wasn't a regular letter is all. It wasn't delivered by a postman."

"My mail, regardless of how I receive it, is none of your business."

It had been Pearlie's intention to ask about the cattle that were being moved. Every day, for the three days Albert had been gone, as many as fifty cows were being cut away from the others and driven away. Because of what Pearlie had overheard in the saloon in town, he suspected something was going on right under Richard's nose. Smoke had left him here to help Albert, so with or without Richard's approval, or even knowledge, Pearlie decided to investigate.

When fifty more cows were cut away that afternoon, Pearlie followed the two cowboys, Keefer and Higgins, keeping far enough behind and using the lay of the land so as not to be seen.

The cows were driven to the extreme west end of the ranch and there they were met by three other men. One of the new men gave Keefer some money then took the cows.

Pearlie followed Keefer and Higgins back, with the intention of telling Richard about what he had seen. The money in Keefer's pocket would prove his charge. But, to Pearlie's surprise, Keefer gave the money to Richard. Pearlie had been wrong in his suspicions.

Two days later, Albert returned to the ranch.

"Albert," Richard said. "What are you doing here?"

"What do you mean, what am I doing here? I live here."

"Yes, but, well, I didn't expect you back yet. I . . . uh, received a letter saying you had been taken from the train, and I was to pay a ransom for your return."

"Did you pay the ransom?"

"No, I was in the process of trying to raise the money. Five thousand dollars is a lot of money."

"Oh," Pearlie said. "That's what it was all about."

Both Albert and Richard looked at Pearlie with a confused expression on their faces.

"That's what *what* is all about?" Richard asked, mouthing the question for both of them.

"The cattle that Keefer and Higgins have been cutting out and selling."

"Keefer and Higgins have been selling cattle?" Albert asked.

"Yes, two hundred and fifty head, so far," Pearlie said. "I followed them once and saw them sell fifty head to some men who met them at Lodgepole Creek. At first, I thought they had been stealing the cattle, until I saw them giving the money to Richard, uh, that is, Mr. Barrington."

"You are lying!" Richard said. "They gave me no money. I have no idea what you are talking about."

Pearlie raised his finger. "Look here, Mr. Barrington, out here, a man's word is his bond. I don't lie, and I'll not stand by and let anyone accuse me of lying. Perhaps you being new to the West and all, you don't fully understand what you just did, but falsely accusing someone of lying can get a man killed."

"Are you threatening me?" Richard asked, a vein in his temple throbbing.

"No. You being the brother of a man I respect, this is more of a friendly piece of advice. And my advice is this. Don't be calling me a liar again."

"We could settle this quite easily, Richard. We could talk to Keefer and Higgins," Albert said.

"We'll do no such thing," Richard said, angrily. "All right, I did authorize them to sell a few head, but only so I could raise enough money to meet the ransom payment." He pointed to Pearlie. "But that was none of this man's business, which is why I denied it. I demand that you fire him."

"Well, as he is not, technically, in my employ, I can't actually fire him. And his assistance has been quite valuable. For example, he found two more wells for us."

"By *witching*?" Richard asked. "Really, Albert, you don't put any store in such hokey as witching, do you?"

"It worked," Albert said.

"Blind luck."

"Never the less, I have no intention of asking him to leave."

"Then I shall leave," Richard said.

"I wish you wouldn't do that."

"There is no way you can stop me from leaving."

"No, I don't suppose there is. But I wish you wouldn't leave," Albert repeated.

Richard glared at his brother for a long moment, then turned sharply and walked, quickly, away. Fifteen minutes later, Richard rode off the ranch without looking back and without further challenge.

"I hate to say it," Albert said. "But I am convinced Richard has been stealing from the ranch for some time, now. I wonder if I could prevail upon you to act as my foreman."

"I'd be glad to, at least for as long as I stay here," Pearlie said. "By the way, as your foreman, do I have the authority to fire anyone?"

Albert smiled, and nodded. "You do."

"Who the hell are you to say me 'n Higgins is fired?" Keefer demanded. "There can't nobody fire us but one of the Barringtons."

"One of the Barringtons is gone," Pearlie said. "And the other Barrington just made me foreman. I know you two have been stealing cattle, and the only reason I don't turn you over to the sheriff, is because I also know you were stealing for Richard. Well, he is gone now . . . and so are you."

"You think you can force us to leave?" Keefer asked, reaching for his pistol.

"Yeah, I think I can," Pearlie said, drawing his pistol so quickly that Keefer, who hadn't even cleared leather yet, jerked his hand away from his gun.

"No, no, don't shoot!" Keefer shouted. "We're goin'! We're goin'!"

It was at dinner that evening, that Albert Barrington figured out what Pecorino had in mind.

"My God!" he said, sharing his thought with Pearlie. "What on earth should we do?"

"I'll get in touch with Smoke," Pearlie said. "He'll know what to do."

Pecorino was having his breakfast the next day when Dobbins knocked on the door of his cabin.

"Yes, Dobbins, come in," Pecorino said, wiping his mouth with his napkin. "What is it?"

Dobbins smiled as he held out a piece of paper. "I just got this telegram, and I thought it was something you might be interested in."

Pecorino read the telegram, then smiled. "Yes," he said. "Very good. I am, indeed, interested."

CHAPTER TWENTY-TWO

Sugarloaf Ranch

Smoke and Cal were replacing the wheel of a hay wagon when a young man, wearing a Western Union cap, rode up.

"Mr. Jensen?" the rider said.

"I'm Jensen," Smoke replied. He scratched his cheek, leaving a small smear of grease.

Cal laughed, then handed him a cloth and pointed to the smear.

"What can I do for you?" Smoke asked as he wiped his cheek.

"I have a telegram for you, sir. It's from a man named Barrington."

"Oh, Lord, Smoke, you don't think something's happened to Pearlie, do you?" Cal asked.

"I don't know," Smoke replied with concern in his voice. He took the telegram.

CAN YOU COME TO THREE MOUNTAIN
RANCH SOONEST STOP I AM VERY
CONCERNED ABOUT SOMETHING OF

THE MOST DIRE CONSEQUENCES AND
PEARLIE ASKS THAT YOU COME STOP A
BARRINGTON

"I don't think Pearlie is in any particular trouble, but he is involved in some way, so I'm going back up to Wyoming."

"Do you want me to come with you?" Cal asked.

"No, I don't know what this is about, but I would rather you stay here and look after things."

Fort Regency

"His name is Jensen, Smoke Jensen," Pecorino said, waving the copy of the telegram Dobbins had brought him. "He is coming to Cheyenne, and our friend has suggested that if he gets involved, he could be quite troublesome. It may be that he is Odysseus who would blind the Cyclopes and defeat our movement. And I will not let this be."

"Who is it that's a comin'? I thought you said his name was Jensen? I mean, what kind of name is Cyclone?"

Pecorino was talking to his three lieutenants.

"I was speaking metaphorically," Pecorino said. "Jensen is the name of the man who is coming, and from what I have heard, he is reputed to be a shootist of considerable skill."

"A shootist? You mean a gunfighter?" Logan asked.

"Yes."

"You want the three of us to go up against a gunfighter?" Logan asked. "Look here, General, we ain't nary a one of us gunfighters."

"No, not three of you, just one of you, and a man of

your choosing. I am not asking you to face him down in some sort of demonstration of skill and courage. I'm asking you to kill him in the most expedient way you find to do so. It is worth one thousand dollars to me, and I will promote whichever one of you volunteers to captain. That will make you second in command. And whoever you get from the ranks will be promoted to sergeant."

"I'll do it," Jenner said, speaking up before either of the other two. "It'll be nice having you two yahoos sayin' sir to me," he added with a grin.

"It'll be a cold day in hell before I say sir to you," Logan said.

"You will say sir when you speak to *Captain* Jenner," Pecorino said, emphasizing the word "captain."

"I know there are some among you who neither appreciate nor understand my insistence on discipline and decorum. But discipline means structure, and structure means cohesion. A cohesive force is much stronger than the sum of its numbers. If we are to succeed, we must do it together."

When Pecorino had begun his lecture, he was speaking only to Logan. But as he developed his thought, he was soon addressing all three of them.

"Am I understood on this?" he asked.

"Yes, sir!" the three responded as one.

The serious expression on Pecorino's face was replaced with a smile. "Remember," he said. "The rewards for what we are doing in this revolution are beyond calculations. Wealth, land, and power for each of you."

"I'm goin' to have me a thousand-acre ranch!" Logan said.

"Not me. I'm goin' to have me a whore house," Moss

said. "No, I'm goin' to have me four whore houses in four different towns, 'n that way, no matter which one o' them towns I'll be in, I'll have me a woman."

"Ha," Jenner said. "That's the onliest way you'll ever have a woman, is iffen you own the whore house."

Jenner and Logan laughed.

"I've only got one question, General," Captain Jenner said.

"What's that?"

"We'll sort of stand out in the army suits though, won't we?"

"You do have a point. For this operation, you are authorized to wear mufti."

"Wear what?"

"You can wear your ordinary clothes," Pecorino said. "There will be no need for uniforms."

"All right, I'll go pick out my man now."

"I'll go with you," Moss offered.

"No, I'll not risk more than one of my officers on this mission," Pecorino said. "It wouldn't do to have two of you killed."

"Kilt?" Jenner asked, in alarm.

"With any gamble, just as there is reward, in this case you are being promoted to captain, there is also risk," Pecorino said. "And your risk is that you could get killed. As I said, Smoke Jensen is quite proficient with both revolver and rifle. It is up to you to use every skill and device to minimize any such risk."

"Ha! You still want to do this, Captain Jenner?" Logan asked.

"You're damn right I do, Lieutenant."

A short while later when Jenner saw Parker playing

mumblety-peg with a few of the other men he called him away.

"Yes, sir?" Parker said after they walked some distance from the others.

"How would you like to be promoted to sergeant?" Jenner asked.

"Ha! Who do I have to kill?"

"Funny you would ask that."

Cheyenne, Wyoming Territory

As the train rolled into the Cheyenne Depot, Smoke was just leaving the train when he heard himself addressed by a nondescript man who had all the earmarks of an out-of-work cowboy.

"Yes?"

"I was told to give you this here letter when you got down from the train."

"How did you know who I was?"

"I asked the station master if he know'd who you was, 'n he pointed toward you 'n said you was him. So if you is him, this here letter's for you."

"Thank you, yes, I am Smoke Jensen," Smoke said, giving the man a quarter for the letter.

"Yes, sir, thank you, sir!" the messenger replied, smiling with the knowledge that he was holding five beers in his hand.

Not until Smoke was some distance from those who had come to meet the train, did he open the letter. This wasn't Pearlie's writing.

> I've got your frend Perly. Iffen you want to
> see him alive agin come to the

123 stabel west of town. dont brang nobdy els
with you. When you git there take off
yur hat and wave it sos well no its you.

"Tell me," Smoke said, speaking to the station master a moment later. "Do you know where the 123 Stable is?"

"Oh, Mr. Jensen, you won't be able to rent a horse there, the 123 is closed. It's been abandoned for more 'n two years now. Truth to tell, you wouldn't of wanted to rent your horse there even when it was open. It always was of the lowest grade."

Smoke smiled. "Oh, I had no idea of renting a horse there. It's just that I heard about the place and was curious about it, is all."

"Well, if you actually wanted to just take a look at it, it's about a quarter of a mile beyond the west end of town, right after you go around the first bend. You'll see it on the left side of the road, the building is still standin' there, all kind of gray 'n washed-out lookin'. Near 'bout half the roof is gone. You can't hardly miss it."

"Thanks," Smoke replied.

Smoke loosened the pistol in his holster, then walked through town, returning the greetings of those who either nodded, or waved at him. A quarter of a mile out of town the road curved to the left, and just as he reached the curve, he saw what had to be the 123 Stable.

The station master had done a good job of describing it. The corral fencing was gone entirely, probably taken by someone who intended to use it somewhere else. What remained of the building was sun-bleached, the boards gray and splitting. If there had been any doubt as to whether this was the right place, that doubt was assuaged by the barely legible sign that was painted on front of the building.

123 Stable
Horses Boarded and Rented
Thomas Hunsinger Owner

"Hey, Cap'n Jenner, here comes someone."

"Thank you, Sergeant Parker."

"You reckon it's him?" Parker asked.

"I don't know. I ain't never seen 'im before."

The approaching man stopped, and, as directed by the letter, removed his hat and waved it.

"That's him, all right," Jenner said.

"You climb back down 'n get just inside the door," Jenner ordered. "Call out to 'im, 'n get 'im to come on up to the barn. He'll be payin' attention to you 'n won't even see me up here. When he gets in easy range, I'll shoot 'im, 'n he'll never have no idea where it even come from."

"How am I s'posed to get him to come up here?" Parker asked.

"We told 'im we had Pearlie. Tell 'im we've got 'im here, 'n we'll cut 'im loose for . . . oh, say a hunnert dollars."

"All right," Parker agreed.

Smoke had waved his hat as the letter had instructed, but so far he had neither seen nor heard anything that indicated that Pearlie or anyone else was in the stable.

"Pearlie?" Smoke shouted. "Pearlie, are you in there?"

There was no reply to his hail.

"Pearlie?"

"He's here," a voice called back. The voice came from just inside the main door, which was only an opening, the doors themselves long gone by now.

"Let me see him."

"Come closer," the voice said.

"Bring him to the door, I can see him from here."

"You got a hunnert dollars?" the voice called.

"Yes, I have a hundred dollars."

"We'll cut 'im loose for a hunnert dollars, but you'll have to come close enough so's that I can see that you actual have the money."

Smoke took out a dollar bill and held it up, knowing full well that the man in the barn wouldn't be able to determine, from his position, the denomination of the bill.

Smoke didn't like the feel of this, but he approached the building as directed. Smoke had survived many gunfights, not only because of his courage, swiftness, and shooting skill, but also because of the intense intuitiveness he had developed during his many years of living on the edge.

He knew, even as he was approaching the barn, that he wasn't being brought there to pay the kidnappers one hundred dollars for Pearlie. They were using Pearlie for bait.

Very few men would have heard the slight shift of feet in the loft of the barn, and perhaps Smoke didn't hear it as much as he sensed it. But in a lightning draw his pistol was out and he shot the man who was aiming at him from the loft opening.

Even if his perception of danger had not been followed

by a draw that was as quick as thought, the shot, hitting his adversary just above the right eye, which was the only target presented, would have been the stuff of legend. The loft shooter pitched forward, rotating in mid-air to land on his back on the ground just in front of the barn.

"Jenner!" a startled cry came from the man who had already exchanged words with Smoke.

"Come out," Smoke said. "Come out and tell me where my friend is."

With only an anguished scream in reply, the man at the front door stepped out to expose himself, while at the same time he was firing his pistol. One shot came so close that Smoke heard it pop as it passed his ear, and he knew he had no choice but to return fire. It took but one shot and that danger, too, was eliminated.

"Pearlie!" Smoke called, hurrying on up to the livery. Though technically he was taking a chance that there would be nobody else there, the same intuition that had warned him of the shooter in the loft, now assured him that there was nobody else in the barn, and it was safe to approach.

"Pearlie?" he called again, rushing into the barn. There was no Pearlie on the ground floor, and when he climbed into the loft, it was empty, as well.

CHAPTER TWENTY-THREE

Renting a horse from the Cheyenne Livery Stable, Smoke rode quickly out to the Three Mountain Ranch, thinking that would be the best place for him to start his search for Pearlie. But even as he rode up to the big house and all the ancillary structures, he was most pleasantly surprised to see Pearlie standing by the corral gate.

"Smoke!" Pearlie greeted. "I'm glad you came."

"How did you get away?" Smoke asked.

"How did I get away from what?" Pearlie replied.

"I was led to believe you had been captured." Smoke showed Pearlie the letter he had received.

"Huh," Pearlie said. "No, as you can see, I haven't been captured, so I don't know what this is all about."

"I think someone was using you as bait to get me. I walked right into an ambush." Smoke told Pearlie about the shootout, including the fact that he had left two dead men behind him.

He told the same story to Albert a few minutes later.

"If I had to guess, I would say they were a part of Pecorino's army," Albert said.

"Pecorino?"

"Yeah, this fella that's callin' himself a king." Pearlie replied. "His name is Pecorino."

"How do you know?"

"Because he told me his name," Albert said. "Although, the 'king' idea is just a part of his grandiose plans. For now, he is referring to himself as General Pecorino."

"Were these men who attacked you wearing uniforms?" Pearlie asked.

"No."

"Well, it doesn't matter whether they were wearing uniforms or not. I'm absolutely positive that they were Pecorino's men, no doubt sent by him to get rid of you."

"Where are they now?" Albert asked. "The men who ambushed you?"

"I don't know where they are at the moment, but I told the sheriff about them."

"Why don't we ride into town?" Albert suggested. "If they haven't been buried yet, I might be able to identify them."

"You can identify them? How?" Smoke asked.

"I was, recently, a . . . guest . . . of Pecorino at his fort. I saw several of his men. I might have seen these men."

"Yes, that's a good idea. We'll ride back into town," Smoke said. "But here's what I don't understand. They couldn't have set up an ambush for me, if they hadn't known I was coming. How did they know that?"

"I think I can answer that. While I was at the place they are calling Fort Regency, I saw a large amount of telegraph wire, two miles of it, I believe someone said. I don't know where this Fort Regency is, but it is my guess that it is within two miles of a telegraph transmission line, and if that is the case, they may have been able to access the telegram that I sent you, asking that you come."

Smoke nodded. "Yes, that seems a likely scenario," he said.

When Jenner and Parker didn't return from their mission, Pecorino sent Moss to find out why they were delayed. Moss knew where to go to check on them, because the 123 Stable had been his suggestion.

Like Jenner and Parker before him, Moss, too, was in civilian clothes. He decided it wouldn't be a smart move to just barge at the stable until he had done just a little preliminary investigation. It wouldn't be good to blunder in on them in the midst of the actual shooting. For that matter, it wouldn't be good to get there before the shooting either, as his unexpected presence could throw everything off.

He figured that the first place to check should be the saloon. Yes, the thought of a beer sounded good to him, but saloons, he knew, were also good places to come by news.

"They're a' standin' up in a couple o' pine boxes now, down in front of Welsh's Funeral Home," Moss overheard one of the customers saying.

"Who are they, does anybody know?"

"There don't seem to be nobody that knows. The only

thing that's know'd about 'em is that this feller by the name of Smoke Jensen brung 'em both in, belly down over their horses."

"Is he the one that kilt 'em?"

"Yes, same one that shot them train robbers, 'n the same one that shot Ethan Dewey."

"Damn! Sounds to me like this Jensen feller ain't someone you want to get on the bad side of."

"Well, it must 'a been what they call justified killin', or else he woulda never come back in to tell the sheriff. He woulda just left 'em there."

Even before he heard Jensen's name being mentioned, Moss was already certain that the two dead men were Jenner and Parker. Five minutes later, as he stood in front of the two coffins, his certainty was confirmed as he looked at the blue-hued faces of the two men.

"Well now, bein' made a cap'n didn't' work out all that good for you, did it?" Moss said, under his breath.

"You know these two fellers?" someone asked. The questioner had been standing close enough to overhear, if not understand, what Moss had mumbled.

"No, I was just sort of commentin' to myself is all," Moss replied.

As Moss rode back to Fort Regency, he wondered if Pecorino was goin' to appoint another captain. If so, why not him? After all, he was the one that took the chance on ridin' into town to find out what happened to Jenner and Parker.

Smoke, Pearlie, and Albert stopped at the sheriff's office as soon as they rode into town.

"You're just in time," the sheriff said. "I think Welsh is plannin' on buryin' the two of 'em this afternoon. He's took 'em down from where they was standin' to see if anyone could identify 'em, but they're probably still in his funeral parlor."

"Was anyone able to identify them?" Albert asked.

"No, sir, there wasn't nobody that had 'ny idea at all who they was." The sheriff chuckled. "I can see why you're wantin' to find out their names, Mr. Jensen. A couple of no accounts like them two has more 'n likely got some paper out on 'em, 'n you'd be lookin' for the reward."

"Yes," Smoke said, thinking it was easier to let the sheriff think that, than go into a long explanation.

Albert knew the undertaker so it was easy to get permission to view the bodies. Both were lying out on tables in the back of the parlor.

"They have no families, at least, nobody who has spoken for them," Welsh said. "So I probably won't embalm them, as I only do that by request anyway."

Albert examined both of them very closely, but gave no reaction.

"Thank you, Mr. Welsh," he said after a few moments. He looked up at Smoke and Pearlie. "I'm ready to go."

"I recognized both of them," Albert said as the three men took their lunch in the Cattlemen's Club. "I only know the name of one of them . . . Jenner. I don't know the name of the other one, but I did see him at the fort."

"Then there is no doubt, Pecorino did single me out," Smoke said. "The question is, why? I've never even met the man. Does he feel that I'm standing in the way of his revolution?"

"I'm sure that when he read the telegram I sent you, that he realized I have figured out his plan," Albert said. "And he also knows that I intend to share his plans with you."

"What plans are those?"

"I know how Pecorino plans to pull off this revolution. And, begrudgingly, I have to say that it could be fiendishly effective."

"I'm listening."

"Are you aware that the President of the United States will be coming through Wyoming soon?"

"Who isn't aware? It's been in newspapers all over the West." Smoke smiled. "I even know the men who will be driving the President's train, Clyde Barnes and Austin Prouty."

"Oh, that is very good," Albert said. "Perhaps you can warn them, and they can do something about it."

"About what? Albert, are you saying that Pecorino is planning to assassinate the President?"

"No, not assassinate. I believe he plans to take the President from the train, and hold him as some sort of bargaining chip to force the government in Washington to recognize his crazy scheme of creating a kingdom."

"What in the world would give you such an idea?"

"Because he snatched me from a train, and when my brother was unable to come up with the ransom, he let me go anyway. He said that taking me was the rehearsal for a finesse operation. And he stressed the word finesse.

Smoke, I am certain that he plans to take the President hostage."

"Smoke, maybe we should send Clyde and Austin a telegram, warning them," Pearlie suggested.

"I would agree, except for one thing. If we send a telegram, Pecorino will just read it," Albert said.

"You're right, it will do no good to . . . wait," Smoke said, smiling broadly. "What if we send a telegram we want him to read?"

"Is there a way of sending a telegram from here that won't go out over the main wire going west?" Smoke asked the telegrapher, an hour later.

"No, but that doesn't matter," the telegrapher replied. "You see, every telegram has a designated receiving station, and only those stations who hear their call will respond."

"What if someone, who wasn't a designated station, wanted to pick up the message? Could they do it?"

"No, that would be illegal."

"But it could be done?"

"Well, yes, I suppose so. But really, sir, that's nothing you need worry yourself about."

"Perhaps not. But, let's just say that I wanted to send a telegram that couldn't be taken from the main line. Is that possible?"

"It depends on which direction you wish to send the telegram."

"South."

"Ah, well, in that case if you crossed the line into Colorado to the first stop there, Carr, you could originate a telegram there and if it is going south, it won't show up on the main line."

"All right, I'll think about it," Smoke said.

One hour later he was on a train for the hour-long trip to Carr. As soon as he arrived in Carr, he bought a ticket for the first train back to Cheyenne, which would be leaving in two hours. He sent a telegram to Sally.

SALLY TODAY OR TOMORROW YOU WILL
GET ANOTHER TELEGRAM FROM ME STOP
I WANT YOU TO DISREGARD THAT ONE
AS I WILL BE SENDING DISINFORMATION
FOR A REASON STOP WILL BE HOME
WHEN ALL HERE IS COMPLETED AND
EXPLAIN ALL THEN STOP LOVE SMOKE

The next morning Smoke returned to the telegrapher in Cheyenne. "I've been thinking about it, and you are right, there's no need for me to be worrying about someone else reading my telegrams," he said.

"Indeed, there is not, sir. As I explained, even though it is possible to capture a telegram from a trunk line, it is both illegal and highly unprincipled to do so. And, as only a trained telegrapher would be able to do it in the first place, I know of no one in this profession who would violate their code of ethics to do such a thing."

"You have convinced me," Smoke said, as he wrote out the message he wished to send.

CHAPTER TWENTY-FOUR

The day after Sally got the first strange message from Smoke, she got a second, the one she was supposed to disregard.

SALLY, I BELIEVE I WAS LURED UP HERE
SO I COULD BE AMBUSHED STOP DO NOT
WORRY, I SURVIVED THE ATTEMPT ON MY
LIFE STOP I HAVE NO IDEA WHO THE
ATTACKERS WERE BUT THINK THEY MUST
HAVE BEEN SEEKING REVENGE FOR
SOMEONE I MAY HAVE ENCOUNTERED IN
MY PAST STOP NO DIRE CONSEQUENCES
STOP PEARLIE AND I TO RETURN SOON STOP
LOVE SMOKE

"I wonder what this is all about," Sally mused.

"I don't know, but Smoke told us to just disregard the next telegram and this is the next telegram," Cal said.

"Well, something is going on, that's for sure."

"You know what? It's almost like this here telegram is

one that Smoke is wanting someone else to read, like he's wanting to fool them or something," Cal said.

"Yes! Yes, Cal, that's it exactly. That is most astute of you to see that, and I'll even forgive you your grammatical error."

"I made a mistake in . . . oh . . . wait, I said 'this here' didn't I?"

"Yes, you did, but as I said, I'll let this pass."

"Thank you," Cal said.

"And, because you were smart enough to figure out what this is all about, I'll even make you some bear-claws."

A huge smile spread across Cal's face. "Yes, ma'am! Thank you, Miz Sally! Uh . . . are we going to have to save some for Smoke and Pearlie?"

"Oh, I think I can make some more when they come back."

Fort Regency

"General, I don't think we'll have to be worrying about Smoke Jensen anymore," Dobbins said, showing Pecorino the telegram he had taken from the trunk line.

"Good, this is good!" Pecorino said, reading the telegram. "I never was actually worried about Smoke Jensen, Dobbins. But he is someone we would have had to deal with, if he had stayed around, though only as a nuisance factor."

"Yes, sir, well he was a nuisance to Jenner and Parker, that's for sure," Dobbins said.

Pecorino took a short, choppy breath, wondering if Dobbins intended his comment to be insubordinate. He finally decided that Dobbins didn't actually have enough sense to understand the nuance of his remark. Besides, at the moment, Dobbins was indispensable. There were no messages being sent anywhere of which Pecorino wasn't aware. And, most important, he was able to keep track of where the Presidential train was, at any time.

Today, for example, he knew that the President would be arriving in North Platte, Nebraska, within a very short time.

Like Pecorino, Smoke and Pearlie had been following the telegraphed reports of the progress of the President's traveling party, so they took a train east so that they would be in North Platte when the train arrived. There was already a rather significant crowd of people in anticipation of seeing the President, and Smoke and Pearlie stood out on the platform awaiting the train.

An official greeting was planned, and in addition to the gathering of citizens from North Platte, and the surrounding area, there was a military detachment from nearby Fort McPherson, complete with a band, and seven cannons.

The sound of a distant whistle could be heard above the excited buzz of conversation.

"Here comes the train!" someone shouted, though as everyone had heard the whistle, his shout was totally unnecessary.

* * *

When the Presidential train pulled into the depot at North Platte, Nebraska, Austin was leaning out the window.

"Lord almighty, Clyde, would you look at that?" Austin exclaimed.

The depot was festooned with flags and bunting, and as many as a thousand or more people were gathered on the depot platform.

"Looks like they got 'em a welcome planned for the general," Austin said.

Clyde chuckled. "It's more 'n likely for the President, wouldn't you think?"

"Oh, yeah, I reckon it is, at that."

Clyde brought the train to a complete stop, and with one final hiss of steam, he and Austin stood out on the engine deck to watch the proceedings.

After the train stopped, and before any of the dignitaries had emerged, Smoke and Pearlie walked up to the front of the train, where they saw Clyde and Austin standing on the locomotive platform.

"Clyde, Austin!" Smoke called.

"Well, I swan, Clyde, lookie there!" Austin said, a happy smile on his face.

"Smoke Jensen!" Clyde said, responding to Austin's alert. "And Cal, or Pearlie?"

"Pearlie," Pearlie answered.

"What in the world are you two doing here? What brings you to North Platte, Nebraska?"

"We came to see you," Smoke said.

"For certain? Why on earth would you come this far just to see us? Not that me 'n Austin ain't pleased or nothin'," Clyde said.

"The President is in danger," Smoke said.

"What? What kind of danger?"

"I'll tell you all about it. And I'm going to need your help, if you don't mind."

"No, of course we don't mind. We don't mind none at all," Clyde said. What is it? What kind of danger is the President in?"

"Is there someplace where we can go to talk? It's pretty involved."

"Yeah," Clyde said. "Well, we'll have to wait 'til Austin gets the steam down far enough for us to leave the engine."

Their conversation was interrupted by an army band playing *Ruffles and Flourishes,* followed by *Hail to the Chief.*"

After the band played, Smoke heard the command of one of the army officers.

"Ready? Fire!"

The officer's order was followed by a loud boom as the seven cannon fired a powder charge.

"Ready?"

New powder charges were loaded into the breech.

"Fire!"

The procedure was repeated one more time, thus completing a twenty-one-gun salute.

"Huzzah the President!" someone shouted, as President Hayes stood on the bottom step of his personal car and waved at the cheering crowd.

The mayor of North Platte, Joe Felker, stepped up onto the platform.

"Mr. President, on behalf of the citizens of North Platte, let me welcome you to our beautiful community, and may I personally extend to you the courtesy of an obedient servant."

"We've all heard you speak a lot of times, Joe," someone shouted from the crowd. "Now get down off 'n that stage 'n let the President speak."

The shout was met with laughter.

A smiling President stepped up onto the platform and waited until the cheers and applause died before he spoke.

"I want to thank you for your hearty reception. You may wonder what has brought me here, so far from Washington, our nation's capital. I determined upon a transcontinental journey eighteen months ago, General Sherman having shown me that I could make the trip in sixty days. I would have left then, but the extra session of congress interfered.

"I was determined to accomplish the journey this year, so three months ago I caused the fact to be advertised that I would undertake such a trip, so as to draw the fire of criticism if any could be made. I am most happy to say that not a single newspaper nor a single individual uttered an adverse word.

"Why, you may ask, did I embark on such a trip? It is because I am open for information about the Great West, and wish to learn by observation and inquiry of its needs, so that, if possible, I can assist its further development. Among other things, I have learned valuable facts in connection with the business of raising cattle, and I wish to pay tribute to these wonderful Westerners who have the fortitude and enterprise to populate the wild waste of dreary plains and create wealth apparently out of nothing."

After the President spoke, the crowd called for Mrs.

Hayes and, smiling, the President added to the call, holding his hand out in invitation to his wife.

"Clyde, the steam's down now," Austin said. "Unless you want to stay here 'n listen to all the speechifyin' that's goin' to be happenin'."

"We've already heard it a dozen times durin' this trip, they don't none of 'em say nothin' no different," Clyde said. He looked over at Smoke.

"There's a room in the depot that's used just for the train crews. What with all the excitement goin' on around the President and the general, 'n all, why, it's more 'n likely to be empty. We can talk there."

"Good idea," Smoke replied.

As Clyde suggested, the room was empty, occupied only by the aroma of coffee from a large pot that sat over a low-burning flame. The four men filled cups, then found a table.

"Now, you said the President is in danger?" Clyde asked.

"Yes. I think there is a plot to kidnap the President."

"Ha, don't know how anyone's goin' to do that," Clyde replied. "We got not only the President, but the Secretary of War, General Sherman, General McCook, Colonel Barr, and Captain Gutterman with us. Why, he'd practically have to come through the army to get to 'em."

"What other soldiers do you have, other than the generals and the colonels you mentioned?" Pearlie asked.

"They're the only ones," Clyde said.

"Uh-huh. And are they armed?"

"No," Austin said. "They ain't armed. Near as I know, there ain't even a gun on board the whole train."

"It's interesting that you said he would have to come

through an army," Smoke said. "When the truth of it is, there is no army to come through, but there is an army that will make the attempt."

"Damn," Austin said. "We need to tell the President."

"Yeah," Clyde agreed. "Only I think the tellin' should come from you, Smoke."

"Can you get me a meeting with the President?" Smoke asked.

"I don't know, there's so many people out there now, 'n somethin' like this, you'd need to be able to get him aside."

"Fort McPherson," Austin said.

"What?"

"Fort McPherson, remember? After all the speechifyin' 'n such that's goin' on here, we've been invited out to Fort McPherson where some highfalutin' army feller is supposed to feed us dinner."

"Yes, that's a good idea!" Clyde said. He looked back toward Smoke. "We'll take you with us."

CHAPTER TWENTY-FIVE

Fort McPherson, Nebraska

The army had a coach for the President and his family; General Sherman, his daughter, and Secretary of War Ramsey and his wife rode in an army ambulance. Everyone else rode in a couple of open carriages.

Major Phil Purvis, the commanding officer at Fort McPherson, was standing in front of the commandant's house when they arrived, and he invited everyone in where he and his wife would provide lunch for all.

"Who are you?" General Sherman asked, when he saw Smoke and Pearlie for the first time. "You two aren't members of the train party."

"My name is Smoke Jensen, General."

"I brung 'em, Gen'rul," Clyde said. "They got somethin' that I think you 'n the President should hear."

"Oh? And what would that be?"

"General, I have a very strong belief that there is going to be an attempt to capture the President," Smoke said.

General Sherman laughed out loud. "And how do you think someone is going to do that?"

"It isn't *someone*, General. It's several. In fact, they

refer to themselves as an army. An army of liberation, if you would believe them."

General Sherman shook his head. "Who did you say you were?"

"Smoke Jensen. This is my friend, Pearlie Fontaine."

"Gen'rul, don't know if you've ever heard o' Smoke Jensen, but out here most folks have. Most especial folks that live in Colorado. 'N I can speak from personal experience on account of it wasn't too long ago that he single-handed stopped a train robbery 'n saved mine 'n Clyde's lives," Austin said.

"I'd listen to him if I was you," Clyde said. "As the engineer of this train, you might say that I'm responsible for the lives of ever' body that's on it. 'N that means the President 'n his wife, 'n you 'n your daughter, 'n ever' one else."

General Sherman ran his hand through his beard for a moment as he studied Smoke and Pearlie.

"All right," he finally said. "You two just wait here. I'll go see if the President will meet with you."

When General Sherman left Smoke, Pearlie, Clyde, and Austin in the foyer, he saw Major Purvis talking to a sergeant who would be serving the party.

"Do not let the coffeepot get empty," Purvis said.

"No, sir, I won't."

As Sherman approached, both Major Purvis and the sergeant came to attention.

"General," Major Purvis said by way of greeting.

"At ease," General Sherman replied. "Sergeant, you may return to your duty. Major, I would have a few words with you, if you can spare the time."

"Yes, sir, of course I can," Purvis replied.

"I believe I was told that, before you came here, you had been stationed at Fort Sedgwick, in Colorado. Is that true?"

"Yes, sir."

"Have you ever heard of a man named Smoke Jensen? I've been given to understand that he is quite well known in Colorado."

Purvis smiled. "Yes, sir! But not just Colorado. Smoke Jensen is known, and well thought of, all over the West. Why do you ask, General? Have you read one of the books about him?"

"There are books written about him?"

"Indeed, there are, sir, there have been many books written about him. They are novels, of course, but his real exploits exceed anything that has ever been written about him."

"So, what you are saying is that you would trust him?"

"With my life, General. With my life," Major Purvis replied.

"Interesting you should use that particular phrase, Major, because that is just what I will be doing. Not only my life, but that of the President, our families, and everyone on board the train."

The smile left Major Purvis's face. "General, I don't know what you are talking about, but from all I know about Smoke Jensen, and I am quick to tell you that I have never met the man, but from all I know about him, if you are depending on him, your lives would be in good hands. But tell me, sir, if you can, why would such be the case?"

"He is waiting in the foyer to meet with the President, and according to Mr. Jensen, the President may be in some danger."

"Then, assuming it is really Smoke Jensen who is bringing the warning, I would say listen to him."

"I'm quite sure he is who he says he is. Apparently, Mr. Barnes and Mr. Prouty know him quite well, and they have identified him."

"Then I think you should hear him out."

"Is there a room in your house where the President and I can meet with him, privately?"

"Yes, sir, of course. You may use the library."

"If you would then please, Major Purvis, escort Mr. Jensen and the others with him, into the library. I'll summon the President."

"Yes, sir," Purvis agreed.

Smoke examined the bookshelves in Major Purvis's library. The shelves lined at least three walls, all filled with books, and Smoke couldn't help but think of how Sally would approve. He removed from the shelf a book by Kipling, and was looking through it when General Sherman and President Hayes stepped into the library.

"Ah, a fan of Kipling, I see," the President said, by way of greeting.

"Yes, Mr. President." He held the book out. "*The Man Who Would Be King*," he said. "Fitting, I think, under the circumstances."

"Mr. Jensen, as you requested, you have an audience with the President."

"Thank you, General."

"I'm curious about your reference to the title of that book having relevance," President Hayes said. "You wouldn't be insinuating, would you, Mr. Jensen, that I would be king? If so, may I remind you that I didn't even run for reelection?"

"Good," Smoke said, quickly.

"I beg your pardon."

"Mr. President, no, I did not intend to suggest that you had any allusions to being a king." Smoke smiled, sheepishly. "As I voted for Mr. Tilden, when I said 'good' I meant that I'm glad you wouldn't be running again."

"I see," President Hayes replied. "Well, young man, I admire and respect your candor. And you are in good company, more Americans voted for Tilden than voted for me. I understand that you are concerned for my safety. Your Presidential preference won't be getting in the way, I hope," the President added, with a little chuckle.

"No, sir, Mr. President, absolutely not!" Smoke said emphatically.

"Your comment about *The Man Who Would Be King* is relevant, how?"

"The threat to your safety, Mr. President, comes from a man named Clemente Pecorino. Before I get into the specific threats, may I suggest that you read these published articles? They were written by Pecorino. The first is, I suppose, Pecorino's version of the Declaration of Independence. He calls it the Founding Proclamation of Nova Amerigo Regnum."

The President read through everything Smoke gave him, passing the documents to General Sherman as he finished each one.

"Why, this man is insane," Sherman said.

"Yes, but then you might be able to make the same case for John Wilkes Booth," President Hayes said. "His insanity did not get in the way of him assassinating President Lincoln."

General Sherman nodded. "You have a point."

"All right, Mr. Jensen," the President said. "You have my attention. What sort of plot does this would-be king have against me?"

"I can't be certain, Mr. President, but based upon what Mr. Albert Barrington went through recently, I have an idea of what it might be. And I hasten to add, sir, that it is Mr. Barrington who has come up with this theory, based upon what happened to him."

Smoke went on to explain how Barrington had been taken from a train, blindfolded, and led to some mysterious army fort, where he was met by Pecorino's uniformed army.

"Where is this fort?" General Sherman asked. "Are you saying that the United States Army is involved in something like this?"

"No, sir," Smoke replied. "It is a fort, and it is manned by an army of sorts, and they are wearing uniforms. But it is not a U.S. Army fort and the uniforms are not U.S. Army uniforms."

"Is this a foreign army of some sort?" President Hayes asked.

"No, sir, they are all Americans."

"So, you are talking revolution."

"I would say so, but while Mr. Barrington was there, engaging Pecorino in conversation, he learned that the revolution Pecorino has in mind is to be finessed, not fought."

"Finessed? What does that mean?" General Sherman asked.

"By itself, it probably doesn't mean much of anything," Smoke replied. "But there was something else Pecorino said that started Barrington to thinking. Pecorino said that his kidnapping Barrington was a rehearsal for the finesse operation.

"Mr. President, General Sherman, I believe that Pecorino intends to try and take you from the train."

"To what end?" President Hayes asked.

"I believe he intends to hold you hostage, until the federal government cedes him the states of Colorado, Utah, Nevada, California, and the territory of Wyoming."

"The government would never do that," President Hayes said. "No one person's life is tantamount to the survival of the nation as a whole, not even the life of the President. If so, why, we would never be able to field an army."

"I think you are right, Mr. President. His plan has no chance to succeed. But he believes it does, and that is what makes him dangerous to you and to the others on this train. I fear he would be perfectly willing to start killing other members of the train's party, and especially including your own family, in order to force the federal government to respond as he wants."

"But how can one man do such a thing?" General Sherman asked.

"It isn't just one man," Smoke replied. "As I told you, he has his own army."

"Even so . . . a small band like that, he must know that, even if he were to succeed, temporarily, he would still have to face the might of the U.S. Army. What could a few men do?"

Smoke chuckled. "General, you might remember a few people like William Quantrill, Bloody Bill Anderson, Little Archie Clement, and Asa Briggs from the war. As a matter of fact, I rode with Asa Briggs. Now do you really have to ask what a few men can do?"

President Hayes chuckled. "I guess he's got you on that one, Bill."

Sherman nodded. "I have to confess that I do see his point."

"That conceded, Mr. Jensen, what are you saying we should do? Surely you don't expect me to abandon my trip, do you?"

"No, sir. I want you to let Pearlie and me come aboard the train as your personal guards. Well, actually, we would be guarding all of you."

"That's ridiculous," General Sherman said. "The two of you against a guerilla army? You, yourself, pointed out what someone like Quantrill could do."

"You'll pardon me for saying so, sir, but Pecorino wouldn't make a pimple on Quantrill's ass," Smoke said.

President Hayes laughed out loud. "Indeed!" he said. "What a delightful idiom. Where did you ever hear such a thing?"

"From the same place I learned almost everything else I know, from a man named Preacher."

"A pastor taught you such a thing?" General Sherman asked.

Pearlie laughed. "General, I don't think anyone ever made the mistake of callin' Preacher a pastor."

"Very well, Mr. Jensen, you and your friend may continue the trip with us."

"We'll keep you safe, Mr. President," Smoke promised.

CHAPTER TWENTY-SIX

When everyone returned to the train, President Hayes invited all of them to assemble in the dining car so he could introduce Smoke and Pearlie. Those gathered included President Hayes, his wife, Lucy, and their two sons, Birchard and Rutherford, General Sherman and his daughter, Rachel, Secretary of War Alexander Ramsey and his wife, Anna, Colonel Barr and his wife, Sara Sue, as well as General McCook and Captain Gutterman. Both General McCook and Captain Gutterman were unaccompanied. Mule Blackwell and Vernon Mathis, the off-duty engine crew, as well as the service crew of the train, the chef and four porters, were gathered there, as well. Only Clyde and Austin were absent from the meeting, but there was no need for them to be there, they were well acquainted with Smoke and Pearlie.

"Folks, I've invited these two gentlemen to accompany us for the rest of the trip," President Hayes said. "Though we have no specific threat, General Sherman and I have discussed the matter, and we feel that it might be well to have a couple of men act as our bodyguards. And that is the function of these two, Smoke Jensen and Pearlie Fontaine."

"Smoke Jensen?" Birchard said. "You mean, you are for real?"

"What are you talking about, Birch? What do you mean is he for real?" the President asked.

"Pa, are you saying you've never heard of Smoke Jensen?"

"Are you telling me that you have?"

"Sure, I have. He's famous." Birchard smiled and held up a hand. "Just a minute, I'll be right back."

The President glanced over at Smoke. "Mr. Jensen, do you have any idea what this is about?"

"Yes, sir, I'm afraid I do."

"What is it? Don't tell me you are a wanted man."

"No, sir, it's nothing like that."

"Here they are!" Birchard said, coming back into the dining car at that moment. He was holding three books in his hand, and he held them up one at a time, reading the titles as he did so.

"*Shootout of Smoke Jensen, Warpath of Smoke Jensen,* and *The Wrath of Smoke Jensen.* These are all about you, aren't they?"

"Smoke's too humble to tell you, but I'm not," Pearlie said. "Those books are about him, all right."

"Pa, he's a genuine hero," Birchard said. "I've been reading all about him."

The President looked at Smoke, and smiled at Smoke's apparent discomfort in being singled out in such a way.

"Obviously, Mr. Jensen, you've made an impression on my son."

"Those books," Smoke said, with a dismissive wave of his hand. "I want you to know, Mr. President, that I don't have anything to do with them."

"Except provide the inspiration for the writer," the President said.

Smoke was silent.

"General, you're in charge of the train," Captain Gutterman said. "Have you given any consideration as to where these two men will sleep?"

"There are a couple of extra berths in the crew car," one of the porters said. He looked at Smoke. "That is, if you don't mind sleepin' with the train crew."

"What is your name?" Smoke asked.

"Jackson, sir. Troy Jackson," the porter answered. He turned to the other three porters, introducing them one at a time. "Julius Booker, Tibbie Neal, and George McKay."

"The off-duty engine crew sleeps in there, too," a man wearing striped bib overalls said. "I'm Mule Blackwell, one of the engineers. This is my fireman, Vernon Mathis."

"I'm glad to meet both of you," Smoke replied. "Do you second Mr. Jackson's invitation?"

"I do indeed, sir."

"Very good then. Gentlemen, my friend and I would be very pleased to share the crew car with you. And we thank all of you for your hospitality."

"Well, now that that's taken care of, General, if you would, please tell Mr. Barnes and Mr. Prouty that they may proceed as soon as it is practicable for them to do so," President Hayes said.

"If you would like for me to, General, I'll carry the

message for you. I want to speak with Clyde and Austin anyway."

"You know them?" Mule asked, surprised by the announcement.

"Oh, yes, we've met before."

"Yes," General Sherman said. "If you would carry the message for me, I would appreciate that."

After the meeting, nearly everyone left the dining car to return to their normal positions on the train. The three who remained were Leslie Wilkes, the chef, General Sherman's daughter, Rachel, and Pearlie.

Rachel cocked her head and smiled at Pearlie. "Did I hear the President correctly? Is your name really Pearlie?"

"Well, it's actually . . . uh . . . Wes. Wes Fontaine," Pearlie said, speaking a name that had been but rarely on his tongue over the last several years.

"I like the name Pearlie," Rachel said. "That's the one you should use."

"Yes, ma'am. It's the one I do use."

Rachel chuckled. "Oh, for heaven's sake, why are you saying ma'am to me? Do I look like an old maid school teacher?"

Pearlie laughed out loud. "No, ma'a . . . uh, I mean no. You're one of the prettiest women I've ever seen. You sure don't look like a school teacher."

Even as Pearlie spoke the words, though, he felt a twinge of guilt. Sally had been a school teacher. She was no old maid, but she had been a school teacher, and he considered her to be a very pretty woman.

"Would you like to have dinner with me tonight?" Rachel asked.

"Why, sure. Where?" Pearlie asked.

Rachel laughed again. "Here, silly, in this car. When you're travelin' down the road at more than thirty miles an hour, this is the only place we can have dinner."

"All right," Pearlie said. "I'd be glad to."

"You think someone is goin' to actually attack the train 'n try 'n take the President?" Clyde asked as he opened the throttle to get the train underway.

"I have a suspicion that they will," Smoke said.

"What should we do?" Austin asked.

Smoke smiled. "For now, just drive the train."

Rawlings, Wyoming

"I've got the information for you, Mr. Sloan. I've found out as much as I can about the President's train," Chris Dumey said. Dumey was an employee of the Union Pacific Railroad.

"Please, give me all the details," Pecorino replied. Earlier, Pecorino had presented himself as Craig Sloan, a writer for *Harper's Weekly Magazine.*

"Why do you need to know so much about it?" Dumey asked.

Pecorino, who was wearing glasses, took them off, ostensibly to polish them. In fact, as his eyes required no ground lenses, wearing the glasses was giving him a headache. But he considered them an important part of his assumed persona.

"Well, sir, the train is being pulled by the fastest engine the Taunton Locomotive Company makes."

"Just how fast is that engine?"

"It can pull six fully loaded cars, to a speed of little better than seventy miles per hour on a flat track."

Pecorino let out a low whistle. "That's very fast," he said.

"Indeed it is, sir. There may be other engines in the country as fast, but there are none faster," Dumey said. "Of course, there is no way the train will ever travel so fast out here."

"Why not?"

"Well, sir, I don't think there's any track out here that would allow for a train to travel at such a rapid velocity. And for another thing, the train will be carrying the President of the United States, and the Union Pacific would never take the risk of endangering him. I expect that the train will go no further than thirty-five miles to the hour, at its absolute maximum."

"How long do you think it will be before the train reaches Wyoming territory?" Pecorino said.

"Well, sir, the latest information I've got is that they won't be leaving North Platte until around two o'clock this afternoon. And they'll be stopping at Oglala before they get to Bushnell, which as you know is right on the border line between Nebraska and Wyoming. Figure, eight hours of travel, and two hours at Oglala, I would guess that they'll reach Bushnell around midnight, tonight."

"Will the train stop at Bushnell?" Pecorino asked.

"Only for water. It will be the middle of the night then, and I'm quite sure everyone on board will be asleep."

"Mr. Sloan?" the station telegrapher asked, stepping into Dumey's office to interrupt the conversation.

"Yes?" Pecorino replied.

"You have a telegram, sir."

TWO MORE ADDED TO THE PRESIDENT'S
TRAVELING PARTY STOP THE TWO
ADDITIONS ARE SMOKE JENSEN AND
HIS MAN PEARLIE FONTAINE STOP
JEAN GUITTIERE

"Jensen again," Pecorino said to Moss. "I thought Jenner and Parker would take care of him for me, but they failed. Now the worst has happened. They are on the train with the President."

"You need to talk to a man named Stiles," Moss said.

"Who is Stiles?"

"I'll be honest with you, General, I don't think he's the kind of feller we would want in our . . . uh . . . army. But if you need a dirty job done, he just might be the one who can do it for you."

"Where will I find Mr. Stiles?"

"He's down at the Mad Dog Saloon, I just seen 'im not more 'n ten minutes ago."

"Can you introduce us?"

"I s'pose I could. Me 'n Stiles ain't what you would call good friends or nothin', but I know 'im, 'n he knows me, so, I figure I can introduce you."

Five minutes later, after the introduction, Pecorino was sharing a table with Stiles in the back corner of the Mad Dog Saloon, near the now-silent piano. Stiles hadn't given his first name, and Pecorino had been introduced to him as Sloan.

"I'll do anything if the price is right," Stiles said, after Pecorino felt him out.

"There are two men who have become . . . let us say, troublesome, and I would like the trouble removed."

"You mean killed," Stiles replied.

"You get right to the point."

"No need to beat around the bush. Who do you want killed?"

"Smoke Jensen and Pearlie Fontaine."

Stiles was silent for a moment.

"No comment?"

"That's quite a job."

"Yes, I've already made that discovery. I don't expect you to do it alone, and I'm prepared to pay you enough to hire some help. How many men do you think you will need?"

"Enough to get the job done," Stiles replied, without being more specific. He took out the makings of a cigarette.

"From all that I have learned of this man, Jensen, he can be quite a formidable enemy."

"I know all about Smoke Jensen," Stiles said as he curled the paper to hold the tobacco. "I've been wantin' to kill Jensen for a long time."

"Then, why haven't you done so, before now?"

Having licked the paper to close the cigarette, Stiles put it in his mouth and lit it. He took a puff before he answered Pecorino's question.

"I haven't killed 'im, because nobody has offered to pay me for killin' 'im. I don't kill nobody unless I'm gettin' paid to do it."

"Well, I shall be paying you, quite a substantial amount, I might add. But I am more than willing to pay well, because I want the job done. I have additional plans with regard to the passengers on that train, but those plans can proceed no further until Smoke Jensen and the man with him are both dead."

"What are your further plans?" Stiles asked.

Pecorino shook his head. "That doesn't concern you."

"I believe you said five thousand dollars," Stiles said.

"Yes."

"I'll take the money now."

"I'll give you one thousand dollars now, and the balance once the job has been completed."

Stiles took a puff of his cigarette and squinted his already-narrow eyes against the smoke.

"I want fifteen hundred now."

"A thousand."

"Do you want him dead?"

"Yes, of course I do. It was my understanding that, that was the purpose of this meeting."

"If you want him dead, it's goin' to cost you fifteen hundred now. I'll need to hire some good men, and good men cost money."

"All right," Pecorino agreed. "But if you have men to gather, you had better do so quickly. The eastbound train leaves in one hour, and you must take it in order to arrive at Bushnell prior to midnight."

"I have an idea," Richard Barrington said later that same afternoon.

"What sort of idea?" Pecorino asked.

"An idea that can apply pressure on the principals," Richard said.

"Can you be more specific? What sort of pressure?"

"Let's face it, while the concept of taking prisoner

every member of the President's traveling party is a good one, it is going to be quite difficult to attack the train and carry out the plan," Richard said. "But, if we can find some sort of weak link to exploit, we may be able to attain our goal without undue risk."

"Do you have a plan in mind?"

"Yes."

Pecorino listened to Richard's plan, and agreed to put it into operation. He considered sharing with Richard his own plan for taking care of Jensen and Fontaine, but kept the information to himself. He had studied Aaron Burr's plan, and learned from Burr's mistake, not to share authority. And part of that lack of sharing authority included not sharing too much information.

CHAPTER TWENTY-SEVEN

Oglala, Nebraska

There were at least two thousand people gathered at the depot when the train pulled in, and Smoke and Pearlie left the train to keep their eyes on everyone in the crowd. General Sherman and the Secretary of War spoke first, then President Hayes. As Hayes finished his speech, he saw a tall, rather large, man with gray hair and a gray beard. The man, standing in the front row of the crowd, was wearing an army uniform with sergeant's stripes, but it was quickly apparent that the uniform he was wearing was from the Civil War.

When President Hayes caught his eye, the man in uniform came to attention and saluted. "*Willkommen* in Oglala, Colonel," he said.

"Well, I'll be," President Hayes replied, returning the salute. "If it isn't Sergeant Schmidt."

"*Jah. Ist gut* to see an old *kamerad.*"

President Hayes turned to his wife and two sons. "Lucy, Birchard, Rutherford, I want you to take a very good look at this man. If it weren't for Sergeant Conrad Schmidt, I wouldn't be here today."

"What's the story, Mr. President?" Secretary of War Ramsey asked.

"Yes, Mr. President," someone from the crowd called out. "Are you telling us that this old square-head German actually saved your life?"

"He did," President Hayes said. He had stepped forward on the platform to respond to Sergeant Schmidt's greeting, but now he returned to the podium someone had erected, so he could address everyone.

"It was at the Battle of Winchester. I had my horse shot out from under me, I was wounded and bleeding and lying helpless in between our lines. To be honest with you, 'in between' doesn't quite describe it. I was much closer to the enemy lines than I was to our own.

"I had resolved myself to being killed, or at least captured. Then I heard a horse galloping toward me and thought, 'This is it!' But the horse wasn't coming from the enemy lines; it was coming from our own lines, and Sergeant Schmidt was in the saddle. Bullets were flying all around him . . . the Rebs weren't shooting at me. Sergeant Schmidt was their target.

"When the sergeant got to me, without even dismounting, he reached down and snatched me up as if I were no more than a rag doll. Then, with me holding on for dear life, and with shot shell all about, this brave man"—President Hayes held his hand out toward the tall, large, gray-haired man who was wearing his Civil War uniform—"Sergeant Schmidt carried me to the safety of our own lines.

"I recommended him for the Medal of Honor, and I am pleased to see that my recommendation was acted upon, because he is wearing the medal now."

"Hoorah for our blacksmith! Hooray for the Dutchman!" someone in the crowd shouted, and, just as they had cheered for the President when the train had first arrived, now they were cheering for Schmidt.

As the crowd outside cheered the speeches and the man who, during the late war, had saved the President's life, another man was standing at the telegrapher's counter. The telegrapher, who was staring through the window at what was going on outside, hadn't seen him.

"Telegrapher," the man called out, the irritation evident in his voice.

"Yes, sir?"

"Is this the way you run your office? Leaving your customers standing here with no service?"

"I'm sorry, sir. I was watching the President."

"Are you holding a telegram for a Mr. Guittiere?"

The telegrapher smiled. "Yes, sir, I am."

"May I have it, please?"

The telegrapher returned to his desk, looked through a stack of telegrams, then selected one.

"Here it is, sir," he said, passing the message across the counter.

PREPARE TO MEET FOUR MEN IN
BUSHNELL STOP PROVIDE THEM WITH
ANY ASSISTANCE THEY MAY NEED STOP

After he read the message, he tore the message up.

"Oh, sir, have I made a mistake and given you the wrong message? If so, please don't destroy it, it's the only copy I have kept," the telegrapher said, disturbed by what he had seen.

"It's the right message, but I've read it already. I don't need to keep it."

"How very strange," the telegrapher said.

Shortly after the train left Oglala, it was time for dinner, so everyone gathered in the dining car. Smoke sat at a table with General Sherman and the Secretary of War and his wife.

"Thank you for sharing the table with me," Smoke said.

"Yes, well, you're quite welcome. Normally, my daughter and I share the table with the Secretary and Mrs. Ramsey," General Sherman said. "That is, when she isn't with Captain Gutterman."

"Captain Gutterman?"

"Well, he is the youngest officer on the train," General Sherman said. "I suppose her sharing time with him could be a matter of convenience as much as anything else. But now it would seem that my daughter has found someone else who has caught her interest." He nodded his head toward Pearlie and his daughter, Rachel, who had found the only table in the car designed to seat just two people. "Since Captain Gutterman isn't here at the moment, maybe he won't notice."

Mrs. Ramsey chuckled. "Oh, for heaven's sake, Bill, you are missing the point."

"What point is that, Anna?" General Sherman asked.

"Well, it is obvious, isn't it? The whole point is that she wants John Gutterman to see her with Pearlie."

"Anna," the Secretary gasped. "Such a thing to say."

"Oh, for heaven's sake, Alex, you don't really think you went in pursuit of me, do you? You men don't understand anything about courtship. That's why, from the beginning of time, women have let men chase them, until the women caught the men," Anna said.

The others around the table laughed.

"And you think that's what Miss Sherman is doing with Pearlie? Letting him chase her, until she catches him?" Smoke asked.

"Or until she catches John Gutterman. It's really her game to play, now," Anna said.

"All right, Anna, enough of the secret rituals of female courtship. I think you are telling us all more than we really want to know," Secretary Ramsey said.

"Yes, dear," Anna replied compliantly.

"Mr. Jensen . . ." the Secretary started.

"Please, Mr. Secretary, call me Smoke. I'm so universally addressed so, that I sometimes don't even recognize the name when someone calls me 'Mister' Jensen."

The Secretary chuckled. "All right, Smoke it is. Tell us, Smoke, do you know anything else about this man who you fear is going to attack our train?"

"Nothing more than I have shared with you," Smoke said.

He went on to tell how one of Pecorino's men had been killed when they attacked Cal and the others, who were delivering Sir McGinnis. "Sir McGinnis is a prize bull," he explained.

Smoke also told about the robbery of the Bank of Alford.

"There were at least twelve of them, they were all wearing military style uniforms, and, according to all reports, they rode into town like an army unit, robbed the bank as if conducting a military raid, then left with quite a large sum of money," Smoke concluded.

"Well, then, that's what this is all about, isn't it?" General Sherman replied. "This whole 'revolution' thing is just a way of raising money."

Smoke shook his head. "No, sir, I don't think so. My friend, Albert Barrington, was taken from a train by Pecorino. And even though Pecorino had sent a ransom note, he let Mr. Barrington go without collecting. According to what Pecorino told Albert, his being taken from the train was described as a rehearsal for an upcoming operation."

"And, who is this man, Barrington?" General Sherman asked.

"If he had stayed in England, he would be Sir Albert Barrington, Lord of Denbigh. No title here, of course, but he is a part owner and ranch manager of the Three Mountain Ranch, doing so in partnership with an English corporation. He also has some background in the field of psychiatry."

"I'm sorry," General Sherman said. "The field of what?"

"Psychiatry," Smoke said. "It deals with the behavior and mind. Albert said Pecorino is a classic example of someone who has an exaggerated sense of self-importance. And to such a person, recognition is much more important than money. Everything he has done so far, even the money he has raised or stolen, has but one purpose, and that is to help him become king of the new kingdom he wants to create."

"And you actually think such a man is foolish enough to attack a train that is carrying the President of the United States?" Secretary Ramsey asked.

"I feel certain that he is."

"If, as you say, he has at least twelve men with him, then you and your friend Pearlie seem greatly outnumbered," Secretary Ramsey suggested.

"Mr. Secretary, as I am sure General Sherman will bear me out, it isn't how many men you are against, it is how you choose to fight them. You look for their vulnerability, and find a way to take advantage of it."

"Bravo," General Sherman said, clapping his hands lightly. "Mr. Secretary, you could find no better lesson on tactics at West Point."

"Nevertheless, don't you think we should stop, and wait for a military escort?" Secretary Ramsey asked.

"No, sir, I don't," Smoke replied.

"Why not?" the Secretary asked.

"In the first place, we have only Mr. Barrington's idea, and my hunch, that it will happen. And in the second place, if he did have such a plan in mind, seeing all the military on the train might cause him to change his plans."

"Well, isn't that what we would want him to do?" Secretary Ramsey asked.

"No, sir, we would like for him to attack the train," Smoke said.

"Wait a minute, Mr. Jensen. Are you suggesting that

you intend to use the President of the United States as bait?" General Sherman asked, incredulously.

"In a manner of speaking, yes, sir. Better to have Pecorino try something when we are expecting it, than to have him do something when we are not expecting it. Here, I can protect the President. But I've been led to believe that he will be traveling by stagecoach, riverboats, and ships at sea. Is that true?"

"Yes."

"That spreads out the chances for Pecorino . . . too many opportunities for him to find the opportunity to strike, unexpectedly. We will have a much better chance of stopping him now."

"What he says makes sense, Bill," Ramsey said. "I say we turn it all over to Mr. Jensen."

"Thank you, Mr. Secretary," Smoke replied.

Smoke had said nothing about the two men who had attacked him from the 123 Stable. They weren't in uniform, and there was nothing to connect them to Pecorino. And, as far as he knew, Pecorino knew nothing about him, and for certain, had no way of knowing that Smoke was on the train, guarding the President.

"Well," General Sherman said. "Now that that is all settled, let me glance over toward my daughter and see how she is handling Pearlie."

"From my perspective, I would say she is handling him pretty well," Anna Ramsey said.

Everyone at the table glanced toward Pearlie and Rachel.

* * *

"I think we are the center of attention here," Rachel said, smiling across the table at Pearlie.

"Yeah," Pearlie said, looking around. "We do appear to be."

"Are you married, Pearlie?" Rachel put her fingers to her mouth. "Oh, how . . . indecorous of me to ask you such a question. And if I am to ask it, I certainly should have asked the question as to whether or not you are married before I invited you to dinner."

"No, I'm not married," Pearlie said. He paused for a second before he continued. "At least, not any more."

"Oh?"

"I was married once, but not for very long. She died."

"Oh, I'm so sorry. You said not for very long. How long did you have together?"

"About two minutes."

"What?" Rachel gasped.

"Her name was Lucy."

"Lucy? Like the first lady?"

"The first lady?" Pearlie shook his head. "I just thought her name was Mrs. Hayes. "My Lucy was Lucy Goodnature, and we had planned to be married, but she got shot. Among other things, Smoke is a justice of the peace, so, as she was dying, she said that her biggest regret was that she could not call herself my wife. But Miz Sally pointed out that Smoke is a justice of the peace, and he can marry people, so Smoke was able to marry us, even as Lucy lay dying. She died within moments, but not before Smoke finished his words. And she died with a smile. I think it eased her passing to know that she died as my wife."

Rachel's eyes were filled with tears as she reached across the table to take Pearlie's hand in hers.

"Oh, Pearlie, I'm so sorry," she said. "I didn't mean to bring up such an unpleasant memory."

Pearlie smiled and put his other hand on hers. "No, don't be sorry, Rachel. I treasure the memories of Lucy," he said. "It's all I have left of her now."

"You are a good man, Pearlie."

CHAPTER TWENTY-EIGHT

Bushnell, Nebraska

The night was alive with sound, from the singing insects, to the hooting owls, to the occasional yelp of a coyote. There were three men with Stiles, each of them two hundred dollars richer because Stiles had told them that he was given eight hundred dollars in advance to do the job, and they would divide another eight hundred dollars when the job was done.

Stiles had lied about the amount of money he had been given, and he kept nine hundred dollars for himself.

At the moment, Stiles was standing on the track, gazing down along the twin steel rails, which were glistening silver in the moonlight.

"I gotta piss," someone said.

"Well, Nelson, if you have to piss, piss. There ain't no need for you to be askin' our permission."

"I ain't askin' nothin', Waters. I was just sayin' is all."

"Maybe he wants you to come hold it for 'im," the third man said.

"Maybe you'd like me to piss in your pocket," Nelson replied, testily.

"Ha," Waters said. "What do you think, Jones, you think we got Nelson pissed off?"

"Better pissed off than pissed on," Nelson said, and that remark brought a laugh.

"Hey, Stiles," Waters called. "Why don't you hold your ear down to the track 'n see if the train is comin'."

"What's that s'posed to do?" Stiles replied.

"I don't know, but I've seen injuns do it, 'n they say they can hear a train from a long way off by doin' that."

"Yeah, well, injuns has sorta special powers when it comes to things like that," Stiles replied. "The train's s'posed to be here by midnight, 'n I spec' it will be."

The four men were gathered around the water tower, which was about one hundred yards west of the Bushnell depot. There were no more than ten or twelve people standing on the depot platform, waiting for the train.

"Must not be just a whole lot of people wantin' to see the President," Nelson said, buttoning his trousers as he returned to the group.

"There won't be nothin' to see no how," Nelson said, "on account of the train ain't goin' to stop at the depot. It'll be a' comin' on through 'n won't stop 'til it gets here to take on water."

"That's good, for what we got to do," Stiles said.

"Yeah, I reckon it is."

The men heard a distant whistle.

"There it is," Stiles said. "Remember, the two men we want will be sleepin' in the caboose."

"How do we know which two are Jensen 'n his man?" Waters asked. "I mean there's bound to be more 'n just two people sleepin' there."

"Yeah, well it don't make no difference whether we

know which two is them or not," Stiles replied. "Soon as we get into the caboose, we're goin' to kill ever' one that's in there. That way we're sure to get the right ones."

"That's sure goin' to be some surprise to ever' one that's in the caboose when they wake up in the mornin' 'n find out that they're all dead," Jones said.

"What? Jones, you don't make one lick of sense," Waters said. "If they're already dead, how are they goin' to wake in the mornin' 'n find out they're dead?"

"They could know," Jones insisted. "Where do you think ghosts come from?"

"You're as nutty as a peach orchard boar."

"Hush, I hear the train," Stiles said.

By now the train was close enough that they could hear, in addition to the whistle, the chugging of the steam engine.

"All right, men, on the other side of the track, and down into the ditch," Stiles said. "And remember, just as soon as the train stops for water, be ready to climb onto it. Jones, you 'n Waters will climb up onto the front of the caboose while me 'n Nelson will climb up onto the rear. That way we can go into the front door 'n the back door at the same time. That'll more 'n likely get anyone who is inside all confused 'cause they won't know which end to look at first."

"Hey, Stiles, if we climb up onto the back of the caboose, the people that was standin' out there to watch the train go by is liable to see us," Nelson pointed out.

"Yeah, you might be right," Stiles agreed. "All right, we'll all get on the front until the train leaves. Then Jones 'n Waters will stay in front while me 'n you will climb across the top of the car 'n drop down onto the back."

"Ain't that dangerous? I mean climbin' across the top o' the car like that while it's movin'," Nelson asked.

"It ain't no more dangerous for you than it is for me," Stiles said.

"Yeah, I guess you're right."

The four men crossed the track and lay down in the drainage ditch, now dry, that ran parallel with the tracks. As the train rumbled by, they saw that every window in every car was dark, except for the caboose. A dim light did shine from the caboose windows.

"Hey, they's lights on in the caboose. There might be someone awake in there," Waters suggested.

"That may be, but do you think they'll be sittin' there with guns in their hands?" Stiles asked.

Waters laughed. "Yeah, what difference does it make whether they're asleep or awake? It ain't goin' to be hard to kill 'em."

The train stopped with a hiss of steam and a squeal of brakes.

"All right, onto the train," Stiles ordered, and the four climbed up the berm, then onto the small vestibule at the front of the caboose.

"Soon as the train gets a' goin' again, me'n Nelson will climb over to the back," Stiles said *soto voce*.

Stiles and the others waited on the front platform of the caboose until the train got underway.

"All right, Nelson, let's go. Once me 'n you get to the back, we'll all go in at the same time, from both ends of the car."

"How are goin' to know when to go in?" Jones asked.

"I'll fire my pistol. That'll be my signal," Stiles said.

"But won't that warn them?" Nelson asked.

"It won't make any difference. As soon as I fire the pistol, we're going to rush into the room shootin'. Remember, shoot everyone."

Smoke woke up when the train stopped for water. He was about to go back to sleep, when in that almost precognitive sense that had served him well for so long, he perceived danger.

"Pearlie," he said. He spoke just loudly enough for Pearlie to hear him.

"What is it?" Pearlie replied.

"I don't know, but get your gun out and be ready," Smoke said.

Pearlie had been around Smoke long enough to know not to question his instincts. He sat up on his bunk, and like Smoke, drew his gun.

There was a lantern attached to the wall of the caboose, and though the flame was turned down low, there was enough illumination to make out the entire car, from the coffeepot on the little coal burning stove in the middle aisle, to the small table, and to the other six bunks which were attached to the wall, upper and lower bunks, a total of four on each side of the car. The other six bunks were occupied with sleeping men, the four porters, and the off-duty engine crew, which, at the moment, happened to be Clyde and Austin.

There was the unmistakable sound of a gunshot from the rear platform. Almost immediately thereafter both the front and back doors were pushed open.

"What?" Julius shouted.

"Stay down! Ever' body stay down!" Smoke shouted,

and even as he was calling out the order, two men pushed in through the back door, and another two came in through the front door. The men came in shooting, but they weren't aimed shots.

Smoke and Pearlie's shots were aimed and after an exchange of gunfire that lasted only seconds, all four of the intruders were down.

"Was anybody hit?" Smoke called out. Both Smoke and Pearlie were holding smoking pistols.

"I'm all right, I wasn't hit," Austin said.

"Me neither," Clyde said.

"I wasn't hit," Julius added, and the other three porters spoke up then attesting to the fact that none of them had been hit by the shooting.

"Damn!" Clyde said.

"What is it?"

"Look at the coffeepot."

There were two bullet holes, low in the blue metal pot, and coffee was streaming out. The only reason the coffeepot hadn't been knocked off the top of the stove, was that it was sitting inside a secured ring, the arrangement designed to keep the pot from falling over during the normal operation of the train.

"Who the hell was them fellers?" Austin asked. "And how come they was a' tryin' to kill us?"

"I expect they wanted to kill everyone in the caboose so they would have some men aboard when they make their move to kidnap the President," Smoke said.

"I don't know," Pearlie replied. "Look at 'em, Smoke. None of them are wearing uniforms. I don't know if this has anything to do with Pecorino or not."

Smoke didn't reply. Instead, he walked over to the

bodies of the two men who had come in through the back door, and began going through their pockets. He pulled out a roll of money from one of the men, then let out a low whistle.

"Look at this, Pearlie," he said, holding up the money.

"Yeah, both of these men also have pockets full of money. Where do you think men like these got so much money?"

"From Pecorino," Smoke replied. "I believe he paid these men to attack the train."

"Do you think they intended to capture the President?" Pearlie asked.

"No, I think their job was just to make it easier by taking out the President's bodyguards."

"But the President doesn't have any bodyguards," Pearlie said.

"Oh?" Smoke replied.

"Wait. We're the President's bodyguards, aren't we?"

"Yes."

"Then, I don't understand. How did they know we are the President's bodyguards, and how did they know where to find us?"

"That, my friend, is the question," Smoke replied.

"What do we do now?" Pearlie asked.

"Now, we wake up General Sherman. He's in charge of the train and it seems to me like he should be informed."

"Yeah, I think you're right."

"Wait a minute," Julius said as Smoke and Pearlie started toward the front door. "You ain' goin to just leave these bodies here, are you?" He took in the bodies with a sweep of his hand.

"For now," Smoke replied.

"I don't like bein' around 'em."

"Well hell, Julius, they ain't likely to do nothin' to us now, are they?" Austin asked.

Julius laughed. "No, I reckon not."

"I think we should keep this incident a secret from the others," General Sherman said when Smoke awoke him to tell him of the attack. General Sherman, Smoke, and Pearlie were standing in the vestibule between General Sherman's car and the Pullman car that was occupied by Colonel and Mrs. Barr, General McCook, and the others. Captain Gutterman had stepped out onto the vestibule, as well, and though Smoke would have rather kept him out of the conversation, he made no effort to do so.

"We can hardly keep it a secret, General," Captain Gutterman said. "After all, four men were killed."

"Yes, four men who were, no doubt, trying to kill the President," Sherman replied.

"How do you propose that we keep it secret from the President," Captain Gutterman asked. "We can't just dump them off the train, alongside the track, can we?"

"Clyde tells me that the train will have to stop for water in Egbert. It will still be dark, then," Smoke said. "I believe we can sneak the bodies off the train, then deliver them to the mortician."

"What makes you think he'll handle them?" Gutterman asked.

Smoke smiled. "He'll handle them," he said.

CHAPTER TWENTY-NINE

Although it wasn't yet dawn, a streak of gray spread across the eastern sky as Smoke, Pearlie, Julius, and George dragged the bodies through the early morning darkness to leave them in front of the mortuary.

"You three hurry on back," Smoke said. "The fewer of us that are seen, the better it will be. I'll take care of the mortician. Julius, George, remember, don't say a word about this. And you make sure that Troy and Tibbie don't say anything about it either. We have to keep this an absolute secret."

"We'll be quiet," Julius promised.

Pearlie and the two porters returned quickly to the train and not until they were out of sight, did Smoke start pounding on the mortician's door. As the mortician lived in an apartment over the mortuary, Smoke was certain that he would be able to arouse him.

After pounding very hard on the door, a window opened upstairs and a man, still dressed in his sleeping gown, stuck his head out.

"Here, what is the meaning of you pounding on my door at this hour of the morning?" he called down.

"I have some business for you," Smoke said.

"Are you out of your mind? I don't open until eight o'clock."

"Yes, sir, I understand that. But these four men didn't wait until eight o'clock to die."

"Perhaps not, but they will still be dead at eight," the undertaker called down.

Smoke laughed. "Yes, sir, you got me on that one, I suppose they will. All right, I'll just leave them here for you and you can take care of them when you open."

"No, don't you be doing a thing like that. How would that look for my business now? Just hold on, I'll be down shortly."

Smoke waited for the undertaker, unconcerned as to whether or not the train would leave without him. It was now time for Clyde and Austin to relieve Mule Blackwell and Vernon Mathis, and Clyde assured Smoke that he would not leave until Smoke returned to the train.

By the time the door opened, the mortician had lit a lamp inside so that the room behind him was illuminated.

"Who are these four men?"

"I don't know," Smoke said.

"Well, where did they come from?"

"I don't know that, either."

"Do you expect me to just take four bodies like this, without knowing anything about them? Why, in the first place it would be against the law if I didn't report them to the sheriff."

"Oh, you can report them to the sheriff. I don't have a problem with that. It's just that I don't intend to get involved with the law."

"Here, did you shoot these men?"

"If I had killed all these men, do you think I would bring them to you to be buried? I would have just left them."

Smoke's reply wasn't actually a lie. He didn't really deny shooting them. And he hadn't shot *all* of them.

"I suppose you're right. But the sheriff is going to want more information than you've given me, if I'm going to get any burying money from the county," the undertaker said.

"Go through their pockets," Smoke said.

"What?"

"Go through their pockets. I think you'll find enough money there to cover your fee."

"Not very likely," the undertaker said. "Men like these seldom have a nickel on them any longer than it takes to get to a saloon and buy a beer." He stuck his hand down into the pocket of one of the bodies, them came out with a roll of bills. "My word!" he gasped. "How much money is this?"

"Two hundred dollars," Smoke said, having already counted it. "Check the pockets of the others."

Every time the undertaker put his hand in a pocket, he brought out another roll of money until he was holding fifteen hundred dollars.

"What . . . what am I supposed to do with all this money?" he asked. "This is many times more than it will cost to bury them."

"I expect what you do with it would be up to you," Smoke said. He smiled. "Perhaps start a fund to provide burial money for the indigent?"

"Yes," the undertaker said with an enthusiastic shake

of his head. "Yes, that is exactly what I will do. Here, help me get them inside."

"What about the sheriff?" Smoke asked.

"You let me handle that."

Ten minutes later Smoke walked by the locomotive, which was puffing loudly as the relief valve opened and closed to vent steam. Austin was standing on the ground with an over-sized oil can, lubricating one of the huge, driver wheels. Clyde was leaning out the window, with his crossed arms resting on the windowsill.

"How soon are we going to get underway?" Smoke asked.

"How long will it take you to get back on board?" Clyde asked with a broad smile.

"About one minute."

"Then I'd say we'll be underway within one minute."

At breakfast, Smoke and Pearlie were sitting across from each other at a four-person table that still had two empty seats. So far only Secretary of War Ramsey, General Sherman, and Captain Gutterman knew about the attack on the train during the night.

It had not been Smoke's intention to include Gutterman in the information last night, but the young captain had overheard the conversation.

So far as Smoke could tell, the attack last night was still known only by those who had actually been through it, and the three men, Sherman, Ramsey, and Gutterman, that Smoke had told.

Rachel came into the dining car then and with a smiling nod in recognition of Pearlie, took a seat, not at their table, but at the same table she had shared with Pearlie the night before. Only this time her breakfast companion was Captain Gutterman.

"I guess I didn't make that much of an impression on her last night," Pearlie said with a self-deprecating grin. "And how could I? Gutterman is a captain in the army and I'm basically just a cowboy."

"You're much more than a cowboy, Pearlie, and you know it."

Smoke had not shared with Pearlie Mrs. Ramsey's words about Rachel playing the two men against each other.

"She was born and raised in the military; I suppose it just makes sense that she would be drawn to an army officer. Besides, her pa is a general, and not just any general, he's the top general in the entire U.S. Army. That's just a little too high up on the totem pole for me."

"Don't ever sell yourself short, Pearlie. You're as good a man as I've ever known."

"Thanks," Pearlie said.

Smoke smiled. "But don't let that go to your head now."

"Oh, I'll try just real hard not to," Pearlie replied with a chuckle. The smile left his face as the subject changed. "Say, what do you think that was last night? Do you think those four men planned to snatch the President all by themselves?"

"No, if you want to know what I think, I think they wanted to empty the caboose so they could get fifteen or twenty men on. And of course, if we had been killed in the process, there are no other weapons on board so there would have been no way to stop them."

"We sure put a stop to that plan," Pearlie said.

"Yes, but if they had one plan, you can be dead sure they have another to take its place. This man, Pecorino, may be a fool, but he isn't dumb. He'll find some other way of coming after us, so we need to be ready."

Colonel and Mrs. Barr arrived then. "Do you gentlemen mind if Sara Sue and I join you?"

"No, please do," Smoke said, and he and Pearlie stood as Mrs. Barr was seated.

Over at the single table for two, breakfast had just been delivered, and Captain Gutterman began to butter his biscuit.

"Tell me, Rachel, did you enjoy your dinner with Mr. Fontaine last night?" Gutterman asked.

"It was very pleasant. He's quite a sensitive man, you know."

"Sensitive, you say? Rachel, are you aware that he has killed, who knows how many men, in his life?"

"No, I wasn't aware of that."

"Why is it, do you think, that he and Mr. Jensen have been chosen to act as bodyguards to everyone on the train? It is because both of them are quite proficient with the gun. And they have shown a willingness to use that proficiency many times over."

"Perhaps, but surely all of the . . . incidents," she said, searching for an acceptable word, "were necessary and justified. Otherwise, he would be in jail, wouldn't he?"

"As you know, I was born and raised in the West, Colorado to be precise, and I know all about Smoke Jensen and Pearlie. Though I confess, I had never heard his last name before."

"You know them?"

Gutterman shook his head. "I know *of* them. I don't know them. Believe me, Rachel, and I am saying this for your own good, you are much too refined a person to get involved with someone like Pearlie. But I'm curious, just what on earth makes you think that someone like that is a sensitive person?"

Rachel thought of the story Pearlie had told her about his tragically brief marriage with a woman named Lucy. She started to mention it to him, but held back the impulse to do so. She couldn't help but believe that Pearlie had shared that story with her in confidence, and she intended to honor both that confidence and his feelings.

"I don't know," she said. "I've just got that feeling."

Breakfast was over, and though Colonel and Mrs. Barr had left the table, Smoke and Pearlie lingered over another cup of coffee.

"You think Sir McGinnis is pining over Cal?" Pearlie asked.

"Probably not as much as Cal is pining over Sir McGinnis," Smoke replied. Both men laughed.

Captain Gutterman walked by their table, just as Smoke and Pearlie were sharing the laugh.

"Well, I'm glad to see that both of you can laugh this morning, in view of what happened last night," Gutterman said.

"Shhh," Smoke said. "You heard what General Sherman told us."

"I am speaking only to you," Gutterman said. "And doing so in such a circumspect way that only the two of you can understand what I'm talking about. Unless, of course, you intend to violate the general's orders."

"We have no such intention," Smoke said. "In fact, we aren't the ones who brought the subject up. You are."

Gutterman nodded and smiled. "You're right, I'm the one who gave offense by violating protocol here. Please forgive me for my remark."

"No need to forgive you, Captain, for there was no offense taken," Smoke said. "I figure that we're all in this together, now. As long as we're on this train, if something happens to one of us, it happens to all of us."

Captain Gutterman nodded. "You have that right," he said.

Smoke and Pearlie watched him walk away.

"Who is he, anyway?" Pearlie asked. "I mean, what's his role on this train?"

"I asked General Cook that same question. Apparently, before Captain Gutterman went to West Point, he was born and raised out here, and knows the West very well. He has come along as the expert on all things Western."

"Ha," Pearlie said. "I suppose when you are the President of the United States, you can pretty much have anyone you want around you, including somebody that doesn't do any more than answer questions."

"I suppose so," Smoke replied with a little chuckle.

"Where's our next stop?" Pearlie asked.

"Our next stop is Cheyenne. There are rather significant plans in the works for our visit there. I expect the Barringtons will be there."

"Albert will, Richard won't," Pearlie said.

CHAPTER THIRTY

The train rolled into Cheyenne at 10:45 on the morning of September 4. Smoke and Pearlie were in the dining car looking through the window at the crowd that was gathered on the depot platform.

"Would you look at that?" Pearlie said. "Half the town must be there."

"It sure looks like it," Smoke said.

"Wow, look at all those cannons! Twelve of them," Pearlie said.

"Yes, I heard from General Sherman, they are going to fire a thirty-eight-gun salute."

"Thirty-eight, not twenty-one?"

"Thirty-eight, one salute for each of the thirty-eight states."

As soon as the train stopped, the first gun fired, the heavy boom rolling across the crowded depot platform. That was followed by the second, then the third, each gun firing individually. The sequence of the firing gave the earlier guns time to reload so that all thirty-eight gun blasts came without pause. By the time the guns finished their salute, a thick cloud of gun smoke hung over the gathered crowd, causing many of the spectators to cough and wheeze from the heavy smell of expended gunpowder.

"Smoke, Pearlie!" someone shouted.

"You're right, Albert is here, and Richard isn't," Smoke said.

"I told you, Albert and Richard had a falling out, and Richard went on his way. Good thing, too, because if you want to know what is really causing Three Mountain Ranch to lose money, it was Richard. He was stealing cattle from his own brother."

Smoke was unable to respond to Pearlie's charge, because they met Albert before he could do so.

"How exciting all this is," Albert said, enthusiastically. "Why, not even the Queen generates as much excitement."

"Have you heard anything from Richard?" Pearlie asked.

"I have heard nothing from him since he left. I hope he is just upset and will come back so we can mend the fences between us. It isn't right that brothers should be at such cross-purposes with one another."

"I know this isn't my place to say this, but it isn't right for one brother to be stealing from another, either."

"But he explained that, Pearlie. He was only trying to raise money to pay ransom so he could secure my release."

Pearlie was going to respond with his belief that Richard had been stealing cattle all along, and the reason the ranch was failing was all his fault. But he thought that such a comment might anger Albert, and make him defensive on behalf of his brother, so he held it back.

"Mr. Jensen!" someone shouted, and Smoke turned

to see that he was being hailed by Professor Jordahl, the balloon aeronaut.

"Professor Jordahl, what are you doing here?"

"With all the excitement of the President's arrival, I thought I would take advantage of the crowds," Jordahl said. "I shall be giving demonstrations and selling balloon ascensions. Would you like to make another parachute leap?"

"Parachute leap?" Pearlie asked. "What is that?"

"You mean your friend didn't tell you?"

"What is he talking about, Smoke?"

"Why, Mr. Jensen went up in the balloon with me, then from an altitude of one thousand feet, he leaped from the balloon."

"What?" Pearlie replied, literally shouting the word. "Are you trying to tell me that Smoke jumped out of the balloon from a thousand feet in the air?"

"He did, indeed," Jordahl replied with a teasing smile.

"That's impossible," Pearlie insisted. "Why, if he had done that, he would be dead."

"Not if I used a parachute," Smoke said, and when the expression on both Pearlie's and Albert's faces indicated that they didn't know what he was talking about, he described the device that allowed him to float down from the balloon without injury.

"Good heavens," Albert said. "What courage one must have in order to do something like that."

"Damn!" Pearlie said. "I think I'd like to try that. I think it would be great fun."

Their conversation was interrupted by the band playing *Hail to the Chief,* as President Hayes stepped down from the train. After the music the crowd cheered and applauded the President.

The city of Cheyenne had built a platform for the President, Secretary of War, and General Sherman, festooning the platform with flags, and with red, white, and blue bunting. In addition to the President, Secretary of War, and the Commanding General of the U.S. Army, Lucy Sherman, Helen Ramsey, and Rachel Sherman were also led onto the platform.

As soon as all the dignitaries were seated, Mayor Adams stepped up to the podium.

"It is an esteemed honor for me, as mayor, to welcome President Hayes to the great city of Cheyenne."

"Oh, Lord, how long are we going to have to listen to the speechifying?" Pearlie asked quietly.

"I don't know how long anyone else will speak, but General Sherman told me that he and the President had managed to cut their speeches down to no longer than an hour apiece," Smoke said.

"What?" Pearlie replied, literally shouting the word.

Both Smoke and Albert laughed.

"Damn, don't scare me like that, Smoke."

In another part of the crowd, Pecorino, who was in mufti because he didn't want to call attention to himself, was observing the ceremonies.

"As you can see, Smoke Jensen and Pearlie Fontaine are still alive," Jean Guittiere said.

"I'll have to take your word for that, as I've never seen either of them before," Pecorino said. "Can you point them out?"

"Do you see those men standing by the left corner of the speaker's platform?"

"I see four men standing there. One of them is Albert Barrington," Pecorino said. "It is best that he not see me."

"Yes, well, I don't know which one is Barrington, but the man in the blue shirt is Smoke Jensen, the one in the white shirt is Pearlie Fontaine."

Pecorino studied the two men, one was tall, broad shouldered, and clean shaven. The other was nearly as tall, and also clean-shaven.

"Thank you. It's good to know what my two principal adversaries look like," Pecorino replied. "Now, what can you tell me about the four men I sent?"

"They were killed by Jensen and Fontaine."

"I thought as much since I haven't heard anything from them. Obviously, I have underestimated Jensen and Fontaine. Though it's not that surprising. I was told by Sir Richard, that they were quite formidable."

"Sir Richard? Who is that?"

"It isn't necessary that you know," Pecorino replied. "I have purposely kept you separated from the others, none of whom, including Sir Richard, even know of your existence. Compartmentalizing the various players helps to ensure secrecy, and it is safer for the participants."

"Are you going to make another attempt to get rid of them?" Guittiere asked.

"I have tried twice, and both times my agents have failed me. But I think that, in order for my plan to succeed, I'm going to have to get them out of the picture," Pecorino replied.

"Yes, I was pretty much thinking the same thing. I was

also thinking that you might want to change your plan about taking hostage everyone on the train."

"I have no intention of abandoning my plan," Pecorino replied. He smiled. "However, Sir Richard has come up with a suggestion that I think is quite good. It can be initiated easily, and it involves you."

"Involves me how?"

"One might say that you are the principal player. However, your participation will be quite limited, and with very little risk."

"I'm glad to see that you are concerned about risk, as I am already in considerable personal risk," Guittiere said. "I also appreciate your flexibility. I wouldn't want to connect my wagon to someone who is so obdurate as to get in the way of success."

"Only a stupid man would be that obdurate. I am not a stupid man," Pecorino replied.

"What is this plan?"

As the speeches droned on, frequently interrupted by cheers and applause, Pecorino outlined his plan to Jean Guittiere. When he was finished, Guittiere smiled and nodded.

"You are right, you are not a stupid man. That is an excellent plan, and I believe it will be successful."

"Go now," Pecorino said. "I think it best that we not be seen together, especially by Albert Barrington."

"All right, I'll find a place to blend in with the crowd and listen to the speeches."

Guittiere found a place where he could both see the speakers on the stand and keep an eye on Smoke Jensen and Pearlie Fontaine. He had never even heard of them until a few days ago, now they were the greatest obstacles in the course of events that could change his life forever.

Unaware that they were the subject of conversation and scrutiny, Smoke and Pearlie stood, keeping an eye on the stage where the dignitaries were seated. At the moment, General Sherman was speaking. Then, in response to entreaties from the crowd, General Sherman introduced his daughter to say a few words.

"Let's go find a saloon and have a beer," Smoke said.

"What? No, wait, Rachel is about to speak," Pearlie replied.

Smoke laughed. "I thought you didn't want to listen to all the speeches."

"She's different," Pearlie insisted.

"How is she different?"

"She's prettier than any of the rest of them."

Albert and Professor Jordahl laughed.

"He's right, Smoke. She is prettier than the rest of them," Albert said.

Rachel stepped up to the podium, thanked her father for introducing her, then she looked out over the crowd. She was silent for a second, until her eyes found Pearlie. Flashing him a big smile, she began to speak.

"I was told once that the secret to giving a good speech is to find someone in the audience, and to speak as if you are speaking directly to that person. So, I am speaking directly to you."

As she spoke the words, she turned her gaze directly toward Pearlie, held it for a moment, then looked around, to make eye contact with several others in the crowd, so that each of them sincerely believed that they were the one she had chosen.

"Did you hear that?" Pearlie asked. "She's talking directly to me."

"I want to thank my father, General Sherman, for organizing this great and epic trip, and for inviting me to be a part of this exciting bit of our American history. And I want to think the President of the United States for allowing my father to invite me.

"And lastly, I want to thank all of Western America for the way they have greeted and welcomed us.

"But I know you didn't come to hear a young woman speak . . ."

"As pretty as you are, little darlin', you can stand up there and speak for the rest of the day," someone shouted.

The crowd greeted the shout with laughter.

"Thank you," Rachel said, unperturbed by the shout from the crowd. "But I think I had better turn things back over to the master of ceremonies, so that he might introduce the next speaker."

Even before General Sherman had begun his speech, Pecorino was in the Gandy Dancer Saloon, meeting with a man he knew only as Fargo. At the moment, Pecorino and Fargo were the only two customers in the saloon, as everyone else in town was down at the depot, listening to the speeches being given by General Sherman and all the other dignitaries who had arrived on the train. There was only one other person in the saloon, and that was the bartender, though, at the moment, he was standing in the doorway, looking over the top of the batwing doors, trying to hear the words of the speakers.

"Have you ever heard of a man by the name of Smoke Jensen?" Pecorino asked.

"Yeah, I know who Smoke Jensen is," Fargo said.

"Would you recognize him on sight?"

"I've run acrost him a few times, 'n we've passed words."

"Are you frightened of him?"

"Am I a' scairt of 'im? No, why should I be?"

"From all I have been able to ascertain about him, he is quite formidable," Pecorino said.

"What does that mean?"

"It means that many men have tried to kill him, and many men have failed."

"Yeah? Well, I ain't never tried to kill Jensen, 'n it may just be that them as have tried to kill 'im didn't try hard enough."

"Do you think you can beat him?"

"I wouldn't even try 'n beat 'im," Fargo replied.

"Oh? I was led to believe that, perhaps, you might be someone I could count upon to . . . uh . . . perform a certain service for me."

"By performing a certain service, you mean you want me to kill Jensen for you."

"That was my intent. But if you say you won't even try . . ."

Fargo held out his hand to stop Pecorino. "You wasn't listenin' to me right. What I said was, that I wouldn't try to *beat 'im,* on account of that ain't the way you would kill somebody like Smoke Jensen. The way you would handle it is to choose a time 'n a place that he won't be suspectin' nothin'."

"In other words, you are talking about setting up an ambush for him," Pecorino said. It was a statement, not a question.

"Yeah, does that bother you? I mean the thing you want is for him to be dead, ain't it? If you are goin' to kill a man like Smoke Jensen, this here is the best way to do it."

"All right, I can't say that I disagree with you. But I feel that I should tell you that twice I have tried to have him killed, and both times, the efforts were unsuccessful."

"Unsuccessful in what way?"

"They didn't kill Jensen. Jensen killed them."

"Then they wasn't very smart, was they? How much did it cost you?"

The first two who had tried to kill Jensen had been soldiers in his army, and he paid them nothing, but he didn't make mention of that. "Fifteen hundred dollars. I gave them fifteen hundred dollars, and they failed."

"It's goin' to cost you more than that if you expect me to do the job."

"How much more?"

"Twenty-five hunnert dollars."

"That's a great deal of money."

"Look at it this way. So far you've spent fifteen hunnert dollars 'n you ain't got nothin' for your money. If you want Jensen kilt bad enough, it should be worth twenty-five hunnert dollars to you."

Pecorino drummed his fingers on the table for a long

moment. "All right," he finally agreed. "But I don't pay for failure. I will meet your price, Mr. Fargo, but only *after* you have succeeded. And," he added, "if you are successful, I will remember that, and I am sure there will be more than one opportunity for me to make use of a person of your particular talents and the proclivity for exercising same."

Fargo shook his head. "You can find things for me to do, but I have to tell you now, I ain't much for exercisin'."

Pecorino smiled. "That's quite all right," he said.

"When do you want me to do it?"

"They will be having lunch at the commandant's quarters at Fort Russell, then returning for an afternoon reception with the mayor. I tell you that, simply so that you may know where Jensen and Fontaine may be at any particular time, not with any particular suggestion that you should choose one of those two events as the time for you to carry out this task you have undertaken. As you, yourself suggested, the time and place should be of your choosing."

"Wait a minute. Are you tellin' me you want both of 'em, Jensen 'n Fontaine kilt?"

"You said you could recognize Jensen. Can you recognize Fontaine, as well?"

"Yeah, I know 'im. He's the one they call Pearlie."

"If I am going to pay twenty-five hundred dollars, I intend to get my money's worth. I wouldn't want Jensen out of the way, then wind up having to deal with Fontaine."

"All right, I'll do it. But afterward, you had better have two thousand and five hunnert dollars ready."

"Have no fear, I'll have the money."

Fargo chuckled. "You don't understand, do you?"

"What is it I don't understand?"

"I have no fear of the money not being there. You are the one who should fear the money not being there."

"Yes, I understand. And I assure you that the money will be there."

CHAPTER THIRTY-ONE

Fort Russell, located but three miles west of Cheyenne on the north bank of Crow Creek, was established in 1867. Its original purpose was to protect the workers on the Union Pacific Railway, as well as the citizens of the new town, Cheyenne, which grew from one of the railroad construction camps.

President and Lucy Hayes, their sons Birchard and Rutherford, General Sherman and daughter Rachel, Secretary Ramsey and his wife Anna were the only dignitaries of the train to make the drive out to the fort. At General Sherman's invitation, Smoke and Pearlie made the trip, as well.

They did not make the trip from town to the post alone. There was a significant army detail that accompanied them out to the post, principally, an entire company of cavalry, but also the artillery detail that had fired the salute in town when the train arrived. The gun crews were now pulling their guns on caissons behind teams of army mules. The entourage also included the army band, playing martial music along the way.

As a result of the attendant troops and band, the move from Cheyenne to the fort was, in all ways, a parade. And, as for any parade, there were many spectators because for much of the way there were people standing alongside the road or sitting in wagons pulled off the road. President Hayes, who by now was used to such things, returned the waves of all who had gathered to watch him pass.

Smoke and Pearlie were riding just behind the President's carriage, mounted on fine, spirited horses, which they had rented for the ride from the Cheyenne Livery.

Imbedded with the spectators who were standing alongside the road, was a short, swarthy man with a pock-marked face and the ear lobe of one ear missing. This was Cedric Moneypenny, though it had been almost twenty years since anyone had referred to him as such. Now he was called by the only name most people knew . . . and it was a name that caused the blood to run cold in the faint-hearted. This was the man known as Fargo.

Fargo was very fast and accurate with a pistol, and even more accurate with a rifle. And though he had killed several men in the classic face-to-face matchups, he was not a gunfighter in the traditional sense. Fargo had killed as many men with a long gun, from ambuscade, as he had killed with a pistol at close range. It wasn't that Fargo was a coward; it was that he considered himself to be a professional killer who operated from a position that provided the maximum degree of success.

"Here they come!" someone called.

"Oh, do you think the President will notice us?"

"He'll most likely just look straight ahead, but we'll be able to see him, all right."

"What's that music the band's a' playin'?"

"I don't know, but it sure is purty."

Fargo leaned out to watch the approaching entourage. He saw Jensen riding just behind the coach, on Fargo's same side of the road. He and Jensen had met a few times, and he knew that Jensen would recognize him if he saw him, so Fargo slipped back into the crowd, making certain that he kept some people between himself and Jensen.

Fargo had considered planting himself alongside the road between the fort and the town, but that was before he realized that there would be a veritable army accompanying the President and his party, or that there would be so many people lined up alongside the road to watch them pass by.

Fargo had also given some thought to following the party out to Fort Russell. It was an open post, and he would have no difficulty passing through the gate. But the fort was enclosed by a palisade wall, and if he succeeded in killing Smoke Jensen, his escape route would be limited. The President wasn't his target, but the fact that the President was present made the scrutiny much more intense. And because of the large military body, his two targets were just as well guarded as the President himself.

As a result, a situation beyond his control, he abandoned all thought of carrying out his task while Jensen and Fontaine were en route or at the fort. Pecorino had told him that there would be a reception for the Presidential party at the house of the mayor this afternoon and that meant they would have to come back from the post.

"You may have escaped me this morning, Mr. Jensen," Fargo said to himself. "But I will get you on the way back."

Fargo returned to the Gandy Dancer Saloon and sat in the back corner, nursing a beer and eschewing proffers of company from any of the bar girls. He thought about the twenty-five hundred dollars, and he smiled. He had just thrown that figure out, and would have done it for a thousand dollars. The fifteen hundred extra was all gravy.

Even as Fargo sat in the Gandy Dancer Saloon counting his as-yet unreceived money, the President of the United States and his military escort were arriving at Fort Russell. Colonel Caleb Wham, the commandant of the post, had arranged in advance for honors to be paid to the commander in chief. As a result, the entire population of the fort, except for those who were on specific work details, or who were in confinement, were drawn up in formation on the parade ground, wearing their dress uniforms. Colonel Wham called them to attention as the Presidential carriage rolled through the front gate. When the President reached the post flag pole, the driver called the team to a halt, then jumped down and ran back to open the carriage door for the President.

"Present arms!" Colonel Wham shouted at the top of his voice, and four hundred men rendered the hand salute. President Hayes who had served his own time in the army, and admirably so, returned the salute.

"Would you allow me to troop the line, Colonel?" President Hayes asked.

"It would be an honor, sir," Colonel Wham replied, and when the President passed in front of the troops, he didn't limit himself to merely trooping the line, but went into the platoons, passing between the ranks to review the individual soldiers.

Once the President finished the inspection, he returned to the front of the formation and, again, took the salute from Colonel Wham. The post commandant then turned back to the formation.

"Regiment!" he called.

"Company!" the company commanders replied, giving the supplemental commands.

"Dismissed!"

"Hurrah!" the regiment shouted in one voice.

"Mr. President, if you and your entourage would come with me, please?" Colonel Wham said, starting toward the Commandant's quarters.

This was in keeping with the purpose of the President going to the fort, which was to attend a reception hosted by Colonel Wham.

"I can't tell you how thrilled I am to host the President of the United States and the first lady," Millie Wham said enthusiastically, as the President and his party were shown into the commandant's quarters. "I just know it will be something that Caleb and I will remember for the rest of our lives!"

"What about the Secretary of War, and General Sherman?" Colonel Wham asked with a smile. "Aren't we thrilled to host them, as well?"

"What? Oh . . . oh, yes, of course, I didn't mean to . . ." Millie replied, flustered by her husband's remark. "Oh, if I have given offense."

General Sherman chuckled. "You have offended no one, Mrs. Wham. All of us who are making this trip, realize that it is the President everyone is turning out to see."

"Well, I, uh, please, make yourselves comfortable. We have coffee, tea, and some lovely pastries prepared. Just ask Private Anders or Private Lewis if you need anything," Millie said, nodding toward the two soldiers who stood by to serve.

"Oh," Rachel said a few minutes later. "I see that you have a piano. Do you play?"

"I'm afraid not, dear. That piano belonged to the wife of the previous commandant. From time to time, we will invite someone in to play. I'm sorry I didn't think to do it this time, it's just that, well, I was so excited about the prospect of hosting the President . . . uh . . . that is, all of you."

"Would you mind if I played?" Rachel asked.

"What? No, of course not . . . not at all!" Millie replied. "Why, that would be wonderful."

Rachel sat at the piano, then played through the scale once and looked around at Millie with a pleased smile.

"Why, it's in almost perfect tune," she said.

"Yes, one of the enlisted men here on the post is a piano tuner and he keeps it in tune for us."

Rachel paused for just a moment, cocked her head, then began playing, the music consisting of a single theme that wove itself through the movement like a golden thread through a rich tapestry. The music filled the parlor of the commandant's house, and everyone listened intently as they were drawn into it.

Rachel's fingers moved up and down the piano, caressing the keys rather than striking them, drawing from the soundboard a melody that filled not only the room but the souls of everyone present. The music rose and fell, expanded to full chords, then withdrew to single notes, but always, with a distinct golden theme that pulled everything together.

When she finished, the last note hung in the air for a long second before it faded away.

Pearlie was the first to break into an animated applause, and though the others were going to be somewhat more reserved in expressing their appreciation, Pearlie's enthusiasm won them over. Soon, everyone was applauding just as energetically.

"Oh, my dear," Millie Wham enthused. "I have never heard that piano played more beautifully."

"What was that song you played?" Pearlie asked.

"It was *Beethoven's Sonata 14,* better known as the *Moonlight Sonata,*" Smoke said.

"Yes!" Rachel said. "That is exactly what it was. Why, Mr. Jensen, I'm very impressed that you knew the title."

Smoke laughed. "Heavens, Miss Sherman, there is no reason to be impressed merely because someone can recognize the name of the music. It is we who are impressed with someone who can play it so beautifully. But to satisfy your curiosity, my wife loves music, and I have attended a lot of concerts with her."

* * *

Having missed his opportunity to take care of Jensen and Fontaine during the ride out to the fort, Fargo was about to concede that he may have bitten off more than he could chew. Pecorino had been very specific that President Hayes was not to be harmed, but if Jensen and Fontaine were the President's bodyguards, he didn't know when he would have the opportunity to find them separated from the President.

Despite the difficulty of the task, though, Fargo had no intention of backing out. Never, in any job he had ever pulled, had he made as much money as this job promised. And he wasn't going to walk away from it.

"The two finest horses in the Cheyenne Livery they are. 'N not just in the livery, why, what they're ridin' is the two finest horses in all of Cheyenne, if not the county itself," someone said from one of the other tables in the Gandy Dancer's Bar. "And because of that, why, I'll be raisin' the price next time someone wants to rent one of 'em."

"Egan, what the hell are you talkin' about?" the bartender asked.

"Why, I'm talkin' about Harry and Danny. You know them, Cecil, it's them two horses I bought from the Barringtons."

"Yes, I know the horses. But what do you mean you plan to raise the price of the rent?"

"Why, because of who's ridin' 'em, that's why. First of all, one of 'em is bein' rode by Smoke Jensen. You've heard of him, I reckon."

"Yes, of course I've heard of him."

"And if that wasn't enough, he's ridin' 'im alongside

the President of the United States. Him 'n that feller with him, Pearlie, his name is, rented the two horses so's they could have somethin' to ride on when they went out to the fort with the President. That makes Harry and Danny famous."

Cecil laughed. "It don't neither make 'em famous."

"Oh yeah? Well, how many other horses in town has been rode by Smoke Jensen 'n been so close to the President of the United States?"

"I suppose you do have a point there," Cecil agreed.

"I sure do. 'N as a matter of fact, you know what? I'm a' thinkin' now that maybe when they bring them horses back to the stable, I may not even charge 'em nothin'. I'll tell 'em 'cause it was an honor that the horses was rode with the President."

"Well now, Egan, that's just real generous of you," Cecil said. "Especially since you'll be making it all up by raising what you'll be chargin' all the common folk from now on."

"Yeah, it is kinda generous of me, ain't it?" Egan said, not catching Cecil's sarcasm.

Fargo had overheard the discussion when it first started, but it wasn't until he heard Smoke Jensen's name mentioned, that he actually began to pay attention. So the horses they were riding were rented, were they? That meant they would have to be brought back to the livery stable, and that was good information to know.

Pecorino stepped into the saloon then, and, after buying a beer, walked over to join Fargo at his table.

"When do you plan to take care of the job we have

discussed?" Pecorino asked. Pecorino stuck his finger down into the foam, then lifted it to his lips to suck on it.

"As soon as I can," Fargo replied. "I haven't had the chance to do it yet. There's no way I can get to them when they are surrounded by the entire U.S. Army."

Pecorino chuckled. "They are hardly surrounded by the U.S. Army, dear fellow. It was merely a ceremonial escort for the President."

"I am successful, because I am not a fool," Fargo said. "I am not going to try and go through an army to get to them. Besides, there's two of them, and there's only one of me. That means I have to be real careful. I will get the job done on my own time and in my own way."

"If there is too much of a delay, then you are of no use to me. I must get Jensen out of the way as quickly as possible. His continued presence puts into jeopardy the entire operation."

"Just Jensen? I thought you wanted both of them took care of."

"That would be ideal, of course. But from what I have learned, it is Jensen who is the most dominating character of the two men. That being the case, I am convinced that his removal would prove to be so immobilizing as to render Fontaine's role impotent."

"I don't have no idea in hell what all you just said," Fargo said. "But I believe you're tellin' me to forget about Fontaine, and just take care of Jensen."

"Yes, that is exactly what I am telling you."

"Even if he is the onliest one, it's still goin' to cost you the same amount of money as you was goin' to have to pay me for doin' the both of 'em."

"I should protest that, since you used the idea of

having two targets as justification for asking for so much money. However, since the taking of Jensen is of utter importance, and removing him alone may well accomplish the same thing, I'll not argue the point," Pecorino said.

"Just so's you don't back out on me," Fargo said.

"My dear fellow, if you accomplish the task you have been assigned, I will pay the agreed upon fee with no regrets."

Pecorino left then, and Fargo left shortly after. Listening to the liveryman talking about his two fine horses had given Fargo an idea.

CHAPTER THIRTY-TWO

Birchard and Rutherford, the President's sons, had not gone out to Fort Russell with their father and the others, but had remained in Cheyenne. The reason they hadn't gone was because they wanted to see the balloon ascension and the parachute leap. General McCook had accompanied them, while Colonel and Mrs. Barr and Captain Gutterman, who also didn't go out to the post, remained on the train.

The parachute demonstration having been completed, General McCook and the President's sons were walking back to the train.

"We used balloons during the war, didn't we, General?" Birchard asked.

"Indeed, we did," General McCook replied. "General McDowell used a balloon to perform aerial observations of enemy encampments and movements in the First Battle of Bull Run. And a balloon, with a tether and telegraph line, directed artillery onto the Rebel encampment until the shots were landing on target."

"Did they know about making parachute leaps?"

General McCook chuckled. "Why, I don't know. I suppose so, but I scarcely think they would want to leap out of a balloon. What purpose would that serve?"

"Suppose you had a lot of balloons," Birchard said, "and you floated them out over the battlefield, then, when they got behind the enemy lines, why they could make parachute leaps down to the ground, and engage the enemy from behind. It would be like cavalry of the air."

Rutherford laughed out loud. "Perhaps you should write books in the order of Jules Verne. He has written of man going to the moon. You could write of your air cavalry."

"It could happen," Birchard insisted.

As the reception for the President continued back at Fort Russell, Smoke found an opportunity to speak, quietly, with Colonel Wham.

"Colonel, have you ever heard of someone who calls himself Clemente Rex?" Smoke asked.

"Only what I've read in the papers," Colonel Wham replied. "I believe he is the odd duck who claims to be forming a new nation."

"What do you think about that?"

"I think he's insane, that's what I think."

"Have you ever heard of a place called Fort Regency?" Smoke asked.

"Fort Regency? No, I don't think so. And that's strange, I thought I knew the name of every army fort west of the Mississippi."

"Not so strange," Smoke said, "seeing as this isn't an

army fort. At least not a U.S. Army fort. Apparently, Pecorino has built his own fort."

"Pecorino?"

"Pecorino is the man who calls himself Clemente Rex."

"How do you know he has a fort?"

"Do you know Albert Barrington?"

"You're talking about the man who owns Three Mountain Ranch? Yes, I know him."

"Not too long ago, Albert Barrington was abducted from a train and taken, blindfolded, to a place that Pecorino identified as Fort Regency. According to Mr. Barrington it is run just like an army fort, with soldiers in uniform performing the duties as if they were soldiers in the regular army."

"Soldiers in uniform? Who are these men? Under whose command?"

"I'm sorry if I misled you, Colonel. When I said 'soldiers in uniform' I was referring to soldiers who had sworn their allegiance to Pecorino. And their uniforms are not the uniforms of the U.S. Army."

"Well, I'll be. No, I've never heard of such an army, or of this post, Fort Regency. Where is it? I'll send a company of men to take care of it."

"That's just it, we don't have any idea where it is. Mr. Barrington was blindfolded when he was taken there, and blindfolded when they brought him back."

"It seems strange that we have not seen this post on any of our patrols."

"Pecorino seems to be a fairly intelligent man. I

wouldn't think he would build his post anyplace where your patrols might run across it by accident."

"Well, if you're concerned about this Pecorino person starting a revolution, I wouldn't worry about it if I were you. The Confederacy couldn't do it with a million men, I'm sure Pecorino can't do it with no more men than he has."

Smoke chuckled. "I'm sure you are right."

Smoke didn't mention his concern that Pecorino might have, as his target, the abduction of the President of the United States.

Birchard, Rutherford, and General McCook returned to the Presidential Special Train, which had been pulled off the main line and parked on a side-track where it was scheduled to remain for the next twenty-four hours. Captain Gutterman, who also had not gone out to Fort Russell with the President, was in the dining car, speaking with Leslie Wilkes, the chef.

"You shall be required to prepare lunch only for the train crew," Gutterman said.

"But what about you, the President's sons, General McCook, and Colonel and Mrs. Barr?" Wilkes asked. "Won't you be eating lunch?"

"No. Even though we will not join the President at the fort, we will be dining with the others at the mayor's house."

"What about dinner, sir? Will you be here this evening?"

"Yes," Gutterman said. "We will be back for dinner."

"Very good, sir." Wilkes said. He smiled. "That will

give me an opportunity to go into town and do some shopping so I can prepare something special for dinner."

Gutterman held up a finger. "Perhaps you had better let me check with General McCook before you leave," he suggested.

"Is General McCook here? I thought I saw him leave, earlier this morning."

"He did leave, but I just saw him and the President's sons returning."

"Captain, you don't think the general will say I can't go, do you?" Wilkes asked.

"Oh, no, I'm sure it will be all right. It's just that in General Sherman's absence, General McCook is in charge, and I think he would be more comfortable knowing just where everyone is." Gutterman smiled. "Besides, I know Cheyenne, and I might even have a suggestion as to the best place for you to shop."

"All right, go see the general. In the meantime, I'll be making a list of some of the things I need," Wilkes said.

Leaving the dining car, Gutterman stepped into the car that he occupied, along with General McCook, Colonel and Mrs. Barr, as well as the President's sons, Birchard and Rutherford. Whereas the general, and Colonel and Mrs. Barr had their own roomettes, Gutterman, Birchard, and Rutherford had berths that let down for the night. No one who occupied this car had gone out to the fort for the reception, and they were all gathered in the lounge area of the car. Mrs. Barr was reading a *Harper's Magazine*.

"My goodness, would you listen to this?" Sara Sue said, addressing the others. She began to read aloud. "Suppose some clever person could discover a way to connect Mr. Alexander Bell's telephone instrument, to Mr. Edison's speaking machine. If he could do so, grandmother could call her grandchild, and if the family happened not to be in residence, grandmother could speak into Mr. Bell's instrument, her message to be recorded by Mr. Edison's machine, and played back when the family returned home."

She looked up with a broad smile. "My, what a marvelous time we live in for people to think of such clever things."

"Birch has an idea," Rutherford said in a taunting voice.

"Oh? And what is your idea?" Sara Sue asked.

"It's nothing," Birchard replied.

"Oh, but you were so sure of it," Rutherford said, barely able to contain the mockery. "Go ahead, Birch, tell us all about it."

"I said that I thought you could use balloons as an aerial cavalry," Birchard said. "I believe they could carry soldiers and drop them down onto the battlefield."

"Why, that's a marvelous idea!" Colonel Barr said.

"What? Are you serious?" Rutherford asked. "You think my brother's crazy idea has merit?"

"The difficulty of course, is in being able to make the balloon go in the direction you want," Colonel Barr replied. "But I've no doubt but the time will come when that problem has been solved."

"Yes, Captain, is there something you need?" General McCook asked, looking up to see Gutterman just standing there.

"I have given the chef his instructions. I expect that the President and his party will be back from Fort Russell within the hour. I was wondering if you had any specific instructions for me before we are to gather at the house of the mayor."

"No, nothing that I can think of," General McCook replied.

"Pearlie went out to the fort with Rachel," Birchard said. "Tell me, Captain, are you worried that he is going to get your girl?"

"I have made no claim that Miss Sherman is my girl," Gutterman replied.

Birchard laughed. "Perhaps not, but you sure have been spending a lot of time with her."

"Miss Sherman is the general's daughter. I'm just showing the respect due a young lady of her position."

"Really? Well, I'm the President's son, and you don't spend all that much time with me."

Rutherford laughed. "Ha! Is that what you want, Birch? For Captain Gutterman to spend more time with you than he does with Rachel?"

"Heaven's no!" Birchard said, speaking out so sharply that it drew a laugh from everyone, including Gutterman.

"General, Mr. Wilkes has indicated a desire to shop for something special for our dinner this evening," Gutterman said. "Has he your permission to leave the train?"

"Yes, of course he can leave the train. I have no problem with him, or with anyone else, leaving the train," General McCook replied.

"Very well, sir. And because I am familiar with Cheyenne, I have told him that I may even have some suggestions as to where he should go."

"We will see you at the mayor's home for lunch, won't we?" General McCook asked.

"Yes, General, I'll be there."

"Ha!" Birchard said. "Rachel Sherman and Pearlie are both going to be there. You don't really think the good captain is going to just stand by and let a cowboy steal her away from him, do you?"

Again, the others laughed.

CHAPTER THIRTY-THREE

Colonel Wham sent a platoon of soldiers to provide an escort for the three miles back to Cheyenne. When they reached Mayor Adams's house, Pearlie dismounted quickly to help Rachel down from the carriage.

"Why thank you, Pearlie, that was very sweet of you," Rachel said as she offered her arm. "Will you escort me into the house?"

"I, uh, have to go to the livery to turn in the horse I rented," he said.

"Here, now, Pearlie, I wouldn't want a little thing like putting away your horse to get in the way of your being a gentleman," Smoke said. "You go ahead and escort the young lady into the house. I'll take care of your horse."

"Really? Why, thank you, Smoke. I appreciate that."

"I may ask for a return favor someday," Smoke said as he took the reins to Danny, the horse Pearlie had been riding.

"Yeah, I just bet that you will," Pearlie replied with a broad smile.

Smoke rode away from the mayor's house, leading Danny.

"He is such a nice man, isn't he?" Rachel said.

"In my way of thinking, there's no better man in the world," Pearlie answered.

Fargo had been standing across the street from the livery stable for several minutes, trying to figure out the best way to climb up into the loft without being seen. He saw his chance when Egan called for two of his stable hands to help him take hay out to the horses that were being kept in the paddock out behind the livery. Fargo seized upon the opportunity thus presented.

With his Winchester rifle in his hand, Fargo hurried across the street, climbed the ladder, then moved to the wide loft door at the front of the livery. This door looked out over Central Avenue. Fargo lay down so as not to be visible to anyone below, jacked a round into the chamber of his rifle, and waited. Jensen and Fontaine had rented their mounts from the livery, which meant they would be returning the horses, and when they did he would be waiting for them.

This was a perfect setup, because he would be shooting from ambush and he was certain he could get both of them. When he first conceived the plan of ambushing from the livery loft, he realized that his only problem would be in making a rapid getaway. However, he had been studying on it during the time he had been keeping a watch from across the street, and he had formulated a plan for his escape. A stanchion protruded from the top of the loft window, to which was attached a rope and pulley. This was to facilitate lifting bales of hay into the loft. By using that same rope and pulley, Fargo realized that he could lower himself quickly, leap onto one of the two horses that would have been made available, and ride out of town.

He knew just where to go, because during the planning stages, Pecorino had told him of a small house on Wolf Creek.

"I have made this place my remote headquarters," Pecorino said. "After you have accomplished your mission, meet me there and I'll pay you."

Fargo saw two horses approaching, but was concerned to see that there was just one rider. He was relieved to see, however, that the lone rider was Smoke Jensen, and he smiled at how easy this job was going to be. Jensen had one hand on the reins of the horse he was riding, while the other hand was holding the reins of the horse he was leading.

Fargo could hardly contain his excitement. Jensen was totally unaware of Fargo, and even if he saw him at the last minute, he had both hands occupied. That meant that even someone as fast and as skilled with a gun as Smoke Jensen, would be unable to react.

"Well now, what do you know?" Fargo muttered under his breath. "You're supposed to be so great? Well you've sure got yourself into a fix now, haven't you, Mr. Jensen? This will be the easiest kill I ever made."

Fargo moved, just slightly, in order to improve his position, and raising his rifle to his shoulder, waited for the perfect shot.

It was such a small thing that most people wouldn't have even noticed it, but as Smoke drew closer to the livery, he saw a few pieces of straw tumbling down from the loft over the barn. If anyone else but Smoke had noticed such a small thing, they might have passed it off as a wind gust, or if they questioned the oddity of it, and wondered about its source, it would be nothing more than a curiosity to them.

Smoke didn't question, he reacted, and leaped down from his horse, just as he heard the crack of a rifle and saw a puff of smoke drifting from where he had seen the falling bits of hay. The bullet hummed as it passed over the saddle on a trajectory that would have hit Smoke right between the eyes, had it not been for his instinctive reaction.

By the time Smoke hit the ground he had his pistol in hand, and he squeezed off a quick shot, aimed at the lower left-hand corner of the loft window, which was where he had seen both the tumbling straw and the puff of gun-smoke.

"Damn!" Fargo said aloud as the bullet came so close to him that he could hear the pop as it passed by.

How the hell did he miss? How the hell did Jensen know to duck just as he did?

Fargo jacked another round into his rifle and fired a second time at Jensen, who was now running toward the livery. He would have been an easier target if he had run away from the livery instead of toward it. And most people would have run away. Who, but this crazy idiot, would be insane enough to run toward someone who was shooting at him?

The second shot kicked up dirt just beside the charging Smoke Jensen, and because he had to cock his rifle before he could fire again, Fargo didn't get a third shot. Jensen was now in the livery, under the floor, and out of sight.

Fargo felt something that was most unusual for him. He felt fear.

"Jensen!" he shouted. "Jensen, where are you?"

Fargo tossed his rifle aside and drew his pistol.

There was only one way for Jensen to reach the loft, and that was to climb the ladder. Fargo got behind a couple of bales of hay, which would not only conceal him from anyone who came up the ladder, but would also provide cover from gunfire.

Fargo waited.

No one appeared.

"Jensen, where are you? Come on up! Show yourself!"

Smoke was now inside the livery. He knew that if he climbed the ladder that his assailant would be waiting for him. He looked around to see if he could find an alternate way up, but saw none.

As he stared up toward the loft, he saw a little piece of straw drifting down, and he fired at the crack that had been the exit point for the straw.

"Son of a gun!" Fargo shouted as the bullet popped up from the floor. He was certain that the energy had been so spent by passing through the one-inch-thick board that it wouldn't have done much damage, but he also knew that he was now on the defensive.

And that was no place to be.

By now the gunfire had attracted Egan and his two employees back from the paddock, and they came running up to the rear door of the livery to investigate the source of the shooting.

"No!" Smoke shouted at them. "Stay back!" He waved at them with his gun hand.

The look on Egan's face changed from curiosity to fear.

"Listen to the man, boys!" Egan said, and he waved his arms to push the two men who were with him back. The three of them retreated into the paddock.

While Smoke was moving Egan and his employees to safety, he heard a creaking sound and, turning back toward the front opening saw that Fargo had used the rope and pulley to escape from the loft. On the ground now, Fargo, with a triumphant smile on his face was pointing his pistol toward a distracted Smoke.

"I've got you now, Jensen!" Fargo shouted, even as he pulled the trigger.

There were two gunshots then, so close together that they sounded as one.

Fargo missed.

Smoke didn't.

CHAPTER THIRTY-FOUR

Seth K. Sharples, the duly-elected Sheriff of Laramie County, stood looking down at Fargo's body. There were at least thirty or more citizens of the town who had gathered as well.

"You're the one that killed him?" the sheriff asked.

"Yes," Smoke replied.

"I didn't really have to ask now, did I? How many does this make? Let's see, there were the four who tried to rob the train, Ethan Dewey, them two that was out at the 123 Stable, and now this man. Do you know 'im?"

"The only name I know him by is Fargo. I can't say as I actually know him, though we have exchanged words a couple of times, though it has been a while," Smoke said.

"You said you exchanged words. Bad blood between the two of you, was there?" the sheriff asked.

Smoke shook his head. "If there was, I wasn't aware of it. I don't think we ever passed more than half a dozen words between us, and none of them harsh, as I remember."

"Well, if there wasn't no bad blood between you, why do you think he tried to kill you?"

Smoke, recalling the attack on the train, was almost certain this had something to do with him guarding President Hayes. But he was also mindful of General Sherman's admonition that everyone keep quiet about any threat there might be against the President.

"I don't have any idea."

"Sheriff, I can tell you for a fact, that it ain't this here feller's fault," one of the onlookers said, pointing to Smoke. "I seen this feller ridin' up to the livery barn, leadin' another horse behind him. Then I seen this other feller here commence a shootin' at 'im from the loft of the barn." He pointed to the body on the ground.

"I didn't see the start of it," Egan said. "But when me 'n Beans 'n Baggs heard the shootin', we come back just in time to see this feller come down from the loft 'n shoot at Mr. Jensen. Mr. Jensen was bringin' back a couple of horses he had rented, so that's why he was here. I don't have no idea what this other feller was doin' in the loft of my barn, 'cause he sure as hell didn't have my permission to be there 'n I don't even know when he clumb up."

"I've heard of Fargo, Sheriff," one of those who had gathered around the body said. "And from what I've heard, it seems he's the kind of fella that kills for hire. Or at least, he *was* that kind of fella, I mean, bein' as he's dead now."

"So you're saying that someone hired Fargo to kill Mr. Jensen?"

"More 'n likely that's the case, yes," the informative onlooker said.

"How about that, Mr. Jensen? Can you think of anyone who wants you dead enough to pay to have you killed?"

Smoke chuckled. "Sheriff, I expect there are no less

than twenty who, for one reason or another, would like to see me dead. I've lived what you might call an active life."

"Yeah," Sheriff Sharples said. "So I've heard." He sighed. "All right I guess the county has someone to bury, and given what Mr. Cox just said about Fargo, I don't expect any mourners will turn out for it."

Pecorino was one of the several onlookers who had gathered around Fargo's body. Unlike the others, though, he had not been drawn by morbid curiosity, but by commercial interest, seeing as he had a personal investment in the event. Fortunately, the investment was personal and not monetary, so even though Fargo failed to carry out his assignment, at least it didn't cost Pecorino any money.

He wasn't all that surprised to see Fargo lying dead in the street. Neither Jenner and Parker, nor Stiles and the others had succeeded, and it was probably unrealistic for him to think that Fargo would.

"Do you need me anymore, Sheriff?" Smoke asked. "If not, I have someplace I need to be."

"No, bein' as there are witnesses that saw that you were fired upon as you were riding up to the livery barn, you had every right to return fire, and that makes it justifiable homicide. I don't see any reason to get the judge involved."

"Thank you," Smoke replied.

"You come in with the President today, didn't you? I saw you when you got off the train."

"I did."

"And the mayor is holdin' some sort of reception for you folks, isn't he?"

"Yes, I'm supposed to be there now."

"Well, like I said, I got no reason to hold you. You can go on to the reception now, if you want."

"Mr. Jensen," Egan said.

Smoke laughed. "Don't worry, I'll not be leaving until I've paid the rent for these two mounts. They are both might fine horses, by the way."

"Yes, sir, well that's just it. I don't plan on chargin' you nothin' for these horses 'cause I figure what with you ridin' 'em alongside the President, 'n then especially what with you killin' some feller was tryin' to kill you, that's goin' to make the livery stable famous, 'n draw in a lot more business. Can I tell folks that you said the horses was good animals?"

"Yes, of course you can," Smoke replied.

Egan smiled. "I plan to put me a sign sayin' just that on the stalls where I keep Danny and Harry."

The mayor's house was on the opposite end of Central Avenue from the livery, and Smoke caught a ride with a passing freight wagon, in order to return.

"I very much appreciate the ride," Smoke said as he hopped down from the wagon in front of the mayor's house.

"You're mighty welcome," the good-natured driver replied. "Who knows, someday I might need a ride and you'll come by, driving a freight wagon, and offer one to me."

Smoke chuckled at the response, then walked up to the

front door of the mayor's house. His knock on the door was opened by a servant who escorted Smoke into the house.

"Smoke!" Pearlie called, hurrying over to greet him. "I was beginning to think that maybe you weren't coming."

"I had a little adventure," Smoke said, telling Pearlie about the incident with Fargo.

"We've run across Fargo a few times before without ever having any trouble before," Pearlie said after Smoke concluded the story. "I wonder what put a burr under his saddle this time?"

"I'm not sure," Smoke replied. "I have the feeling that he might have been acting as a paid assassin, but, unlike the four men who attacked us on the train, Fargo didn't have one red cent in his pocket."

"Which eliminates it from having anything to do with the President's trip," Pearlie said.

Smoke shook his head. "Not necessarily. It could be that Pecorino learned his lesson last time, and decided he wouldn't pay until the job is completed."

"Yeah, that makes sense," Pearlie said.

Smoke smiled. "Your young lady over there looks like she's pining away, waiting for you to return."

"Yeah," Pearlie replied with a chuckle. "She does, doesn't she? Maybe I should go over to comfort her."

"Maybe you should. But remember, Pearlie," Smoke cautioned, "not a word about what happened."

"I won't say a word," Pearlie promised.

"From everything I've heard about Smoke Jensen he is a man who can handle himself in almost any situation,"

Pecorino said. "And that's not only from hearsay, now we have a couple of actual events from which we can draw our conclusion. The failed operation on the train, and the failure of Mr. Fargo to do the job."

"Are you going to make another try?" Guittiere asked.

"I was hoping I could get him eliminated," Pecorino replied. "I think it would go easier without him, but I can't waste any more time with him. As I'm sure you understand, the success of this plan is time dependent, and in order to stay on schedule, I must move forward."

"What about the other plan? The one in which I am involved. Do you still intend to go forward with it?"

"Yes, absolutely. The fact that Mister Fargo failed to do his job, does not eliminate the need for the next step, for one plan is not dependent upon the success of the other. On the contrary, the next operation is all the more import because Fargo failed."

"Is everything all set up?"

"Yes, Moss and the others have made all the arrangements and are prepared. You are responsible for putting the plan into operation."

"I am responsible, yes. It is a great responsibility, and as I said before, considering both the circumstances, and what I have to lose, I will be doing this at a great personal risk."

"That is true, the responsibility, and the risk are great," Pecorino said. "But no worthy goal is attained without risk."

"Yes, the reward is great," Guittiere agreed. "And were that not so, I would not have agreed to the plan. But don't worry, I won't let you down."

"I hope that you do not fail, for indeed, the future of a

nation now rides upon this very task." Pecorino smiled. "You will be written of in our history books."

"Where's John?" Rachel asked, looking around the large parlor where the mayor's guests were gathered.

"Maybe he decided not to come," Pearlie replied. He flashed a big smile toward Rachel. "I guess you'll just have to spend all your time with me."

"Oh? You don't really expect me to spend all my time with you, do you?"

"Well, if Gutterman doesn't get here, who else will you spend time with?" Pearlie replied.

"Don't worry, Captain Gutterman will be here," Sara Sue Barr said. "While we waited on the train this morning, he told the rest of us that he knew Cheyenne quite well, so he went with Mr. Wilkes shopping for our dinner this evening. I'm sure that between the two of them, they will come up with quite a pleasant surprise."

"John and Mr. Wilkes went shopping together? Knowing John and how gregarious he is and how particular Mr. Wilkes is, wouldn't you love to be able to see that shopping excursion without being observed?" Rachel asked, with a little laugh.

"I'm afraid I can think of a few other things I'd rather do than spend time watching Gutterman," Pearlie replied. "Like having a tooth pulled, for example."

Rachel laughed out loud. "Oh, Pearlie, you are awful!"

"Captain Gutterman, there you are," Colonel Barr said, his booming welcome heard all over the room.

"Well, the wait is over," Pearlie said.

As Captain Gutterman came into the room, the others turned toward him with greetings of their own.

"I do hope that your tardiness is offset by something you helped the chef find for our dinner this evening," Colonel Barr said.

"Even as we speak, Chef Wilkes has a nice buffalo hump roasting," Captain Gutterman said. "I'm sure you will all be very pleased."

"Oh! How marvelous! I've never tasted buffalo," Rachel said. She glanced toward Pearlie. "I expect you have eaten buffalo often."

"Yes, I have. I think you'll enjoy it. Was that your suggestion, Captain?"

Gutterman nodded. "Yes, it was. As you know, I spent my youth in the West, and I had buffalo often. However, it has been a long time since I've eaten it, and I am very much looking forward to it. Also, I thought it would be a treat for the others."

Pearlie smiled. "That was a good idea, Captain. Yes, sir, it was a very good idea."

"Thank you," Gutterman replied, smiling at the unexpected compliment. "Oh, by the way, how was your visit to the fort?"

"It was great," Pearlie said. "It's too bad you weren't there. Why, I'll just bet you didn't know that Rachel can play the piano. And when I say she can play the piano, I'm not talking about someone like you might hear in a saloon. I mean it's like going to one of those real fancy concerts like Miz Sally's loves to go to."

"I've heard her play. She is quite talented," Captain Gutterman replied.

"You two men are just too kind," Rachel said, flashing a huge smile to both Pearlie and Captain Gutterman.

Across the room from the young people, Sara Sue Barr laughed, then leaned over to speak privately to Helen Ramsey.

"Would you look at the way Rachel Sherman is managing those two young men?"

"Yes," Helen replied. "And the funny thing is, neither of them realizes they are being handled."

"Which of the two will she wind up with, do you suppose?" Sara Sue asked.

"Oh, to be honest, I doubt very much that she will wind up with either one of them. I think that they are just temporary travel amusements for her. After all, she is a most attractive young lady, and what can be more fun than playing a young man with as much skill as she plays the piano? Don't you remember your own youth?" Helen asked.

"Oh, heavens, that was so long ago," Sara Sue replied.

"Dear, some things a woman never forgets," Helen said, and both ladies laughed.

CHAPTER THIRTY-FIVE

Pearlie, not wanting to be perceived as competing with Gutterman for the attention of a woman that he knew he would never see again after this trip, drifted away from them to interact with the others at the reception. Smoke, General Sherman, Mayor Adams, and Judge Craig were in an animated conversation that stilled as Pearlie approached.

"That's all right, we can talk in front of Pearlie," Smoke said to the others. "He knows about it, because I told him as soon as I got back."

"If the sheriff is satisfied, I am as well," Judge Craig said, resuming the conversation. Judge Craig was one of the mayor's guests for the reception. "I'm just sorry that it happened while the President is in town. I wouldn't want him to get the idea that we are a town and county without law and order. I am one of the many Wyoming citizens who want our territorial government to petition Washington for statehood."

"I don't think a thing like this would have any negative influence on statehood," General Sherman said. "Why, it could happen anywhere, New York, Chicago, St. Louis."

"Yes, I'm certain there have even been shootings in Washington, D.C.," Mayor Adams said.

"You are quite right about that," General Sherman replied.

There was the sound of a bell being struck.

"Mr. President, Mrs. Hayes, ladies and gentlemen, luncheon is being served," a woman's voice said.

"I must say, Mr. Mayor," Judge Craig offered, "Mrs. Adams seems to have everything under control."

"Yes," Mayor Adams replied. "Grace Ann loves these sort of things. To host the President of the United States? She is absolutely loving every moment of it."

When they gathered for the luncheon, Pearlie purposely chose a seat away from Rachel, surrendering to a very attentive Gutterman, who was sitting just to her right. "You're giving up, are you?" Smoke asked.

"Nothing to give up," Pearlie replied.

"You're probably right . . . I mean, I can't see her moving West, and I sure can't see you moving to Washington. But she is a pretty, young woman, I will give you that."

"I just hate to think of Gutterman winding up with her," Pearlie said. "There's something about him that I don't like."

"I wouldn't worry about that, if I were you. I'd be willing to lay odds that, after this trip, Gutterman will never see her again."

"Really? Now you're going to make me feel sorry for him."

CHAPTER THIRTY-SIX

"Rachel, I'm about to return to the train to check on the chef," Captain Gutterman said later, after the luncheon was over. He smiled. "Perhaps you are enjoying these long, drawn-out receptions, but if you aren't, I would be glad to escort you back to the train."

"How very perceptive of you, John," Rachel said. "Yes, I believe I would like to return to the train. Oh, do you think Chef Wilkes would let me taste the buffalo in advance?"

"I'm sure he would. He and I have become friends. I'll insist that he honor your request."

"Oh, good. Yes, by all means, let's return to the train now. Before we leave though, if you'll excuse me, I'll have to tell Papa that I'm going. That is unless you want to tell him."

"No, thank you," Captain Gutterman replied. "I am the lowest ranking person on this entire trip, and I've been around generals and colonels enough."

Rachel laughed. "All right, if my father frightens you, I'll go see him myself."

"I'll wait right here," Gutterman said, pointing to the floor beneath his feet.

Leaving Captain Gutterman at his self-assigned spot, Rachel looked for her father and found the general standing near the punch bowl table, just observing the ebb and flow of the reception.

"Hello, dear," General Sherman said, greeting his daughter with a smile.

"Hello, Papa."

"Are you enjoying the reception?"

"It's been very nice," Rachel said. "But now, if you don't mind, I would like to return to the train."

"Oh? Why?"

"I'm sort of out of place. There aren't any other single young women to talk to; in fact, I am quite the youngest here. If I left now, I don't think that either the President or the mayor would take offense." She chuckled. "In fact, I don't think either of them would even notice my absence."

"I don't know," General Sherman replied. "I'm a little reluctant to let you walk back by yourself, under the circumstances."

"Circumstances?" Rachel said. "What circumstances?"

The general was thinking not only about the incident on the train the night before, but also about the information Smoke had shared about the shootout at the livery. He didn't want to mention either of those, specifically though, so he made the "circumstances" more general.

"Yes, circumstances. You were present in the dining car when we introduced Mr. Jensen and Mr. Fontaine, and you know the reason they are with us," General Sherman said. "However, I suppose I could ask Mr. Fontaine if he would walk you back to the train."

"There's no need for that, Papa. John will take me back to the train," Rachel said.

"Captain Gutterman is leaving, as well?" Sherman asked.

"Yes, he has to check with the chef about dinner this evening. We are having roasted buffalo," she said excitedly.

"Rachel, I know you have been seeing a lot of Captain Gutterman since we began this trip . . ."

"And Pearlie," Rachel added with a broad smile.

"Yes, and Mr. Fontaine. You are a very attractive young woman, and as such, you are going to draw attention from a lot of young men. I just don't want you to be hurt."

Rachel laughed. "Papa, I can only be hurt if I invest more into the relationship than the pleasant passing of time. And believe me, that is all this is."

"But that brings up another question. What are these two men investing in you? I mean if they seem to show more than a casual interest, can you handle it?"

"Papa, young women have been 'handling' young men since the beginning of time. Don't worry. I'm perceptive enough not to let it get out of hand, neither with me, nor with John or Pearlie."

General Sherman put his hand on his daughter's shoulder. "I know that you are. All right, come along, I'll speak with your young captain."

By now Pearlie had joined Captain Gutterman and they were standing together when Rachel and her father approached them.

"Captain Gutterman, Rachel has expressed a wish to return to the train, and I understand that you have offered to walk back with her."

"Yes, sir, I have offered to walk Rachel . . . that is, Miss Sherman back to the train." Gutterman laughed. "As a mere captain, I'm afraid that I feel very much out of place here anyway."

"All right, Captain, I appreciate you looking after my daughter. But Rachel, for my own peace of mind, please stay with the young captain, and don't leave the train until I get back."

"Oh, but what is the fun of coming West if I don't get to enjoy any of the towns? So far I've seen nothing but railroad depots in any of them."

"I tell you what," Pearlie said. "When this reception is over, and I get back to the train, I'd be willing to take you around town. Uh, that is, with the general's permission, of course."

"I think that would be fine," General Sherman said.

Rachel glanced at Captain Gutterman, before she responded.

"Yes, I think it would be very nice to have Pearlie show me the town," Rachel said, flashing a large smile toward Pearlie.

"You're sure it wouldn't be out of place?" Pearlie asked.

"Out of place?"

Pearlie looked directly toward Captain Gutterman. "I mean with 'the young captain' and all." Having overheard the general's comment, he mimicked it now.

"Well, I mean if you would rather not do it," Rachel said.

"No, no, I'll be glad to do it," Pearlie said.

"Good. I'll be waiting patiently. John, your arm?" Rachel said, offering her arm to the "young captain."

With a triumphant smile toward Pearlie, Captain Gutterman extended his arm, then walked Rachel to the front door.

Pearlie watched Rachel and Captain Gutterman leave, then turned to see that Smoke had come up to join them.

"I'm not going to lose my best man now, am I, Pearlie?" Smoke asked.

"What? No, what do you mean?"

"You're not planning to run off somewhere with the general's daughter?"

"No, I'm just . . . being nice, is all."

"You know what I think?" Smoke asked.

"What's that?"

"I believe the beautiful general's daughter may be playing you and Gutterman against each other."

"Maybe to get Gutterman," Pearlie said.

"Where's your confidence, Pearlie? How do you know she's not playing Gutterman to get you?"

"You just said why," Pearlie replied.

"I just said why?"

"You called her the 'general's daughter' didn't you?"

"Yes."

"That's why."

"I see what you mean."

Shortly after Rachel left, Mrs. Adams approached the President's wife with a guitar.

"Mrs. Hayes, I have read that you play the guitar, and that you have a beautiful voice. I know this is a terrible imposition on you, but I also know that everyone would be just thrilled if you would sing something for us."

"Ha!" President Hayes said. "You're right, Lucy does have a beautiful voice, and she does play the guitar. But trust me, Mrs. Adams, you aren't imposing on her. Lucy has been known to sing, anytime she can find someone to listen to her."

"Rutherford," Lucy said. If she was chastising him, it was in a voice that was so soft, and so without challenge, that any chastisement was lost.

For the next several minutes the First Lady of the land entertained everyone with a concert of songs, from bouncing little tunes that brought a smile, to more-melancholy songs that caused everyone to give pause to think about the words and music.

She had just finished a song when the front door to the mayor's house was pushed open, and Captain Gutterman staggered in. His uniform was soiled and torn, and his hair was in disarray, and he was holding his hand to the back of his head.

"Captain Gutterman!" General Sherman said. "What happened to you? Where is Rachel?"

"She's gone, General," Captain Gutterman said.

"Gone? Gone where?"

"I don't know, sir. We were on the way back to the train, just talking, and someone stepped out from the corner of a building and hit me on the head. When I came to later, whoever it was that hit me was gone, and Miss Sherman was gone, as well."

"Good Lord, Captain, and you did nothing?" General McCook responded in a sharp and condemning voice.

"I . . . there was nothing I could do," Captain Gutterman said. "As I said, I was knocked unconscious, and when I came to, Rachel was gone."

"Who would do such a thing?" General Sherman asked.

"Someone must have recognized her from the little talk she gave when the train arrived," Mrs. Adams said.

"But, what would that have to do with it?" General Sherman asked.

"Ransom, General," President Hayes said. "It could just as easily have been one of my sons. But your daughter was available, and obviously vulnerable."

"Vulnerable, yes," General Sherman replied. He glared at Captain Gutterman. "I hold you responsible for that, Captain. You were charged with the mission of getting my daughter safely back to the train. And you failed."

"I . . ."

"General Sherman, I know you are upset," President Hayes said. "But let's not be too quick to assign the blame."

General Sherman pinched the bridge of his nose, and closed his eyes for a long moment. Finally, with a sigh, he took his hand down and spoke to Gutterman.

"The President is right, Captain," Sherman said. "It wasn't your fault. Please forgive me."

"Nothing to forgive, General," Gutterman said. "You are her father. It is perfectly understandable."

"I'll tell you what, General, we will stop our Western tour right here. This train will not proceed one mile farther until Rachel is safely returned."

"Thank you, Mr. President. I appreciate that."

By now everyone at the reception, including the mayor,

knew that General Sherman's daughter had been taken, and all, including the mayor, were standing around in open-mouthed shock.

"Oh, what a terrible thing to happen," Mrs. Adams lamented.

"And in our town," another said.

"You saw nothing?" Smoke asked of Captain Gutterman.

Gutterman shook his head. "I don't remember a thing until I came to on the ground. Then I realized that Rachel was no longer with me. She had been taken."

"Mayor Adams, may I request that you get the sheriff and the city marshal on this as quickly as possible?" General Sherman asked. "I want my daughter returned, safely, to me!"

"General Sherman, it might be best not to involve anyone else yet. At least, not at this point. I think we should keep this incident as secret as we can," Smoke suggested.

General Sherman ran his hand through his hair. "But this is my daughter we are talking about."

"Give me twenty-four hours to see what I can come up with," Smoke said.

"She could be dead in twenty-four hours."

"I don't think so. If they wanted her dead, she would already be dead. Whoever took her has something else in mind, and whatever it is, they will need to keep her alive."

"I think Mr. Jensen is right, Bill," the President said. "I think that Rachel, and we, would be best served if this entire incident is kept secret."

"All right," General Sherman agreed, reluctantly. "But

if we haven't found her in twenty-four hours, I intend to get every soldier at Fort Russell involved."

Several were standing around now, in shock and concern over what had happened, and President Hayes turned toward them, then lifted his hands to get their attention.

"I'm sure all of you know, now, that Rachel has disappeared, and we fear that she has been taken by someone. Mr. Jensen believes that the chances of successfully recovering our dear Rachel would be improved by keeping this whole thing a secret. So far her disappearance is known only by those of us in this room and whoever it is that took her.

"So, I'm going to ask, now, that everyone here take a vow of secrecy. Please say nothing to anyone. Rachel's life may depend upon it." The President looked over toward the mayor. "Mayor Adams, I'm going ask that you, your wife, and your employees take that same vow."

"You have our promise, Mr. President," the mayor replied.

"Just find her, Smoke," General Sherman said, the pleading obvious in his tone of voice. "Please find her, and bring her back safely."

"We will," Pearlie promised. "We'll find her, General. You don't need to worry about that."

CHAPTER THIRTY-SEVEN

When Rachel came to, she had no idea where she was or how she had gotten here. She remembered only feeling a hand pressed across her nose and mouth, then she inhaled a cloying smell, grew dizzy, and passed out.

At the moment she was tied, hand and foot, to a long bench, in a small room. She was looking at a wall, and turning her head to the left and right could see only the adjoining walls. There were no windows and no doors that she could see.

"Hello?" she called. "Hello? Is anyone here?"

The door opened and a well-dressed man stepped into the room.

"So, Miss Sherman, you are awake, I see." The well-dressed man came around to stand in front of her.

"Who are you? Where am I? How did I get here?"

"You do seem to be full of questions," the man said.

"Wouldn't you be, if you had awakened to find yourself in a strange place with no idea as to how you got there?"

The man chuckled. "I suppose you do have a point, my dear. And I must say, I do admire your composure. I didn't know what we would get, and was fully prepared for a screaming, crying prisoner."

"Prisoner? So you admit that I am your prisoner?"

"What else would you call yourself? You did not come here of your own accord, so yes, I would say that you are a prisoner."

"What about the questions I asked?"

"Yes, well, I shall take them in order. I am Clemente Pecorino. You are in a temporary holding facility for now, brought here by some men who are under my command. Soon you will be taken to Fort Regency, where I am the commandant."

"You are the commandant of Fort Regency? I've never heard of such a fort. Where is that?"

"Oh, it's quite near here," Pecorino replied.

"By what right have you brought me here? Is it because our itinerary did not include this fort you speak of?"

"Oh, no, under the circumstances, I don't think a visit to Fort Regency would be appropriate."

"But, you plan to take me there?"

"I do."

"Against my will?"

"Yes."

"What if I refuse to go?"

"I'm afraid you have no choice. You will be my guest at Fort Regency."

"Surely you know that my father is the Commanding General of the U.S. Army. If you are the commandant of this fort that you are speaking of, then you are under my father's command, and I demand that you release me at once."

"Oh, but I am not under your father's command."

"What are you talking about? Everyone in the U.S.

Army is under my father's command," Rachel insisted. "He is the commanding general of the entire army."

"Ah, my dear, but as Hamlet says, *therein lies the rub*," Pecorino said. "Because you see, I am not in the U.S. Army. I am the Supreme Commander of the Army of Nova Amerigo Regnum. I am also the king of that nation."

"You're a king? King of Nova Ameri . . . Ameri . . . whatever that is you said. What nation is that? I've never heard of such a place."

"The nation is Nova Amerigo Regnum," Pecorino said, slowly enunciating the words. "Your father and the President of the United States, as well as every other official of the U.S. government on that train, could have been guests, if they had but followed international protocol. They did not, and as a result, they are illegal trespassers."

"International protocol? What are you talking about?"

"They should have applied for permission to cross the border into my kingdom, and had they done so, I would have gladly extended all the courtesies due from the leader of one nation to the leader of another."

"What do you mean illegal trespassers? Mr. Pecorino, you aren't making a lick of sense. We aren't in a foreign country. We are in Wyoming!"

"I must ask that you call me King Clemente. And while this was Wyoming when it was a part of the United States, Wyoming no longer exists. What was once Wyoming is now but a non-specific geographic land area located in the Kingdom of Nova Amerigo Regnum."

Rachel stared at Pecorino as if he had lost his mind. It wasn't until then that she remembered Captain Gutterman.

"John! Where is Captain Gutterman, the man who was

with me?" Rachel asked. "Is he here, as well? What have you done with him?"

"He is none of your affair."

"Did you kill him?"

"No, we didn't kill him, nor did we find it necessary to take him as our prisoner, for he would serve absolutely no purpose. You, on the other hand, are, as you have been so anxious to inform me, the daughter of the commanding general of the entire army of the United States. I think that he, and even the President, would go to great lengths to secure your release. Not so, however, for your escort, so we let him go."

"You let him go free?"

"Yes, why not? He is but a small player upon the drama of the birth of a new nation. We are patriots, founding fathers, you might say." Pecorino smiled. "One hundred years from now, school children of Nova Amerigo Regnum will study us, and they will revere our names."

"Why did you take me? What are you going to do with me?"

"You, my dear, are what you might call leverage. You are going to play an instrumental role in the liberation of my new kingdom."

"My God," Rachel said, shaking her head. "You are insane."

To her surprise Pecorino, instead of growing angry over her charge, laughed.

"I suppose, in a way, I am slightly insane," Pecorino replied. "But in great men the line that separates insanity from brilliance is quite narrow. And it is often difficult to ascertain upon which side of the line that great man stands."

"So now, you are calling yourself a great man?"

"The designation of greatness, I suppose, requires a qualitative analysis from someone who has the advantage of historical perspective. It may well be that now, in this time, an objective observer could declare me insane, but I propose to you, Miss Sherman, the thesis that there can be no objective observer in our time.

"No. It will be one hundred years from now, well into the twentieth century, before an objective study can be done that will recognize my true genius. And of course, due to the fact that I will be recognized as the founder of a kingdom that has taken its place among the nations of the world, I have no fear that I will be so adjudged."

"Please, I beg of you, let me go."

"You will be free of me soon, Miss Sherman, one way or the other."

"Here," Gutterman said. He had led Smoke, Pearlie, and General Sherman to the corner of Evans and 18th Streets. "We got this far, I think."

"Why in the world did you come this way if you were going back to the train?" Smoke asked. "This is at least three blocks out of the way. Why didn't you just come on down Central?"

"Under the circumstances, I mean with a threat against the President, I thought that taking a more circuitous route back to the train would be the safest way," Gutterman replied. "Someone made an attack on the train last night and, thanks to the two of you, he failed. But I was afraid someone might make another try, and who would be a better target, and an easier target, than the general's daughter?"

"He may have a point there, Smoke," Pearlie agreed.

"Thank you," Gutterman said.

Pearlie nodded. "We may be rivals for her interest but equal in our concern for her safety. I know you wouldn't consciously do anything to put her in danger."

"All right, maybe you do have a point. But I still want you to tell me what happened," Smoke said.

"I wish I could tell you," Captain Gutterman said in all sincerity. "But all I can say is that when we got right here, someone stepped out from this alley, and struck me over the head. It must have knocked me out, because when I came to, Miss Sherman was gone."

"You didn't see who hit you?" Pearlie asked.

"No."

"If you didn't see him, how do you know he came out from that alley?" Smoke asked.

"Oh. Well, that's a good question," Gutterman replied. "I suppose I just guessed that he came from the alley. The truth is, I saw no one, so I don't have any idea what happened. But someone did step up behind me, and whoever it was hit me on the head."

Smoke nodded. "All right, I guess I can understand that," he agreed.

"If you don't need me any longer, I would like to go back to the train," Gutterman said. He put his hand to the back of his head. "Whoever hit me, gave me quite a blow, and I'm still dizzy."

"Yes, go ahead, we'll take it from here," Smoke replied.

"I'll go with you," General Sherman said. "If they are holding my daughter, they may try and get hold of me, and they would expect me to be at the train. I wouldn't want to miss any attempt at contact."

"No, nor would I want you to," Smoke replied. "I think you are right. I think you should return to the train. But I would feel better if one of you were armed, so . . ." Smoke held out his hand toward the general, and there was a pistol in his hand.

"I can't take your gun," the general said. "I can't leave you unarmed while you are searching for the brigands who did this."

Smoke smiled. "This is my holdout gun," he said. He patted the pistol at his side. "I'm still armed."

As General Sherman and Captain Gutterman walked away, Smoke and Pearlie stayed at the site where Rachel had been taken. Pearlie began to examine the alley where the assailant or assailants had waited. Smoke looked around on the street.

"Whoever did it, they're damn good," Pearlie said.

"Why do you say that?" Smoke asked.

"Look around. Do you see any sign of where anyone was? If they waited back here for even five minutes, they would have left something to show they were here, but there is nothing . . . not even so much as a footprint."

"Maybe they wiped it away," Smoke suggested.

"They would have had to do that after they took the girl. And you'd think they would have wanted to get her out of here as fast as they could."

"Yes," Smoke said. "And the only way they could have done that would be to put her in a vehicle of some sort, a closed wagon, a cart, something that would make it easy for them to carry."

"And to hide," Pearlie said.

"If they did that, wouldn't the wagon have to be standing by somewhere, waiting. And I sure don't see anything to indicate that."

"I don't either," Pearlie agreed. "Do you think maybe the captain is confused as where they were?"

"I think that is a distinct possibility," Smoke replied.

Chapter Thirty-Eight

As Rachel sat, tied to a bench in the small cabin where she had been taken, she thought of the strange man who called himself a king. He told her that she had been taken for leverage, to be used in establishing his kingdom. She had read stories about such madmen, but she always thought they were just stories. She had no idea that such a person could actually exist.

Pecorino had left just a few minutes ago, and Rachel assumed that she now alone. But because her back was to most of the room, she had no way of really knowing. She had tried to turn the bench around so she could see, but the bench was too long and she was unable to do so. She was equally as unsuccessful in freeing herself from the ropes that had her bound.

Was she actually alone? She couldn't get over the tingling sensation on the back of her neck that suggested someone was in the room with her, but when she called out, there was no answer. And she had heard nothing, no movement, not even the sound of someone breathing.

She had just about come to the conclusion that she was alone, then someone spoke to her.

"Are you actually the daughter of General Sherman?"

This was not Pecorino's voice, this was a voice that she had not heard before.

"Who are you?" Rachel asked.

"Is that true?"

"Please, come around so I can see you. I don't like speaking to disembodied voices."

To Rachel's surprise, her response was met with a laugh.

"Disembodied voice, oh, that is quite a delightful elucidation." There was a decided English accent to the voice.

"Please, come around so I can see you," Rachel said again, this time her voice more beseeching than demanding.

"Very well, Miss Sherman, I shall do so."

The man who stepped in front of her was a short man with dark hair and a goatee. He rubbed his finger along the mustache in what Rachel was sure was a subconscious move.

"Now that I am here so that you can see me, will you answer my question? Are you the daughter of General Sherman?"

"Yes, I am. My name is Rachel. Are you an Englishman?"

"Oh, that is most astute of you, my dear. Yes, I am Sir Richard Barrington, late of England, but now a resident of the United States." Richard held up the finger that had been stroking his mustache. "Please notice that I said I am a *resident* of, and not a citizen of, the United States. Though, if everything goes as planned, I shall be a subject of the new kingdom of Nova Amerigo Regnum."

"Oh," Rachel said, resignedly. "That means you are as crazy as the other man. What was his name? Pecorino?"

"Crazy? No, inspired perhaps, but not crazy."

"What is going to happen to me?" Rachel asked.

"Nothing is going to happen to you if your father co-operates with our demand."

"What demand? Money? Papa is a general and I suppose you could even say that he is famous. But, as Papa says, the only military officers and politicians who get rich are the crooked ones. Papa is as honest as they come, and he has very little money. So if you are holding me for ransom, I'm afraid you are going to be very disappointed."

"You misunderstand. The ransom that we demand has nothing to do with money."

"Then what do you want?"

"Official recognition of Nova Amerigo Regnum as a new nation."

"And you think holding me will get that? Why, you are as insane as that other man, the one who calls himself king."

Richard shook his head. "You don't understand, you, alone, won't bring about recognition of our status. You are but the first step."

"You're crazy," Rachel said again. "You are both madmen."

Richard chuckled. "Perhaps so. But there is method to our madness. We will try and make you as comfortable as we can while you are our guest."

When Richard stepped back outside, he saw Pecorino with two of the men of his "army." Neither of them were wearing the distinctive uniform. Instead, they were dressed as farmers.

There was also a farm wagon there, loaded with hay. Beneath the pile of hay was a long narrow box that could be closed off, then concealed by the hay. It had been this wagon that transported Rachel from where she had been taken.

"Put her in the wagon and take her out to the fort," Pecorino ordered.

"Yes, sir," Moss replied.

Moss and a man named Abernathy, a recent recruit, went into the cabin and returned a moment later with Rachel.

"Get in there," Moss ordered, pointing to the compartment that had been constructed under the pile of hay.

"What? You really think I'm going to get in there?"

"I don't think you are, I know you are," Pecorino said. "Gag her," he ordered.

"What? No, I . . ."

The only sound that issued from her mouth after those three words was a barely audible squeak. The gag, consisting of a cloth tied around her mouth, was very efficient.

Pecorino and Richard watched the wagon drive away.

"Do you really think General Sherman will deliver the others to us to retrieve his daughter?" Richard asked.

"I shall demand of the general that he deliver the Secretary of War and his wife, as well as the President and his family to me, in order to have his daughter returned. But the general, being a man of honor and resolve will, no doubt, refuse."

"You mean, you expect him to refuse?" Richard asked, surprised by the response.

"I do, indeed."

"If you don't think General Sherman is going to accede to your demand, why did you take his daughter?"

"I intend to use the young lady as a demonstration of our resolve. If General Sherman refuses to deliver the others, as I'm sure he will, then I will return his daughter to him."

"Then I don't understand. If you are going to return his daughter to him, what have you accomplished?"

"As I told you, she will be a demonstration of our resolve. I will return his daughter to him . . . dead."

Richard gasped. "You are going to kill her?"

"We are engaged in a revolutionary war. Admittedly, it is a war unique among wars, but it is a war, nonetheless. And, in war, people die. The tragedy is when the deaths are of no particular purpose. But the death of this young lady, the daughter of America's most famous general, lamentable as it may be, will have a significant effect in accomplishing the goals of our revolution. But, by showing our firmness of purpose, I believe that we will be able to come to a rapprochement with the United States government, that will grant us our independence." Pecorino smiled, triumphantly. "And consider this. My name will go down as accomplishing one of the most bloodless revolutions in the annals of history."

"How do you plan to deliver your demand to the general?" Richard asked.

"Why, I intend to use you, of course."

"Me?"

"Yes. You are estranged from your brother, but, as yet, your association with me is not known. That provides you with freedom of motion, and it will allow you to take a letter from me to the general."

"How am I to explain that I have the letter?"

"You can say that it was delivered to you by a messenger that you don't know."

Richard was quiet for a moment.

"Oh, for heaven's sake, Sir Richard, you won't be in any danger. You can still maintain a separation between us. In fact, your continued 'separation' from Nova Amerigo Regnum makes you all the more valuable to us."

"All right," Richard said. "I'll deliver the letter."

"Before you go, I must tell you that we have an ally within their very midst. I think you should make contact with him before you deliver the letter, though do so in a way that does not compromise his position."

"Who is this contact?"

"He is an army officer who wishes a rapid promotion to general," Pecorino said. "We have been using the name Jean Guittiere in all of our communications, but that is merely to protect his real identity. His real name is Captain John Gutterman."

"Richard!" Albert said joyfully. "You have come back!"

"Yes," Richard said. "Albert, Pearlie was right. I was stealing cattle, and I come to you now to apologize and beg your forgiveness."

"Nonsense," Albert said. "The cattle were half yours anyway. No forgiveness is necessary. You are my prodigal brother, and I would be fully prepared to kill a fatted calf . . . if you have left any," he added with a laugh.

"Albert, I . . ."

"Hush," Albert said, holding up his hand. "I was teasing you, Richard. I truly welcome you back. We are brothers, and being brothers is a relationship that never ends."

Albert spread his arms, and the two men embraced.

"Albert," Richard said a moment later. "Do you still have contact with Smoke Jensen?"

"Yes, I saw him only this morning, when the President arrived in Cheyenne."

"Then it is true, he is guarding the President?"

"Yes, he and Pearlie are."

"I need you to take me to him."

"Well, I don't know if he is still in Cheyenne. The President's train may have left."

"The train is still there. They won't be going anywhere for a while," Richard said.

"Oh? I hadn't heard that."

"Please, Albert, it is very important. You must take me at once to see Smoke Jensen."

"All right, if it's that important to you," Albert said. He smiled again. "And while we're there, we'll have dinner at the Cattlemen's Club to celebrate our reconciliation."

CHAPTER THIRTY-NINE

The sun had already dipped below the Seminole Mountain Range when Albert and Richard Barrington approached the Presidential train that was parked on a side track.

"Good, there are Smoke and Pearlie standing outside the train. We won't have to go on board to look for them. Smoke!" Albert called.

Smoke and Pearlie were in an intense conversation, but Smoke looked up when he was hailed.

"Hello, Albert," he called. Though his expression registered some surprise at seeing Richard with him, Smoke said nothing about it.

"My brother has come home," Albert said, happily. "And to celebrate, we are going to have dinner at the Cattlemen's Club. We would like for you and Pearlie to join us."

"Pearlie, I owe you as much of an apology as I do my brother," Richard added. "I do hope you can join us."

"I thank you for the invitation," Smoke said. "But something has come up that is going to require the attention of both Pearlie and me."

"Rachel Sherman," Richard said.

Smoke opened his eyes wide in shock. "What?"

"You said something has come up. You are talking about Rachel Sherman, aren't you?"

"Yes, but how did you know?" Smoke asked. "Who violated their vow of secrecy?"

"Nobody that I know of," Richard replied. "I was instructed to give this letter to General Sherman, but I've decided to give it to you instead."

Smoke took the proffered envelope, then removed the letter.

General Sherman

> *The successful secession of the Kingdom of Nova Amerigo Regnum, as well as the fate of your daughter, now lies in your hands. If you want to see your daughter alive, again, you will deliver the President and his family to me, where an exchange will be made.*

> *The bearer of this letter, who is a trusted emissary, can tell you where the exchange is to take place.*

> *If you cooperate fully, you will not only get your daughter back, but I am prepared to make you the prime minister of my kingdom.*

Clemente Rex

Smoke looked up in surprise. "You?" he said. "You are in cahoots with this crazy man?"

"I was," Richard answered.

"You were?" Albert asked, shocked at the revelation.

"The operative term is, I *was*," Richard said. "Call it

temporary insanity, call it vanity, call it anything you want, and I'll not dispute it. But I swear to you I no longer wish to have anything to do with him. Mr. Jensen, he intends to kill Miss Sherman to make some sort of point."

A few minutes earlier, General Sherman had given to Captain Gutterman the pistol he received from Smoke, with instructions to return it. Captain Gutterman had just left the car to do so, and was standing on the vestibule between two cars, when he overheard the conversation between the four men who were standing out on the depot platform. With Smoke's pistol in hand, he kept his presence unknown, as he listened to the conversation.

"I can't go along with anything like that," he heard Richard Barrington say. "What I once admired as pure genius, I now recognize as lunacy. You have to rescue her."

"Do you know where she is?"

"Yes, she has been taken to Fort Regency."

"That does us no good unless we know where the fort is."

"It is about fifteen miles north, between Lodgepole Creek and Twin Mountains."

"How many men are in this fort?" Smoke asked.

"No more than ten, counting Pecorino himself."

"We can get us a company of men from Fort Russell," Pearlie suggested.

"No, don't do that," Richard said. "If the fort is attacked, there is no doubt in my mind that he will kill her. Somehow you are going to have to sneak into the fort."

"It would still be ten men against two," Albert said. "What chance would they have."

"We can get Captain Gutterman to go with us," Pearlie said. "That'll cut the odds down somewhat. And since he is the one who lost her, I'm sure he'll want to make up for it."

"Captain Gutterman, you say?" Richard asked. "John Gutterman?"

"Yes."

Richard shook his head. "Gutterman didn't lose her. He's the one who captured her. He is in league with Clemente Pecorino."

"You double-crosser!" Gutterman shouted, stepping down from between the cars. Even as he shouted the oath, he was pulling the trigger, and Richard went down with a bullet in his chest.

Gutterman turned the pistol toward Smoke, but was shocked to see that Smoke had already drawn his gun. Smoke fired before Gutterman could get off a second shot, and Gutterman went down.

General Sherman was the first one off the train and he saw Gutterman down and Smoke holding his own pistol.

"What happened? What is this?" General Sherman shouted. "Why did you shoot my officer?"

Gutterman was dead, but Richard was still clinging to life.

"He had no choice, General," he gasped.

"Who are you?"

"I was in league with Pecorino. As was Captain Gutterman." His last four words were barely audible.

"What? Are you telling me Captain Gutterman is a traitor?"

"My brother can't answer you, General. He is dead," Albert said, kneeling over.

Smoke showed General Sherman the letter Richard had delivered.

"I'll get a company from the fort," General Sherman said.

"No!" Smoke repeated the warning Richard had given them. "Let Pearlie and me try first."

"You are too badly outnumbered," General Sherman said. "There was a Confederate general that was my enemy during the war, but he had an idiom about warfare that you can't dispute. General Nathan Bedford Forrest said to win a battle you must get 'fustest with the mostest.' Well, sir, Pecorino is first, because he is already there. And he has the most men."

"No more than ten," Smoke said. He smiled. "And between Pearlie and me, we have twelve bullets."

"A bit of a breeze has come up," Pearlie said, as he and Smoke started toward the livery to rent a couple of horses. "It may cause us a problem."

"How's that?"

"The wind's coming from the south. If they've got anyone standing watch, this wind could carry the sound of our coming."

"Yeah, it might, but we'll just have to . . ." Smoke paused in mid-sentence and a big smile spread across his face. "Birchard is right!"

"What?"

"Rutherford was telling me about something Birchard said. Rutherford was mocking him for talking about an air cavalry, but Birchard was right."

"Smoke, I don't have the slightest idea what you are talking about."

"You did say you would like to make a parachute leap, didn't you?"

"What? This is a fine time to be talking about parachute leaps."

"This is the perfect time," Smoke said. "Especially if we were to make a parachute leap down into Fort Regency in the middle of the night."

"Between Lodgepole Creek and Twin Mountains, you say?" Professor Jordahl asked.

"Yes," Smoke said with a smile.

"Yes, I know exactly where it is, for I have seen it during several of my ascensions. I thought it was a stable of some sort, and I thought it rather odd that it would be there, so far from any ranch."

"There is a wind coming from the south. If we go aloft, untethered, can you get us there?"

"Yes! With my sail rudder!" Professor Jordahl replied excitedly. "I have used it before, and as long as I have the wind at my back, I can alter the angle of my travel. I can't go cross wind, and I can't go against the wind, but I can go with the wind."

"All right, here is the next question. Do you have two parachutes so that both Pearlie and I can leap down into the fort?"

Professor Jordahl shook his head. "You won't need two," he said. "Both of you can use the same one. Your rate of descent will be only marginally faster."

* * *

It was dark by the time Professor Jordahl got the balloon inflated, and less than an hour later, after drifting north on the wind, Jordahl pointed over the edge of the gondola.

"There are lights there, and I believe that would be the fort."

"You believe?" Pearlie asked. "You mean you aren't sure? I thought you said you had seen it."

"I saw it in the daylight, not at night," Professor Jordahl replied. "But there is Lodgepole Creek."

They could see a stream of water, a dim, silver gleam in the darkness below.

"And there are the Twin Mountains." Two large dark mounds could be seen against the night sky.

"We're just going to have to take the chance that it is the fort," Smoke said.

"What's going to happen to you after we jump?" Pearlie asked.

"I will descend as soon as I can once you two leave. If you are successful, you can send someone to retrieve me tomorrow. If you aren't successful, well, I'll just have a long walk ahead of me." He chuckled. "And at that, I would be better off than you two."

"We'll send someone for you," Smoke promised.

"All right, climb over and get into the parachute," Jordahl ordered a few minutes later. "I'm going to drop you right down into it."

"You think you can do that?" Pearlie asked.

"Mister, if there is one thing I can judge better than just about anybody else in the entire world, it is the effect of the wind on airborne bodies. I promise you, you will descend right in the middle of that fort. Trust me."

Pearlie chuckled. "Trust you? We don't have any other choice, do we?"

"You'll both be sitting in the strap, so I suggest you straddle it, and both of you should be looking the same way, that way you can run out the landing easier. Pearlie, you'll grab hold of one ring, Smoke you'll hold on to the other."

The two men climbed over the side, and mounted the parachute seat.

"All right, I'm cutting you free of the gondola now!"

The chute fell away from the basket then, a moment later, they heard the snapping sound as it popped open over their heads.

They descended quietly through the night, and were relieved to see that Professor Jordahl had accurately predicted the wind.

At first, they thought the fort was empty, but as they came lower, they saw a man standing on a platform on top of the wall, looking south toward the approach to the fort. He had not the slightest idea to look up, as Smoke and Pearlie dropped down from the night sky.

Smoke climbed the ladder.

"That you, Simon? Hell, you got another hour before you're supposed to . . ." the sentry said. He was interrupted in mid-comment when he turned and saw a stranger.

"Who are . . ."

That was as far as he got before he was taken out by a blow to the chin by Smoke's steel-hard fist.

Smoke climbed back down the ladder, then joined Pearlie as the two began their search for Rachel.

Smoke had a miner's lamp with him, and he lit it. The projected beam showed that there were only three buildings inside the compound, one long and narrow, a building that was obviously a stable, and a small house.

Smoke shined the beam toward the house, and exchanging nods, the two men started toward the house.

Opening the door, quietly, Smoke cast the beam around and saw Rachel, tied to a bunk.

"What are you doing in here?" a gruff voice called. "No one is authorized in here."

"Well now, isn't that just too bad," Smoke replied.

"Mr. Jensen!" Rachel called out.

"Jensen?" the voice said.

"You must be Pecorino," Smoke said, playing his beam onto Pecorino.

"How did you get in here?"

"We flew in," Pearlie said with a chuckle.

"Pearlie, help me get Rachel untied," Smoke said.

As the two men worked to untie Rachel, Pecorino jumped through the window that was just over his bed.

"Turn out! Turn out!" Pecorino shouted. "We have intruders!"

"He got away!"

"We'll deal with him later. We need to get Rachel free, first."

Working quickly, the two men untied Rachel, then moved to the front door.

"Pearlie, I'm going to take the lantern, and run to the left. If there is anyone out there, the light should draw their fire. You take Rachel to the stable. We're going to have to have some horses to get out of here."

"All right. Rachel, when we run toward the stable, you bend way over at the waist, like this," Pearlie said, demonstrating. "That way they won't have much of a target."

"Ready?" Smoke asked.

"Ready."

Smoke, holding the lantern so that the beam was cast into the middle of the quadrangle, dashed to the left as soon as he exited the building.

"There they go!" someone shouted, and several shots erupted, the muzzle flashes lighting up the shooters.

"Go," Pearlie hissed, and he and Rachel raced through the darkness toward the stable.

"Oh!" Smoke shouted, and the lamp fell to the ground and rolled forward.

"We got the bastard!" someone shouted excitedly. At least four men started forward.

"No, you didn't," Smoke replied calmly, and four shots brought all four men down.

Smoke picked up the lantern and, once more, cast the beam out across the ground. The beam caught two more, and they went down under fire from Pearlie.

Suddenly a galloping horse sprung from the stable, its rider shooting toward the lantern. Smoke returned fire, and the rider was unseated.

"They got the general!" someone shouted. "They got Pecorino!"

"Let's get out of here!" another called.

Smoke saw some men running toward the front gate, but because they offered no danger, he held his fire.

* * *

Smoke and Pearlie were standing on the depot platform next to the train as it was preparing to leave the next morning.

"Mr. Jensen, Mr. Fontaine," the President said. "I wish I could bring both of you to Washington, and before congress, so that I could give each of you a medal. Surely, no American in history has done more to protect a sitting President than did the two of you.

"But General Sherman and Secretary Ramsey have convinced me that this frightening experience we have been through, and the bravery you two"—he paused in mid-sentence and looked at Rachel—"you three have been through," he amended, "must forever remain secret. It would not be good for the American public to know that such a plot was ever conceived.

"When historians write of this trip out West, they will write only of the great welcomes we have received from the wonderful and industrious peoples of this land. It is to be, forever, regarded as a trip eventful only because I became the first sitting President to make such a journey."

"What about Pecorino's men who got away?" Pearlie asked.

"Colonel Wham's troops killed two of them. The survivor will spend the rest of his life in prison, and nobody will ever pay any attention to his mad ravings," General Sherman said.

"Well, Mr. President, I have to confess that I didn't vote for you," Smoke said. "But it's too bad you aren't running again, because I would gladly vote for you now, if I had the chance."

President Hayes laughed. "Mr. Jensen, your affirmation to do so is enough for me."

"Pearlie?" Rachel said. "Aren't you going to tell me goodbye?"

"Sure," Pearlie replied. He stuck out his hand. "Goodbye."

"Not that way, silly," Rachel said, and with a broad smile, she put her arms around his neck and kissed him, deeply, on the mouth.

"Young man," General Sherman said sternly, after the kiss ended. "I would ask you what your intentions are with regard to my daughter." He smiled. "But you have surely earned the kiss from her."

"Smoke," Pearlie said later, as the two of them watched the Presidential train retreat in the distance. "You won't tell Cal anything about this, will you?"

"You don't want Cal to know that a very pretty girl threw herself in your arms?"

"No, I don't. I mean, her being a general's daughter and all, there's no way anything could have ever come of it. But, if I keep it a secret, why, it'll belong to just me for the rest of my life."

"I understand," Smoke said. "And your secret is safe with me."

A distant train whistle put a coda to their agreement.

CHAPTER ONE

"You charge a helluva lot for a shot of this rotgut whiskey you're sellin'," Dan Short complained to Marvin Davis. "You oughta be payin' us to drink this stuff."

"Two bits a shot ain't bad when you think about where you're headin'," Marvin replied. "You said you was headin' across the Red River to Injun Territory, and there ain't supposed to be no whiskey sold there a-tall. You'd be smart to buy a couple of bottles to take with you."

"Hell, I heard there was a lotta places to buy likker in Injun Territory," Tiny Wilson spoke out. "Ain't that right, Dan?"

"Yep, lots of places."

Dan and Tiny were really heading for Arkansas to join up with Duke Thacker's gang, holed up near the little railroad crossing called Texarkana. They'd told Marvin they were heading to The Nations in Oklahoma Territory, in case any Texas Rangers might show up at the saloon asking about them.

Ned Bates was standing at the front door, looking out across the prairie. "Hey, Dan. Lookee here."

"What is it?" Dan asked, not inclined to bother. When Ned called him again, he walked over to the door. "What is it?" he repeated.

"Lookee yonder," Ned replied, and pointed out across a wide grassy plain. That's a nice little herd of horses. I don't see but three fellers tendin' 'em, and one of 'em is headin' this way."

Dan squinted as he took a hard look at the rider approaching the trading post. "Young feller. Not much more 'n a boy."

Overhearing their remarks, Marvin said, "Most likely some of the boys from the Triple-G. Their range starts about five miles west of here. They're a pretty big outfit. Some of their hands stop in here from time to time."

After a few minutes, Sonny Rice pulled his horse up at the hitch rail and dismounted. Dan and Ned, still standing in the door, stood aside to let him enter.

"Howdy," Sonny said with a nod as he passed them. "Howdy, Mr. Davis," he greeted Marvin and nodded to Tiny, who was staring openly at him. "I need to get some bacon and some flour, and some coffee, too, if you've got some roasted."

"I've got some roasted and I can grind it for you, if you want," Marvin said. "Ain't seen you in a while. Where you headin' with those horses?"

"We're drivin' 'em to the Double-D Ranch, just over the Arkansas line. We're just short a couple of things," Sonny replied.

"Well, I can fix you up with those," Marvin said. "You

need a bottle or two of whiskey? Sounds like you boys are gonna be on the trail for a few days."

"No, sir, I reckon not," Sonny replied. "It's just me and Perley and Possum. Neither me nor Perley are much for drinkin', and if Possum wanted any, he'd a-told me."

Over by the front door, Dan and Ned exchanged wide-eyed glances.

Dan whispered low, "You know, sometimes ol' Lady Luck just walks up and lays it down right in front of you."

"She sure does," Ned agreed and walked out onto the porch to get a better look. "Those are some pretty good-looking horses. Ain't no nags in that bunch." They were still on the porch calculating the worth of the herd when Sonny walked out of the store with his packages.

"Need a hand, there?" Ned offered politely, thinking he would most likely want Sonny's purchases as well.

"No, sir. Thank you just the same," Sonny replied. He tied his sacks to his saddle, then climbed up.

"Reckon you boys will be driving that herd till dark," Dan commented. "It's a ways yet before you strike the Arkansas line."

"We ain't in no hurry to get there," Sonny said. "We want those horses to be in good shape when we get 'em to the Double-D. Perley might be plannin' to make camp right there by that creek tonight."

"Well, that's always smart thinkin' when you're sellin' horses," Dan declared, "especially if you're sellin' off your old horses."

"Oh, there ain't no old horses in that herd," Sonny was quick to inform him. "There ain't a horse there that's over five years old."

It just gets better and better, Dan couldn't help thinking. He couldn't resist asking, "How much are you sellin' 'em for?"

"I don't know what the price was," Sonny answered. "Perley knows, if you wanna come ask him."

"Oh, that's all right," Dan said. "I was just curious."

"Well, good day to ya." Sonny wheeled his horse and started back to the herd.

"You know what I'm thinkin', don't you?" Dan said as they continued to watch Sonny ride away.

"You're thinkin' we could take that herd without no trouble a-tall," Ned answered.

"That's what I'm thinkin'," Dan confirmed. "And I'm also thinkin' there ain't no sense in cuttin' Duke and the others in on it. We'll just be a little late gettin' out to Arkansas to join Duke's gang."

"Where you reckon we can sell 'em in a hurry?" Ned wondered.

"We'll worry about that after we get the horses," Dan said. "It don't matter how long it takes. It'll be more money in our pockets than any splits we're fixin' to get riding with Duke Thacker."

Sonny reined his horse up beside the campfire and dismounted. He untied his purchases, then pulled his saddle off the paint gelding he called Lucky, then turned the horse loose to join the others by the creek. "I took a little look up ahead, then circled back around the creek. Everything looks peaceful. I hope you two ain't drank up all the coffee," he said as he pulled his coffee cup out of his war bag.

"I was fixin' to drain that pot," Possum Smith japed, "but Perley said I had to save some for you. So I poured a couple of swallows back in the pot."

"Pay him no mind, Sonny," Perley said, "that pot's still half-full."

Possum chuckled in response to Perley's remark then asked Sonny, "Why did you name that roan Lucky?"

"'Cause he was lucky *I* picked him out to be my horse," Sonny replied, "instead of somebody like you that's hard on a horse."

Perley shook his head as if impatient with their juvenile behavior. Sonny had recently celebrated his eighteenth birthday while Possum, with his gray ponytail, was considerably up there in years. No one knew how old Possum really was. He was not willing to confess his age. In fact, he wouldn't even divulge the date of his birthday, as if refusing to have any more birthdays, and consequently, stay the same age forever.

Perley suspected that Possum was afraid if Rubin knew how old he was, he might fire him. The thought brought a smile to Perley's lips. Possum should know by now that Perley's brother, Rubin, would have to go through Perley to fire him.

When Rubin had asked Perley who he wanted to take with him to move a small herd of horses to Arkansas, he'd picked Sonny and Possum. Perley figured the two of them would entertain each other. All three of them could enjoy a few days away from the chores at the Triple-G, a trip that would actually take about a week to go to Texarkana and back.

The herd they were moving to the Double-D was only thirty-five horses. And they were taking it nice and easy, pushing the horses about thirty miles a day, so as to deliver fresh stock to Donald Donovan. The Double-D Ranch was about 115 miles east of the Triple-G, just across the Arkansas border, southeast of Texarkana.

Sonny poured his cup of coffee and sat down to join them.

"I reckon ol' Marvin Davis is still kickin'," Possum commented.

"Yep," Sonny said. "He wanted to sell me some whiskey, but I told him didn't none of us drink the stuff. I told him especially Possum didn't have no use for it."

"Huh," Possum snorted. "You might think you're japin', but I ain't got much use for that rotgut he sells. One of the boys gave me a drink of some he bought from Davis and it like to peeled my throat skin off."

"There was three fellers at the store," Sonny said. "They were drinkin' it. They were mighty interested in this herd of horses. Asked me how far we were gonna drive 'em tonight, if there was any old horses in the bunch, and I don't remember what else." He didn't notice the look Perley and Possum exchanged in reaction to his comments, but he didn't miss the fact that both of them got up and came to stand over him.

"You say they asked you a lot of questions about the horses, huh?" Perley prodded. "Did they wanna know anything about how many we were? Anything like that?"

"Well, they know there's three of us," Sonny answered,

at last realizing why Perley was anxious to know. He didn't confess that he'd volunteered the information about their number before any of the three fellows had a chance to ask.

"I expect it'd be a good idea to keep watch over the horses tonight," Perley said. "I sure wasn't expectin' any trouble between here and Texarkana. But this time of year is when a lotta drifters are riding the grub line. If some rustlers got their hands on the thirty-five horses we're herdin', they could sell 'em for a pretty good price."

"How much you reckon they'd be worth?" Sonny asked.

"They could sell 'em for a better price than what Donald Donovan's payin' for 'em," Perley answered. "Rubin is makin' him a special price of sixty dollars a horse. Even that'd be a pretty good payday if they were to sell 'em at that price."

"I reckon." Sonny thought about it. "How much would that be?"

"Figure it out," Perley said. "Just like they taught you in school, you got thirty-five horses at sixty dollars apiece. Didn't Miss Bessie Sanford teach you multiplication?"

"I must notta been there that day," Sonny said. "Can you figure it out?"

"Not in my head," Perley replied. "I'll show you how to do it, then maybe you'll remember some of your schoolin'." He found a bare spot of ground, took a stick and scratched out the numbers. Then he went through the numbers as he did the multiplication to come up with the answer. "I expect they'd try to get more money than that for 'em. A good ridin' horse, like Buck or Possum's dun, would cost a hundred and fifty."

When Sonny heard the total Perley came up with, he was duly impressed.

Possum, on the other hand, was not fascinated with the arithmetic lesson. He was more in tune with the present-day world. "That's mighty interestin', Perley," he began sarcastically. "Now, if those three jaspers Sonny met at the store get it in their heads to take this herd of horses off our hands, why, then, we can tell 'em how much money they're gonna make. And if any of us make it back to the Triple-G, we can tell your brothers what happened to the horses."

Perley nodded in response to Possum's comments. "You're right, Possum. We need to be thinkin' about whether we need to get the horses movin', or if we're better off sittin' right here."

"I say we oughta set right here and let 'em come after us," Possum said right away. "We'd be able to handle 'em easier if we're hunkered down on each side of the herd and knock 'em outta the saddle. Especially if they come whoopin' and hollerin' in here."

"I expect you're right," Perley allowed. "'Course we ain't got any idea if those three men are outlaws or not. I hope we're wrong about 'em." He looked at Sonny and asked, "What did you make of those fellows?"

"I don't know," Sonny replied and tried to think back on his conversation at the store. "They just looked like every other drifter that rides through town."

When Possum asked if they were young or old, Sonny said, "Oh, they was older. Not as old as you, but older than Perley." He paused, then asked, "How old are you, Possum?"

Perley couldn't stifle his chuckle when Possum responded. "None of your damn business. You don't go around askin' people how old they are. I didn't ask you how old you are, did I?"

"I'm eighteen," Sonny said, baffled by Possum's reaction. He looked at Perley for help in his confusion over Possum's sudden fit of temper.

Smiling, Perley said, "Possum ain't comfortable tellin' anybody his age. He's afraid if folks find out how old he is, they'll wanna ask him questions about how it was around here back in Biblical times. Ain't that right, Possum?"

"I reckon we'd best decide what we're gonna do with these horses," Possum responded unemotionally, signaling the end of the horseplay.

Taking charge then, Perley made the decision. "We'll stay here tonight, make camp right where we are. The horses are in a good spot. They've got grass and water by this little creek and we weren't gonna push 'em much farther today, anyway. In case we have visitors, we'd all best take night watch tonight, one of us on the other side of the creek."

"Don't look like we're gonna have to wait till dark," Possum said. "Those three friends of Sonny's just left Marvin's store and they're headin' this way right now." That caused Perley and Sonny to set their cups down by the fire.

"Might be a good idea to spread out a little," Perley suggested. It wasn't necessary to advise them to make sure their weapons were handy. "Is that the same three," he asked Sonny.

"Looks like 'em," Sonny said as the riders continued a path directly toward them.

"Looks like they ain't takin' no chances, Dan Short commented as the three men approached the camp by the creek. "They're spreadin' out and holdin' on to their rifles, so don't make no sudden moves."

Tiny and Ned grunted in response.

"Howdy," Dan called out when they were about twenty yards short of the campfire. "Mind if we come in?"

"Not at all," Perley called back. "What can we do for you?"

Dan didn't answer until they pulled up before the fire. "We was talkin' to that young feller there over at the store." He nodded toward Sonny. "He said you boys was drivin' a herd of horses over to Arkansas. Me and my partners are in the horse breedin' business. We're on our way right now to an army post up in Injun Territory to work with the soldiers breedin' mares with some of them wild range horses."

"Is that a fact?" Perley replied. "Breedin' horses for the army. What fort's doin' that?" He waited for an answer.

But Dan couldn't think of an army fort in The Nations. He looked quickly from Tiny to Ned, but both wore the same blank expressions.

"Fort Grover?" Perley asked.

"Right," Dan quickly answered. "That's the one." Tiny

and Ned both echoed the name while nodding vigorously. "Well, your young man there—"

"Sonny," Perley interrupted.

"Right, Sonny," Dan repeated. "He was tellin' us what fine stock you boys were drivin', so we just thought we'd take a look at 'em. They look like pretty decent horses at that and I'm thinkin' this might be your lucky day when you bumped into us. I expect we can get you a helluva lot better price for them horses at Fort Grover. Not only that, we'll help you drive 'em up there to Fort Grover. It must be a lotta work with just the three of you. You could most likely use the help."

"It ain't but thirty-five horses," Perley said. "They ain't much trouble for us."

"Fort Grover's a lot closer than Arkansas," Dan insisted. "You'd have your money and be on your way to the saloon before you got close to Arkansas."

"I'll say this for you, mister," Perley responded. "You made a right temptin' proposition. The truth of the matter is, these horses ain't ours to sell. They've already been paid for. We're just deliverin' 'em. And there ain't no place in The Nations named Fort Grover. Somebody's been pullin' your leg about breedin' horses for the army. I'm sorry we're the ones who had to tell you."

Dan didn't say anything for a long moment, feeling the full effect of having stuck his foot in his mouth.

Ned and Tiny were speechless as well, until Tiny made an effort to salvage their scheme. "Maybe you ain't been up in Injun Territory in a while. Fort Grover ain't been built very long."

Dan's anger for having been exposed so easily at first

caused him to become tense with thoughts of reaching for the army single-action .45 he wore. He was stopped short of that by the sight of the three men facing him, trying to appear casual as they held cocked rifles at the ready. Gradually, his anger began to dissipate, and a wry smile formed on his lips. "Well, friend, I reckon you saw right through that one. You can't blame some of us who've had some hard times, from tryin'. No harm done. We'll be on our way."

Unable to remain silent any longer, Possum asked, "Just what were you plannin' to do after you turned our horses toward Injun Territory? What were you gonna do with us on the way to this new fort you claim?"

Dan had no answer for him. He wheeled his horse and said, "Come on, boys. We're wastin' our time here. We got places to go."

Neither Ned nor Tiny objected and they filed out behind him, leaving the three Triple-G men scratching their heads.

"I reckon they shoulda worked on their plan a little longer before they came ridin' up to ask us to turn the herd north," Possum commented. "They musta thought the Triple-G didn't hire nobody but idiots." He turned toward Perley. "You reckon they really thought we might just turn the herd and go with 'em?" Back to Sonny, he said, "You musta made a right smart impression on them fellers."

"I don't think there's any question about who the idiots are," Perley said. "They'd decided they were gonna take this herd away from us. I expect they were plannin' to just shoot us down and take the horses. When they saw us ready for 'em with our rifles in hand, the one that did all the talkin' decided to make up that little story about the soldiers wantin' to buy horses. If we bought it, then it would be less risky to shoot us in the back while we were driving our horses toward The Nations. Ain't that how you see it, Possum?"

Possum and Sonny nodded in response.

"That don't mean they've given up the idea," Perley continued. "They're still comin' after these horses. They're just gonna wait to jump us after dark."

"I think you're right," Possum said. "We need to be ready for 'em." His concern at that point was for Sonny, who had never shot a man before. Possum asked him, "You gonna be able to set your sight on one of those fellers and pull the trigger?"

"I guess so," Sonny answered, not really sure.

"Make no mistake about it," Possum said, "when they come ridin' back in here tonight, they'll be hopin' to put a bullet into all three of us. Men like that don't think twice about killin' a man to make that big a payday. Ain't that right, Perley?"

"He's right, Sonny. They'll kill for a lot less than these horses will bring. It might make it a little easier on you, if you remember the law usually hangs a man for stealing a horse."

"That's right," Possum spoke again. "If you was to nail one of 'em, you'd be doin' the law's work for 'em."

Sonny didn't say anything for a few moments while he looked back and forth from one to the other. Finally, he spoke his peace. "You're both wastin' your time, tryin' to talk me into shootin' some feller who's tryin' to shoot me.

I'm eighteen years old. Perley, I don't reckon I have to be told to do whatever it takes to save my behind. If I was you or Possum, I'd be more worried about what Rubin would do if we lost these horses."

He'd most likely think Perley stepped in another cow pie, Possum said to himself, recalling Perley's brothers' favorite saying, "If there wasn't but one cow pie between the Triple-G and the Red River, Perley would step in it."

CHAPTER TWO

Dan Short held his horse to a lope for almost two miles before he reined him to a stop and waited for Ned and Tiny to catch up with him. Out of sight of the camp by the creek, he wheeled his horse around to meet them as they rode up.

"Well, that went just about like we wanted it to, didn't it?" Ned Bates asked sarcastically. "I thought for a minute, there, they was gonna turn them horses right around and head for the Red River with us."

"You go to hell," Dan responded. "I had to think of somethin' to tell 'em, when we rode up there and found the three of 'em standing apart with their rifles ready to shoot at the first move we made. It damn sure changed my plans to shoot 'em down before they knew what hit 'em. I noticed you and Tiny didn't make any moves to get the party started either."

"Hell, we thought you was callin' the shots, didn't we, Tiny?" Ned responded.

"That's right," Tiny answered him. "Leastways, we got a good look at them three fellers. Ain't nobody but that young boy, an old man, and that other jasper that did most of the talkin'. Didn't none of 'em look like they'd give us much trouble. We might shoulda gone ahead and drew on 'em. Most likely woulda gunned 'em down before they got them rifles up to shoot."

"Whaddaya think, Dan?" Ned asked. "Wanna ride back and go in blazin' while all three of them are right there together?"

"Why take a chance on one of those jaspers gettin' off a lucky shot and hittin' one of us?" Dan replied. "Might as well wait till dark and shoot 'em in their blankets. We'll keep an eye on 'em to make sure they're still plannin' to camp right there tonight. It ain't too long now before it'll be gettin' dark."

"That suits me just fine," Ned commented. "We might as well get us a fire goin' and fix somethin' to eat while we got the time." He looked at Tiny and winked. "I never like to rustle horses on an empty stomach."

Using some of the fresh coffee that Marvin Davis had ground up for Sonny, Possum set up a new pot. They wanted to make sure they stayed awake that night.

"I don't think I'd be able to go to sleep, if I drank a lotta coffee or if I didn't," Sonny confessed.

"Well, don't think you're the only one that ain't a little edgy," Perley assured him. "I don't know what direction they'll come at us from. Whaddayou think, Possum?"

"I expect they'd try to sweep through our camp on this side of the creek. 'Cause it'd be easier to stampede the horses outta the trees and into that flat east of us," Possum speculated. "'Course, that 'ud be the smartest way to flush 'em outta there, and they could shoot us when they rode through the camp after the horses. But after our little meetin' with those three, I ain't too sure what they'll do."

"I think you're right," Perley said. "So, I reckon we'd best have two of us on this side of the creek. The other one can watch our backs from the other side, and we'll use the creek bank for cover. Might as well go ahead and pick us a spot, maybe take your shovel and dig you out a little hole to make you a smaller target. It'd be a good idea to saddle your horse, in case we have to go after the herd real quick."

They made their defensive preparations, hoping they were wrong and the three drifters weren't willing to risk a raid on the horses. Perley decided to station Sonny on the other side of the creek, telling him his young eyes were better than Possum's. The truth of the matter was Perley figured Possum a better shot and wanted him on the nearside with him.

As darkness approached, they built up the fire, saddled their horses, and led them back into the trees, hoping to tie them out of the line of fire. As the last touch, they rolled up some cottonwood branches in three blankets on the off chance the rustlers were dumb enough to think they were three sleeping bodies.

As the night crept over the creek and the darkness deepened, there were no sounds to be heard other than the steady chirping of the crickets and an occasional snort from the horses standing in the cottonwood trees.

The hours dragged by with no sign of the anticipated rustlers until Possum, some five yards down the creek bank, whispered loudly. "I don't know. Maybe we figured these jaspers wrong. I'm about ready to fry up some of that bacon Sonny picked up today."

"I can't say as I'm disappointed they didn't come to the party," Perley whispered back to him. "I'll cross over the creek and see if Sonny's awake." He got up from the hole he had dug out of the bank and started down to the water when pandemonium broke out in the form of gunfire and yelling. Perley, his reactions always lightning fast, spun around to see the three rustlers charging into the camp, firing at the bundles of cottonwood branches.

Without consciously realizing he had drawn his six-gun, he pulled the trigger, and Tiny bolted straight upright, then slid out of the saddle. Aware then of the trap they had ridden into, Dan and Ned veered away from the camp, but not before Possum put a .44 rifle slug into Dan's back. He fell forward to lie on his horse's neck but remained in the saddle as his horse galloped away from the creek after Ned's horse.

"Reckon that was enough to run 'em off for good?" Possum asked when Perley ran back from the creek bank.

"I don't know. Maybe," Perley answered as they hustled over to check Tiny's body.

"Don't have to worry about this one," Possum declared. "You nailed him plum center of his chest." He bent down to get a closer look. "He's a big 'un, ain't he?"

Sonny hurried up from the creek to join them. "I swear," he exclaimed excitedly, "that's the one called Tiny! Who shot him?"

"Perley got him," Possum answered him. "I shot one of the other two, but I don't know how bad. They was runnin' flat out. The feller was layin' on his horse's neck. Dead or not, I don't know."

"I swear," Sonny repeated. "You reckon they'll come back?"

"Not unless they want some more of what they just got," Possum said. "Ain't that what you say, Perley?"

"It would surprise me if the other two tried it again," Perley answered, "since there ain't but one of 'em that ain't been shot. I expect we'd best stay awake for the rest of the night anyway, in case that one comes sneakin' back just to get a shot at one of us. I figure they ain't in any shape to drive a herd of horses, even one this small, but they might want some payback for this 'un." He tapped the bottom of Tiny's boot with his toe.

Possum turned and looked back toward the trees by the creek. "It was over so fast, there weren't enough time to stir up the horses much. That volley of gunfire wasn't enough to cause them to panic. I reckon we were lucky we was rustled by some greenhorn outlaws." He took a look at the holes in the blankets they had wrapped around the tree branches. "Ain't no doubt what they had in mind for us."

Approximately one and a quarter mile from the camp by the creek, Ned Bates reined his horse back to a walking gait and guided the sorrel through a little patch of pines to a stream beyond them. Dan's horse followed, the wounded man still lying on his horse's neck. Tagging along behind them, Tiny Wilson's dun gelding with an empty saddle walked down to the stream where the two packhorses were tied and waiting.

Ned dismounted and went immediately to help Dan off his horse. "How bad is it?" he asked, attempting to brace himself to catch him.

"I don't know how bad." Dan groaned painfully, the back of his shirt soaked with blood. "It hurts like hell. My back feels like it's on fire." He let go of the horse's neck and slid cautiously over to the side.

Holding on to him and set to take the load of his body, Ned staggered when he caught the full weight of Dan's body but managed to lay him gently on the ground. Dan moaned as Ned tried to examine the wound.

"They was waitin' for us," Dan said. "I saw Tiny get hit, just before we tried to run. Did he make it?"

"No, he didn't," Ned answered.

Dan's question brought back the image of the shooter and the lightninglike move when he'd turned and fired. There was enough light from the fire to see him when he got up from the creek bank and started to walk down the bank. Ned was sure it wasn't the old man or the kid. It was the one who'd done all the talking when they were there earlier.

"I saw who shot Tiny. He turned and fired so fast Tiny never had a chance." Ned paused a few moments while he tried to get Dan's shirt off him, but every way he tried was met with difficulty and pain. He took his knife and cut a hole in the back of the shirt, then ripped it apart, so he could see the wound. "You need a doctor," he announced after studying the angry-looking wound for a few minutes.

"That slug is in your back pretty deep. It's too dark for me to see real good, but it looks bad. You want me to try to dig it outta there? There ain't no doctor around here," Ned told him. "Maybe that woman at Marvin's store can do some doctorin'. We could go see her in the mornin'."

Dan didn't like that idea.

"I don't know what else to do for you, Dan. We ain't got no money to pay Marvin's wife to take care of you, anyway."

"Well, I need some help now. I'm bleedin' like a gutted hog," Dan complained. "I can't do it on my own."

Ned was aware of Dan's complaints, but his mind was on something he considered more important than the bullet hole in Dan's back. "What the hell am I gonna tell Mavis?" he mumbled over and over. When Dan asked him what he was saying, Ned repeated, "What am I gonna tell Mavis?" He'd promised his younger sister he would take care of her husband and bring him home safely. Mavis had tried to talk Tiny out of going with Dan and Ned, but he wanted to go.

Ned spoke to Dan. "I promised her we weren't gonna do nothin' dangerous. Now I gotta tell her I got him killed on his first job with me."

With no interest in Mavis Wilson's loss, Dan recalled something Ned had said. "You said Tiny's horse followed us back here. We could give Marvin Davis that horse for his wife's doctorin'."

"I've gotta pay that gunslinger his due for killin' Tiny. That'll help make it right with Mavis," Ned said.

"You ain't listenin' to me," Dan blurted. "I might be dying here. It ain't your damn sister layin' here with a bullet in her."

Ned got to his feet and stood looking down at the suffering man for a few long moments before saying, "There ain't nothin' I can do to ease your pain. You just lay there and try to be still, so you don't aggravate that bleedin' any worse than it is. I'll get a blanket to spread over you. You just lay still, and in the mornin', we'll go back to

Marvin's store." He walked over to the packhorse Dan used to carry his possibles and pulled out a blanket, then went back and spread it over his wounded partner.

"I 'preciate it, Ned. Tough luck about Tiny, but he shoulda known the chances you take in this business. I 'preciate you takin' care of me."

"You oughta know I ain't gonna leave you out here sufferin'," Ned said. "You just lay still now." He took a couple of steps toward the horses again, then stopped. Turning back toward Dan, he held his pistol in his hand and paused briefly to look at the wounded man, now seeming to be quiet. His mind made up, he took a step closer and aimed the .44 at the back of Dan's head.

The last sound Dan Short heard on this earth was the clicking sound of a hammer being cocked.

"There weren't nothin' I coulda done for ya, Dan, but I weren't gonna leave you to lay out here and bleed to death. It was nothin' but bad luck with them fellers. I've gotta go after that gunslinger and I couldn't take you with me, so I did the next best thing I could think of." He holstered his weapon, unbuckled Dan's cartridge belt, and pulled it out from under his body. Then he checked Dan's pockets for any cash he might have. "You wasn't always real truthful about whether or not you had any money left, but I reckon this time you weren't lyin'. Maybe I can sell your horse and saddle. That oughta help out a little."

Finished talking to Dan's corpse, Ned decided he owed it to him to dig a hole to keep the scavengers away from him. He got the short-handled shovel from the packs and found a spot where the ground didn't look too hard. When he had a shallow hole that looked big enough, he dragged the body over and rolled it into the grave. By the time he finished filling in the grave with the loose dirt, the first light of morning had begun to break over the little stream. It occurred to him that he was hungry and was in desperate need of a cup of coffee.

In the light of a new day, he was still committed to his vow to avenge Tiny Wilson's death. It occurred to him that he would be avenging Dan's death as well. If it hadn't been for one of those men shooting Dan, he would still be alive today.

Ned knew he needed food and a little rest after the night just past. His plan was to follow the herd of horses and wait for a chance to ambush the gunslinger. He couldn't just ride into their camp and call out the man. All three would most likely shoot him on sight. So he gathered enough wood for a fire, made some coffee, and cooked some bacon.

He awoke with a start, not sure for a moment where he was. Feeling the sun on his face, he sat up and realized he had fallen asleep after eating some breakfast. He looked across the ashes of his fire to focus on Dan Short's grave and reminded himself once again that it had been the best thing to do for his old partner. He thought then of the three men driving the herd of horses. No doubt they were well on their way again. He could catch up to them in plenty of time, and took his time getting his horses ready to go. He had five to take care of now, so he rigged up a lead rope for four of them and started back to the camp he had fled the night before. He felt confident the herd would be gone but thought it a good idea to look over their campsite and find the trail they left on.

Entering the deserted camp from downstream the creek, just as he and Dan and Tiny had done the night before, Ned remembered approximately where he'd been when he saw the man turn and fire. That was the end of Tiny. He was knocked off his horse, and had it not been for his own immediate turn away from the creek, Ned might have been the next one to get shot. With that in mind, he walked his horses into the clearing, looking right and left, until he was stopped suddenly by the sight of Tiny Wilson, laid out flat on the ground.

Ned dismounted, walked over to stand by the body, and muttered, "I swear, Mavis, I'm sorry for what they done to him. And they just left him for the buzzards to feed on. Well, I reckon I can dig a grave for my sister's husband." He wanted to be able to look his sister in the face and tell her he took proper care of her dead husband. Already suffering sore muscles from one grave digging, Ned soon found that the interment of Tiny was going to be an altogether harder job than Dan Short's. For Tiny was a huge man. In bulk alone, he would make two of Dan.

Ned was committed to do the proper thing, so he got his shovel out again and picked a spot to dig. He labored away to dig a hole that he thought adequate for one of Tiny's bulk. When it was ready, he dragged the huge body to the grave then dragged it into the shallow grave by holding a boot under each arm and walking the corpse into it like a horse pulling a wagon. He pulled Tiny into the grave until his head dropped in, then he released the boots and let them drop. To his great relief, head and boots fell within the grave.

Ned took a few moments to rest before beginning to fill in the grave. He soon encountered another minor problem. With Tiny lying on his back, Ned had not dug the grave deep enough, for the toes of Tiny's boots were just even with the top of the hole.

"Dadgum it." Ned snorted as he considered the problem. *I could haul him outta there and dig a little hole at that end for his boots to fit into. Then I can turn him face-down and his toes could go in the hole.* He really didn't want to remove the huge body and dig the grave deeper, so he continued to think about it. The toes of Tiny's boots were really just level with the top of the grave. *If I pulled his boots off, his toes ought not to stick up that high.*

That seemed to be the simplest solution, and there would be a little mound of dirt to cover the grave, anyway. Removing Tiny's boots was not the simple task he anticipated. He didn't know if the big man's feet had swollen overnight, or if the boots were just too small for his feet. Ned had to strain with all the strength he could muster before one, then finally the other one, came off.

While pausing to catch his breath, he noticed the boots were better looking than the old pair he wore, and they didn't look that much bigger than his own. He pulled off his boots and tried on Tiny's. They were too big, but not by a lot. He decided to keep them, hesitating for only a moment when he wondered if Mavis would notice. "Nah, she ain't gonna notice, and I deserve somethin' for killin' that coyote that shot Tiny." For want of a better idea for what to do with his old boots, he put them in the grave with Tiny. There wasn't much room in the hole he'd dug, but they fit nicely with one boot under each of Tiny's arms. All done, he filled in the grave, feeling he could honestly tell his sister he had given her husband a decent burial.

With a trail easy to follow, Ned Bates set out to track the herd of thirty-five horses.

"You sure you know how to find this place?" Possum asked when they struck the Sulphur River. "You ain't never been this far east in your life."

"I'm just tellin' you what Rubin told me," Perley replied. "He said if we kept drivin' 'em straight east, we'd eventually strike the Red River where it swings down a little farther south, and to just follow it till we get to Texarkana. He said we leave the river where it loops around north of the town and head south for about twelve miles." Possum looked unsure, so Perley added, "He said, if we get to the Louisiana border, to turn around and come back. We'd gone too far."

Ignoring Perley's japing, Possum said, "Might save a lotta time if we park this herd somewhere outside Texarkana and go into town and ask somebody how to get to the Double-D."

"Maybe," Perley allowed, "but we'd just be drivin' the horses a few miles more to get close to Texarkana. Rubin says the Double-D ain't as big as the Triple-G, so if we go like he told me, we'll most likely be on Double-D range right after we cross into Arkansas. Even if we don't find the headquarters, we'd at least be on their range. We've struck the Red about where he said we would, so let's follow it and see if he knew what he was talkin' about."

So, that's what they did, driving the horses on an old trail that started out to the east. After traveling a distance they figured to be at least eighteen or twenty miles, they decided to stop and rest the horses. They picked a spot with a wide grassy gap in the short oak trees that lined the banks of a creek. As soon as their horses were taken care of, Perley got a fire going and charged up the coffee-pot, while Possum attempted to make some pan biscuits.

Not one of the three men mentioned the possibility of a lone rider, who had been following them all morning.